CW00523940

Best Wishes

Creation

Vicky Garlick

VICKY GARLICK

All rights reserved. No part of this publication may be reproduced or transmitted by any means, electronic, mechanical, photocopying or otherwise, without prior permission of the author.

First published 2017

Copyright © 2017 Vicky Garlick

ISBN: 1545433844
ISBN-13: 978-1545433843

For my family

CONTENTS

ACKNOWLEDGMENTS

Firstly I want to thank my sister, Jo for once again taking the time to create the cover for my novel. She's an Artist and I like to think she's in this book as much as I am.

Thank you also to my entire family who continue to support and inspire me. I wouldn't be doing this without you.

A very big thank you to those who read and gave feedback on Creation before it was published. Your input was invaluable and I'm very grateful you volunteered.

And thank you to *you* for buying this book, I hope you enjoy reading it as much as I enjoyed writing it.

Prologue

Nilla hummed contentedly to herself while she scrubbed at the pots in a large sink and watched her young daughter play in the tiny garden at the back of their one storey house. She could hear Aggie chattering to herself but couldn't see what she was doing, not that she had anything to worry about anymore; four years had passed since her husband had been taken and the stigma around her had finally settled. She smiled at Aggie, who looked so much like the father she would never know; the curly, jet black hair and bright green eyes could only have come from Charlie. Nilla pushed her own pale brown strands behind her ear and continued scrubbing.

Aggie sat facing away from her house pushing damp, clay rich soil into piles in front of her, "This will make things better," she said to herself. She patted the first mound into a horizontally oval shape and grinned as she added several small spheres of soil to the oval's base. Aggie glanced over her shoulder towards the kitchen window and grinned at her mother who watched her from the sink. "Mama will like it," she concluded as she patted another, larger sphere of damp soil onto the oval one.

She could hear her mother humming, she loved hearing her mother sing; her voice was cool and calming and always managed to send Aggie to sleep, no matter how bad her dreams were. She added more water to the soil and started rolling two pieces into lengths, which she then flattened and began to shape, these were eventually added vertically to the sphere on top of the oval. Aggie sat back and stared at her creation frowning, it didn't look quite right; then she giggled to herself and picked up a final clump of clay rich soil, moulding it into a small ball between her hands and added it to one end of the oval piece. Then she poked at the large sphere producing two dents in the surface, she smiled feeling satisfied and wished her little rabbit could be real. She took a deep breath and let out a happy sigh; thin tendrils of pale yellow mist began to swirl in the air.

"Finished mama!" she shouted over her shoulder to her mother who smiled at her and left the window.

Nilla emerged from the door, an apron over her loose beige shirt and wide legged trousers, "What is it?" she asked drying her hands on the apron.

Her daughter got clumsily to her feet, "I made you something," Aggie said running towards her mother. "Look." Nilla followed her daughter's dark, outstretched hand and gasped, throwing her hands over her mouth. A small, deformed brown-red rabbit was hopping clumsily around their small garden. Aggie squealed in excitement and began chasing the small creature while the colour drained from Nilla's face as she felt a cold dread sweep over her.

"Aggie, where did you get that?" she asked quietly, crouching by her daughter as she petted the crudely made rabbit.

"I made it for you," she said grinning, Nilla started to check over her daughter, much to Aggie's annoyance and finally found the grubby graze on her right knee. She collapsed to the ground and Aggie looked confused.

"What's wrong mama?" she asked climbing onto her mother's lap, the rabbit now forgotten.

"Aggie you have to promise me something, this is very important," Nilla said as her daughter stared up at her with wide eyes. "You must never do this again." She spoke softly, trying hard not to sound angry or scare her daughter, trying desperately not to let the fear she felt leak out and infect her daughter.

"Did I do something wrong?" Aggie asked, her lower lip trembling.

"Of course not," Nilla said hugging her daughter tightly. "But there are some people who won't like what you can do and they might try to take you away from me," she heard Aggie begin to cry and she tried hard to hold back her own tears. "Please Aggie, promise me you'll try not to make anything ever again." Her daughter nodded a tear stained face and Nilla got to her feet, her daughter still in her arms. She took Aggie inside, then returned to the garden to dispose of the rabbit.

Chapter 1

Flicker sat in a sparsely furnished room at a simple and horrifically unsteady desk writing the 260th letter to his brother, whom he knew would never receive it. He'd been writing one a week since he'd arrived at the palace and even though the officers swore they mailed all letters he knew it was a lie, because Redd had never replied. He set the pen down and stared out of the bolted window at the vast and elaborate gardens within the palace boundaries and the glistening sea beyond. He'd almost forgotten what the sand felt like between his toes and longed for the days when he and Redd had built sandcastles, but those were long gone now and he'd never experience them again.

He sighed as a knock came at the door, he didn't even know why they bothered knocking, it's not like they cared much for privacy. A tall, muscular officer walked in, picked up the folded letter and pen and left the room, without closing the door. Flicker sighed again as he closed it behind the man and ran a pale hand through his unkempt red hair. He grabbed one of the few books he was allowed to have from a slanted shelf and lay on his bed, staring at the crinkled pages without reading them.

Had it really been five years? Trapped in this lavish yet barren building? He threw the book against the wall and yelled in frustration. Why did they even bother to keep him here? It's not like he cooperated, it's not like he wanted the power he had. If they just let him go he'd promise never to use it, but he knew they never would, because he'd begged them every day for a year since he'd arrived. Their response had always been the same; 'Your talent serves the Emperor.' Except that it didn't because from the moment he'd arrived he'd refused to use it and no matter how much they'd tortured him, he'd never broken. So now he was stuck, 'teaching' others, though he usually just slept at his desk while the class did as they pleased. Really they should have just let him go, or maybe killed him. There was another knock at the door and this time a short, elderly woman with shoulder length bushy grey hair entered and smiled at him, Flicker smiled back.

"Rough day?" she asked in a cracked voice and sat on the unstable chair by the desk.

"Same as every other day Jack," he replied throwing his stained jumper to the floor.

Jackie frowned, "You could try to be more cooperative," she suggested inclining her head. "They might actually mail your letters."

Flicker snorted, "They don't mail anyone's letters, no matter how cooperative they are, do you know anyone who's had a visitor since they arrived?"

Jackie hesitated, head to one side in thought, then slowly she shook her head, "You'd definitely get a better room," she pointed out, looking at the small, empty box that was Flicker's home.

He shook his head, "I prefer this room, it reminds me how cruel the Emperor really is to us."

"He's not that bad you know."

"Oh really? Then why does he keep us here against our will? Why does he refuse to let us see our families? You've probably been here the longest Jack, how can you still see the good in him?"

Jackie smiled sadly, "Because in a way he's the only family I've got now, I doubt my husband is still alive and my children left Shanora years ago, I've got nothing out there."

Flicker fell silent and his weary, haggard features softened, "I'm sorry Jack, I really am. You're one of the few people I can stand to be around in here, I don't want to argue with you."

Jackie chuckled, "That wasn't an argument," she said shaking her head. "If you'd seen me and my Cam go at it you'd realise what we were having was a polite discussion." She grinned at him and he smiled forcefully back. Jackie got to her feet. "Just try to be more helpful," she said placing a hand on his shoulder. "I know you take pride in your resistance, but this is your home whether you want it to be or not and really, it's not so bad." She clapped him on the back and left the room, closing the door quietly behind her. Flicker unclenched the hands that had unconsciously balled into fists and got to his feet; there were still a couple of hours of daylight left so he decided to walk the gardens.

The palace grounds were actually beautiful; tended to by the best gardeners, they were peaceful and calming, or at least they would be if it weren't for the constantly patrolling officers. There was a chill in the air as Flicker walked unconsciously towards the sculpture garden; he was always drawn to it, probably because it's what he missed the most. The sculptures he strolled around had all been made by those living in the palace and they were incredible. The detail on them was exquisite, making every creature look as though it could come to life at any moment. He stared for a particularly long time at a large lizard with dragon characteristics, which he knew must have been scaled up in size in order to be displayed in this part of the grounds. He smiled to himself at the thought of it coming to life and terrorising the palace, *If only*, he thought.

There weren't many others out at this time, which suited him as it meant he didn't have to make small talk with people he disliked. The officers eyed him suspiciously as he weaved between sculptures of a proud looking fox and a snuffling badger and he sighed to himself.

"Honestly, you try to escape a few times and suddenly you're on everyone's watch list, maybe they should have just read between the lines and let me go." But he knew that would never really happen, the Emperor would never allow it. The only way you were allowed to leave was in a coffin and he had seriously considered it; if it wasn't for the fact that they were watched almost all the time, he probably would have been successful.

Jan, one of the more tolerable officers, who was tall and had short dark brown hair, sauntered over to the bench Flicker was laid on; he pretended not to notice.

"Hope you're not thinking of trying to leave us again," he said pushing the shorter man's feet off the bench so he could take a seat.

Flicker snorted, "I gave that up long ago," he replied.

"I thought maybe you'd formed a new plan; make yourself so dirty and foul smelling that we couldn't come near you without choking on the fumes." He smiled, the skin around his blue eyes crinkled and Flicker, despite himself, allowed a brief chuckle.

"I guess I just don't see the point in keeping up appearances," he said, his face returning to its natural frown "I mean, who am I really trying to impress?"

Jan chuckled, "You know some people like to stay clean for *themselves.*"

Flicker snorted again, "I'm perfectly happy as I am thanks, anyway," he said sniffing under his arms. "I don't even smell."

Jan raised an eyebrow, "If you can't smell what we all can then you definitely need a wash," he said getting to his feet. "I could push you in the pond if you like?"

Flicker appeared to consider this, then shook his head, "I'm not sure I should be in the same vicinity as the swans."

Jan laughed, "You got something against swans?"

"No, they've got something against me, every time I go near them they try to attack me."

"I'm not surprised if you approach them smelling like that!"

Flicker glanced at the darkening autumn sky and began to grumble, "I suppose I should get myself inside," he said bitterly.

Jan looked suddenly apologetic, "Honestly Flicker you've brought this on yourself, if you'd just cooperated from the beginning you wouldn't have had these restrictions placed on you." He seemed genuinely sorry when he spoke but it didn't stop Flicker scowling and cursing internally.

"Ever thought that maybe you're on the wrong side?" Flicker said getting to his feet and starting back towards the palace before Jan could respond.

Instead of going straight to his room he stopped by the bathrooms and took a shower. Officers stood by the door of the large, open planned room, watching him and several others in case they tried anything, but what exactly were they going to try in here? Flicker let out a long breath as the warm water cascaded over his pale, slim form and wished he could stay in one of the exterior buildings, but that wouldn't happen, he'd burnt too many bridges and now, this twenty-four hour guard was his punishment.

He was escorted back to his room, where the officer waited as he changed from one set of ragged clothes to another, slightly cleaner set, then took the, 'caked in dirt' ones and the towel. People like Flicker weren't allowed spare clothes or towels in their room, it was a miracle he was allowed sheets on his bed. Since he was a flight risk - in more ways than one - anything that could be considered potentially dangerous, or, 'useful' to him was removed, his door couldn't lock and an officer would check on him at three hour intervals. In all honesty he was getting tired of being treated like a child and both Jackie and Jan's words returned to him as he lay on his bed staring at the ceiling.

The following morning, when an officer checked on Flicker's class, she was astonished to see him actually teaching. She double checked it was definitely him in the room and walked out almost in a daze. Flicker smiled at her confusion; she wasn't the only one to be bewildered by his sudden change, his entire class had stared at him blank faced for five minutes. It had made him chuckle. After their initial shock his students had quickly gathered their materials and started working; they weren't a large group, nine in total and they varied in age. Unless those who were older had some previous experience, they often struggled to keep up, while the younger members picked up the skills easily.

Flicker had his own mound of clay on his desk and he showed the group various techniques to shape and mould it. He was thankful that they hadn't wasted their lessons with him, even if he'd not actually helped them, they'd always attempted to sculpt animals and objects. It meant his work with them now was far easier than if he were starting from scratch. He had a feeling they'd also been talking to the other teachers. It felt a little strange to be working with clay again after all this time, he actually couldn't remember the last time he'd sculpted something, but the techniques flooded back as if no time had passed and the feel of the clay beneath his fingers felt natural.

Flicker was an Artist, like everyone else who lived in the palace grounds, except for the Emperor, officers and most of the support teams. He had the ability to bring his creations to life using a few drops of his own blood and for that reason he was forbidden to live outside the palace grounds. He wasn't like the majority of the other Artists though because he hated his, 'gift' and other than a couple of accidental occurrences, he'd never brought anything to life.

He'd spent most his life working with his brother as an artisan, creating furniture, ceramic vessels and garden sculptures, until one afternoon when the eagles he'd just fired for a customer had come to life. Flicker had been mortified and his brother, Redd had simply stared in shock while the customer had fled their shop screaming at the top of his lungs. It hadn't been long until the officers had arrived to take him to the palace. He had soon discovered the creation process wasn't as simple as he'd assumed; although anything you made could be brought to life, it wouldn't look or act, 'real' unless it was incredibly detailed, accurate and ultimately perfect. The Artist also needed to mix a small amount of their own blood into their chosen medium and essentially breathe life into the finished product. That had been his problem, he must have accidentally got some of his blood mixed into the clay he'd been working with and his next breath had sealed his fate.

There were subtle differences for creating, for example solid objects like weapons were better moulded out of clay and then fired, while organic items like animals should have the clay remain wet as it holds more elasticity. Drawings or paintings worked in a whole different way; it didn't matter what medium you used, as soon as you breathed life into them the object would lift and rise from the page in a three dimensional format. They never seemed to have the same stable structure as objects sculpted from clay though, which was why so much of the palace Artists focus was on sculpting.

Flicker despised being an Artist, he honestly couldn't see how he was helping the Emperor or the city with his, 'gift' though perhaps that was because since he'd arrived at the palace he'd never really used it. When he'd arrived the officers had spouted some rubbish about the Emperor protecting their safety, but honestly, he just thought they were trying to stop them using their power for their own gain, after all what was to stop him creating a pile of gold bars? He didn't actually know what it was the Artists did for the Emperor, since all he'd been asked to do in the end was teach, and until now he'd not even done that. There were rumours of course about the city being in trouble but there wasn't any proof. Once he'd asked Jackie about it, but she hadn't known either and considering she actually followed the rules and was generally well respected in the palace, it seemed suspicious.

He'd always been happy with his decision to do nothing, to be a giant pain for everyone, but recently he'd started to feel tired, he missed being active, he actually missed working with his hands and he missed the outside world. He didn't think he had much chance of getting out of the palace grounds, after all he'd tried several times in the past and had failed every time, but Jackie's words the other day had haunted him, 'this is your home'. She was right, it was his home, as reluctant as he was to be there, and it would be his home for the next fifty or so years, did he really want to continue living how he was? Constantly watched by the officers, refused personal possessions except a few ragged books?

No. If he couldn't have his old life back, and he knew that wasn't a possibility, then he wanted at least a slightly easier one than he had, even some privacy would be a blessing. So Flicker had made the decision to be more cooperative, more helpful and perhaps he'd even start actually using his, 'gift' if they asked it of him. In all honesty, he had started to get a little curious of what their power was used for, of what it was the Emperor actually wanted with them, and maybe this way, maybe by changing his attitude, he'd find out.

Chapter 2

Aggie raced home, stumbled several times on the cobbles and narrowly avoided colliding with a large shire horse. The other pedestrians gave her odd looks as she raced past them but she couldn't help it, she was so excited, today was the day, finally something good was happening. She burst through her front door and almost fell into the kitchen where her mother was cooking and humming to herself; she threw her arms round her mother and hugged her tightly.

"You're home early," Nilla remarked glancing at the clock on the wall.

"I couldn't help it," Aggie said still squeezing her mother. "I ran all the way here," she grinned at her mother, who smiled softly back.

"Okay, wait here," she said removing her still smiling daughter from around her waist. Nilla left the room and returned moments later with a beautifully wrapped box; Aggie hopped from one foot to the other in excitement, "I hope it's what you wanted," she said apprehensively. Aggie ripped off the colourful paper and flung the lid off the box, gasping as she gazed at the contents; inside was a hand woven navy blue wrap with fine and elaborate deep purple and silver decoration. As Aggie ran her small, pale brown hands over the soft, smooth fabric she noticed the silver threads glistened; she gasped again.

"Is this real silver?" she asked and her mother nodded as Aggie threw her arms round her and said in a muffled voice. "This is the best gift you could have ever given me." She pulled away suddenly and there was a slight frown on her face. "How can we afford something like this?"

Nilla just smiled at her daughter, "You let me worry about that," she said stroking her daughters long black hair. "You only turn sixteen once you know." Aggie grinned again and instantly threw the wrap round her shoulders, admiring herself in the small wall mirror. Her mother watched her daughter and a sad smile crossed her face, yes it had been a lovely gift, and the best one she could offer since what she knew her daughter really wanted - to see her father - would never happen. Nilla busied herself back at the counter while Aggie continued to fondle her new wrap, which hadn't actually been as expensive as she'd implied. Everything except the silver thread had been sold to her at a discounted price since she was a weaver by trade and then she had made the garment herself in her spare time, but even if it had cost her several months pay it would have been worth it to see the smile on her daughters face.

"How was school?" she asked slicing a carrot into rough chunks.

"It was okay," Aggie replied twirling in front of the mirror to watch the colours on the wrap swirl.

"What did you do?"

"Maths, history, science and art." Nilla inhaled sharply and her daughter stopped twirling. "Don't worry, we were just decorating plant pots."

Nilla released her breath and smiled apologetically, "I'm sorry darling," she said putting the knife down so she could look at her daughter. "We just can't afford

14

another accident."

"I know and I'm really sorry about that, I hadn't even realised I'd cut my hand until-" Nilla nodded causing her daughter to stop mid-sentence; she didn't need reminding of the mouse her daughter had accidentally brought to life at school. They had only avoided the officers coming in and assessing everyone because the teachers had found a nest, which they had assumed the mouse belonged to. It had been too close and Nilla hadn't reacted well when her daughter had told her. She'd realised later that she'd overreacted but the anger had sprung from fear, the fear of losing her daughter to the Emperor, just as she'd lost Charlie.

After they had eaten Aggie went to her room with the intention of doing her homework but the paints she had concealed under the bed called to her and she took them carefully from their hiding place. She pulled a sheet of paper from her sketch pad and began to quickly and lightly draw the outline of some flowers; she had to be extra careful, she couldn't afford to have mistakes for these flowers. She needed them to be perfect, indistinguishable from the real thing. Once she was satisfied with her effort she started to fill in the colour with her special paints, the ones that contained a few drops of her blood. She worked quickly but carefully, adding colour, texture and shading to each of the flower heads, leaves and stems until eventually a colourful bunch of wildflowers stared at her from the paper. Aggie glanced quickly towards her door, took a deep breath in and let out a long breath; fine, pale yellow mist flowed from her mouth and began to twirl round the painted flowers.

The paper began to quiver and the image of the flowers started to inflate as if air was being pumped into it somehow; Aggie grinned as she watched the bunch of wild flowers slowly lift off the page and settle on its surface. She picked them up and smelled their sweet scent; it still fascinated her how accurate the creations were. She looked at the paper, which had browned and aged in the creation process as it always did and threw it into the bin. Aggie cracked opened her door and peered into the hallway listening for her mother; silence followed, which meant she was probably reading. Aggie crept along the hallway and towards the back door, which lead to the garden, once outside she wandered round, making it look like she was picking flowers in case her mother saw her from the window.

Of course she could have just picked flowers from their garden in the first place, but ever since the incident with the rabbit when she was small she had been in love with her gift and even though she had promised her mother she wouldn't use it again, she had, a lot. She'd tried to be careful, and the incident at school had really been an accident. Aggie made sure now that she only used her gift where she felt safe. She wished more than anything though that she could talk to someone about it; there was so much she still didn't understand and so much she felt she could learn. When she felt she had wandered the garden long enough she went back inside and found her mother in the living room reading a book, Nilla looked up when she entered and smiled at the flowers, which were presented to her.

"What's this?" she asked taking them from her daughter.

"They're a gift, to say thank you for the wrap."

Nilla smiled warmly at her daughter and smelt the sweet, calming scent of the flowers, "They're lovely," she said getting to her feet. "I'll put them in some water."

Aggie smiled and went back to her room, the next bit would be tricky; Aggie had found out quite quickly that objects created using her gift, no matter how real they looked, didn't work like the real thing. The plants she had created never seemed to age and any animals she'd brought to like had never seemed to need food or water. She had no idea why it happened but it meant the flowers she had given to her mother would have an unnaturally long life, unless she swapped them for a slightly altered version every few days. It was more work than simply picking real flowers but it gave her an excuse to keep using her gift and this made her grin.

Aggie had managed to replace her mother's flowers with a slightly altered version five days later, though she had almost been caught in the process. Nilla had been out at the market and Aggie, seeing that the flowers still looked as perky and fresh as the day she drew them thought it was best to create a more aged version. They didn't need to be altered by much but it was important to keep up appearances, after all her mother was extremely observant. She had been that way ever since the incident with the rabbit; she thought Aggie didn't notice her watching her every move but she did. She didn't really mind though, it just meant she'd had learnt to be extremely careful.

It hadn't taken long to create the slightly altered version of the flowers; because her mother had been out she'd been able to use the original bunch for reference. With the new bunch in the vase, Aggie only had to dispose of the old one, which could have proved to be tricky if they hadn't lit the fire that morning. Aggie threw the flowers into the flames and watched as they smoked for what felt like hours before finally catching fire. It was then that she heard the front door. She swivelled round, eyes wide as she stared at the door, then she turned back to the fire and tried to place a log on top of the flowers, which were now burning happily but were also still clearly visible.

"I'm home!" her mother called from the hall and Aggie, having made sure the flowers were now hidden under several logs, rushed out to meet her.

"Let me help with those," she said grabbing several of the bags from her mother's hands and taking them to the kitchen.

"What have you done while I've been away?" She asked as her daughter started to unpack the fresh fruit and vegetables from the bags.

"Trying to finish my homework," Aggie replied, frantically trying to remember if she'd moved her paints back into her bedroom.

"How much have you got left?"

"No, I should get it finished this morning, then I might take a walk outside since the weather's nice."

Her mother nodded, "Yes, it's lovely out there, why don't you ask some of your friends to go with you?" Aggie nodded absentmindedly and sighed internally as she remembered shoving her paints back under her bed before putting the flowers on the fire. "You could invite them round here instead if you'd prefer?" her mother added, peering at her daughter intensely.

Aggie smiled, "It's such a nice day, I'll see if they want to take a walk to the beach." Her mother smiled at her but frowned internally, she couldn't understand why her daughter continued to lie about having friends. Nilla knew she'd put pressure on her to be careful, she knew that her own fears about her daughters gift had made Aggie shy away from others but she'd always tried to encourage her to have friends. Unfortunately it seemed as though she either wasn't interested or was too afraid.

Aggie took one of the transport vehicles towards the edge of Shanora later that afternoon. It was early autumn and the weather was bright and warm with a clear sky and a gentle breeze, which meant the beach would be busy; luckily Aggie wasn't actually going to the beach. Before she reached the narrow trail that lead down to the walled and patrolled beach she hopped off the vehicle and veered off down a side street.

She was in the fishing district now; it made sense for the fishermen to live close to their livelihood but she wasn't staying there either. She reached an abandoned house at the end of the narrow street, closest to the city wall and slipped inside. Aggie had stumbled on the house quite by accident on a day she had been trying to escape some of the children from her school. She'd never told her mother she was being bullied, it didn't seem necessary to give her something else to worry about.

The house couldn't have been abandoned for long, the doors and windows were still intact and the spiders hadn't quite taken over yet. It wouldn't be that much longer until it was reported or the officers found it, so she had to make the most of it while she could. She moved into the back room and grinned as a small, black spaniel rushed to greet her. She crouched down and threw her arms round the creature as it licked her face; she laughed and fell to the floor while the dog clambered on top of her.

"Cassie!" she giggled as the spaniel continued to clamber over her and lick her face. She eventually managed to push the energetic dog from her and with as stern a command as she could muster told the dog to sit, which she did and remained motionless. This was Aggie's biggest secret, this was the thing her mother would never forgive her for if she ever found out. Creating flowers every now and then in her own home was one thing, but creating a spaniel and hiding it in an abandoned house was another.

The whole situation had been an accident; all Aggie had wanted to do was use the abandoned house to practice and hone her, 'gift'. She'd made plenty of other objects and creatures before she'd made Cassie but none of them had seemed as *real* as the spaniel. Aggie knew the danger of her gift, she knew what it would mean if she were found out, so she had always made sure she'd disposed of whatever it was she'd created before she'd left this building. Except for Cassie. No matter how hard she'd tried she could never bring herself to kill the dog, to kill *her* dog.

That was part of the problem, from the moment the spaniel had been created she had been real, far more real than anything else Aggie had ever made. Without thinking Aggie had named her and from that moment she had been unable to kill her, but she couldn't take her home either. Being made from clay, Cassie didn't eat anything, if she took her home it wouldn't be long before her mother became suspicious and she'd have to admit everything. She couldn't bear the thought of her mother killing Cassie, so she stayed in the abandoned building instead.

Cassie was still motionless as Aggie contemplated what she could do with the spaniel but when no solution sprang to mind she allowed the dog to move again and she sprang towards her master and creator. Aggie giggled again as Cassie earnestly tried to cover her face in saliva and decided she would tackle this problem another day.

Chapter 3

Flicker had received a lot of attention since he'd started actually teaching his class, which at the moment still caused him some amusement. After the first officer had checked on him, word had spread and over the past week he'd probably seen every officer in the grounds peer into his classroom. Jackie was thrilled of course and that made him smile, because he genuinely did care for her; she'd taken him under her wing when he'd first arrived and had treated him like family. He'd always regret how he pushed her away during those first few months and he was constantly trying to make up for it. Thankfully Jackie wasn't one to hold a grudge, either that or she thought constantly barging in on his life would be punishment enough.

Jan was the most astounded, not only had Flicker washed, but he was also now actually teaching. "Are you dying or something?" he asked one afternoon when Flicker's students were busy creating lifelike animal statues.

"If I am then it's news to me," Flicker replied as he carefully surveyed his class.

"Then why the sudden change?" he asked with a hint of suspicion.

Flicker shrugged, "I guess I finally realised I'm here for the long haul and there's only so much disruption I can cause before I become tired of it."

Jan shook his head in disbelief, "I have to say, you lasted longer than any of us thought, we even had a poll going for a while, but honestly, after the first couple of years we thought you'd never come round."

"Maybe you should try rebelling," Flicker said with a smile. "And see how long you last."

Jan grinned and gave Flicker a gentle shove, "I have to say you're a lot easier to be around when you don't smell so bad."

Flicker snorted, "I wish I could say the same for you." Jan laughed unexpectedly loudly causing a young girl to jump and behead her half sculpted lizard. "Honestly Jan," he said walking over to the girl to try and help her salvage the reptile.

"My apologies," Jan replied as he made his way to the door. "Will you be out in the grounds later?" Flicker nodded, while helping to re-sculpt the lizard's eyes and Jan left the room with a smile.

Despite his new – if not slightly forced – positive attitude, Flicker continued to eat his meals alone. Jackie had offered him a place at her table with her friends but he couldn't stand the way they looked at him and he definitely didn't want to sit with his students no matter how many times they offered. So he ate alone, which suited him fine. It was strangely the only time he felt really and truly alone with his thoughts, even when lying in his room at night he knew there was an officer just outside and he knew they were always listening for him. At mealtimes however, no one was paying attention to him, or to anyone for that matter, which meant he could be alone, he could finally breathe.

A man in his mid-thirties, with dark skin and even

darker hair sat opposite Flicker and proceeded to stare at him with intense green eyes. Flicker paused with a fork of food halfway to his mouth and stared back.

"Can I help you?" he asked with weariness at having his isolation disturbed.

"That depends," the man replied.

"On what?" he sighed as he returned his fork to his plate.

"On whether you want to trade classes," the man said with a hopeful glance, Flicker shot a confused expression his way.

"You want to trade classes?" he asked still confused and the man nodded. "What's wrong with your class?"

"Most of them aren't interested in learning anything," the man said in an exasperated tone. "And I know you like to be a bit free and loose with the rules."

"Sorry," Flicker said with a half apologetic smile. "I thought everyone would have heard by now but I've recently turned over a new leaf, I'm actively teaching now."

The man opposite cursed loudly and rose to his feet, "Thanks anyway," he said and trudged out of the hall.

"That was odd," Flicker muttered to himself and continued eating as the piercing green eyes remained etched in his memory.

The evening autumn air was cool but there was still some warmth to it as Flicker stepped out into the gardens sometime later and wandered towards the gaming lawn. Several Artists' were playing croquet and another few were having a go at quoits. He wasn't there to play – he was never there to play – but occasionally he enjoyed watching the others, so long as he didn't have to actually engage with them. He positioned himself on one of the benches furthest away and sniggered as one of the Artist's hit his croquet ball in completely the wrong direction.

"Do you think you could do any better?" Jan asked from behind causing Flicker to jump.

"Probably not," he admitted. "But then, I'm not the one trying to impress Faye."

Jan raised an eyebrow as he sat next to Flicker, "Is that what Mace has been doing?"

Flicker laughed, "You wouldn't think it to look but yes."

"Well good luck to him," Jan said with a smile, then he turned to Flicker.

"No," Flicker said as Jan opened his mouth.

"You don't even know what I was going to say."

"Yes I do and the answer is no," he said in a firm tone.

Jan grinned, "Why not? It's not like there's much else to do."

Flicker looked at him and his face was grim, "I can't think of anything worse than getting into a relationship under the scrutiny of the Emperor," he said getting to his feet and walking away from the lawn games.

Jan jumped to his feet and followed, "Who said anything about a relationship, I just thought you could have some fun."

"Fun? Tell me if the idea of having officers listen outside your door while you've got someone in your room sounds like fun to you."

Jan fell silent and the smile fell from his face, "I hadn't thought about it like that."

"That's the problem," Flicker said bitterly. "You don't think about what life is really like for us, all you see is that we're provided for and protected but we're not." He stopped abruptly and turned to face Jan; his hands

24

had balled into fists by his sides. "We're told when to eat, when to sleep, we're watched day and night, we're prisoners! It doesn't matter how much you sugar-coat things that's what we are!"

"I thought you said you'd turned over a new leaf," Jan pointed out and Flicker relaxed his hands.

"Give me a break," he said sighing heavily and continuing to walk towards the lake. "It's only been a week."

Flicker's class improved significantly in the weeks that followed, Jackie had told him he'd caught the attention of the people upstairs and when he'd asked who they were she'd simply smiled and said, 'you'll see'. He couldn't explain why but those two words made him feel uneasy.

He was halfway through a class when it happened, when a petite young woman with short blonde hair was escorted into his class by an officer. She wore a long dark skirt and a white blouse, and carried a clipboard.

"Is everything okay?" Flicker asked as he walked over.

The young woman smiled and looked down at her clipboard, "Flicker is it?" she asked in a cool voice, he nodded but remained silent. "I've been asked to audit your class."

Flicker's eyebrows raised an inch, "An audit?" he asked in confusion. "I've never had an audit before."

The young woman smiled again and looked at him pointedly, "You've never taught your class before." The officer at her side let out a chuckle while Flicker continued to look stunned.

"What do I need to do?" he finally asked after several minutes of silence.

"Just continue teaching as normal, I'll take a seat in

the corner."

Flicker turned back to his class who quickly busied themselves with their sculptures. Suddenly feeling very self-conscious, he moved to the front of the room and addressed his class.

"I've uh, I've taken a look at the work you're doing at the moment and uh it's coming along nicely." He cursed himself internally, wondering why he suddenly cared what this woman thought. A glance to his left saw her scribbling notes onto her clipboard; he turned back to his class and took a deep breath.

"Your basic animal forms are improving significantly," he said gesturing to a small fox at the front. "But you need to pay more attention to the smaller details." He turned to the small clay cat sat on his desk and beckoned the students forward. "Take a look at the texture and detail I've included on the fur, the tiny indication of claws on her paws, now take a closer look at her facial features." The students crowded round his desk and began scrutinising his work; he suddenly felt far more relaxed and had almost forgotten the woman scribbling furiously to his left.

"To be able to fool someone, to have them think the creature is real you have to make your creation think it's real." Several confused faces turned towards him. "Take a look at that hawk," he said pointing to a clay bird on one of the nearby tables; the creator blushed. "The basic form is excellent, there's even detail on the feathers, but look closely at the facial features, at the legs and talons, it lacks definition, which means it won't act the right way when brought to life."

The hawk's creator blush deepened and Flicker smiled kindly, "You're all improving at an astonishing rate considering you've had a terrible teacher," they chuckled at that. "In order to make your creations perfect you must pay attention to the little things as well as the big. I suggest you spend the afternoon in the animal sanctuary to really get to grips with their likenesses." The students returned to their desks and continued with their sculpting while Flicker sat behind his desk and watched. He didn't notice the woman approach him and jumped when she spoke.

"You have an interesting way of teaching Flicker," she said looking down at her notes.

"What do you mean?" he asked with a hint of nervousness.

"Most teachers would mention the importance of detail at the start of the year, before their students have even touched the clay."

"I think we can both agree I'm not like most teachers," he replied with a hint of a smile. "Personally though, I like to see what people can do before I start imparting my *wisdom* on them."

"Do you not think that by imparting your wisdom from day one you can ensure they use the correct methods from the beginning?"

Flicker winced and turned to fully face her, "You're not an Artist are you?"

"Actually I am."

He looked surprised, "Have you taught before?"

She shook her head.

"I didn't think so, you see if you had then you would know that there aren't correct and incorrect techniques. Yes there are techniques that are useful, that achieve the best result, but quite frankly everyone has a different style when it comes to art. For me to tell someone what they're doing is wrong when they're getting the right results would itself be wrong."

He hadn't meant to but he'd started to raise his voice and the woman had taken a step back from him, it was only when the door opened and an officer peered in that he took a deep breath and spoke in a more appropriate tone.

"I'm sorry," he said looking apologetic. "Some of my students haven't the best artistic ability and I'm simply doing my best to encourage them."

The young woman nodded and scribbled a few more notes on her clipboard. "Thank you for your time Flicker," she said as she walked towards the door. "You'll be receiving a report from me in the next few days." She left the room quietly and it was only then that he realised she hadn't mentioned her name.

Chapter 4

The sun was setting and dusk had appeared in Nilla and Aggie's garden where the latter sat sculpting something from the clay rich soil. Normally she wouldn't try something so risky, but since her mother was working late, she thought she would be safe. The garden was small and fenced, with a number of shrubs and plants that were beginning their hibernation process. Aggie continued to glance around her but it was getting difficult to see and the fence surrounding the garden was tall so she wasn't really expecting trouble. She didn't know why but she was itching to use her gift today, perhaps it was because she hadn't been able to use it as much lately or perhaps it was because she knew she was good at it.

She had finished the basic shape for her creature, a simple blackbird, and was now adding detail with a small wooden tool she had taken from school. It was perfect for adding fine detail to the feathers, face and legs. She had probably been working on this bird for over two hours, carefully making sure that every detail was as precise as possible. Really she shouldn't have chosen such an unpredictable creature; unpredictable inasmuch as birds tend to fly away as soon as they're created. At the same time, it would be harder for people to track the bird back to her if it didn't look or act like it should.

It didn't take long until she was satisfied with her

work, then she decided to test the theory she'd been working on. It went back to Cassie, the spaniel that seemed so much like a real dog. She'd tried to work out why the dog was so much better than her other creations, why she was so much more lifelike and she thought she had the answer.

It wasn't just about simple mimicry, any good Artist or artisan could make a spaniel sculpture look the way it should. Anyone with artistic ability could add fine detail to make the creature *look* real but not anyone could have that creature *act* real once brought to life.

When she'd brought the rabbit to life all those years ago, she'd wished it were real as she'd accidentally breathed life into it. But with Cassie she'd imagined the spaniel moving and acting as a real dog would, then she'd brought the dog to life. Now she wondered whether it was that level of thought, along with the breath of life that made the creations so real.

She glanced quickly round the darkening garden once more, took a deep breath, pictured a majestic blackbird in her mind, flitting round the garden, chirping happily, searching for food and let her breath go.

A fine pale yellow mist was exhaled along with her breath and began to swirl around the blackbird sculpture. Slowly, the colour of the bird's body and legs darkened to a deep brown/black, while the beak and a thin ring around the eyes brightened to a soft yellow. At the same time the bird solidified, no longer looking like a statue. The feathers ruffled and the head twitched towards her where two beady eyes stared straight at her. Aggie gasped; the bird looked just like all the others that frequently visited the garden. It ruffled its feathers once more, took a few hops forward, spread its wings and took to the skies. Aggie gazed after it in wonder and amazement and grinned to herself; her creations were going to look so much better from now on.

"What was that?" A gruff voice to her right made her jump and she swivelled round on her knees to see who had spoken. A thin faced, grey haired man was watching her with narrowed eyes over the fence.

Aggie's heart quickened, "A blackbird," she said trying to make her voice sound normal though she was sure it wavered. "I saw it on the ground and thought it was injured." The man eyed her suspiciously and Aggie hoped the increasing darkness was hiding her dirtied clothes and hands.

"You shouldn't go near such things," the old man said in his gruff voice. "Could be carrying a disease." Aggie nodded and got to her feet, trying to make her way to the house as quickly and as normally as possible. The old man followed her with dark eyes as she left, then he glanced at the disturbed earth close to where Aggie had been sitting and frowned.

Aggie was roughly shaken awake the next morning and saw her mother's concerned expression through bleary eyes.

"What's wrong?" she asked through a yawn.

"What happened in the garden last night?" Nilla asked in a stern voice laced with worry.

Aggie's heart began to pound but she tried not to show her alarm, "What do you mean?" she asked in as confused a voice as possible and thankfully the fact that she'd just woken helped significantly.

"I've just had Glen at the door," Nilla said as she began pacing the room. "He said he saw you doing something to a bird and that there was disturbed earth." Nilla stopped her pacing and looked sternly at her daughter. "Please tell me you didn't create something."

Aggie sat up slowly and swallowed hard, she wasn't good at lying to her mother but she was going to try. "I thought I saw something moving in the garden, so I went to see what it was," she began while her mother's gaze bore into her. "When I got closer I saw it was a bird, I don't know what had happened but it looked injured, I went to help it and it just flew away."

"And the disturbed earth?"

There was an accusatory tone and Aggie winced, "I don't know, maybe I scuffed it when I was trying to help the bird?" She tried her best to sound innocent, tried to will her mother to believe her story. Eventually, after what felt like hours her mother relaxed and sat on the bed next to her daughter.

"I'm sorry, I know I'm hard on you sometimes but I don't want to lose you."

"I know mother," Aggie said throwing her arms round Nilla's neck. "I'm sorry I worried you." Her mother smiled and left the room while Aggie felt a knot of guilt in her stomach, she was going to have to be more careful.

She made sure she didn't use her gift at all for several days and the only thing she was seen doing by the old man in her garden was her homework; she needed him to think she was normal. When she felt the heat had died down she decided to go and see Cassie in the abandoned building, assuming it was still abandoned. She hopped on one of the transport vehicles close to her house and sat humming to herself until it was time to hop off again.

She tried to look casual as she strolled down the streets of the fishing district, noticing how unusually busy it was for the time of day. She found it difficult to maintain a slow, steady stride; the excitement of seeing Cassie again, and maybe creating something else was almost too much. Once she was almost out of sight of the main street her pace quickened and a grin spread across her face at the thought of seeing her spaniel creation.

She turned into the narrow street where the abandoned building was and stopped abruptly, her face fell as she saw a number of officers milling about at the other end.

"Oh Crafts!" she said under her breath as she turned quickly to leave the narrow street. She wasn't fast enough though and an officer called to her, Aggie turned back towards them and one of the officers jogged towards her. She did her best to look innocent.

"Are you from round here?" the officer, a middle aged woman with cropped, dark brown hair, asked. Aggie shook her head and the officer looked suspicious. "What are you doing here?"

Aggie swallowed hard, "I heard from some of the children at school that there was a secret tunnel to the caves on the beach somewhere round here." The answer, which had sounded good in her head, sounded ridiculous once she'd said it. The officer continued to stare at her with suspicious eyes, Aggie cleared her throat and tried again. "I was meant to be meeting some friends here to try and find it," she shrugged her shoulders in an attempt to look casual. "I guess they saw you and fled." She remained under the scrutinising gaze of the officer for what felt like several hours until the woman finally turned back to her colleagues.

"Go home kid," she said, not looking back at Aggie. "There's no secret tunnel to the caves round here." Aggie heaved an internal sigh of relief and turned to go when she heard several loud barks. She swivelled round and saw

Cassie bounding towards her and the officer; the officer cursed and pulled out her firearm.

"No!" Aggie cried, running towards the oncoming spaniel and throwing herself between her and the officer. The woman lowered her weapon and stared at Aggie with renewed suspicion.

"It's just a stray dog kid," she said holstering her weapon as Cassie bounded around Aggie.

"I'll take her home," Aggie said crouching down and putting her arms round Cassie's neck, who proceeded to try and drown her in saliva. The officer shrugged and walked back towards her colleagues, Aggie heaved a sigh of relief and scampered back out into the main street with Cassie at her side.

"That was a close one Cass," she said as she continued to jog away from the narrow street; the spaniel bounded at her heels and when she felt she was far enough away from the officers she slowed to a walk. They continued walking through the fishing district and then as animals weren't allowed on the transport vehicles, they continued on towards her home near the main market square.

The sky was darkening by the time they reached the one storey house and Aggie's stomach flipped as she thought about what she would say to her mother. She pushed open the door and Cassie bounded across the threshold and into the living room where Nilla yelped in surprise. Aggie ran after the spaniel and looked apologetically at her mother who was trying to avoid being licked to death by an energetic dog.

"Aggie?!"

"I'm sorry mother," Aggie said, pulling Cassie from Nilla's lap. "She's a bit enthusiastic."

"Where in the Emperor's name did she come

from?!"

Aggie took a deep breath, "I found her in the fishing district, she was going to be killed and I couldn't let that happen." The statement was only half true but she hoped her mother would believe her. Nilla stared open mouthed at her daughter and sighed heavily as she saw the look of pleading in her eyes.

"Alright," her mother said in a resigned tone. "She can stay," Aggie's heart leapt and she squealed in excitement. "But you must be the one to look after her," she said in a stern tone. Aggie nodded her head furiously and wrapped her arms round the spaniel who wagged her tail enthusiastically.

"Come on Cassie, let's go to the gar-"

"You've already named her?" Aggie froze mid-step and turned to her mother who was eyeing her with suspicion.

"I-I named her on the walk home," she stammered. "I needed to call her something."

"She seems to have taken to you awfully fast," Nilla indicated how the spaniel remained at her daughter's heels and Aggie felt herself blush.

"I saved her from being killed."

Nilla raised an eyebrow, then focused on the book she had been reading, "It's late Aggie, you'd better get yourself to bed." There was a lack of warmth behind her mother's words, which made Aggie cringe and she went silently to her room, with Cassie following at her heels.

"I'm such an idiot," she hissed to herself when they were safely in her room. "I should have just brought you here from the beginning." Even as she said the words she knew it wouldn't have made any difference, there was a special bond between her and Cassie and the spaniel had obeyed her from day one. "I don't know what she'll do when she figures it out," Aggie said as Cassie stretched out on the carpet. "But I promise I won't let her hurt you, I don't care what she does to me, but I won't let anyone hurt you." She scratched softly behind Cassie's ears and the dog yawned contentedly.

Outside, Nilla listened by the door.

Chapter 5

Flicker cursed as he ran down the darkened corridors of the palace; he could hear the footsteps of those who chased him, they were only minutes behind. He cursed again as he nearly ran into a door and skidded to the left where he continued to run at full speed. *How could things have gone so wrong so quickly?* He thought as he tripped, fell and sprawled across the floor; he quickly picked himself up and started to run again.

His breathing was heavy and he felt sweat trickle down his face. He reached the familiar corridor and saw the door leading to his room. Flicker threw himself inside, flung himself under the sheets and tried with all his might to slow his breathing. His face was probably bright red but he hoped they wouldn't notice in this light; they'd clearly check his room first, after all, he had a bad history.

His door creaked open and he could hear the shuffling of feet as at least two officers came into his room. Flicker practically held his breath as shadows fell across his closed eyes; they were inspecting him, trying to see whether he looked like he'd been running. It felt like they stared at him for an age, and he tried to keep his breathing slow and steady, trying to mimic someone who was sleeping.

The shadows finally receded and the shuffling footsteps left the room and went back into the corridor.

Flicker heard his door creak as it was closed but the absence of a click told him it hadn't been shut completely. He heard lowered voices in the corridor outside,

"If it wasn't him then who was it?" a deep, male voice said.

"I don't know," replied a distinctly feminine voice.

"Are we sure he was asleep?" the male voice asked.

"I don't know," the female voice said again, then she whispered something to the man that Flicker couldn't catch. He heard the sounds of footsteps getting quieter down the corridor and heaved an internal sigh of relief though he didn't dare move. He remained lying in his bed facing the wall, eyes closed and continued to breathe deeply.

He must have remained that way for half an hour and had almost drifted off to sleep when the door burst open and the female officer leapt into the room, her firearm raised. Flicker sat up in alarm and stared wide eyed at her. The officer pointed her firearm at Flicker and eyed him suspiciously, he stared at her in confusion, almost forgetting what he'd been doing earlier that night.

"Is…is something wrong?" he asked in his best innocent tone.

"Someone just tried to break into the Emperor's private rooms," she said, firearm still aimed at Flicker's face. He adopted a shocked expression and looked around his room as if expecting to see the culprit hiding somewhere. "Don't play dumb," the officer snapped. "I know it was you, you're always causing trouble."

Flicker smiled innocently, "Breaking in isn't really my style, I'm usually trying to break out." The officer moved forwards and smacked him across the face with her firearm; a spark of pain flooded his face.

"Crafts!" Flicker yelled throwing a hand to his face.

"What was that for?"

"Admit what you did," she said sternly, levelling the firearm at him again.

"I haven't done anything," Flicker replied angrily, his face burning beneath his hand.

The officer finally lowered her firearm but didn't holster it, "Your little act isn't fooling everyone," she said turning to leave. "I'm going to be keeping an eye on you from now on." She slammed the door behind her and left Flicker in near darkness. He let out a loud sigh and rubbed the side of his face, he would have a cracking bruise in the morning.

It had been a stupid idea, he'd known it from the start, the problem was he wasn't good at being patient. It had started several months ago, after he'd received his first class audit; the review had been surprisingly good. He'd been almost certain the woman would slate him but had been pleasantly surprised to read a glowing review. He'd thought that would be the end of it, but the woman continued to visit every few weeks and even started to test the students. He hadn't been aware the students needed to be tested but then he'd not actually taught them before.

The woman, whose name he now knew was Lucie, brought illustrations of various animals, plants and everyday objects into the classroom and expected the students to sculpt them within the day. These tests also required them to mix their blood with the clay and bring their creation to life at the end.

Flicker had protested at first, his students were still learning, they weren't overly confident with their skills and she was placing pressure on them, which had caused a number of them to slip up. He was convinced the quality of their work had declined because of these tests and he couldn't see the point of them. When he asked Lucie she simply told him not to worry and that his students were on target. When he'd questioned that, she'd simply failed to answer.

In the last couple of months he'd almost forgotten why he'd decided to change his attitude, why he'd decided to cooperate. But in that moment, when Lucie had told him they were on target it came rushing back. He wanted to know why they were there, he wanted to know what it was they were doing for the Emperor and he wanted to know why it was so important that their creations were perfect.

Flicker had started to talk to the other Artists, had decided to ask about their classes and about their personal lives. Although he despised small talk with people he really had no interest in, he'd found it was a great way to get people to relax, and when they relaxed, they let little things slip. So far he'd already found out that class audits took place every month in every classroom and the students were graded. When a student consistently achieved the same grade over several weeks, they were removed from the class and when he'd asked around a bit more, he'd found out they hadn't ever returned.

It seemed he was getting more questions than answers; what was the purpose of the audits? Where were the students being taken? What did the Emperor want with them? And why had it been so long since anyone had seen him? Nothing had made sense. He'd tried asking Jackie about the vanishing students but even she hadn't seemed to know what was going on.

"I expect their just doing the Emperor's work," she had said, not really giving it much thought.

"Yes but what *is* the Emperor's work?" Flicker had pressed. "Doesn't it bother you Jack? They're taking the best Artist's from our classes and we've no idea where they're going or what they're doing."

"I'm sure they're doing work to help protect the city, you know Endore and Flintai have made an alliance."

"If that were the case why not just tell us? I'm telling you Jack there's something weird going on."

"What makes you think that?"

Flicker looked frustrated, "No one sees the Emperor anymore. That man is meant to be hundreds of years old and yet no one's claimed to have seen him in decades. We've been told the other cities have allied against us, that they're planning to invade and yet nothing has happened. Tell me that doesn't seem a little odd to you?"

Jackie looked at him thoughtfully then just shrugged and continued to read her book.

Flicker was frustrated and restless. As far as he could tell, the students weren't being removed from the palace. He'd talked to Jan about whether Artists were ever taken out of the palace and he'd sighed and shook his head, clearly thinking Flicker was reverting to his old ways. Although he hadn't actually Flicker an answer, his response had told him everything; Artists didn't leave. He'd then tried to follow a couple of officers as they escorted one of the students away from a classroom but was quickly stopped and prevented from moving any further. As far as he could tell from the direction they were walking, they had headed towards the main stairs.

He hadn't ever really explored the palace, he knew lots of the Artist's had when they'd first moved in to the palace but he'd been so angry and miserable when he'd arrived that he hadn't really been interested in what secrets his new home might hold. He'd been more interested in getting as far away from it as possible, but now he *was* interested, because there was clearly something going on, something the officers and the Emperor – if he even existed anymore – didn't want the Artists to know about.

He'd started his, 'plan' by wandering corridors he'd never been down before to see whether they were actually forbidden or not and he found the whole experience fascinating. The places he'd walked on a daily basis were all fairly mundane to him now, always the same paintings, sculptures and tapestries. But these new corridors were amazing; he hadn't realised just how impressive and varied the artistic ability was in the palace. The paintings were vibrant and detailed; he could tell that every brush stroke had been carefully positioned in order to make the image as realistic as possible. He'd spent so long staring at the pieces of work that he'd almost forgotten why he was there. He'd found it surprisingly difficult to tear himself away from the artwork that adorned the walls and floor but a stern reminder that something underhand could be happening to the Artists and the city, brought him back to reality.

It had taken several weeks of exploring until he had finally found what he was looking for, or at least what he assumed he was looking for. He'd wandered down a completely new corridor, which was surprisingly sparsely decorated and as he rounded another corridor he came face to face with a couple of officers.

"What are you doing down here?" A tall, burly man asked.

Flicker stumbled back in surprise, "I'm sorry," he said as he tried to regain his composure. "I was just taking a walk to stretch my legs."

The burly officer grunted and eyed Flicker suspiciously, "What's wrong with getting some fresh air?"

"Have you seen the weather lately?" he asked and when the officer's stared back with black expressions he elaborated. "There's a huge storm raging outside, no one's allowed out until it clears."

The second officer, a shorter, stocky man stepped in front of his colleague and addressed Flicker, "I think you had better find somewhere else to walk." He put a hand to his hip where his firearm rested and Flicker backed away before turning to leave. His heart had been pounding but he'd managed to get a glimpse of the corridor behind the officers. There had been several doors, spaced well apart and all had been padlocked. If the student's really were doing the Emperor's work, Flicker would put money that it was in those rooms.

He had thankfully been taken off twenty-four hour watch several weeks ago, which had meant he could proceed further with his, 'plan' and he had started sneaking out of his room at night. He spent weeks finding out where and when the officers patrolled through the night, ensuring he could find a quick and clear path back to his room if the need arose. He was surprised to find there weren't really any regular patrols; officers guarded the main entrance and every couple of hours a couple of them would walk the main corridors, but that was pretty much it.

He'd managed to make his way back to the forbidden corridor only to find it was guarded and it seemed no matter how long he waited the officers remained at their posts. It was almost two in the morning when he thought about giving up just as the two guards walked down the corridor away from him and out of sight. He'd thought about trying to get past the locked doors there and then but it seemed too risky and he didn't want to blow the plan before he'd actually been able to properly try it.

Instead he waited silently until two new officers arrived and stationed themselves partway down the corridor. Flicker had been counting under his breath until they'd arrived and guessed it had been about ten minutes. That didn't leave much of a window of opportunity but he'd have to find a way to work with what he had.

That brought him back to this evening when he'd gone back to the corridor to try and pick one of the padlocks and sneak into a room. Pickling locks wasn't like it was in the books he'd read though, they made it seem quick and easy, both of which it was not. The new set of officers had seen him as they turned the corner, or at least they'd seen someone, he'd had the sense to cover his face and hair and they'd set off after him.

Although he knew he would be bruised and tired in the morning he hadn't seen the evening's activities as a failure. The answers he wanted were definitely inside those padlocked rooms, the female officer's reaction to what had happened had told him that. He would have to be patient, he grimaced at that thought, and he'd have to work on his lock picking skills but he vowed there and then that he'd find out what was in those rooms if it was the last thing he did.

Chapter 6

Everything had been a bit hard for Aggie lately, her mother had hit the roof when she'd found out the truth about Cassie. Nilla had burst into the room, scolded her daughter severely, then taken the spaniel away from her. Aggie had cried and been miserable for days, she'd refused to acknowledge her mother or that what she had done was wrong.

She had returned from school one afternoon to find Cassie waiting for her just inside the door. She'd squealed and thrown her arms round the spaniel's neck, hugging her tightly while Cassie licked her face. Her mother had stood in the doorway to the kitchen and Aggie had looked up at her, beaming and Nilla had found it difficult not to smile herself.

"This doesn't make what you did okay," Nilla had said as she walked back into the kitchen.

Aggie had trailed behind, "I know," she'd said quietly while Cassie skipped around her feet. "I'm really sorry mother, I didn't mean any harm."

Nilla had sighed heavily, "You're just not taking this seriously, Aggie," she'd said sitting down at their small wooden table. "What do you think the officers would do if they found out we'd been lying about you all this time? What do you think they'd do to me?"

Her eyes had widened as the realisation hit, "I'm

sorry," she'd said loudly and with tears pricking her eyes. "You're right, I didn't think, I promise I'll be more careful."

"It's not about being careful Aggie!" Nilla had snapped, getting to her feet. "You shouldn't be using your gift at all!"

"You don't know what it's like," Aggie had protested. "My insides itch until I use my gift, it's part of me, I can't just ignore it."

"You'll ignore it Aggie," Nilla had said quietly and with an underlying threatening tone. "Because if you don't, one day you'll come home and Cassie won't be here." Aggie's eyes had widened again and this time the tears spilled down her cheeks as she screamed curses at her mother and ran from the room.

Eventually everything calmed between Aggie and her mother and the latter reluctantly agreed not to use her gift. As if that wasn't enough, her mother gave her a vial filled with her blood, so that if anyone asked her to prove she wasn't an Artist, she could cheat. Her mother in turn had asked for a small amount of Aggie's blood; she'd been hesitant to give it, saying there'd be no need if they both used, 'normal' blood but her mother had insisted, stating it was only a precaution and Aggie had eventually given in.

She was frustrated that she couldn't use her gift, her insides itched at her to create something and she suddenly remembered the paints under her bed. She excused herself from the living room, claiming she had homework to do and went to her room. She started rummaging frantically under her bed and began to panic when she couldn't find what she was looking for.

Her heart pounding, she started grabbing everything

and anything and pulled it from under the bed until eventually there was nothing left and she still hadn't found the paints. She stared with a look of horror and a noise behind made her turn.

"Are you looking for these?" her mother asked, holding up the box of paints.

Aggie's face reddened, "I wasn't going to-"

"Don't lie to me Aggie!" Nilla snapped. "Do you think I'm an idiot? Do you think I don't know you've been creating? I know those flowers you gave me weren't real, but I chose to ignore it, I chose to believe you were going through a phase and as long as you used your gift inside and on little things then what did it matter." Aggie opened her mouth to speak but her mother cut her off before words could escape. "Crafts! Aggie you've become reckless, you've been using your gift outside! You almost got caught! Is this all just a game to you? Don't you even care that you'll be taken away."

"I do care!" Aggie yelled. "But if I don't create something soon I'll go crazy! You don't understand how it feels, you're not special like me!"

"Do you know what it's like for me?" her mother asked her voice suddenly quiet but powerful; Aggie looked confused. "I had my husband taken from me before we'd had chance to settle into our new life, I was left to raise our child alone. The only piece of him that I've got left is you Aggie," her daughter shifted uncomfortably. "I've done my best to keep you safe all these years. I should have turned you in myself after finding out you were like him, but I couldn't, I couldn't lose you too. Do you not see you're playing with fire? Sooner or later you'll slip up and someone will find out, you'll be taken from me and we'll never see each other again. It's almost happened once as it is! Do you understand why I need you not to use your gift?"

Aggie nodded, tears filling her eyes and her mother bent down to hug her. "I'm sorry Aggie, in an ideal world I'd have you creating all the time because I want to see you happy, but this world is far from ideal and I refuse to hand over the only good thing in my life to the Emperor." She kissed her daughter on the forehead then left quietly and closed the door. Aggie crawled into her bed and began to sob, not only at what her mother had said, but also at the loss she felt over her gift.

Aggie ensured she didn't use her gift but she was becoming more miserable by the day because of it. It wasn't just the loss of her magic, it was her awful school life; she didn't have any friends and she was treated badly by the other children and the teacher. It was no secret that she was artistic, many people were, it's why there were so many artisans in the city of Shanora. But what most people didn't seem to understand was that you could be artistic and not be an Artist. Of course in Aggie's case this wasn't exactly true, but the other children didn't know that, they simply didn't like her because she had talent.

Her teacher was almost as bad as the children, she didn't actually tease Aggie of course, that would have been unprofessional, but she did treat her differently. She kept her distance, ignored her hand when it was raised to answer a question and just generally tried to pretend Aggie didn't exist.

It was frustrating, and normally Aggie would create something small at home to calm her mind but now she felt like an exposed nerve. Events at school had begun to escalate, though she'd no idea what had triggered it; the other children had started calling her harsh, insulting names and began to mention her father during art class. She had never really known her father, he'd been taken to the palace when she was very young and she barely remembered anything about him; there weren't even any pictures.

"I heard your dad was scum you know," a boy with greasy blonde hair and a crooked face said one day while they were using pastels. Aggie tried to ignore him but he continued, egged on by his friends. "I heard he'd been creating things for years before he got caught," he said loudly to a girl next to him who had long brown hair, tied back in a braid.

The girl, known as Stephie sneered, "What kind of things Jason?" she asked with mock interest. Aggie knew where this was going; she'd heard it far too many times before. It didn't make her any less angry.

"Money," Jason said and Stephie gasped a little too loudly, Aggie tried to ignore them.

"Money?" Stephie asked in mock disbelief and Jason nodded. "That would mean he'd been cheating the Emperor."

"Oh yeah," Jason said as Aggie tried not to clench her fists. "It's the reason they've got that house and those nice clothes. They definitely couldn't have afforded things like that with their normal wages."

The pastel in Aggie's hands snapped as she clenched her hand round it and she spun on her heels to face the boy and his accomplice. She opened her mouth to respond when the teacher, Mrs Rhodes finally looked up from her desk.

"Settle down children," she said turning back to whatever she had been reading.

"I'll bet she's an Artist too," Jason whispered, grinning cruelly at Aggie. "Look at her work, she's definitely got the ability." He nudged Stephie who glanced at Aggie's picture of a mountainous landscape.

"Probably is one," Stephie almost hissed. "Like father like daughter, I'll bet she's creating money just like he did too."

"Crafts! Will you two shut up!" Aggie snapped, getting noisily to her feet. Mrs Rhodes shot her a stern look but Aggie was too far gone to care. "You don't know anything about me or my family, none of you do, so shut your Emperor loving faces!" The room fell silent and she knew she'd gone too far. Mrs Rhodes rose silently from her seat and took Aggie by the arm, she led her from the room and into a tiled corridor.

"There was no need for that outburst Miss Sanders," Mrs Rhodes said in a stern, unforgiving voice.

Aggie remained defiant, "Was I supposed to let them bad-mouth my family like that?"

"You shouldn't rise to them, you know they do it to wind you up."

"They do it because they know they'll get away with it," Aggie said before she could stop herself.

"Just what do you mean by that?" Mrs Rhodes asked sharply, folding her arms.

"Nothing," she said quickly, trying to backtrack. "I'm sorry Mrs Rhodes, I didn't mean what I said."

"I should hope you don't, I'll expect you to remain behind today for half an hour." Aggie deflated and nodded her head but her insides burned with hatred towards these people, why on earth should she be the one being punished when it had been the others who had started the whole thing?

It was quiet and cold when Aggie finally left the school grounds, the other children having left over half an hour ago while Aggie had been cleaning up the classroom. She grumbled and muttered to herself on the walk home until she came across Jason and Stephie hanging around a darkened alley. They were with several of their friends and they turned to Aggie with wicked grins on their faces.

"Crafts," Aggie said under her breath as she tried to walk past them.

"What's the rush?" Jason asked grabbing her by the arm while Stephie and several others barred her path.

"I just want to get home," she said quietly and tried to remove Jason's hand from her arm, he gripped tighter and she winced.

"But we wanted to talk about what happened earlier today," Jason said.

"What about it?" Aggie asked, a sense of dread flowing over her.

Stephie grinned, "We want to know how long you've been hiding your ability."

Aggie froze and her heart missed a beat, she remembered to breathe and tried to look as normal and as innocent as possible, "Excuse me?"

"Don't give us that," Stephie replied taking a step closer to Aggie. "You're an Artist aren't you." It wasn't really a question but Aggie shook her head furiously.

Jason snorted, "Oh please, you must think we're as stupid as Mrs Rhodes, we know you created that mouse, we've heard rumours you created a bird in your garden, and where exactly did that dog come from?"

Aggie's heart was in her throat, pounding away, threatening to burst from her chest if she didn't calm down and control herself.

She forced a smile, "Nice story," she said, hoping her voice wasn't wavering too much. "I wish I could tell you it was true, but I can't. The mouse was part of a nest, the bird in my garden was injured and the dog was a stray I found in the fishing district, ask the officers who found her."

The group stared at her, clearly unconvinced but Aggie didn't care anymore, she just wanted to get out of there. "I wish I *was* an Artist," she continued, wrenching her arm from Jason's grip. "Then I'd finally be able to get away from all of you." As they stared at her in stunned silence she bolted and raced down the street before they had a chance to realise she'd gone. They stared angrily after her as she ran and she heard Jason shout several incomprehensible curses after her, then something clearer came through and it sent a shiver down her spine.

"You can't hide Aggie! The officers will find you! You'll get what you deserve!"

Chapter 7

It had been surprisingly easy for Flicker to stay out of trouble and look innocent, though the officer who'd hit him clearly wasn't convinced and continued to check up on him. After the disaster he'd had trying to break into the padlocked rooms he decided he needed to be more prepared next time. He'd managed to persuade the kitchen staff to lend him one of their padlocks, claiming he needed a hobby and he now sat desperately trying to pick the lock. He let out a loud curse as Jackie entered his room.

"I'm not sure that language is appropriate to use around a lady," she said in her cracked but kind voice.

Flicker grinned, "You're no lady Jack."

She chuckled, "What on earth are you doing?" she asked peering at the padlock.

"I've taken up a new hobby," Flicker replied setting the padlock to one side. "It passes the time."

Jackie looked suspiciously at him, "And why exactly have you chosen lock picking as your new hobby?"

"Because I was able to get a padlock, what else was I supposed to do? We're not exactly overflowing with resources here, unless they're linked to art that is."

Jackie looked unconvinced, "This doesn't have something to do with the attempted break in does it?"

Flicker felt his heart miss a beat but he maintained

his calm exterior and forced mock hurt into his voice, "Come on Jack, don't tell me you believe what that officer's saying."

"I didn't say that," Jackie said with a sly smile. "In fact I didn't accuse you of anything, but your reaction screams guilt, you might want to work on that." Flicker looked shocked but Jackie just smiled. "You know I won't say anything," she reassured him. "But where exactly were you trying to break in to?"

"That's just it Jack," he said leaning forwards. "I don't know." She stared at him with a, 'you really are an idiot' look, and he pressed on. "Student's go missing, I thought maybe they might be being held somewhere."

"Why don't you start from the beginning," she said, taking a seat at the desk.

Flicker took a deep breath, "Ever since I started actually teaching my classes have been monitored and my students tested."

"That's common across all classes."

Flicker nodded, "Of course I wasn't aware of that until recently. Then I heard from a couple of the other teachers that their most promising students were either taken from their classes or simply didn't show up one morning."

"Again that's been a common occurrence for as long as I can remember."

"But *why* Jack? Why on earth are the best students removed from class? Why aren't they seen again? And why is it that so many of the classes focus on sculpting?"

"Because it's more useful," Jackie pointed out. "Items that are created through sculpting are far more durable than those drawn or illustrated."

"I don't know Jack, it's suspicious to me. I thought I'd take a look around, I've never really explored this place. That's when I came across a guarded corridor with several padlocked doors." Jackie stared at him expressionlessly, Flicker sighed in exasperation. "Padlocked doors Jack, why on earth would there be padlocked doors?"

Jackie smiled affectionately, "You're thinking too much about it Flick, those rooms probably just hold some of the Emperor's possessions."

Flicker shook his head, "I don't think so Jack, I think something's going on, something the Emperor – if he exists – doesn't want us to know about."

A frown settled on Jackie's face, "I really thought you were trying," she said sadly and Flicker looked confused. "I really thought you were trying to make this your home-"

"I am Jack-"

"No you're not," Jackie said shaking her head and getting to her feet. "You're causing trouble again, they might not know it's you yet but if you carry on this way then they will. They won't give you another chance Flick, think about that." She smiled sadly at him and quietly left the room. Flicker stared after her, then picked up the padlock and idly fiddled with it.

Thinking about what Jackie had said, Flicker decided to try and ignore the corridor of padlocked doors. He wanted to prove to Jackie he'd changed, even if he wasn't sure he had and he threw himself into his teaching. It was torture. He knew there was something going on but Jackie was right, he was on thin ice at the moment, one officer was already suspicious of him and if he slipped up again…he shuddered and walked out into the palace grounds. It was bitterly cold outside and Flicker wrapped his threadbare coat tighter round him; there was a small smattering of snow on the grounds and it gave the grounds a peaceful look.

Jan strolled over not long after Flicker had entered the perfectly trimmed hedge maze and he wondered where the officer had come from.

"Is there some kind of secret tunnel through this maze?"

Jan smiled, "Not exactly," he replied evasively. "Everything okay?" Flicker nodded but his face remained grim. "What's wrong?" Jan asked with genuine concern.

"It's nothing," Flicker said forcing a smile.

"No, it's something," Jan said with a touch of hurt to his words. It's just nothing you want to talk to me about."

Flicker stopped and turned to face him, "Can you really blame me? I know your loyalties lie with the Emperor, I'm not about to bad-mouth him in front of you." They continued walking in silence for some time until Jan finally broke the silence.

"It's not true is it?" he asked and when Flicker looked confused he elaborated. "Some of the other officers are saying you tried to break into one of the Emperor's private rooms."

"Would you even believe me if I told you it wasn't?"

Jan stopped abruptly and when Flicker looked back at him his face was full of hurt, "I get that you don't want to talk to me about the Emperor, I get that you might not want to tell me the truth about whatever happened in that corridor." He was silent for some time, face full of concern and Flicker wondered whether he should say something.

Jan sighed heavily, "I like you Flicker, I have from the beginning, you didn't care what anyone thought about you and you looked past the fact I'm an officer; I thought we'd become friends. I didn't think I'd given you any reason to doubt my friendship. Whatever you told me about that night I'd believe you and it would remain between the two of us."

It was Flicker's turn to be silent, he thought back to all of the conversations they'd had over the years, back to all of the times Jan had caught him trying to escape and conveniently forgot to report it. He *was* a good friend, but he was also an officer of the Emperor.

It was several minutes before he finally spoke, "I think the Emperor is up to something," his voice was quiet. "I don't know what it is but I intend to find out." He hadn't actually admitted to anything but saying what he had was a test. If Jan really was on his side then nothing would happen, no one would come for him, he wouldn't be tortured and he wouldn't be questioned. But if he wasn't...well, hopefully it wouldn't come to that.

Jan sighed, "Flicker listen to me, I've been in those rooms, I've seen every part of this palace, there's nothing secretive going-"

"Then what's inside the rooms?"

Jan looked at Flicker, apparently deep in thought, "Workshops," he answered as Flicker looked confused. "You might not know this, it's not exactly something the Emperor wants to advertise, but Shanora has been in trouble for years." Flicker's look of confusion deepened and Jan sighed again, he dragged Flicker deeper into the maze until he was sure no one else was around.

"You may or may not know that Endore and Flintai have allied against us," Flicker nodded. "The Emperor has cut all ties with them, even trade, he's heard rumours they're planning to invade so he's put Shanora on lockdown, which means we've no way to get fresh resources."

"He has the best Artist's creating the supplies we

need?" Flicker asked.

Jan nodded, "No one knows about this except the Emperor's administration staff and the officers, the people only know about the possible threat of war, they know nothing about the lack of resources. You can't say anything Flicker, I shouldn't have told you and I'm trusting you, just like you're trusting me." He was right, Jan had trusted him, he'd trusted him with something far greater than what he himself had revealed. Perhaps they really were friends.

"I won't say anything," Flicker assured him.

"Will you stop snooping around?"

"Yes."

It was only after Flicker had returned to his room that he started to wonder whether what Jan had told him really was the truth, or whether it was some clever ploy to keep him from entering those workshops and seeing what was really going on.

"Maybe I'm just paranoid," he said as he collapsed onto his bed; it creaked unnervingly.

"Talking to yourself again I see," Jackie said as she entered the room.

Flicker sat up quickly, "Jack! I'm so sorry about before, I really am, I-"

"Forget it," she said with a smile. "What were you chattering about before I entered?"

He sighed and ran his hands through his shaggy red hair, "What's wrong with me Jack?"

Jackie grinned, "Do you want the list?"

"I found out what's going on in those padlocked rooms," he said and Jackie's expression faltered. "I didn't break in," he said quickly and he features softened again. "I asked someone and they told me, only now I'm wondering whether they actually told me the truth or not. So what's wrong with me? Why can't I trust people?"

Jackie took a seat next to him on the bed and took one of his hands in hers, "You spent a long time pushing everyone in this place away-"

"Not everyone," Flicker interrupted.

"Most people then," Jackie corrected. "You convinced yourself they were evil because they worked for the Emperor and even though you're trying to make this your home, it's difficult for you not to see things as you always have. You'll start to trust people eventually Flick, you just have to be patient and give it time."

"I'm not good at being patient," Flicker said with a grin.

Jackie patted his hand, "You'll get there. Out of curiosity who was it who told you?"

"Jan."

Jackie chuckled, "Oh you can trust that one, there's not a bad bone in his body. I liked him from day one, so polite and caring, not like some of the others." Flicker thought back to the beatings he'd had not long after he'd first arrived; it's what they'd tried to make him cooperate. After sending him to the hospital wing on several occasions they finally gave up, that was until he started trying to escape. He winced at the memory. But Jackie was right, Jan wasn't a bad person, he'd never taken part in those beatings and he'd never done anything to suggest he wasn't on Flicker's side. Well nothing except serve the Emperor but was that really his fault? Everyone had to make a living, perhaps he had a family to support, perhaps that was why he was so kind hearted.

"You're right Jack, he's one of the good ones."

Jackie chuckled, "Of course I'm right, I'm always right, haven't you learnt that by now."

Chapter 8

Aggie was terrified; the fight with her mother, the incident with her classmates, everything had suddenly become real to her. She didn't want to be taken to the palace, she didn't want to lose her mother and she didn't want to lose her freedom. He mother was happier after Aggie had explained everything and had even started to relax her grip, allowing Aggie to leave the house for something other than school.

As it turned out she wasn't really in the mood for leaving the house anymore; the only reason she used to go out was so she could practice her gift or visit Cassie and since she wasn't doing that anymore there didn't seem much point. She was also terrified of being caught.

School hadn't really improved, her classmates, led by Jason and Stephie continued to imply she was an Artist and continued to taunt her. It was only a few days after the original incident, when everything became too much for Aggie and she snapped.

A balled up piece of paper hit the back of her head and when she unfolded the crinkled, white sheet she read the words, 'Artist scum'. She scrunched the sheet and threw it back at Jason, whom she assumed was the one to throw it in the first place. Several more balls of paper hit the back of her head and as the unfolded them one by one, the insults got worse. Mrs Rhodes left the room for a brief moment and Aggie got to her feet and turned to face the sniggering group.

"Why can't you just leave me alone?"

Stephie smirked, "Because everyone knows Artist's are inferior, why else would they be the servants of the Emperor?"

"Artist's are not inferior!" Aggie said sharply.

"Why do you care so much if you're not an Artist?" Jason challenged.

"I don't," Aggie said quickly, unclenching her hands, which had unconsciously balled into fists. "But Artist's are people just like us, they shouldn't be treated differently."

"You know what I think?"

"What!?"

"I think you *are* an Artist, I think you're trying to hide out among us and I think I'm going to turn you in."

Aggie's face darkened, "Meet me by the shed at the end of the day, I'll prove to you that I'm no Artist."

Jason got to his feet, "And what are you going to do when we actually show? How will you cheat your way out of this one?"

"I don't need to cheat," Aggie said firmly. "I'm not an Artist and I can prove it." Jason sniggered again and sat back down but not before agreeing. Mrs Rhodes re-entered and Aggie took her seat and continued her work, her heart hammering in her chest at what she'd just done.

Aggie waited nervously by the shed; it was quiet where she was, the shed rarely got used except to tidy the school grounds once a week and it was the perfect place for what was about to happen. Snowflakes floated lazily around her and settled on the frozen ground while she rubbed her hands together to keep them warm. She'd concealed the vial of her mother's blood in her sleeve and hoped she would be able to use it without the others noticing. What had she gotten herself in to? Her mother would be furious if she knew what was happening; Aggie was meant to be keeping a low profile but what else could she have done? This seemed the only way to get her classmates to leave her alone. She clenched her hands into fists, suddenly angry at herself for letting her temper get the better of her, she should have just ignored Jason and Stephie.

Ten minutes passed and no one had shown so she got ready to leave just as two figures strolled around the corner of the large school building, their gang trailing behind them.

"Crafts!" Aggie cursed under her breath but tried to maintain a calm exterior. "You actually showed then," she said trying to sound bored.

Jason grinned, "Oh I wouldn't have missed this for the world." They crowded round her and Jason held out a blade for her to cut herself. Aggie took a deep breath and held the blade to her palm, she'd practiced the next bit at home, her mother had insisted. As Aggie drew the blade across the fleshy part of her palm she made sure the sleeve of her uniform covered the area and she flipped the blade over so the blunt edge was drawn across. She had already loosened the top of the vial and now let the blood inside flow across her palm, as if from a fresh cut. She dripped the blood into a well in the clay she had placed on the ground and then wrapped some cloth around her palm to, 'staunch the flow of blood'.

Aggie began to knead the clay until the blood had fully combined with the soft, elastic medium and then proceeded to mould it into the shape of a small lizard. The group stared at her intensely as she worked; she knew it didn't need to be perfect, it wouldn't come to life no matter how lifelike it was but she truly loved her artistic talent and the clay felt natural beneath her fingers. She worked for a good half hour until she was satisfied with the basic shape of the lizard; she hadn't bothered to texture the skin but *had* outlined the details of the face. She frowned slightly at the lack of detail; it just didn't feel right to leave something looking so unfinished.

Aggie took a deep breath and realised her heart was pounding, then she exhaled and to her relief nothing happened, no swirling mist and no creation. She breathed an internal sigh of relief, stood up and faced Jason and Stephie.

"See, I told you I wasn't an Artist," she placed her hands on her hips for emphasis.

"I still don't believe you," Stephie said.

Aggie stared at her in disbelief, "Weren't you watching just then? I mixed my blood, I attempted the breath of life, what more do you want?"

"I think you cheated, I want to see your hand," Stephie said taking a step forwards.

Aggie instinctively took a step back, "You want to what?"

"I want to see your hand, how do we know you really cut it?"

"How about the fact that my blood is on the blade and you saw me drip it onto the clay," Aggie subconsciously clutched her bandaged hand and Stephie's eyes narrowed.

"We saw you drip someone's blood onto the clay, how do we know it was yours?"

"Are you serious?" Stephie continued to stare at her accusingly though the others, including Jason averted their eyes and remained quiet. "You're crazy!" Aggie turned to leave.

"Why won't you just show us? What are you hiding?" Stephie taunted.

Aggie faced her once again, "I'm not hiding anything, I've just proved I'm not an Artist, it's not my fault you're crazy and can't see what's right in front of you."

"I know you're an Artist," Stephie said in a low voice. "I don't care how many times you try and trick us into thinking you're not, I've *seen* you create things, and I'm going to make sure you pay."

Aggie turned and slapped her without thinking; Stephie stared dumbstruck at her, then Aggie barged her way past a couple of the group who had been staring idly at the ground and now they lay on their backs staring at the darkening sky in surprise having slipped on ice. Stephie recovered herself quickly and ran after her, shouting curses and insults but Aggie was faster and she managed to lose her with little difficulty. She didn't stop running. She stopped only when she fell through her front door; her mother walked into the hall to investigate the noise, saw the bandage and her daughter's tears and her heart almost stopped.

"What happened?" Nilla asked, her voice laced with fear and worry as she picked her daughter up off the floor.

"I'm sorry, I'm so sorry," Aggie sobbed as her mother sat her down in the living room, Cassie came to sit by her and rested her head on Aggie's knee.

"It's okay," Nilla said in a gentle voice, though her insides were filled with dread. "Tell me what happened."

Aggie recalled the events through loud sobs and a lot of stuttering. When she had finished, her sobs coming out as more of a whimper now, she stared at her mother with a mixture of fear and regret. Nilla just wrapped her arms around her daughter and hugged her tightly. If she really was about to lose her then it wouldn't do either of them any good if she scolded her.

They waited together, Aggie curled up on her mother's lap, while Cassie lay on the floor by Nilla's feet. Mother held daughter tightly and stared intensely at the clock on the wall waiting for the inevitable banging on the door. When several hours had passed and no one had come crashing through their door, she put Aggie to bed but remained in the living room, the dread that coursed through her keeping her awake.

Aggie refused to go to school the following morning and after a lot of shouting and crying Nilla finally agreed to let her stay home. She wasn't sure it was the best course of action, if anything it probably screamed guilt, but Aggie was in no fit state to leave the house, so Nilla had relented. She allowed Aggie to remain at home for the remainder of the week and sent a message to Mrs Rhodes, explaining that she was unwell. Aggie managed to calm down after several days when the officers still hadn't come for her and Nilla was pleased to see her daughter finally smile.

It happened on the seventh day. Aggie was in the garden playing with Cassie and Nilla was putting a casserole on to cook. There was a faint knock at the door. Nilla wiped her hands on her apron, hummed quietly to herself and opened it; several officers stood in the doorway and Nilla's breath caught in her throat. She took a step back and moved to close the door but one of the officers, a young, well-built man stopped her.

"Mrs Sanders?" she nodded her head. "We've had reports that someone in this household has been displaying artistic gifts, most accusations have implied your daughter. We've come to see whether there's any truth to them." She suddenly felt dizzy, she couldn't breathe and was thrown back fourteen years to the day they came for Charlie. They had said the same thing back then, that there had been reports of him using his gift. She had cried back then and begged them not to test him, begged them to let him stay. They'd held her back while Charlie had sliced a dark finger and created a mouse. They hadn't let him say goodbye, hadn't let him see his tiny daughter one last time. On that day a piece of Nilla's heart had broken and it had remained broken.

The officer repeated himself and Nilla was jolted back to the present, the officer tried to walk past her on seeing Aggie enter the house through the back door but Nilla barred his way, her face set.

"My daughter isn't an Artist," she said firmly and Aggie shrank back.

The officers stared and the well-built man smiled, "Mrs Sanders, do not think you can prevent us testing your daughter."

"I don't," Nilla said, trying to stop her voice from shaking. "You won't find anything though."

"We know someone in this building is an Artist, we've received reports from multiple sources."

Nilla inhaled sharply and the officer smiled knowingly. They were sat at the kitchen table; the officer placed a number of supplies in front of them and handed Aggie a knife.

Aggie chose the paints for a change, she would illustrate a bunch of colourful flowers, just like those she'd created for her mother, only this time they wouldn't be brought to life. She pressed the blade against her finger and allowed blood to be drawn but before it could drip into the paints she managed to get her mother's blood from the vial and into the paint. To the officers, it looked like her blood had mixed with the paints. It didn't take long for her to sketch the flowers and fill them with colour, after all she didn't need them to be accurate. She took a deep breath, crossed her fingers for luck and exhaled. Her mother let out a relieved sigh as no pale mist was released and the flowers weren't brought to life.

The officer frowned and looked to Nilla, "Now you."

She inhaled sharply and with a shaking hand took the fresh knife that was offered to her. She sliced her finger and allowed not only her blood but the blood from the vial, Aggie's blood to drip onto a small lump of clay. She started to knead it and after a few minutes began to mould it into a small rabbit just as Aggie had showed her to do. The next bit would rely solely on luck; she took a loud, deep breath and next to her, Aggie quietly did the same. They released their breath's together, Nilla loudly and Aggie silently. Whether the low winter sun had obscured their vision or the officers had simply seen what they wanted, they never knew.

The small, crudely made clay rabbit began to solidify, its fur changed to a grey-brown and started to puff up in places. The tail fluffed into a small while ball and the long, slender ears twitched as the rabbit was given sentience. It was far from perfect; the body was lopsided, one ear was longer than the other and the facial features were crooked, but it didn't matter, the fact is the creature had been brought to life and the officers believed Nilla had done it.

"You're coming with us," the officer said as he grabbed Nilla by the arm and the other officers drew their firearms and trained them on her. A female officer took her by the arms and led her to the front door.

"Mother!" Aggie cried as she tried to reach Nilla; the officers barred her way and Nilla glanced back at her terrified daughter.

"Everything will be okay," she said trying to reassure her daughter with a trembling voice. She was escorted from the small house and the newly created rabbit was killed and left on the kitchen table. The officers left the building noisily and without care, Aggie cried for her mother and was eventually left alone with the empty silence. Cassie trotted over to Aggie who was sobbing on the kitchen floor, laid down next to her and began to nuzzle her hand.

Chapter 9

Lucie watched, her face impassive as the students created the animal of their choice and scribbled on her clipboard. Flicker fidgeted in irritation, he had tried every time she entered his class to find out what she was testing for to no avail.

"Your students seem to be improving significantly," Lucie said in her cool voice. "I will be recommending that one or two of them be moved into the advanced classes."

Flicker's interest peaked, "The advanced classes?" he asked, trying hard not to sound too eager; Lucie nodded. "What exactly are the advanced classes?"

Lucie smiled but her face gave nothing away, "The students will be trained to work for the Emperor."

Flickers insides flipped and he took a deep breath to steady his nerves, "And what exactly does that entail?"

"I'm afraid that's classified information but I wouldn't worry, your students will be involved in very important work that will benefit Shanora. I'll submit the paperwork for Nhiall and Serena this afternoon, expect a couple of new students in a few days." Lucie left the classroom before Flicker could ask further questions and he was sure she did that on purpose. He looked to his students; Nhiall and Serena were looking at him with confused and worried expressions and he smiled to try and reassure them.

"It looks like you're being promoted," he said light-heartedly. "I expect you'll receive instructions of where to go later today." Flicker instructed the class to continue with their sculptures while he sat at his desk wondering how he could get the answers he was desperate for.

He had tried to accept what Jan had told him, had tried to forget about the padlocked doors but he couldn't. He was certain what Jan had told him was partially true, but it was only the truth in *his* eyes. He believed that whatever Jan had been told was a lie, which made him smile because if Jan didn't know the whole truth then he wasn't as deep in the Emperor's pockets as the others.

Flicker had started to plan another break in, he'd been practicing picking locks again and had even been successful several times. He was fairly certain every time the lock had sprung open it had been a fluke but he just hoped that luck would stay with him when he reached the padlocked rooms.

He had told Jackie what he was planning, there had been no point in lying to her and in truth he hadn't wanted to. She hadn't scolded him, which had shocked him.

"Truth be told," she began, re-tying her grey hair as she sat at her usual spot at the desk. "I've been thinking about what you said, and I'm starting to wonder if there isn't something going on myself."

Flicker's heart leapt, "Do you mean that Jack?" she nodded and he grinned.

"What made you change your mind?"

"After the last time we spoke I decided to do a little digging," Jackie said in mock innocence. "You may not know this Flick but I've a few friends in the Administration department."

His eyes widened in surprise, "You've never told me that Jack."

Jackie grinned, "Yes, well, we all need a *few* secrets. I decided to ask them about the Artists who are removed from class-"

"What did they say?" Flicker interrupted, incapable of holding back.

Jackie shot him a look, "They gave me the same answer that Jan gave you."

Flicker deflated, "That's it? I was hoping for something more."

She scolded him, "No Flick, you don't understand, they gave *exactly* the same answer."

He sat up, suddenly interested, "Really? Are you sure?"

She nodded, "It was strange Flick, their faces went blank almost as if they'd said the same phrase hundreds of times."

Flicker frowned, "That does seem odd."

"I thought so too."

Suddenly Flicker grinned, "Glad to have you on board Jack, I could do with a wingman."

"Wing-woman," she corrected with a smile. "Now what exactly do you need?"

"A diversion, something to keep that corridor clear, there's no break between shifts anymore, whatever their guarding they're stepping up their game."

"I guess that's what happens when someone tries to break in," she shot him a wide grin and he smirked back. "Give me a few days, I think I can organise something."

Jackie was as good as her word, she had wandered to the kitchen, where she had persuaded the staff to make her a snack and while they were distracted had stolen some oil and several matches. She turned up to Flicker's room with a wide grin.

"This should do the trick," she said throwing them on the bed.

"Crafts, Jackie! Just how big a fire are you planning to start?"

She grinned again, "You said you needed a significant distraction, what's more distracting than your home going up in flames?"

Just after midnight, Flicker left his room and crept around the palace until he neared the padlocked rooms, then he crouched down in the shadows and waited. It wasn't long until he heard the yells and cries for help and several officers hurtled past him from the direction of the forbidden corridor. He crept out of his hiding place and edged his way to the corridor opening, he peered round the corner and saw, with relief that it was empty. He hurried along to the first padlocked door and crouched down beside it.

Jackie turned up minutes later, "I don't know how long you've got," she whispered in her familiar cracked voice. "I started three in the end, but those officers are quick and they already had one out when I left." Flicker nodded and continued working; he had two thin pieces of metal inserted into the keyhole of the padlock; one remained stationary while the other was being moved carefully. He had managed to push three of the pins out of the way and was now working on the final one.

It took several painfully long minutes until he heard the small, 'click' as the final pin was pushed into position and the lock sprung open. Flicker gasped and Jackie's eyes widened.

"We better check this out quickly," Flicker said while glancing over his shoulder. "Who knows when they'll be back. Jackie nodded as Flicker turned the handle and pushed open the large wooden door.

It was completely dark inside the room and Flicker fumbled for the light switch; eventually a dull glow illuminated the room. They stared round, amazed and a little disappointed; the room was a large workshop, just as Jan had said. Cupboards, shelves and drawers were labelled and organised with various materials and Flicker wandered the room's exterior looking at each in turn. There was an exceptionally large quantity of clay stored there, but that was no real surprise. What Flicker did find odd was the large quantities of metal stored around the room; did the Emperor have the Artists making weapons? Or were they really creating resources as Jan had said?

"Flick," Jackie whispered and Flicker crossed the room to where she crouched.

"What is it?"

Jackie indicated with her hand and Flicker crouched to examine the box she had opened; it was long, narrow and filled with planks of wood. Flicker glanced at the label on the lid, 'Wooden planks (resources)'.

Flicker's heart sank and he visibly deflated, "I was wrong Jack," he said miserably. "Jan was telling the truth, they really are creating resources."

Jackie placed a comforting hand on his arm, "It's okay Flick, we're all wrong occasionally, let's talk about this tomorrow, we need to get out of here before the officers return." Flicker nodded and they left the room silently, remembering to place the padlock back on the door before they left.

For the first time in months, Flicker didn't feel like teaching his class. He was miserable, he had been sure there was something more going on, something darker, but he had been wrong. The excursion to the padlocked rooms had been a failure in his eyes, all it told him was the Artist's really *were* doing something useful and that the Emperor might not be so bad after all. He shuddered at that thought, no, the Emperor was still evil, he held them here against their will and refused to let them see their families or friends. No one who did that could have an ounce of good in them.

He was about to tell the class to do as they pleased for the day when the door opened and two new students walked in. *Of course,* he thought, *Lucie did warn me I'd be receiving new students.* He sighed heavily and got to his feet to greet them.

"New recruits," the officer said before leaving without another word.

"What are your names?" Flicker asked with little enthusiasm. The first student, a nervous looking boy in his late teens with blonde hair spoke first.

"My name's Gabe," he said with a wavering voice.

Flicker nodded and the teenager took the empty seat near the back of the room. He turned to the second new student, a woman in her early thirties who had pale brown hair, kind blue eyes and a comforting smile. She didn't seem nervous but Flicker could see the worry in her eyes and he wondered who she'd lost.

"My name is Nilla," she said calmly and took a seat near the front of the class. Flicker instructed the main group to sculpt something they enjoyed so he could focus on the new arrivals. He asked them to sculpt a pot to start with; it was always good to start easy and he watched them with interest. He was particularly interested in Nilla, whom he was sure had something to hide.

Gabe didn't seem to have any trouble with the pot; he'd obviously had some practice with a potter's wheel and it was possible he'd been training to be an artisan before he'd been sent here. He probably wouldn't have much trouble when it came to sculpting more complex items. Nilla on the other hand was terrible; she'd clearly never even *seen* a potter's wheel. It wasn't her fault, and it wasn't the first time it had happened. Flicker sighed; it would mean a lot more work.

He walked over to Nilla who was cursing loudly as the potter's wheel spun too quickly and a large clump of clay hit the wall.

She looked to Flicker as he reached where she sat, "I'm sorry," she said glancing at the splattered clay. "I'll clean that up, I've never actually used one of these."

He smiled and he hoped it looked sincere, "It's okay," he said indicating she move so he could take the seat. "I'll show you the basics." He placed a fresh lump of clay in the centre, wet his hands and began using the pedal to move the wheel slowly. Nilla watched with fascination as Flicker used his palms and fingers to mould and shape the uninteresting mound of clay into a wide rimmed pot. Her heart began to thump as the realisation of what she'd done hit her full force, *Oh Crafts! What am I going to do?* Flicker glanced up and noticed the glazed expression on Nilla's face.

"Look, I know making pots isn't the most exciting thing in the world but you've got to start somewhere and I need to know your experience level."

"I can help you with that last part," Nilla said, snapping back to reality. "I've no experience, I've never made or created anything"

Flicker's eyes narrowed, "You must have done something or you wouldn't be in here."

Nilla's heart thumped again and she felt her cheeks flush, "Well, yes of course I've created something, but it was an accident, I've not made a habit of it and I wouldn't know the first place to begin with something like that." She gestured to a sleek clay cat on the nearest desk and her sense of worry deepened.

"Not a problem," Flicker said, removing himself from the potter's wheel. "That's what I'm here for." He indicated that she take a seat again and watched her as she tried to mimic his movements; she really was awful. It got him thinking; usually people with the gift are aware on some level, and usually there's an urge to create. He'd managed to keep his at bay by occupying his mind with other things, but surely this woman would have wanted to test her limits? Most people did at first, even Flicker had, until he'd realised the full scale of what being an Artist meant. This woman looked like she didn't have a clue about her gift, and it looked like she hadn't tested or experimented. Flicker frowned, how had she managed to get caught if she hadn't been experimenting? Something definitely didn't add up with this woman.

When the group broke for lunch, Flicker asked Nilla to stay behind, she felt her heart pound again and took a deep breath to try and calm herself.

"How long have you been aware of your gift?" he asked watching her carefully.

"Not long," Nilla replied, trying to keep her voice steady.

"Surely you must have been aware that there was something different about you?"

Nilla nodded, she knew from both her husband and daughter that there was an unexplainable feeling inside that alerted a person to their power. She also knew from her husband that it was able to be ignored if you remained busy.

"My husband was taken from me fifteen years ago

for being an Artist, when I began to notice that something inside felt different, I suspected what it might be and I put all of my effort into ignoring it."

"But why?" Flicker asked puzzled. "If your husband is here then surely you could have revealed yourself and been reunited with him."

Nilla heard her voice waver as she spoke the next words slowly, "I have a daughter."

Flicker nodded, *So that's who she lost.* "How exactly did you get caught if you don't mind me asking?"

Her heart began to pound, "My daughter has always liked art, she wanted to try and make something with some clay. I must have got some blood mixed into it and when I breathed…well you know." He nodded. "Our neighbour saw what happened and called the officers before I could stop him."

"I'm sorry, that must have been difficult for you."

She nodded, "It was, and I know I haven't half as much talent as the rest of the Artists in here."

"I'll do my best to help you as much as I can," Flicker said walking her to the door. "I'm not holding out much hope though, you really are awful." He said it light-heartedly and with a smile and Nilla forced one back.

Chapter 10

Almost a week had passed since her mother had been taken and Aggie hadn't left the house; she'd barely left the kitchen. She had remained on the floor of the kitchen weeping for her mother and, without realising for her father. She had managed to lose both parents, she would never see them again, and it was all her fault. Cassie continued to lie next to her; she whined occasionally and tried to lick Aggie's tears away.

If she had listened to her mother in the first place none of this would have happened; the children wouldn't have teased her and perhaps she'd have even been friends with them. They wouldn't have called the officers and her mother would still be there.

She finally extracted herself from the kitchen, suddenly feeling how cold the house was and shuffled towards the bathroom to take a shower realising partway through that there wasn't any soap which set her off all over again. She curled up on the shower floor, warm water cascading over her, mingling with fresh, salty tears. *How can I support myself?* she thought as she struggled to catch her breath between sobs.

"I'm sorry," she cried looking towards the ceiling, as if that gesture would allow her mother to hear her. "I'm so, so sorry," she hugged her knees and loud sobs tumbled from her.

Eventually the water turned cold and Aggie dragged herself from the room, wrapping a thick towel round herself in the process. She entered the living room, built up the fire and sat by it drying her hair for several minutes before noticing the dwindling supply of firewood. Her breath caught in her throat but this time she managed to hold back the sobs, *there's more wood outside*, she reminded herself and took a deep breath. Cassie trotted into the room and curled up on the floor by her legs. She was so grateful to the spaniel; if Cassie hadn't been there she didn't know how she would have survived this long.

"I suppose I'll have to look for work," she said to Cassie as she stroked the thick, dark fur. "I wonder what I can do?" She looked down at her dog as if expecting an answer who sighed in response. "I can't weave like my mother," Aggie continued, rubbing her hair with a smaller towel. "I don't dare become an artisan, I can't fish, I have nothing to sell or trade. What am I going to do?" She sighed helplessly and Cassie licked the hand that had fallen to her lap in despair. "I'm so glad I've got you Cassie," she said leaning down to wrap her arms round her dog. "I don't know what I'd do without you."

It took a few more days before Aggie found the courage to venture outside and it was awful. The weather was as harsh as the other citizens. She was avoided in the streets as if she had some kind of unsightly illness; no one looked in her direction and no one talked to her. She drew her coat more tightly around her large snowflakes swirled in the breeze and tried to get lost in the crowds, which didn't work, because the crowds continued to move away from her.

The market wasn't much better; Aggie had found a bit of money in her mother's room and thought she would buy some of the essentials they no longer had, she swallowed hard, that *she* no longer had. The shop owners were reluctant to take her money but at the same time took pity on her. After only an hour Aggie had what she needed and hurried back to the safety of her home.

She had turned down one of the side streets, hoping to take a shortcut and three tall, broad figures barred her way. Aggie stopped suddenly, her heart began pounding and her breathing quickened, she started to back away from them and bumped into something else. Her breath caught in her throat and she turned slowly round to see another tall figure. Aggie dropped her basket and fell backwards onto the snowy ground.

"Filthy scum," one of the men spat and Aggie shuffled backwards through the snow until her back was against a wall.

"Can't believe you dare show your face," another said kicking the basket and its contents away from Aggie causing them to scatter.

"You're a disgrace," the first man said again crouching low to face her. "You should have reported her to the officers, filthy, stealing-"

"What's going on here?!" The men straightened and turned to see a female officer aiming her firearm at them.

"Nothing miss," the first man said backing away from Aggie, the others followed suit.

"I think you'd better be on your way," the officer said, not taking her eyes off the men; they dipped their heads and retreated. The officer holstered her weapon and moved towards Aggie who remained against the wall tears rolling down her face. "Are you okay?" the officer asked gently. Aggie looked into soft blue eyes and tried to nod her head thinking that she looked familiar; the officer helped her to her feet and dusted the snow from her coat.

"You stay there, I'll get your things," the officer started gathering up Aggie's purchases and placed them back into the basket. She ran a hand through her cropped brown hair as she handed the basket back and Aggie realised where she knew her from; she had been at the abandoned building.

"Thank you," Aggie mumbled, clutching the basket with both hands.

The officer smiled, "You're welcome, my name's Flora, do you live close by?" Aggie nodded. "Do you want me to walk you home?" Aggie nodded again. They walked in silence, Aggie still trembled from the ordeal and her breathing hadn't settled. Flora remained with her until they had reached her house. "Will you be okay?" she asked as they reached Aggie's house, with what seemed like genuine concern.

"Yes," Aggie said in a small voice.

"I patrol this area quite a lot," Flora said gently placing a pale hand on Aggie's shoulder. "You let me know if you have any more trouble okay?" Aggie nodded again and scurried inside where she collapsed to the floor and allowed more tears to flow as she shook with fear and exhaustion.

As another week went by with Aggie refusing to leave her house more of her supplies dwindled. She woke one morning to find she had run out of food and something finally snapped inside her.

"This is ridiculous," she scolded herself. "It's time I took charge." She got herself cleaned up, threw on her cleanest and smartest clothes and headed out into the streets. People still looked at her with suspicion but she held her head high and tried to ignore them while her heart raced. She still wasn't sure what she was qualified to do, so she aimed for one of the small shops close to her home.

"Excuse me," she asked in a polite voice to the shopkeeper who seemed desperate to pretend she didn't exist.

She saw him sigh before he turned to her with a forced smile, "What can I do for you miss?" the balding shopkeeper asked while he adjusted his glasses.

"I'm looking for work and-"

"I'm sorry, I'm not looking for anyone right now," the shopkeeper interrupted and turned abruptly away. Aggie's shoulders sagged and she slipped back out into the street. She walked a bit further from her home and saw a 'help wanted' sign in another shop window, her spirits lifted a little and she walked into the building where a small bell chimed. The shopkeeper, a small, plump woman turned with a smiling face, it faltered for a split second when she saw Aggie.

"Can I help you?" she asked in a high pitched voice.

"I couldn't help but notice your sign," the woman's smile faded. "I'm looking for work and-"

"Oh I'm sorry dear," the woman said bustling over to the window and yanking the sign from its resting place. "That's an old sign, I must have forgotten to remove it." She walked to the door and stared at Aggie, indicating the conversation was over; Aggie made her way back outside into the chill air.

"Thank you anyway," she said with a slight waver in her voice. She exited the shop and began to walk away then glanced over her shoulder and saw the woman replace the sign; she took a deep breath to steady herself. *I'll just have to keep trying.*

She spent her whole morning being rejected, mostly kindly, and decided shops might not be the way to go.

She wandered towards one of the small pubs and made her way inside. It was dimly lit and smelt strongly of alcohol and smoke; she wandered to the bar, looking around at the sparsely occupied building. She smiled at the barman as she approached and he frowned at her.

"We don't serve minors," he said in a gruff voice.

Aggie smiled, "Actually I'm looking for work-"

The barman shook his head cutting her off, "I'm sorry but we don't employ minors either, folk tend to get a bit rowdy in here." Aggie nodded, thanked him and left, she didn't know whether he had been lying or not but at least he had let her down gently, which was far more than anyone else had.

She must have enquired about work in over ten pubs and each rejected her in the kindest way but she was starting to feel hopeless. She had also tried several more shops but they had dismissed her without a kind word and in a couple of cases had refused her entry altogether. She was cold, her fingers feeling frozen, her legs ached, she felt exhausted and on the verge of tears when she walked into the last pub in the surrounding area; The Fisherman's Fancy. She walked up to the bar and a large, broad man with wiry dark hair and beard looked at her while cleaning glasses. She had just decided to walk straight back out again when he spoke with a surprisingly gentle accented voice.

"Everything okay lass?"

Aggie took a deep breath, "I was wondering if you had any work?"

The man looked at her for several minutes before answering, "I wish I could lass, we're busy enough, but I'm not sure you'd be able to handle the crowd that comes in here." Aggie nodded, felt tears prick her eyes and turned quickly towards the door, she had almost reached it when a large hand rested gently on her shoulder. "What's wrong?" the large man asked as he crouched next to her.

The words tumbled from her mouth before she could stop them; how she didn't have a father, how her mother had recently been taken to the palace and how she had no one she could turn to and no money to her name. The large man listened without comment as she sobbed her way through her story and he handed her a tissue when she had finished. She sighed loudly and suddenly felt exhausted as if a weight had been lifted. She looked up at the large man who was staring at her silently.

"My name's Wolf," he said with a smile.

"Aggie," she replied in a wavering voice and stared back at the floor.

"Well Aggie, I think something might have just opened up here."

She stared at him wide eyed and swallowed hard, "Really?" she asked, not daring to hope.

Wolf nodded, "I can't guarantee it'll pay well and the sorts we get in here can be a bit on the wild side but I can't let a young lass starve. You come back here tomorrow at seven and I'll show you the basics."

Aggie smiled tentatively and blew her nose before getting to her feet, "Thank you," she said quietly, hardly daring to believe his offer of work.

Wolf smiled again and walked her to the door, "Tomorrow at seven then lass," he said as she started for home. "Now you take care of yourself."

Chapter 11

Nilla had been working hard to try and improve her sculpting skills; it had taken a number of very long attempts but she had finally, and successfully, sculpted a pot. She had started staying an extra hour after the other students had left and without the pressure of them being around her technique had improved, though only slightly. She had just finished another satisfactory vessel and Flicker placed it with the other objects to be fired.

"What happens to them?" she asked as Flicker washed his hands.

"Haven't you explored the palace yet?" Nilla shook her head. "The sculptures, if they're good enough, are used to decorate the interior and grounds." He indicated the pot in front of her. "This will probably be used in the kitchens."

Nilla smiled, feeling proud of her small achievement, "Thank you for letting me stay a bit longer these past couple of weeks, I think the other students were making me feel self-conscious, they're so talented."

Flicker nodded, "I know it can be difficult but you'll get better."

Nilla shook her head, "I'm not so sure," she paused and glanced at Flicker who was watching her carefully. "I'm not who-" she was cut off as an officer opened the door.

"Thought I heard voices," Jan said cheerfully.

Flicker smiled, "I've just been providing extra tutoring to one of my newest recruits."

Jan smiled at Nilla, then turned back to Flicker, "Could do with talking to you later, will you be out in the grounds?"

Flicker nodded, "I'll grab something to eat and come find you." Jan nodded and retreated back into the corridor.

Nilla eyed him suspiciously, "You're friends with an officer?"

Flicker shrugged, "Jan's not like the others, he's a good man."

"I don't think I've ever met a good officer," Nilla said sceptically.

"You have now," Flicker said with a smile. "Trust me, he's okay."

Not yet knowing anyone else at the palace Nilla sat with Flicker to eat, though she could tell he'd have rather eaten alone. She wasn't normally bothered about being alone but this was a strange place full of strange people who were all so very different from her and it made her feel completely and utterly alone.

She didn't bother making small talk with Flicker over dinner, she could already tell he wouldn't appreciate that, so instead she decided to watch those around her. There wasn't anything exciting happening, just people having dinner, but what was interesting was that there appeared to be a group system going on. People clustered together as they always did but Nilla noticed when people had received their food they knew exactly where they were going to sit down. It wasn't a case of looking for a free table, they knew which was *their* table with *their* friends;

how on earth was she going to survive in this place?

An elderly looking woman walked over, smiled and sat opposite Flicker, he sighed and she looked annoyed.

"That's hardly the way to greet a friend," she said in a cracked voice.

Flicker smiled wearily, "Sorry Jack, it's been a long day and I thought you'd come over to chide me."

Jackie chuckled, "As if I'd do a thing like that. I noticed you weren't sitting alone like usual and thought I'd introduce myself to your-"

"She's one of my new students," Flicker cut in and Nilla felt an odd sense of hurt; this woman had obviously been going to say, 'friend', which she knew she technically wasn't but it still bothered her how Flicker had dismissed it so quickly.

Jackie frowned at Flicker and turned to smile at Nilla, "I'm Jackie, don't mind Flick, he's grumpy with everyone, please join our group for meals whenever you like."

"Thank you," Nilla said with a genuine smile. "I'm Nilla, I'm very new here, it's all a bit overwhelming."

Jackie nodded, "Don't worry, you'll settle in eventually, it just takes a bit of time. Make sure you explore the palace, there's some lovely works of art dotted round." Nilla nodded and Jackie got up to go but before she did she cuffed Flicker round the ear who cursed loudly.

"Crafts! What was that for?"

Jackie grinned evilly, "That was for being a bad host," she winked at the two of them and Flicker scowled in return.

Nilla took Jackie's advice and decided to explore the palace after dinner, she already knew she couldn't continue to tag along with Flicker since he was going to meet Jan and she knew she would be less than welcome. It also seemed fairly evident that Flicker would only tolerate so much of her and since she needed mountains of help with her creations she would do her best not to annoy him.

The palace was beautiful, she didn't think she'd ever seen anything quite as magnificent or ornate. The corridors were carpeted with a deep red, which didn't seem to show any wear and she wondered whether they were replaced on a regular basis. The walls remained pale, though they had elaborate and delicate mouldings consisting of a repeating floral design, which was highlighted in places with gold. She must have spent several long minutes examining the mouldings before she finally moved on.

There were numerous paintings adorning the pale walls that almost looked as though they could be real – and in this place she supposed they could be. She noticed stormy seas and snowy mountain ranges as well as immaculate illustrations of the city and gentle rolling hillsides. The level of talent needed for pieces like these paralysed Nilla, she had no chance of ever being this good or producing something this realistic. It was true that not everyone with the gift had artistic ability, but it was also true that having the gift increased your receptiveness to learning artistic techniques. Even someone with no ability would be able to produce a piece of art like this after a few years. Nilla would be the exception, and how long before they realised what she was? Or rather what she wasn't? What would they do with her then? Would they return her to her home only to take away her daughter? Or would they punish her for deceiving the Emperor?

Her heart quickened while her breathing became

erratic and she had to will herself to move, to take one step and then another. She managed, with great effort to leave the corridor full of impressive work only to stumble into another almost identical one. This corridor contained fewer paintings and more sculptures. They adorned a variety of plinths and were made up of a mixture of technically perfect creatures.

She collapsed next to an impressive looking tiger and felt tears run down her face. It was becoming ever more realistic that the sacrifice she had made so her daughter could have a life would be for nothing unless she could trust someone enough to tell them what she had done and beg them to help her. But who could she trust? Flicker? Jackie? No, she'd just met them and had no idea where their loyalties lay.

Nilla sobbed for what felt like hours, despair almost suffocating her; she couldn't get enough air into her lungs and eventually coughed with panic. She needed to calm down, she tried to take slow, deep breaths. She would just have to put in the extra effort to learn the techniques, she would spend every waking hour in the classroom if necessary in order to sculpt something as impressive as the creations she was surrounded by. She glanced at the tiger again and noticed a tiny inscription on the plinth, 'Charlie Sanders'. Nilla gasped and stared, almost forgetting to breathe, then she smiled and dragged herself to her feet.

"Of course," she whispered. "There *is* someone I can trust."

It was only when dawn arrived that she began to panic about trying to find her husband. It had been years since she'd seen him and although she could trust him when they'd been together, how did she know she could trust him now? Fifteen years was a long time, what if he'd learnt to embrace his gift? What if he supported the Emperor? What if he'd found someone else?

This last thought made her breath catch in her throat and she had to steady herself. In the fifteen years they'd been apart she hadn't found anyone else, she hadn't wanted anyone else but that didn't mean he hadn't wanted to find someone else. What would she do? How would she react if she saw him with someone else?

Questions swirled round her head as she entered Flicker's classroom and barely acknowledged the instructions he issued. He walked over to her when he noticed she hadn't moved and when he asked if she was okay she just nodded and went to take a seat at the potter's wheel. She heaped a lump of clay into the centre, dipped her hands into a bowl of cool water and began to manipulate the clay.

She was barely paying attention to what she was doing, thoughts concerning her husband bombarded her and she couldn't get the idea that maybe he'd moved on out of her head. She glanced briefly at the tall jug in front of her before she picked up some wooden tools and began to carve simple designs into the body.

Her mind was solely focused on her husband so she didn't notice Flicker watching her with interest as she carved and incised a simple swirling pattern. Only when Flicker clapped his hands and informed them that it was lunch did Nilla realise what she'd sculpted. She stared at the jug in front of her, it had a wide rim with a small triangular pouring lip but a narrow neck, which smoothly widened to a spherical body before narrowing again at the base. She leant closer to inspect the decoration she'd applied; the base appeared rippled and she realised she had impressed her thumbs to create it. The body was home to a simple swirl decoration, almost as if she were trying to mimic the waves of the sea.

She looked up as Flicker approached and realised she was the only one left in the classroom.

Flicker leant against one of the desks and eyed her suspiciously, "You seem to have improved somewhat," he said nodding to the jug.

Nilla looked a little bemused, "I'm not really sure what happened, I wasn't really paying attention to what I was doing…" she trailed off as a thoughtful look crossed Flicker's face. "What?" she asked.

"I think," he began slowly as if mulling over the words carefully. "That your talent is hiding within you." She looked confused and he elaborated, still speaking slowly. "We've both seen your attempts at sculpting, it's not that you can't do it, but it takes a lot of concentration. Today was different, you say you weren't concentrating, you weren't paying attention to what you were doing, well I think that's how your gift is manifesting. Since it's never really had the chance to surface, it's choosing to come out when your mind is focused on other things."

Nilla nodded slowly because she knew of course that she had no gift, "I suppose that could be true."

"We'll test the theory more over the next few days, but this could be the way to improving your skill. I'll show you the techniques you need, you can spend some time focusing on them and then we'll try and get you unfocused and see what you can do." Nilla smiled and hoped that it seemed sincere, he seemed so enthusiastic, like he'd suddenly realised she wasn't a lost cause after all. Her heart sank as she left the room and walked towards the dining room; how on earth was she going to get herself out of this mess?

Chapter 12

Aggie's mood had improved by the following evening as she dressed in the only smart clothes she owned ready for her first evening at The Fisherman's Fancy. She had no idea what she would be required to do or how much she would be paid but she felt grateful to Wolf for taking a chance on her. She knew deep down he either didn't actually need any help or he couldn't afford to take her on but he had offered her work anyway and she was determined to prove she could be useful.

She arrived just before seven and Wolf beamed at her from behind the bar as she entered. The Fisherman's Fancy was lit mostly by natural light from the fire and a few smaller bulbs around the exterior. There was a large bar towards the back of the main room, where several patrons were already drinking heavily; other customers sat at circular tables around the room with drinks and food, and there was a quiet hum of chatter that was oddly soothing.

"Evening lass," he said as he emerged from behind the bar. "You're looking smart," Aggie smiled broadly and Wolf guided her to one of the back rooms where it was quieter. "Nice and simple to start with, I'll have you clearing and washing glasses, once you're okay with that you can start to take drinks to the folks." Aggie nodded enthusiastically and Wolf smiled kindly at her as he handed her a small, black apron. They entered the busy front room again and Aggie set about clearing glasses, making sure to be extra careful when carrying the tray towards the bar.

It wasn't easy work and she was exhausted after only a couple of hours, but the crowd inside didn't look like it would let up anytime soon so she kept on going. Wolf smiled at her every time she passed him and she hoped she was doing a good enough job that he would want her to come back. She was clearing glasses from a small table in the corner when a familiar soft, female voice spoke close by.

"I'm trying, but it's not as easy as you might think," Aggie glanced in her direction and her suspicions were confirmed; it was the female officer, Flora, who had walked her home. She was sitting with a man who had scruffy, deep chestnut hair and a frown on his face.

"You've been trying to sort this for months and we've yet to see any progress," the man said in a deep voice; he ran his hands through his hair and Aggie noticed a large scar along his left forearm.

Flora sipped her drink and looked sternly at him, "Crafts! It's not going to happen overnight, these things take time, they don't let just anyone in there you know." The man sighed heavily and folded his arms in annoyance; Flora ignored him and the two sat in silence for some time. Aggie snapped back to reality and continued clearing glasses, hoping that Wolf hadn't seen her eavesdropping; she glanced in his direction but he was busy with a customer.

It was late by the time the majority of the customers filtered out and stumbled towards their homes. Aggie having cleared all of the visible glasses began to wipe the spilled alcohol from the tables. There were only a few small groups left in the pub, including Flora and her friend, who didn't seem to have spoken again since Aggie had overheard them. She noticed the man glancing round the room occasionally, sigh in what looked like exasperation, then turn back to his dwindling drink. She was wiping down a table close to them when Wolf wandered over.

"How are you holding up lass?" he asked and Aggie straightened up to look at him.

"I'm okay," she lied as exhaustion swept over her.

Wolf smiled knowingly, "You've done a grand job this evening but I'll take it from here, you get yourself home and get some rest." Aggie nodded and carried her tray with the few glasses that littered it to the bar, Wolf followed her but first glanced at Flora and her friend. Aggie removed the apron she had been wearing, which was now sticky in several places and Wolf held out his hand to take it from her.

"I can take it home and wash it," she offered but Wolf shook his head.

"Don't you worry about that lass, I'll sort it. Here take this," he handed her several coins and a loaf of bread and she stared up at him stunned. She opened her mouth but Wolf cut her off before she could speak. "No point arguing with me lass, either take it now or I'll find where you live and deliver it that way." She said nothing but nodded and then without thinking threw her arms round the large man and squeezed as tightly as she could. He patted her on the head somewhat awkwardly. "Go on lass, get yourself home and I'll see you at the same time tomorrow." Aggie drew back, threw a wobbly smile his way and nodded before scampering out of the door and to her home.

"You're too nice for your own good," the man

sitting with Flora said.

Wolf walked over and sat with them; they were now the only ones left in the pub, "She's got no one left," he explained. "I couldn't just send her away."

"You're a good man, Wolf," Flora said and the other man snorted, Flora snapped round to look at him. "You could learn a thing or two from him Redd." The man known as Redd scoffed and took another swig of his drink.

Wolf scowled at him, "You'd better get used to her, she's not going anywhere, not while I'm here."

"Fine," Redd said with annoyance. "Now can we please get down to business."

Aggie continued to work in the evenings for Wolf and she was soon delivering drinks as well as clearing classes. She found herself holding her head high as she weaved between the tables in the pub and made sure every glass sparkled before being put back on the shelves. Wolf continued to pay her far too much and although she started to protest he ignored her and often sent her home with a loaf of bread or leftovers.

She had noticed that Flora and her friend Redd came into the pub most nights and always seemed to take the same small table near the window. Although it wasn't unusual that customers would come in on a regular basis, it did seem odd to Aggie that they came in every night and stayed until closing. She wondered if perhaps they were close friends of Wolf's though she didn't yet dare ask.

Flora had recognised her after a few days and had seemed concerned for her wellbeing; Aggie had smiled and explained that she was fine but Flora hadn't looked convinced. Redd seemed disinterested in anything but his drink whenever Aggie was close by and she noticed that he stopped talking if she got too close, which made her wonder what they were talking about.

She decided that although she liked Flora, she didn't like her companion, Redd. He seemed cold and hostile towards her and reminded her of the children at her old school. Flora smiled at her whenever she passed, whereas Redd scowled and glared at her over his drink. He would ignore her if she came to their table, despite Flora's best efforts to introduce her to him. On a number of occasions he'd even been rude and Wolf had once found her in the back room crying into her apron. When he'd found out Redd had teased her for breaking a couple of glasses he had stormed out and when Aggie had finally emerged Redd was nowhere to be seen.

Although Redd clearly disliked her, Aggie found herself being drawn to him; he was clearly hiding something and seemed incredibly bitter. She wondered if perhaps he had lost someone to the Emperor as she had, or maybe it was something linked to the large scar on his left arm. Aggie decided one evening after days of hostility and teasing to give Redd a taste of his own medicine. She saw Flora wave her over and she smirked to herself as she arrived.

"Good evening Flora," she said smiling at the other woman and conveniently forgetting to acknowledge Redd who frowned at her. "What can I get you this evening?"

"It's nice to see you looking so well Aggie," Flora said smiling. "I'll have my usual if you don't mind." Aggie smiled and turned to walk away, she heard a loud clearing of the throat and turned back to the table to see an irate Redd glaring at her.

"You didn't ask for my order," he said.

Aggie smiled politely, "Oh I'm sorry, I didn't see you

there," Flora stifled a laugh as Redd looked taken aback. "What can I get for you?" Redd remained silent and Flora, unable to hold on anymore burst into laughter. This seemed to snap Redd out of his stupor and he scowled at both Flora and Aggie.

"I'll have another pint please," he finally said through gritted teeth.

"Of course, I'll bring that right over," Aggie said with a smile and walked towards the bar where Wolf was watching, she suddenly felt cold and realised how unprofessional she'd been. "I'm sorry," she said as she approached. "That was wrong of me, I-"

Wolf started to chuckle and slammed his fist down on the table making several glasses clink together. Redd glanced over and scowled once again, Wolf wiped a tear from his eye and beamed at her.

"I think you're one of the best workers I've ever had," he said and Aggie looked confused. "I don't think I've ever seen someone stand up to Redd but by the Emperor did he deserve it!" Wolf began to laugh again and Aggie allowed herself a small smile.

From that moment on Redd's hostility towards her softened somewhat, he still wasn't exactly pleasant but he acknowledged her when she approached, even if only in the form of a nod. He still tended to halt his conversation with Flora when she drew near and that made her wonder even more what they were talking about. She had no doubt it was something legitimate and lawful since Flora was an officer, but what on earth could they be talking about that they wouldn't want her to hear?

The evening was drawing on and the majority of customers had long since left, Aggie had washed the remaining glasses and was in the process of cleaning the tables ready for the following day. She noticed Wolf sitting with Flora and Redd and all three were talking in hushed voices. Although she was desperate to know what they were talking about, she kept her distance and continued with her job.

"Come over here lass," Wolf called unexpectedly and Aggie jumped in surprise, she walked to the small table near the window and Wolf pulled over a chair for her. She sat somewhat nervously and stared at the surface of the table as if trying to determine how old the tree had been before it was felled. There was a heavy silence and finally Aggie looked up, all three were staring at her.

"Have I done something wrong?" she asked nervously.

Wolf smiled kindly, "Not at all lass, Redd just wanted to apologise to you," Aggie looked across at Redd and saw him looking about as uncomfortable as she felt. Flora and Wolf frowned at him and eventually he heaved a sigh.

"I'm sorry I've been less than pleasant to you," he said with little sincerity. Aggie knew Flora and Wolf were making him do this and she decided as a kindness not to prolong his agony.

"Don't mention it," Aggie said getting to her feet with a genuine smile. She was making her way to the opposite end of the room to continue wiping tables when five burly men crashed through the door. Aggie spun in fright and was knocked heavily to the ground by a large clenched fist. Wolf, Redd and Flora were on their feet in seconds and rushed towards the intruders.

Aggie's face throbbed and her vision swan. She dragged herself to her feet and began to clamber towards the bar; one of the men caught sight of her and lumbered towards her. She glanced frantically round for some sort of weapon and grabbed for the only thing within reach. The large glass smashed into the man's face and he roared with anger; he reached her in two large paces and slammed her against the bar, one large hand round her neck pinning her in place. She tried to scream but no sound emerged, she tried to pry his hand away but his grip was firm; he raised his other fist and she braced herself.

The blow never came but his grip slackened and she crumpled to the floor as the man toppled backwards. Redd stood behind him with a large cudgel in his hand. His face was a picture of thunder and Aggie felt herself cower before him.

Something snapped him back to reality and he knelt beside her, "Are you okay?" he asked with genuine concern, Aggie nodded, not convinced her voice wouldn't tremble. Redd helped her to her feet as Wolf and Flora cuffed the five men who lay strewn around the now dishevelled pub. Flora raced into the streets and Wolf joined Redd and Aggie at the table by the window.

Concern was etched across Wolf's features, "Are you okay lass?" he asked checking her over for wounds,

"I think so," she managed to croak out and realised her neck and throat were throbbing along with her head. She turned suddenly to Redd. "Thank you for-"

"Don't mention it," Redd said quickly. "I'm glad you're alright." He turned away quickly as Wolf continued to check her over and watched the unconscious men until Flora returned with several more officers.

They dragged the men from the pub and Wolf began to clear away the shattered tables, damaged chairs and broken glass. Aggie got up to help and Wolf waved her back to her seat.

"Don't you worry about this, lass," he said as he swept up the glass she had used as a weapon. "You get calmed down and I'll walk you home."

"I'll take her," Redd said getting to his feet. "I think you should keep an eye on your pub, I'll see that the girl gets home safely." *Girl?* Aggie thought with a frown as she got to her feet and tried to straighten her clothes and re-tie her curly black hair into something presentable. Wolf didn't look happy about letting her out of his sight. "I can take care of us both," Redd tried to reassure him. "I promise I won't leave her until she's safely in her house." Reluctantly Wolf nodded and Redd guided Aggie from the chaotic scene.

They walked in silence for some time and Aggie began to feel uncomfortable, she glanced at Redd and saw his face was grim and he stared straight ahead.

"Something on your mind?" he asked without looking at her.

"No," she said quickly and this time he did look at her.

"I can't guarantee you'll get another chance to speak freely around me so you might as well do it now."

There was more silence as Aggie built up the courage to croak out her question, "Why do you act so hostile towards me?" From his expression it wasn't the question he'd been expecting then he smiled unexpectedly.

"If you knew me well enough girl, you'd know I'm hostile towards most people."

Aggie frowned, "My name's Aggie, not *girl*."

He smiled again, "My apologies, Aggie," his face turned serious again. "I didn't mean to offend but I don't trust others easily and that includes you."

"I can understand that." They walked again in silence and Aggie felt more relaxed in his presence. Redd was true to his word and ensured she entered and locked her door behind her but not before catching a glimpse of Cassie. He frowned.

Chapter 13

Flicker sighed heavily as he and Nilla stared at the collapsing vessel on the potter's wheel.

"You're still trying too hard, you need to get back to that same state of non-focusing."

Nilla folded her arms, forgetting that her hands were covered in wet clay, "It's actually a lot harder than you might think to become unfocused, especially when you're *trying* to become unfocused."

Flicker ran a hand through his shaggy red hair and looked apologetically at Nilla, "I'm sorry, I'm pushing too much aren't I?"

She nodded, her face remaining stern, then her face softened, "I will keep trying but I think it will be hard to replicate the conditions of that first time."

He looked at her curiously, "Do you mind me asking what was going through your head that first time?"

Several minutes passed while she stared at him, contemplating her answer. She still didn't know if she could trust him, but he was the closest thing to a friend she had and maybe he would be able to help her.

"I was thinking about my husband," Flicker looked surprised but said nothing, Nilla sighed heavily. "I've been wondering whether I should try and find him but I'm not sure if I'm ready for that yet."

"Why wouldn't you want to find him?"

"Because he might have moved on, he might have found someone else, someone just like him-"

"What do you mean just like him?"

Nilla froze, realising she'd slipped up, she racked her brain for a way out but couldn't find one, "I don't know," she finally said, trying to sound exhausted. Flicker looked at her suspiciously and Nilla started to clear away the collapsed pot. "I just meant that he might have found a new life here, perhaps he's happier here than he was with me."

"I think at some point you'll have to try and find him," Flicker said gently and it surprised Nilla; Flicker smiled. "I know I come across as a miserable old git but I promise I'm not."

"I know I'll have to find him eventually, it's better for him to find out I'm here through me than through someone else." They continued to tidy the potter's wheel while Nilla felt a sense of unease in her stomach.

Weeks passed and Nilla's artistic ability was consistently hit and miss. She had been present for several class audits and Lucie was unimpressed with her creations. On several occasions after examining her work she had spoken quietly to Flicker and Nilla was getting worried that her cover would soon be blown. Flicker continued to try and help her improve but Nilla could see he was getting frustrated since she wasn't progressing as quickly as the other new student Gabe.

He had asked her to take a walk with him around the palace grounds and Nilla could tell it wouldn't be a pleasant experience. They had entered the sculpture garden when Flicker sighed heavily and sat on one of the benches. It was quiet and deserted in this part of the grounds and Nilla suspected that's why he'd chosen it.

"I don't know what to do Nilla, they're not happy at the moment."

"Who's not happy?" Nilla asked shoving her hands in her pockets and not really sure if she wanted to know the answer.

"The managers, they're not happy with your progress, and I don't know what else I can do to help you improve."

"What will they do if-" she couldn't finish the sentence.

"I don't know," Flicker said shaking his head. "This has never happened before, it's almost like you're not an Artist." Nilla's breath caught in her throat and Flicker spun to stare at her; his eyes narrowed and Nilla felt panic rising inside her.

Flicker got to his feet and stared at her, "Crafts! You're not are you? That's why you need to find your husband. Crafts! Nilla what have you done?"

She broke down, tears trickling down her face, "I couldn't let them take her," she managed to say through the tears.

"Her?" Flicker asked. "Your daughter?" Nilla nodded through the tears. "But why would they..." His eyes widened. "Crafts! Nilla, is your daughter an-"

She nodded frantically cutting him off, "I just couldn't let them take her," she said miserably.

Flicker exhaled heavily, sat next to her and put his head in his hands. He was silent for a few minutes. "You took her place to protect her." It wasn't a question.

"Yes," she said quietly. "I didn't want her life to be over."

He placed a comforting hand on her shoulder, "I understand, you wanted to protect your daughter but you've put yourself into a terrible position. Now neither of you are safe. If they find out what you've done they'll more than likely kill you for lying to the Emperor and then they'll find your daughter and bring her here anyway." Nilla sniffed loudly and Flicker noticed Jan walking towards them.

"Crafts!" he hissed and Nilla glanced up, she saw Jan on a collision course with them and tried her best to hide her tears. "It's okay," Flicker said, trying to reassure her. "I won't tell him anything, I'll just say you're finding it difficult to adjust, it's not that uncommon." He left her sniffing on the bench and walked to meet Jan who had a concerned expression on his face.

"What have you done to her?"

Flicker shot him a look and spoke sharply, "She's new, and she's finding it difficult to adjust to life here."

Jan raised an eyebrow, "I thought you'd turned over a new leaf?"

"It's difficult to think what we're doing in here is helping when someone like her gets thrown in after being ripped from her family."

Jan shifted uncomfortably, "I know it must be hard, I honestly couldn't imagine not being able to see my wife and children whenever I want, but what you're doing is protecting our city." Flicker looked unconvinced, so Jan continued. "I mean it Flicker, for years now we've been on the verge of war, but the work you all do is keeping us safe. Imagine how many more lives would be lost if our neighbours invaded."

Flicker considered his words, he still didn't believe what he had been told but he could also see from Jan's expression that he truly believed it. "Sometimes it's difficult to believe what we're doing is the right thing, especially when someone like her is thrown amongst us." He walked back to Nilla before Jan could retaliate and the latter knew better than to follow, so he left them alone.

Nilla was silent when he approached spoke in a hoarse voice, "I'm so sorry," she said, blowing her nose loudly. "I'm normally able to keep myself together."

"You've been through a lot in the past few weeks, everyone breaks down at some point when they enter this place."

Nilla took a deep breath, "So what am I going to do?"

Flicker smiled, "*We* will find a way to improve your skills." Nilla choked back another sob and smiled.

It wasn't easy, Nilla spent almost every waking hour with Flicker in the classroom trying to improve her skills. Months passed and her plan to find her husband had slipped to the back of her mind. Instead her focus was solely on fooling the managers into thinking she was an Artist. Flicker seemed to be impressed with her progress, she had almost caught up with Gabe, the young man who had started at the same time as her. Thankfully several of Flicker's top students had been promoted and several new recruits had arrived, meaning she was no longer the weakest student.

Flicker grinned at her across the table in the dining room, and she looked at him quizzically.

"What's going on with your face?"

Flicker continued to smile, "I honestly didn't think I'd ever get you to the point that I was confident with your ability, you're really starting to fool them."

"*We're* starting to fool them," she corrected. "I wouldn't have been able to do any of this without you."

"Well, whatever the case, we'll have to be careful from now on, we don't want you getting *too* good."

Nilla looked confused, "Why not?"

Flicker looked at her intensely, then decided to let her in on everything; he told her about the padlocked workrooms and the work that's apparently done in them, and the fact that once the students are, 'promoted' they're not seen again.

Nilla still looked confused, "But surely if I get to that point then I've succeeded in pretending I'm an Artist."

"And what happens when you're required to create things?"

Nilla faltered and her face fell, "You know, somehow I'd forgotten. I'd forgotten who it was that lives here and what it was that these people have to do. Of course I can't be seen to get any better, if I really did have to create things then I'd be found out for sure."

Flicker cocked his head to one side, "However…"

Nilla narrowed her eyes, "What's going on in that head of yours?"

Flicker snapped back to reality, "Nothing," he said smiling. "Absolutely nothing."

They were about to leave and take a walk round the grounds when a familiar male voice sounded, Nilla's breath caught but she didn't dare look up.

"I have a proposition for you," the voice said and Nilla realised he was talking to Flicker.

"Yes?"

"I'd like to trade a student with you."

Flicker raised an eyebrow in surprise, "Why?" Nilla dared a glance at the man and her eyes widened as she was greeted with familiar jet black hair and piercing green eyes. *Charlie!* She lowered her gaze quickly before he noticed.

Charlie sighed and took a seat, "I have a troublemaker, she's driving me insane, no one will take her, you're my last chance."

Flicker chuckled, "I'm surprised you didn't think of me first considering I used to *be* a troublemaker. I take it she's new?"

Charlie nodded, "Got her a few weeks back."

Flicker nodded thoughtfully, "Can I swing by tomorrow and take a look at her?"

Charlie nodded eagerly, "Any time tomorrow, my door is always open." He got up to leave, then hesitated, Nilla willed herself to speak but found herself frozen. "Thank you," he said to Flicker before he walked away.

Nilla let out the breath she'd been holding and Flicker gave her an interested look, she just smiled, "Do you think you'll take the student?"

Flicker shrugged, "It depends entirely on how much potential I think she's got."

"Artistic potential?"

"Something like that," he grinned mischievously.

The girl joined their class several days later and immediately starting causing havoc mostly by sneaking blood into her clay and bringing her creations to life. Flicker grinned as several imperfect lizards and snakes roamed the room and informed his class to ignore her. Nilla sat at her desk attempting to sculpt a small cat and wore a troubled expression, for some reason she hadn't revealed to Flicker that the girl's former teacher was her husband. She couldn't even understand what had caused her to freeze in his presence, she'd been missing him for so long and finally he was there and what had she done? Nothing.

"Is everything okay?" Flicker asked at the end of the day.

Nilla gazed at her half finished cat and sighed,

"There's something I should have told you days ago.

Flicker tensed, "Go on."

"The man you spoke to the other day, the one who begged you to take that girl," Nilla paused and bit her lip. "He's my husband."

Flicker raised an eyebrow and pulled a chair over, "Why didn't you say anything when you saw him?"

I don't know," Nilla said shaking her head. "Maybe I was scared."

"Scared?"

"I practically abandoned our daughter."

"You did what you did so she could live her life the way she should."

Nilla sighed and began pacing, "But what if I made the wrong decision? What if she's struggling out there? Maybe I should have let her come here, maybe she would have been happier."

"Don't ever think that!" Flicker said suddenly angry. "It might seem okay to you, you've only been here a few months, I've been here five years and believe me I'd rather be anywhere else. Your husband has been here far longer, imagine how he feels. Your daughter's so young, think what it would do to her to be thrown into this place, knowing she would remain here until she died."

She took a deep breath, "You're right, I just miss her."

"I know," he replied. "Believe me I know." Nilla pulled away and looked quizzically at him. Flicker sat back down. "I have a brother, he was my best friend, he *is* my best friend, being in here doesn't change that. We had a business together, we were artisans, I loved my job and I loved my brother and once I found out about my *gift* I panicked. We kept it hidden for as long as we could but I messed up," he sighed and put his head in his hands.

"I'd cut myself, I don't know how I did it but I did, I'd been making several eagle statues for a client, who wanted them to adorn his living room. The day he arrived to collect them I wheeled them out and could almost see them ruffling their feathers. I took a deep breath and exhaled without thinking and by the time I'd reached the customer the eagles were sprouting feathers and twitching their necks as if they were searching for prey."

He looked up at Nilla who had her hands over her mouth in horror, "you were reported?"

Flicker nodded, "The client scrambled away as quickly as possible and grabbed the nearest officer, they tested us there and then, there was nothing we could do, I couldn't cheat my way out of it like you did," he smiled bitterly and Nilla put a comforting had on his.

"I'm sorry," she said softly.

Flicker shrugged, "I've spent most of my time here trying to escape, I've never formed close bonds with anyone except Jackie, I just didn't see the point, I was convinced I would break out."

"What changed?"

"Reality hit I suppose, I started to realise I wasn't going anywhere and if I wanted an easier life I had better change my attitude."

Nilla frowned, "That's not what you think at all."

Flicker looked at her with surprise, "What makes you say that?"

"The padlocked rooms."

"What about them? They're just workrooms."

Nilla shook her head, "I can see you don't really believe that, you think there's something more to them," the surprise on his face confirmed her suspicions. "Are you going to tell me your theory then?"

"That's just it Nilla, there isn't one."

"What do you mean?"

"I mean exactly that, no matter how much I think those rooms are a front for something else I've no idea what that something else is."

Nilla smiled, "Then why don't we try and find out?"

Chapter 14

In the few months since the incident at the bar, Redd had started to warm towards her; he wasn't exactly friendly like Flora but he was civil and seemed vaguely concerned for her safety. She wasn't sure whether it had been the fact she had been so helpless or that while walking her home he'd realised she wasn't as bad as he thought but he had started to smile at her when she arrived for her shift. At first she had found it quite unnerving, something which caused Wolf endless joy and he had laughed at her when she first mentioned it, but as the days passed into weeks she had started to relax and it had been nice to have another friendly face in her life.

There had been no other incidents, though Wolf had had to improve the security and there were now several bolts that slid across the door at the end of the night. He also made sure that Aggie never walked home alone.

On one of the occasions Redd was escorting her, he seemed quite interested in her personal life. He had mentioned he'd seen Cassie and seemed to be vying for information as to where she came from. Aggie told as much of the truth as she dared and mentioned that Flora had allowed her to take the dog from an abandoned building. Redd had looked unconvinced but knowing he could easily verify the details he seemed to accept it, if not a little reluctantly.

"So both your parents are at the palace?" he asked one cool, spring evening on the journey to her house, she had nodded but said nothing. "And you've not shown any signs of having the gift?"

His question was innocent enough but Aggie felt her heart rate increase, "No, I've never displayed any signs." She probably answered a little too quickly and forcefully and Redd raised an eyebrow in response.

"That's interesting, I know they say being an Artist isn't genetic but usually if both parents are found to have the gift the child does too. I'm surprised they didn't take you to the palace for observation."

Aggie shrugged and tried to sound calm, "I don't know what to tell you, they tested me but I failed, or passed depending on your view."

"I'd be careful, they'll be keeping an eye on you and you'll probably be re-tested again at some point."

Aggie felt her heart miss a beat, "Really?" she asked in surprise. "That was never mentioned." Redd nodded and she paused before throwing him a shaky smile and tried to sound confident. "I've got nothing to hide." Redd looked at her intensely but said nothing.

"Why's he suddenly so interested in me?" Aggie asked Wolf one evening.

"I think he's just trying to make up for his earlier behaviour," Wolf replied unconvincingly.

"I don't know," Aggie said looking thoughtful. "How long have you known him?"

"Long enough lass, I trust him with my life." Aggie nodded feeling slightly foolish and set to work taking drink orders and clearing glasses.

Redd and Flora entered sometime later and both smiled at Aggie as she passed, she thought she heard

112

Flora talking about entering the palace but then someone called her over and she didn't have a chance to hear any more.

It was towards the end of the evening when she caught a few more snippets of their conversation.

"It's looking promising," Flora said and Redd looked hopeful. "I don't know when, but they *have* said they're looking for transfers, they know I've registered an interest so keep your fingers crossed."

"If that's the case then we should probably finalise the plans, once you're in, we may not get much of a chance to meet out here." Flora nodded and Aggie was called away again. *I wonder what plans they're making and where exactly is Flora trying to get in to? Maybe I should ask Wolf.* She frowned at this last thought, if she asked Wolf then he'd know she'd been eavesdropping and he might let her go.

She decided to take the plunge at the end of the night when Wolf was putting some leftovers together for her in one of the back rooms.

He looked up at her and a concerned look crossed his face, "Something wrong lass?"

She was quiet for several minutes while she decided what to say, "I'm worried," she said finally.

Wolf frowned, "About what?"

Aggie paused again and Wolf sighed in exasperation, "Redd and Flora."

Wolf stood up straight and turned to face her, "What exactly is causing you to worry?"

There was concern in his voice and Aggie swallowed hard, "I heard something when I walked past," Wolf stared at her with piercing eyes and she knew she couldn't turn back now. "I'm worried they might get into trouble."

Wolf suddenly chuckled, "Oh lass there's no need to

worry, they know what they're doing and everything's in hand."

It was Aggie's turn to look concerned, "Wolf, are you in on it too?" his smile faltered, which told her everything she needed to know. "Please tell me it's nothing illegal, I couldn't bear to lose you too." There were tears welling up in her eyes and Wolf pulled her into a tight hug.

"Now don't you worry Aggie, nothing is going to happen to any of us, we've been organising this plan for almost a year."

Aggie struggled to extract herself from Wolf's embrace, "What are you planning?"

He stared down into her eyes, which were brimming with tears and sighed heavily, "I'm sorry lass it's not up to me to tell you, this is all Redd's doing." Aggie huffed, turned and stormed from the room before Wolf had a chance to stop her.

The Fisherman's Fancy was empty now except for Redd and Flora, sat at their usual table by the window. Aggie marched over and slammed her fists unimpressively down on the table; they turned to look at her.

"Aggie what's wrong?" Flora asked in a concerned tone.

Aggie ignored her and stared at Redd, her gaze trying to bore into his soul, "What are you planning?"

His face remained impassive, "I don't know what you're talking about."

Aggie snorted and threw her head back, "Don't give me that, I heard you two talking earlier, where are you sending Flora? And why are you involving Wolf?" Tears had started to well in her eyes. Wolf appeared behind her and tried to pull her away from the small table.

"Come on lass, take a seat," Wolf managed to get Aggie to sit at the adjacent table; Redd continued to look unfazed by her outburst while Flora crouched next to her. A few tears rolled down Aggie's face and sniffed loudly.

"What's wrong Aggie?" Flora asked in a calm and gentle voice, she glanced into her soft, kind eyes and buried her face in her hands.

"I told you she wouldn't be strong enough," Redd said harshly to Wolf.

Aggie's head snapped up, "What did you say?"

Redd shrugged, "Nothing."

Flora tilted Aggie's head back towards her, "Aggie talk to me, why are you so upset?"

She wiped tears from her face and when she spoke her voice wobbled, "I don't want to lose you," she said quietly.

"Oh Aggie you won't lose us," Flora said wrapping her arms round the young girl.

"But he's planning something," she said trying to glare at Redd and failing, "and if I lose you then I'll have no one. You're the only ones who've taken a chance on me, you're the only ones who are protecting me, without you they'll come for me and I won't be able to stop them this time." The words spilled from her mouth before she could stop them and the three adults stared at her.

"Who will come for you?" Wolf asked slowly.

Aggie suddenly looked terrified, she jumped up quickly from her chair and made for the door but Redd blocked her path,

"You're an Artist." It wasn't a question. Aggie collapsed to the floor too exhausted from keeping her secret to protest. Wolf and Flora looked shocked and confused but Redd continued to stare unemotionally down at her.

"Aggie what is he talking about?" Flora asked but Aggie remained in a crumpled heap, head in hands waiting to be taken away.

Wolf made his way over to her, crouched down and placed a hand gently on her shoulder; she flinched but didn't look at him.

"No one's going to hurt you lass," Wolf said trying to sound reassuring.

"We're not going to turn you in," Flora added.

"You need to tell us everything," Redd said sitting opposite her. "How is it that the officers didn't catch you? Especially with that creation of yours."

Aggie looked shocked, "My what?"

Red gave her a look, "Your dog, it's a creation isn't it?"

Aggie nodded, "How did you know?"

Redd smiled, "There was just something a bit odd about her."

Aggie nodded and Wolf gently nudged her to tell them everything. She remained quiet for what felt like hours, she was terrified to reveal her secret, but part of her guessed that Redd already knew what she would say.

She took a deep breath and began to explain. She told them of how her father had been taken when she was so young that she didn't even remember who he was and that her own power had developed when she was small but her mother had begged her to hide it.

"It wasn't that easy though was it?" Redd asked staring at her with intense unblinking brown eyes.

Aggie shook her head, "It's like an internal itch," she explained, rubbing her hands and staring at the floor, "the only way to scratch it was to create something, my mother didn't understand."

She took another deep breath and told them about

the day when the officers finally arrived. She explained in detail how they had tricked the officers and how they had taken her mother to the palace instead.

"Oh Aggie you poor thing!" Flora threw her arms round her and hugged her tightly, she heard Wolf sigh heavily.

"I wish you'd have said something sooner lass."

"How would that have helped?" Aggie said suddenly frustrated. "My mother's been taken, she's in the palace all alone and she's no clue about how to act like an Artist. She should have just let them take me instead."

Redd placed a hand on her shoulder and spoke uncharacteristically softly, "You must see that she couldn't let them take you, she couldn't let them ruin your life. She wanted you to be free, to grow up and live your life however you choose."

"But they have ruined my life, they've taken my parents from me."

There was a long silence, which was eventually broken by Wolf, "I think we should tell her."

Redd shook his head, "I still don't think she's strong enough."

"She might be able to help," Flora interjected."

The conversation carried on around Aggie for several minutes before she finally stood up and they turned to look at her. "Don't talk about me like I'm not here," she said quietly but with some force.

"Sorry lass," Wolf said. "We didn't mean anything by it, why don't you sit down and we'll tell you everything." Aggie returned to her seat and as she glanced at the three of them she could see clearly that Redd was deeply unhappy with the current situation.

"I promise you can trust me," she said staring directly into his eyes. "You now know my deepest secret,

I promise I will keep yours in return."

Chapter 15

Nilla trembled as she walked down a long corridor high up on the sixth floor. She had been asked to speak to Lucie privately and all she could think was that they'd found out she wasn't an Artist. They'd probably question her, maybe even torture her and it would only end when they finally took her daughter away. When they had what they wanted, they'd almost certainly kill her. Her heart pounded as she stopped by a door with Lucie's name on, took a deep breath and knocked. A light voice called for her to enter and she stepped inside.

Flicker had been worried when the message arrived; to his knowledge it had never happened before. The staff viewed and tested the students, they took the students away from the classes but they never asked for a meeting. It had made him panic; what if they had found out what was going on?

They had spent months trying to devise a plan for uncovering what was really happening behind the scenes in the palace. They had started by mapping out the interior and exterior layout, trying to identify all of the areas within the palace grounds. They had quickly found out that the palace was a lot larger than either of them had thought. There were seven floors in the main building – that they knew of - and ten smaller three storey buildings within the grounds.

The majority of rooms were designed to accommodate the Artist's who lived there; bedrooms, bathrooms, comfortable relaxation areas. Every building had a kitchen and a dining hall and there were the classrooms in the main building but they also found a number of store rooms, which they assumed held artistic supplies. Just one of the buildings in the grounds housed the officers who slept on site.

The top three floors were a bit more of a mystery to them and would require some careful scoping; the administration team worked and were housed on one of them and it was thought that the Emperor himself occupied the entire seventh floor though they didn't have confirmation. The padlocked workshops were located on part of floor five though the remainder of that level was still unknown. To Flicker's knowledge there was also a basement but as far as he knew it held the kitchen supplies.

Nilla had concluded that whatever was really going on must be on one of the top three floors since they knew very little about them and she believed that might be where the 'promoted' students were staying.

She had tried to calm Flicker down after his initial panic had set in, "There's no way they can know what we're doing," she tried to reassure him.

"We've been drawing maps," Flicker insisted, "what if they've seen them?"

Nilla shrugged, "So what if they have? We could easily claim we were passing time, perhaps we're trying to find out how many rooms the palace has." Flicker looked unconvinced but Nilla assured him she'd be in no danger.

She wished desperately that she felt now as calm as she had sounded back then. She exhaled as she stepped into the light, spacious office. Lucie was sat behind a large pale wooden desk; papers littered the top and she appeared to be writing reports. She smiled politely as she glanced up from her work and indicated a seat in front of the desk. Nilla took the seat and waited for Lucie to finish.

"I'm sorry I won't be a moment," Lucie said glancing up for a second time.

"Don't worry," Nilla said as she began to look around the bright room. Lucie had a number of impressive paintings adorning her wall, though Nilla wasn't sure why she was so surprised, there were works of art everywhere. Then she saw the signature on the one behind Lucie's desk; she let out a quiet gasp and Lucie looked up.

"Is everything okay?" she asked, she nodded and Lucie returned to her report. Nilla tore her eyes away from the painting, which had been created by the office's inhabitant and wondered whether Lucie was an Artist or just an artisan. They knew so little about the administration team and where they came from. The paintings were the most impressive things in the office, the remaining floor space was filled with low bookshelves, cabinets most likely containing files and papers and a large comfortable sofa with a small table in front of it. There was also a limp looking plant in one corner and Nilla wondered how much of the office's contents had been made by Artist's. She was snapped back to reality by Lucie's calm voice.

"How are you settling in then Nilla?"

Nilla tried not to look confused, "Fine thank you," she replied politely.

"You've been here quite a while now so we thought we would check in and make sure you're adjusting to life in the palace."

She felt her heart increase, this wasn't normal procedure, she knew it wasn't but she tried to sound calm when she spoke. "Is there some reason that I'm the only person having this, 'check up'?"

Lucie smiled, "Straight to the point, I like that," she sat back in her chair and stared at Nilla with calm, unblinking eyes, "I have a proposition for you," she said finally.

"What sort of proposition?" Nilla asked cautiously.

Lucie got to her feet and walked to a large window that overlooked the palace gardens, "I'd like you to join our team." She glanced over at Nilla who was sat in a state of shock.

Nilla was silent for several minutes, trying to process what had just been said; they hadn't found her out, they weren't going to discover her daughter, they wanted her on their team?

"What team?" she finally asked.

Lucie smiled and walked back to her desk, placing her hands on the back of the chair, "our administration team," she explained. "We're always looking for bright new talents to assist with the work we do and you seem to have taken to this place like a duck to water."

Nilla still sat in a state of shock but she sent a wavering smile towards the woman, "Why me?"

"Because I can tell from watching you that creating isn't really the path you want to take. Yes you're good at it, you're improved exceptionally from when you first arrived, but you're not passionate about it and that's okay," she said trying to sound reassuring. "The Emperor understands that not all of his Artist's will have the enthusiasm for creating, which is why he employs the rest of us to take care of the day to day paperwork and general running of the palace. I think you'd fit in perfectly up here," she smiled again.

Nilla's heart started to race again but for an entirely different reason; if she were part of the administration team she would be able to find out what was located on the top three floors. She also wouldn't have to endure the tedious classes anymore and would no longer need to spend hours learning how to sculpt. She might also be able to find out if the Emperor really was up to something. She felt excitement dancing inside her but she tried to remain calm and neutral.

"What exactly would I be required to do?"

Lucie smiled as if she'd already sealed the deal, "Nothing too strenuous to begin with," Nilla guessed that was her way of saying she wouldn't have access to anything important but she nodded anyway. Lucie continued, "You'll start with filing and organising while also shadowing various team members to see what it is we do. If you have a specific interest then we will try our best to accommodate, if not then we'll put you where you're most needed."

Nilla nodded again, "It sounds very much like my type of work."

Lucie almost beamed, "I thought as much, I'll give you a few days to really think about it but if you're happy to accept then we'll sort out getting you moved up here to work. You'll remain in your current room for the time being, we have a short probationary period and there's no point getting you settled into a room up here if you don't end up liking it."

Nilla smiled and nodded, "How should I get a message to you?"

"Just hand it to one of the officers, they'll be able to pass it along to me. I do hope you'll accept," she said moving round to Nilla's side of the desk. She assumed this meant the meeting was over and rose from her seat to move towards the door, Lucie stopped her as she was about to open it. "It's important that you understand the full implications of moving up here," she said suddenly sounding serious. "You cannot continue to fraternise with the other Artists, we spend our time watching them and grading them, it wouldn't be right for you to have your judgement clouded."

"I understand, I'll have an answer for you in a few days," she said as she smiled and left the room.

Flicker wasn't sure what to make of the whole thing, he had started by showing enthusiasm and excitement, just like Nilla, he had thought she could use this new position to act as a double agent. Then she had revealed the whole truth, everything that Lucie had told her about, 'fraternizing'.

He frowned, "I'm pretty sure we could find a way around that little complication, we wouldn't necessarily be able to meet up as often but I'm sure we could find a way."

"I hope you're right," Nilla said with concern in her voice. "Because I don't want to take this position, uncover something sinister and secretive only to find out I can't actually do anything with the information."

"Whenever Jan and I needed to talk privately we would meet in the maze, I'm sure we could do something similar." Nilla nodded and Flicker suddenly looked concerned. "What are you going to do about Charlie?"

She looked suddenly tired, "I don't know," she said shaking her head, "I want more than anything to see him again and to talk to him but I'm terrified of what might happen or what he might say. I've also been here for several months now and I'm not sure how he'll react if he finds that out"

"What do you think would happen if those administration people found out you were married to someone in here?"

"I've no idea and I'm not entirely sure I'd like to find out," she sat heavily on a desk in the classroom. "What am I going to do Flicker?"

He shook his head, "I've no idea, but we'll think of something, I promise."

Nilla and Flicker sat in the centre of the maze enjoying the cool spring air as the sky began to darken, Nilla was unusually quiet and Flicker decided not to push her to talk, she'd be doing plenty of that in a few minutes. They heard the sound of voices drawing nearer and Nilla's heart began to pound while she felt her stomach flip.

"What on earth can be so important that you had to drag me away from my work?" The voice was unmistakably Charlie's and Nilla held her breath.

"Just be patient, you'll find out soon enough," came Jackie's curt reply. The two of them fell silent and as they rounded the corner Nilla let out the breath she'd been holding. She felt her stomach flutter with nerves and had to concentrate on keeping her food down. This was it, after all their years apart they were finally reunited

"Hello Charlie," she said, her voice wavering as the husband she hadn't seen or spoken to for fifteen years stared at her in disbelief. He ran a dark hand through his black hair and his mouth opened and closed several times as words failed to be spoken.

Nilla's heart quickened as they stared at one another, *What if he's not happy to see me?* She thought, suddenly terrified she'd made the wrong decision.

"We'll leave you to talk," Jackie said grabbing Flicker

and dragging him away.

"We won't be far though, just call if you need anything," Flicker added flashing a concerned look at Nilla who forced a smile before turning back to Charlie.

He was still staring at her with those piercing green eyes in disbelief, "How are you here?" he asked almost in a whisper.

Her voice was unsteady as she answered and she spoke in a whisper, "Aggie's an Artist."

Charlie's eyes widened and he sat with a thud on a bench in the clearing, "Are you sure?"

"She manifested her gift when she was five, I'm sure."

Charlie sat silently for several minutes before looking with confusion at Nilla, "If Aggie's the Artist then how are you here?" Nilla sighed heavily and sat next to her husband, she recounted as much of her tale as she could manage and Charlie sat silently throughout listening intently. Her voice was shaky as she spoke; she was terrified of what he might think of her and she failed to make eye contact, choosing instead to stare at the ground.

The silence was heavy when she finished and after several minutes Charlie exhaled loudly, "I understand why you did what you did," he said and Nilla looked up half hopeful. "But I don't think she's any safer now than she was before and she's alone, how can you be sure she won't get caught?"

The words stung though Nilla knew there was truth behind them, "She won't be caught, not now, I'm sure of it."

"If she's any sense she'll leave the city."

"If she does leave it won't be for some time," Charlie looked at her questioningly, "the officers guarding the gates require papers to prove who you are, they would have record that I'd been taken recently and if she tried to leave too soon it would look suspicious."

"They'd test her again."

Nilla nodded, "She wouldn't stand a chance."

They sat in silence again while Charlie processed what Nilla had told him; it was a lot to take in, just seeing her had been overwhelming. Tentatively he placed his hand on hers and she turned to look at him,

"I've missed you Nilla," he said softly and she felt her heart flutter.

"I've missed you too Charlie." She placed her head on his shoulder and they sat in silence once more.

Chapter 16

Aggie sat silently while Flora and Wolf looked to Redd, who stared at the ground. He took a deep breath and looked up making eye contact with Aggie who felt unnerved by his hard gaze; she shifted in her seat but made a conscious decision to continue staring at him. She noticed the flicker of a smile and he started talking, maintaining eye contact the entire time.

"I'm an artisan," he began and saw the brief surprise on Aggie's face before she managed to regain her composure. "I've a small business, which I ran with my brother, it was what we had wanted to do ever since we were children. We were popular and we were busy, we were both happier than we had ever been, it was the perfect life." There was a hint of sadness in his voice and Aggie wondered what had happened to his brother.

"Flicker was by far the better of the two of us when it came to sculpting creatures, he had a great eye for detail that I just couldn't seem to mimic no matter how hard I tried." Redd smiled fondly at the memory and it seemed as if he'd forgotten the others were in the room. "We'd actually started talking about expanding the business, we were thinking of taking on an apprentice, but we never made it that far," he trailed off momentarily and his face darkened.

"I didn't have a chance to say goodbye before they

took him," Aggie's eyes brimmed with tears as she thought about her own separation from her mother. "I knew Flicker was an Artist of course, it's why he was so good with the detail, but I also knew he hated his gift and wanted nothing to do with it. He never used it; the act of sculpting without creating was enough for him to keep the urge at bay."

"What happened?" Aggie whispered.

Redd sighed heavily, "He must have cut himself without realising and some of his blood was mixed into the clay he was working with." Aggie's eyes started to widen as she guessed what had happened next.

"He had sculpted several eagle statues for a client and as he wheeled them out I saw yellow mist and then they started to-" Aggie gasped loudly and threw her hands over her mouth, Redd nodded grimly; Flora and Wolf who had remained silent throughout also looked grim.

"The eagles became real, I swear the whole thing happened in slow motion but there was nothing I could do to stop them or the client. It was almost like I was watching it happen from afar; I was frozen, staring as they took flight while my brother looked on in horror. The client bolted for the nearest officer, I begged Flicker to run, I thought if he left there and then that he might make it to the gates in time. He wouldn't go, he was convinced they'd torture me until I gave him up and in all honesty he wouldn't have got far, officers crawl over this city like ants. He just waited, calm and patient until they arrived."

"Did they test you?" Aggie asked; he voice was hoarse and she realised tears were running down her face.

Redd nodded, "We were both tested, I was clean, Flicker wasn't; they took him there and then." Redd sighed again and looked seriously at Aggie, "I spent a long time being angry with the officers, with the Emperor and even with my brother. My life began to spiral out of control and I'd probably still be lying in a gutter somewhere if it hadn't been for Wolf."

"Well you were in *my* gutter and it made the place look untidy," the attempt to lighten the mood fell flat but Redd forced a smile anyway.

"We started planning not long after that, and we've been planning ever since."

"Planning what?" Aggie was getting curious now and there was a hint of excitement as she dared to hope what it was they were going to attempt.

Redd grinned genuinely for the first time, "We're going to break into the palace and get my brother out."

Aggie gasped again and a heavy silence followed until she was finally able to calm down enough to speak, "You're trying to get transferred to the palace?" she asked turning to Flora who nodded. "But how are you involved in all of this? you're an…" she trailed off, hoping the implication wasn't realised; she was disappointed.

"Flora can be trusted," Redd said sternly and Aggie shrank back slightly.

"I didn't mean anything by it," she said quickly.

Flora smiled, "I'm not offended, you're new to all this, how could you know."

"How did you become part of it?" Aggie asked timidly.

Flora smiled reassuringly, "You may find it hard to believe but not every officer agrees with the way the Emperor runs the city. A few of us are actually part of an underground resistance-"

"A what?" Aggie asked in confusion and awe.

"We do our best to reach the Artists before the other officers, it we manage it then we tell them to lay low for several weeks until the rumours die down. After that we advise them to leave the city, of course we don't know what conditions are like elsewhere but we like to believe they're better than here."

"So you help Artists?"

Flora nodded, "I wish I had been able to get to you before the others," she whispered into Aggie's jet black hair and Aggie squeezed her tightly before pulling away and throwing her a shaky smile.

"I'd like to help," she said turning to Redd, her face resolute.

Redd shook his head, "I'm sorry Aggie, I just don't think you're strong enough to cope with this, you're so young-"

"I can handle this," she said forcefully. "Please let me help, my mother is in there and she has no idea what to do, I need to get her out."

Redd sighed again and noticed the looks Flora and Wolf were giving him, "Let me think about it."

Redd's expression darkened once Aggie and Flora had left The Fisherman's Fancy and he turned to Wolf expectantly.

"Don't give me that look," the other man said as he cleared away their glasses.

"Why are you so intent on putting a young girl in danger?"

"She's already in danger," Wolf said, irritation lacing his voice. "She's an Artist Redd, one who'll be tested regularly; she'll be in danger her whole life!"

"Don't you think I know that!"

"I don't know, do you? Seems as though you only care about your brother, but what about all the other Artist's in that place? Don't they deserve to be set free and reunited with their families?!"

Redd fell silent, "I'll think about including her," he said finally but without conviction and Wolf let out a loud sigh.

"I know this is hard for you, you've been waiting five years to free your brother, but you're starting to get tunnel vision, it's not just about him anymore, it's about all of them."

Redd stayed silent for several minutes, "I promise I'll consider including her," he said again but this time there was clear sincerity and Wolf smiled.

Flora entered sometime later and confirmed Aggie was safely at home.

"It gets harder and harder to leave that girl," she said with a grim look on her face. "I invited her to stay with me but she won't leave her home."

"Can you blame her?" Redd asked while staring at a stain on the table. "It's the only thing she's got left that links her to her family, I'm not sure she'll ever be ready to leave it." Wolf shot him a look but Redd didn't notice, instead continuing his train of thought as if the others weren't there. "If she's not willing to part with her house, to part with her mother's memory, then how can she be useful to the plan? What will she contribute? How useful will she really be?" Redd was snapped back to reality by a glass slamming on the table in front of him.

"Sometimes I think you only see and hear what you want," Wolf growled and Flora got to her feet ready to intervene if necessary. "Didn't you see her face when she pleaded? She wants more than anything to have her mother back with her, she might not want to leave her house right now but if it's between a house or her family she won't hesitate. That girl is stronger than you think and she'll be more use than you think."

A stony silence followed as the two men stared each other down while Flora unconsciously held her breath.

Eventually Redd shot him a half smile, clearly defeated, "You're probably right old friend," he said quietly and somewhat reluctantly. "I've spent so long thinking about my brother that I've forgotten the bigger picture and I suppose it couldn't hurt to have an Artist on our side."

Flora released the breath she'd been holding, "We had better start telling her the plan."

Wolf grinned, "I think we had better alter the plan."

The following evening, after Wolf had closed up, the four of them sat round the small table by the window. Aggie looked attentive and eager, while Redd still looked at her sceptically.

"At the moment we're waiting to find out whether Flora can be transferred into the palace, it will be far easier to break in if we've actually got someone on the inside."

"But how will you know when?" Aggie asked, not managing to sit quietly.

"Palace officers don't stay there all the time," Flora explained gently. "There are a number who live there permanently but the rest are on a rota, two weeks on, four days off. Those four days are your own and since many officers have their own homes anyway they return for their days off."

"So you'll be able to keep us updated?" Aggie asked.

Flora frowned, "I don't know," she admitted. "Having never worked in the palace I don't yet know the full extent of the rules and restrictions."

"How will you let us in?" Aggie asked and Redd shot her a look that told her she hadn't yet officially been accepted; she shrank back.

Redd answered, "Once Flora is inside and we've been able to communicate with her on the layout, security, and whether she's managed to find Flicker, and your mother." He added as an afterthought, "We will agree on a day and time to enter into the palace."

"Wouldn't it be easier if we were already inside?" Aggie said thoughtfully.

Redd scoffed, "We will be inside once Flora lets us in."

"No," Aggie said shaking her head. "I mean wouldn't it make more sense if we were inside from the start? at the same time as Flora?" Silence followed as the words she'd spoken sank in and eventually Wolf smiled.

"She's a smart lass this one."

"It's an interesting idea," Flora said thoughtfully. "But I don't think it's wise for you to enter the palace straight away." Redd suppressed a smile as Wolf and Aggie looked surprised.

"But it could really help-"

"I know," Flora interrupted. "But I think it would be wise if I scoped out the place first, I can report back to you and we can stagger your entry into the palace. To have you all enter at once could look suspicious, and it will give me a chance to find your brother, and your mother." Eventually they all nodded, realising that to be cautious made the most sense.

"How close are you to being transferred?" Aggie asked, suddenly feeling terrified at the thought of losing another person in her life.

Flora smiled reassuringly, "It shouldn't be for another few weeks, there's a lot of testing and training involved, but don't worry, I'll make sure I still find the time to check in on you."

Aggie felt herself relax, "Is there a plan for when we get in to the palace?" she avoided looking in Redd's direction, knowing he was probably scowling at her for still assuming she would be joining them.

"We're still working on it," Wolf informed her, scratching his bushy beard. "It's difficult to plan when we don't know a lot about the layout, that's why most of our planning has been theoretical and hearsay."

"It's a shame we can't get some inside information before you go in," Aggie said while chewing on her bottom lip. "Have you never received anything from your brother?" she asked finally looking at Redd who was still scowling. "I've tried writing to my mother a few times but the officers I give my letter to always say she's probably too busy to write back."

Redd let out a bark of laughter, "They don't deliver the letters," he said sharply and instantly regretted it as he saw the look of pain cross Aggie's face. He tried to soften his tone, "I don't know why they do it, maybe they don't want the Artist's to remember they have family, but they never deliver the letters." Aggie looked with teary eyes to Flora who just shook her head.

"I'm afraid I don't know either, we're all told the same thing and it's what we're meant to tell the inhabitants of the city."

"How do you know-" she trailed off, too afraid to finish the sentence in case Redd's reaction was harsh again.

"Flicker would have written back," Redd said softly, trying to make up for his earlier outburst. "He wasn't just my brother, he was my best friend, he would have written to me." Aggie nodded slowly but didn't say anything, she could feel something igniting deep inside her almost as if her insides were burning and she realised with surprise and horror that what she felt was hatred. Pure hatred, towards the Emperor and towards those who supported him.

Chapter 17

Nilla and Charlie's reconciliation had been brief. After they had talked and Nilla had told him all about their daughter, Flicker and Jackie had returned with concerned looks on their faces.

"What is it?" Nilla asked getting to her feet.

"There's an officer looking for you," Flicker said in a low voice. "I think they want your answer."

"What answer?" Charlie asked also getting to his feet.

Nilla turned to look at him, "I've been offered an administration job," she explained as a look of confusion crossed his face. "Someone in that department has noticed creating isn't really my calling in life and she's provided me with an alternative."

"Are you going to do it?" Charlie asked seemingly reluctant as if he feared her answer, Nilla nodded and a look of hurt and anger crossed her husband's face. "So you fling yourself back into my life only to hurl yourself away again?" His fists were clenched and Nilla glanced at Flicker and Jackie as if they would be able to help.

She took a deep breath and placed a hand on his arm, "It's not that simple Charlie," she said softly though his features didn't alter. "I'm not an Artist, we all know that now-" there was a sharp intake of breath from Jackie and Nilla cursed herself for her stupidity. She spun round to look at Jackie who had thrown her hands over her mouth in shock, Flicker was whispering in her ear and Nilla felt her heart quicken while thoughts of torture raced through her head.

Jackie slowly lowered her hands and eventually she grinned mischievously, "I knew you weren't an Artist," she said taking a seat on one of the benches. Nilla's mouth hung open in shock and surprise while Jackie continued to grin. "This one," she gestured to Flicker, "seems to think I was born yesterday." Flicker started to protest but Jackie waved him away, "I've been here a long time," she explained, "and I've seen a lot of Artist's come through here, I couldn't tell straight away but eventually it started to make sense, especially the extra help Flick was giving you."

Nilla felt tears prick her eyes as she approached the older woman, "Why didn't you turn me in?" she asked in disbelief.

Jackie continued to smile, "Because Flick likes you, and because I liked the look of you."

Nilla threw her arms round Jackie briefly before turning back to her husband, who clearly still wanted an explanation. "You need to understand that I've been finding it difficult, I'm no Artist and I'm no artisan. Flicker has helped me fool the administration staff and the officers but I don't know how much longer I can keep it up. I need to take this other position so I can try to lead some sort of normal life here."

Charlie let out a sharp laugh, "Normal life? There's nothing normal about living here Nilla, we're simply glorified prisoners." She felt rather than saw Flicker and Jackie glance at one another, but they all knew better than to reveal their thoughts and plans to someone they couldn't completely trust.

The thought sent a sharp pang of guilt through her

but the truth was she really didn't know if she could trust her husband anymore. They had spent fifteen years apart and in that time she had no idea what he'd been through. Perhaps he really did despise his living situation or perhaps he was trying to catch them out. She hoped more than anything that he could be trusted.

As if sensing her thoughts Charlie took her hands in his, "I won't tell anyone about you, I promise I'll keep your secret, and not just for our daughter." She smiled and threw her arms round her husband, realising just how much she had missed having him near her.

"I promise I'll try to keep seeing you," she whispered in his ear and he squeezed her tightly.

Charlie eventually left them alone, clearly sensing they had something private to discuss; Nilla almost collapsed on the bench, suddenly exhausted. She looked up at Jackie and the older woman just shook her head.

"No need to say anything, you're obviously going to help try and find out what's going on in this place, and if that's the case then you're okay by me."

Nilla smiled at her, then turned to Flicker with an accusatory look, "Why didn't you tell me that Jackie was on our side?"

Flicker cleared his throat, "Technically you're on our side," he said with a grin, "I had to keep you both secret from one another or suspicions might have been raised." He looked specifically at Nilla, "I didn't think you wanted anyone else to know about your non-Artist status." Then he turned to Jackie, "And I wasn't sure how happy you'd be to find out I'd accepted a potentially untrustworthy stranger into the ranks." The two women feigned annoyance but eventually they smiled and Flicker felt himself relax.

Nilla started her new job several days later and felt her stomach squirm with nerves; she knew she needed to make a good impression and she worried about how much contact she would be allowed with her former, 'colleagues'. Although she was now working for the administration team she was still living in her old room, which meant she would also have to eat in the main dining room.

Lucie had explained that some interaction would be tolerated, but anything more than polite and brief conversation would be deemed inappropriate and her position would be terminated. As such, she had agreed to only polite conservation with Flicker and Jackie out in the open but they had agreed to meet in two days time in the maze so she could update them on her progress.

Lucie showed Nilla to a small box of a room, which would be her office for the foreseeable future, "I've left you several useful folders on your desk, which I'd advise you to read and become familiar with. Tomorrow you'll start shadowing others and we'll see what it is you're good at." She smiled at Nilla, who reciprocated the gesture while looking round her sparsely furnished office. "It's fine for you to decorate your office as you see fit," Lucie explained, taking a seat on the small sofa in the corner, "but I'd advise you to hold off until we make your position permanent." She smiled again and Nilla nodded.

"Do you know who I'll be shadowing first?" She asked, sitting behind her desk to see how it felt.

Lucie nodded, "I'll be taking you tomorrow, I've two classes to check in on and thought it would be best to start with something you're already partially familiar with."

"Is there information on the monitoring process in

these files?"

Lucie nodded again, "I was going to suggest you start with that, then I'd move onto our filing system since you'll be doing a lot of that." Nilla started making notes on a sheet of paper she'd found in one of the desk drawers and Lucie looked impressed.

"I won't be required to meet the Emperor will I?" She tried to sound nervous and a little terrified, while masking her underlying intention to uncover information for Flicker and Jackie.

Lucie laughed kindly, "Oh no, I wouldn't worry about anything like that, only the most senior staff deal with the Emperor." She tried to look relieved but inside she deflated; she wondered whether to push her luck and ask her next question but the decision was made for her as Lucie studied her features. "The Emperor lives on the top floor," the other woman explained and when Nilla looked genuinely shocked she elaborated. "I guessed you wanted to ask, it's okay," she added. "It's only natural to be curious. You wouldn't believe how many times I'm asked about it on a daily basis."

"Does he ever-" she paused trying to think of how best to work the question.

"Show himself?" Lucie finished and Nilla flushed. "He does occasionally, but he's a very busy man and he likes to keep himself private."

"Have you ever met him?"

Lucie glowed a little with pride, "Once, a few years back now."

"What was it like?"

"Amazing," she breathed wistfully. "He radiated power and knowledge, I'll never forget it. Perhaps one day you'll get to meet him too." Nilla nodded and smiled, trying to portray the look of someone who had had their curiosity satisfied, though in reality she itched to bombard the other woman with more questions about their seemingly absent ruler.

Lucie left several minutes later and she began shuffling through the files on her desk until she found the ones on the filing system and the classroom audits. She opened the latter and set it out in front of her ready to read but found her mind wandering to the Emperor.

It had been confirmed that he lived in the palace and was on the top floor; although it had been something they suspected, they hadn't known it for sure. She also knew that many of this, the sixth floor was taken up with offices and Lucie had mentioned that should her position become permanent she would be moved up here into one of the apartments. She decided to shuffle through the files again and see if there might be a map of the palace or a floor plan but was left disappointed. She desperately wanted to ask Lucie about the layout of floors five and six but knew she would have to wait until the other woman trusted her or she could wander freely. With a loud sigh, she finally focused on the file containing information on the classroom audits and began to read.

Nilla joined Lucie the following day in front of Flicker's classroom, her insides squirmed again but she felt she had more of a legitimate reason to feel uncomfortable, after all this *had* been her old classroom.

Lucie glanced over and noticed the nervous expression on her face, "Will you be okay going in there?" she asked with little sincere concern.

Nilla tried to make her expression neutral, "Of course, I'm pretty much indifferent to the people in there."

"Good," Lucie replied without emotion. "That's the

way it should be." It struck Nilla that Lucie's demeanour altered when she was in the privacy of the sixth floor; she seemed relaxed, calm and friendly, while at the moment she radiated stiffness and a lack of emotion. She guessed this was how she portrayed her professionalism.

They entered as Flicker threw a lump of clay across the room; the two women drew up short in order to avoid being hit by the flying grey mass. Flicker swivelled in their direction, his face red with anger and frustration then instantly he froze and tried to calm himself.

"Hello Lucie," he said with an edge to his voice.

"Good morning Flicker, do I take it you're having some problems?" She opened her notebook and looked at Flicker expectantly.

He grimaced, "Everything is fine," he said through gritted teeth. "Do what it is you came for," he turned from them and sat, arms folded behind his desk. It had only been a day but he already missed Nilla's presence in his class, having her hover behind Lucie wasn't the same thing since he dared not look at her.

Lucie addressed the class, "Please continue working on your sculptures, I will be walking round with my colleague to examine your progress."

Flicker watched as they moved between the students, examining the form of their sculptures and the fine detail. Lucie always asked them questions about their techniques and what they enjoyed sculpting most. He glanced over at his newest student, the girl he'd received from Charlie; she was a pain and he seriously regretted his decision to take her on, especially now Nilla was no longer around.

He hadn't minded the girl, whose name was Zara, creating chaos to begin with, it had reminded him of his own behaviour when he'd first arrived, but it was starting to grate on him and his other students were beginning to suffer. He had thought about trying to trade her off though he was sure no one would take her, then he had tried to talk to her, one on one but she hadn't listened.

He was actually thinking about reporting her when he noticed Nilla talking to her quietly. He sat up in his seat as he saw the look of horror on Zara's face and as Nilla walked away to where Lucie waited by the door the young girl began moulding and sculpting the lump of clay in front of her.

He got to his feet and walked to the door, "What on earth did you say to her?"

The corner of Nilla's mouth twitched in a smile but when she spoke she was distant and professional, "That's not something for you to worry about," she replied and Lucie nodded her approval. Flicker felt a pang of hurt and had to remind himself that this was all part of the act, or at least he hoped it was. He shook his head and scolded himself internally, *It's only been one day, there's no way they could have turned her that quickly.*

"The majority of your class are doing well," Lucie said looking at her notes, "A few of them are on track for promotion but I don't think that will occur for another few months." Flicker nodded absentmindedly and Lucie turned to Nilla, "I normally break for lunch between audits, I'd advise you to do the same. Meet me in an hour outside Corman's classroom, do you know where that is?" she nodded and watched as Lucie left the classroom.

Nilla heaved a sigh of relief, "I'm so sorry," she said turning instantly to Flicker.

He smiled and felt a wave of relief wash over him, "No need, I know it's all part of the act."

Nilla nodded, "It is, but it doesn't mean I feel good about it."

"You had better get yourself to the dining room,"

Flicker said pointedly. "I'll bet Lucie is waiting around to see how long it takes you leave."

Nilla looked shocked, "Really? Do you think so?"

Flicker nodded, "I'll bet she and the others will be watching you really closely over the next few weeks. They'll want to see whether you're committed to them or not."

She felt her heart quicken as she thought about how long it had been since Lucie left. "I'll see you and Jackie tomorrow," she said walking quickly to the door.

"Keep using that cold demeanour," Flicker said with a grin. "You'll fit in perfectly," Nilla shot him a look before she smiled and left the room.

Chapter 18

Aggie looked and felt miserable as Flora explained she had passed the palace training sessions and would begin working their within the week.

"Chin up lass," Wolf said as Flora talked quietly to Redd. "This won't be the last we see of her."

"I know," Aggie said shakily. "I'm just worried, we haven't exactly had time to formalise a plan."

"We'll figure it out," Wolf said reassuringly and he patted her shoulder. "You forget we've been planning this for years, we might not have everything ironed out but we're far from blundering around in the dark." Aggie smiled up at him and somehow felt a little calmer. They spent that evening finalising some of their more concrete plans.

"I doubt I'll find out anything useful in the first few weeks, it always takes a bit of time to earn trust, but I *can* keep an eye out for Flicker and your mother."

"I think it would be best if we didn't meet again after tonight until the last of your days off in about two weeks."

"Why so long?" Aggie asked in surprise.

"The other officers might start tailing her," Wolf explained gently. "They're always a bit suspicious of new arrivals."

Aggie didn't like the idea of not seeing Flora for two

weeks, she had quickly become attached to her as the only female influence in her life now.

"Don't worry," Flora smiled, "I promise I'll be fine, I doubt anything exciting will happen to me in the first week, I'll probably just be learning how everything works." Aggie still felt uncomfortable but remained silent as Redd began talking.

"Once we know how things are inside and whether you've found Flicker, we'll start working on getting the rest of us inside." Aggie felt a pang or hurt and frustration at the lack of mentioning her mother. "I don't think it's wise to move in too early, I'd rather we were poised to strike as soon as we entered-"

"That won't work," she finally burst out, louder and with more hostility than she had intended.

Redd turned to face her, his expression one of annoyance and amusement. "And why not? The more surprise we give the officers the better."

"I agree," Aggie said and three confused faces stared at her, "but I've been thinking about this and the fact is we don't actually know what will happen once we're inside. It might take us some time to actually find one another and no one actually knows what happens to the Artist's as soon as they enter the palace."

Redd tried to remain calm and patient but there was an edge to his voice, "That's exactly why Flora is going undercover inside, so she can inform us of what to expect, so we can be ready for every possibility when we arrive ourselves."

The smug feeling she'd felt moments earlier, believing to have thought of something they hadn't were instantly squashed and she felt her cheeks go hot. "I didn't realise," she said quietly as Wolf put a protective arm round her shoulders."

"It's alright lass, you weren't to know."

Redd looked frustrated, "I really think we should reconsider her role in all this," he spoke as if she wasn't there and this hurt Aggie even more.

"She'll be okay," Flora assured him but he didn't look convinced.

"I know you think I'm pretty useless," Aggie said quietly while looking at the floor. "I know I don't really have a clue what's going on, but in my defence you haven't really told me anything."

Redd opened his mouth to speak but Wolf cut across him, "She's got a point there, you've been against her helping from the start and maybe if you'd included her she would be able to contribute more."

Aggie tried to ignore feeling as if she had been insulted once again; mentally telling herself that Wolf wouldn't have intended it that way.

"I promise you I'll do what I can to help, I want to free the Artist's as much as the rest of you, I promise I won't let you down." Redd sighed heavily and went to get some fresh air where he could clear his head and think; there was a heavy silence in the pub when he left.

"He's never going to accept me is he?"

"Believe it or not he's already accepted you," Flora replied and Aggie shot her a look.

"She's right," Wolf agreed. "He's hostile because he's struggling with his conscience, he knows how important you'll be, you're the only one of the three of us that's actually an Artist. But you're also only sixteen, and it doesn't sit well with him to put you in unnecessary danger."

"Neither of you seem bothered," Aggie pointed out, suddenly wondering why they were so quick to throw her in harm's way.

Flora smiled, "Redd doesn't see what we see," she replied. "He only sees a terrified, young, naïve girl who-"

"What do you see?"

"We see someone with determination and strength," Wolf said gently. "Someone who has managed to evade the officer's for sixteen years and someone who has something more important than us to fight for." Aggie smiled and felt a warm feeling spread through her.

Redd entered the pub again sometime later and promised to be more upfront with her from now on, she beamed at him and promised again that he wouldn't be disappointed. They finalised their plans and discussed some of the smaller details before Flora left; Aggie hugged her tightly, not wanting to let go.

"You'll see me soon enough," she said giving Aggie a squeeze.

"I wish I was able to enter the palace with you."

"Don't be silly," Flora said pulling away and grinning mischievously. "I need someone to keep an eye on these two for me."

The Fisherman's Fancy was quiet and sombre once Flora had left, Redd was trying to encourage them to continue planning but Aggie no longer felt enthusiastic, instead feeling concern for Flora.

"She'll be okay," Wolf said quietly as Redd put his head in his hands in frustration. "She's been an officer a long time and she knows how to be discrete."

"I'm sorry," she said looking at Redd.

He looked up in surprise, "What for?"

"For getting upset, I know you don't think-"

"It's fine," Redd cut her off and threw her an unconvincing smile. "Why don't we call it a night."

"I'll walk you home lass," Wolf offered while getting to his feet.

"It's okay, I'll take her, you finish up here." Aggie's insides squirmed as she walked in silence next to Redd, she could tell he wanted to say something to her; his expression was hard.

"I promise I won't disappoint you," she finally said, unable to take the awkward silence any longer.

Redd was silent for a few minutes before he replied, "I don't think you're going to disappoint me. I know I'm hard on you, I know I've been blowing hot and cold with regards to your involvement in all this, but I don't like the idea of sending you into danger. You've got your whole life in front of you and I don't think you should be wasting it on something that could fail."

Aggie stopped in her tracks and looked at him, her expression showing frustration, "Do you honestly think I haven't considered the risks?" Redd opened his mouth but she continued, "Believe me I've weighed up the risks, I know we might fail, I know the whole plan might be a non-starter." She looked at him now with almost pleading eyes, "I can't just sit and do nothing Redd, my mother has given up her life so I can have one but I can't leave her in there, because she is my life and without her I'm lost. No matter what happens, I know the risks and I accept them."

Redd smiled at her and they continued walking, "Wolf and Flora were right about you," he said before they settled back into silence, Aggie with a faint smile on her face.

"Are you sure you don't mind lass?" Wolf asked with concern, Aggie shook her head with a smile. They had been discussing possible ways of entering the palace for several nights and it seemed that their original idea, which had been to wait for Flora to unlock the main doors was now fully redundant as it seemed too risky.

Redd had finally agreed with Aggie that having them all pose as Artists was the best idea, though Wolf, who had previously campaigned for Aggie's involvement, seemed suddenly reluctant.

"I don't think any of us have thought of a better idea," she pointed out.

"Don't you think it will look suspicious if we're all caught together?"

Redd cocked his head and frowned, "Crafts! You may be right." They sat in silence for several more minutes.

"I could tip them off about you," Aggie suggested with a grin. "Then I could breathe life into the creations for you, it's not much different to what me and my mother did."

"You could do the same with me," Redd suggested. "The officers test me regularly, I believe I'll be receiving a visit within the next few months."

"How will I know when they're coming?"

"I guess you'll have to work for him lass," Wolf said with a grin. "They normally test you during work hours don't they?"

Redd scowled at him but nodded his head, "Then you can get yourself taken fairly easily, since you're the only one with any actual power."

"A vial each should do it," Aggie said, fishing two small, glass containers from her pocket; she made a small cut on her finger and began to fill the first of the vials.

"What do we do with these then?" Wolf asked as she handed him a small vial of her blood, she rolled her eyes and Redd answered.

"They'll ask us to create something, you'll need to pretend to cut yourself, or you could actually do it, doesn't really matter, as long as you put some of this into the medium you use."

Wolf coughed nervously, "Won't they expect me to be artistic?"

"I can teach you if you like," Aggie said helpfully. "I did the same thing with my mother, I taught her something simple that wouldn't look suspicious."

Suddenly Aggie was busier than she had ever been; she started her day working for Redd, which she loved since she was able to use her artistic ability and he seemed to finally be enjoying her presence. She usually stocked up on supplies after working for Redd and spent a bit of time with Cassie; she felt guilty that she had been ignoring the dog lately but thankfully, not being real, she was very low maintenance.

Finally she continued to work for Wolf in the evenings, something she also thoroughly enjoyed, in part because the regulars all seemed to have taken a shine to her. She completed her day by attempting to teach Wolf how to sculpt, which was proving to be incredibly frustrating. He didn't have any artistic talent, and wasn't grasping the instructions she gave him. Redd, being terribly unhelpful, sat laughing in the corner.

"You could come over and help," she scolded, which only made him laugh harder.

"And miss this fantastic show? Not a chance!"

"I actually think you've got worse," she said to Wolf, who looked frustrated with himself."

"I think you're fighting a losing battle," Redd called as Wolf cursed loudly. "Some people just don't have any artistic talent."

Aggie frowned and looked suddenly worried, "What are we going to do then?" When Redd looked confused she elaborated. "The officers are hardly going to believe he's an Artist when he's got no artistic ability."

Redd was suddenly; serious, "I hadn't thought of that, we might have to think of an alternative way to get him inside the palace."

"Other than officers and Artists, who actually goes into that place?" Wolf asked in a gruff tone that displayed his annoyance at himself.

"I've no idea," Redd replied shaking his head. "Let's hope it's something Flora can help us with when we next see her."

If we see her, Aggie thought with worry.

Chapter 19

It seemed as though Nilla had passed Lucie's test, she seemed a lot more relaxed around her now and was even starting to discuss what area she might like to join.

"I know both Alies and Perunia were impressed with you and would happily have you as part of their teams."

Nilla couldn't imagine working for Alies, he was an awful old man with no respect for anyone, it didn't matter how interesting it would be to help the new arrivals adjust, she wouldn't be working for him. Perunia, however was a lovely woman, she was gentle and kind and never had a bad word to say against anyone. She didn't think the woman lead the most interesting team, the others were all a bit bland but the work would be far more interesting than the people.

They dealt with the not so mysterious workrooms on floor five and Nilla thought that would be the best area for her to be a part of, especially considering what Flicker had been doing. A lot of the work was similar to what Lucie did; they audited the classes, but they also dealt with the end products of the creation process; what better way to find out once and for all what was going on.

"Any thoughts?" Lucie prompted with a smile.

Nilla returned the gesture, "I'd love the opportunity to work with Perunia again, she and her team made me feel very welcome."

Lucie made a note on a piece of paper, "You'd be happy with the work? It can get a bit repetitive."

"I'd be more than happy with the work," Nilla replied, "I found it fascinating."

Lucie finished what she was writing and looked at Nilla, "I think you've made the right decision and I think you'll really flourish with her team." Her smile faltered for a second and she lowered her voice, "Just between you and me, Alies is a total idiot."

Nilla let out a short burst of laughter and Lucie giggled in response; she knew she wasn't meant to actually like these people or form ties with them but Nilla had found them, well most of them, to be friendly and pleasant. At the end of the day they were in the same boat as everyone else, forced to live and work here for the Emperor without really knowing why, it was hard not to feel a bit of sympathy for them.

She was moved up onto the sixth floor a few days later and when she saw her new room she stared open mouthed in shock; it was huge. The word room was actually an understatement since she had three. She walked in to a cosy, well lit living room with a comfortable looking green sofa, a writing desk and chair. From there she went through into a spacious bedroom, with a large double bed, another green sofa and a couple of drawers for her clothes and meagre possessions. Finally she had a small, clean white bathroom with an elaborate looking bath; she had absolutely no idea what she would do with all the space.

The room she'd had before was just that, a room; it had been small and dingy with a simple, single bed and a small desk with a chair. She had use of a shared female shower at the end of the hall and there was a communal sitting area close by.

It had certainly been a bit of a shock when she'd arrived since she'd been used to a lot more space and freedom but she had been rather surprised at how quickly she had adjusted to the change. Now she stared round the large living space she once again had and felt slightly lost. She wished, not for the first time, that she could go and find Flicker and Jackie to update them on her situation and the line of employment she'd chosen.

She sighed heavily and slumped down onto the green sofa, which was so soft and comfortable that she let out an involuntary mumble of satisfaction. She hadn't been sitting long when there was a loud knock at the door; she heaved herself off the enticing sofa and opened the door to find a young male officer.

"Can I help you?" she asked with only the slightest twinge of nerves.

The young officer handed her what looked like a magazine, "You're required to choose some clothing and personal items from here," he said while looking incredibly bored with the task."

Nilla flicked briefly through the magazine and noticed clothing, furniture and small trinket items, she looked confused, "I don't understand, I don't have any-"

"Your new role will require smarter clothing," the officer replied, looking, if possible, even more bored. "The Emperor will organise payment of ten new outfits and any other items you require. New clothing will be offered every three months, send your order to your supervisor."

She looked like she'd been slapped in the face but before she could speak the officer had turned and walked away grumbling. She stared down at the magazine again and slowly walked back to the comfortable sofa, clearly in a state of shock. She couldn't believe she would just be given new clothes, how on earth could the Emperor really be as bad as they all said when he had provided her with this wonderful living space and would be supplying her with fine, new clothes.

She shook her head, suddenly angry at herself, "No wonder they all love the Emperor, he must be brainwashing them with possessions." She could almost see how easy it would be, normal Artists didn't have fine clothes or even several different outfits, they all wore the same brown trousers and beige shirts. To be taken from that and a small room with shared amenities to this – she gazed round her living room again in awe – and to be provided with new clothes and extra gifts, how could someone not be swayed to the Emperor's side? Once an Artist had experienced this type of luxury, would they really want to give it all up?

She would have to be careful how she reacted to this treatment; she would order some new outfits, it seemed as though she would have to as there would be no way they'd let her keep walking around in her current uniform. And if there were any items that would be functionally useful then she might also ask for them, but she wouldn't allow herself to acquire any luxuries, after all, if all went according to plan, they might not remain in the palace much longer.

To say that Flora had been overwhelmed during her first few days at the palace was an understatement. One of the more established officers had shown her round and had provided her with several maps so that she wouldn't get lost in her first few weeks. She had also been informed of the Artists' daily routine; they appeared to be on a short lead.

She would be shadowing several officers to begin with while she found her feet and settled into her new routine. Although the palace was huge and the grounds were spacious and decorative she was already finding her new environment a little claustrophobic; she had only been there several days and was already missing the bustling city outside the large palace walls.

The other officers seemed friendly enough, though she could already tell they took immense pride in their jobs and were loyal to the Emperor to the end. So far she hadn't met anyone who she thought might help her when the time came, though it was early days.

She also hadn't been able to start searching for Flicker; her tour of the palace had been a blur as there had been a lot to take in and the palace interior was amazing to look at. She had been informed that the Artists spent their time teaching, learning, creating or providing administrative assistance in the classrooms and workrooms so she assumed he must be in one of those areas. She knew which floors the classrooms, workshops and administration teams occupied, though she had no idea how easy it would be to gain access; she still wasn't really sure what would and wouldn't look suspicious.

She was currently having her new rota explained to her by a large man called Trist; he had informed her that her first full week would be split between the gatehouse and the palace grounds, while her second week would be spent inside the palace itself. This would form the basis for her rota for the foreseeable future.

She smiled but cursed internally as she thought how hard it might be to find Flicker and Aggie's mother out in the grounds. If she had been inside for her first week then she would have been able to make her way methodically around the classrooms, workrooms and administration offices to start crossing them off her list. She knew now that she would have to deliver bad news to her first meeting with Redd, Wolf and Aggie and that didn't sit well.

The large man had now left her to continue studying her rotas and the plans of the palace; the information swam dizzyingly round her head.

"It won't take too long for it all to sink in," came a pleasant, deep voice. Flora looked up and met a pair of intense blue eyes. She smiled and the tall officer, with short, dark brown hair, smiled back.

"I hadn't thought there would be so much information," she admitted then held out a hand, "I'm Flora and as you've already guessed, I'm new."

"I'm Jan," he said grasping her hand and shaking it firmly. "And trust me, it will all sink in reasonably quickly."

"Really?" she asked sceptically.

"Definitely, we spend most of our days patrolling, it's hard not to subconsciously memorise the hallways and passages."

Flora smiled as Jan sat down next to her, "How long have you been here?" she asked,

"Just under ten years," he replied almost in disbelief, "I can't actually believe it's been that long."

"Do you like it here?"

Jan nodded, "We've had a few people transfer back to the city recently claiming the work inside the palace was too dull, but I personally think it's great. I don't think I've ever had two days the same. The excitement has settled down in recent months but I'm sure it will pick up again once we have some newcomers."

"What do you mean?" Flora asked while tidying away her stack of papers.

"As I'm sure you're already aware, not everyone wants to be in here," she nodded. "Well we've had quite a few attempts at escape in the past from a number of individuals."

Flora's stomach lurched but her face remained calm, "I assume they weren't successful?"

Jan shook his head and let out a short laugh, "No of course not, but we did have to tighten things up after a few of the attempts."

"Did someone get close?" Flora asked suddenly feeling annoyed at whoever it had been.

Jan nodded, "They would never have actually succeeded but it sent a shock through the ranks and the Emperor was furious."

"The Emperor?" Flora started. "He directly addressed you?"

"Oh no," Jan laughed. "But someone from his administration team came down and…well, words were exchanged."

"You've never seen him then? The Emperor I mean?"

Jan shook his head then peered over at her schedule, "Looks like we're on the same rota," he said smiling. "If you need any help finding your way around, just give me a shout." Flora thanked him as he got up to leave, then turned back to her pile of paper and pretended to study it once more.

Artists had already tried to escape, *Crafts!* She cursed at herself. *Of course they would, why didn't we consider that possibility?* She frowned at herself and bit her bottom lip in thought, they would probably have to spend a lot longer planning their escape than they had first realised. She wondered whether any of the officers in here were secretly part of the underground resistance but quickly dismissed that idea; it was highly unlikely.

She would have to meet with Redd and the others and give them even more bad news, but it was better that they came across this hurdle now than later. This was partly the reason she'd suggested she transferred to the palace in the first place; they needed to know what they were dealing with. They would now need to come up with a detailed plan that covered every eventuality, she guessed they would only get one shot at this, and they couldn't afford for it to go wrong.

Chapter 20

Aggie had started wiping down the tables in The Fisherman's Fancy early to try and keep herself occupied; Flora was meant to have arrived half an hour ago and although the other two seemed calm, Aggie was panicking.

"She'll turn up lass," Wolf assured her while tidying the bar area.

"Has she ever been late before?" Aggie asked nervously.

Redd shook his head, "But she's also never been an officer in the palace before, we've no idea what's been going on in there or whether they're keeping a closer eye on her while she's back in the city than we thought."

"You're not worried then?"

"If she can't make it tonight then she'll turn up another night," Redd informed her, though Aggie thought there was a hint of uncertainty. She chose not to press on and instead continued to tidy the tables and chairs.

Once the two hour mark had passed Redd finally slumped his shoulders and let out a loud sigh, "She must be being watched."

"What if they've found her out?" Aggie asked worriedly.

"They won't have," Wolf said, resting a comforting

hand on her shoulder. "She's a smart one, it's more likely they're watching her to make sure she's not going to betray them."

"I thought she said they'd done all the background checks?"

"They'd be idiots if they didn't continue their checks," Redd pointed out as he got to his feet and stretched. "The best way to find out if someone's a traitor is to find out what they do in their own time."

"What if they don't stop watching her?" Aggie asked with slight panic.

"They can't watch her forever and she's smart, she'll find a way to slip away from them, even if it's only for a few minutes. Come on, I'll walk you home."

"How is it you're not worrying?" Aggie asked quietly on their journey.

Redd shot her a grim smile, "I am worrying," he admitted and she tried to hide her look of surprise. "I know I seem indifferent but that's just how I cope, Flora's a good friend and she's putting herself in danger for people she's never met, so yes, I'm worried."

"But why-"

"Because it won't help the situation, if I sit and obsess over everything that might have happened then I'll descend into madness, I need to stay focussed, no matter what happens I need to get to my brother." They walked in silence until they reached Aggie's home where Cassie greeted them enthusiastically. Aggie crouched down to hug her and noticed a piece of paper on the floor.

Briefly ignoring the spaniel, she grabbed the scrap of paper and saw two lines of neat handwriting on the surface, she showed it to Redd.

I think I'm being followed, I'm going to lay low for a few weeks,

"You were right," she said quietly as she and Redd slipped inside her house while Cassie bounded after them.

"I'm not surprised, they're suspicious of everyone, even their own officers,"

"Who's they?" Aggie asked, stoking up the fire so they could burn the paper.

"The Emperor and whoever's working with him."

"I'm glad she's okay," Aggie said as she watched the paper blacken and curl before catching fire.

"So am I," Redd agreed. "Will you be okay tonight?" Aggie nodded as she put another log on the fire. "I'll tell Wolf about the note, and I'll see you at the workshop tomorrow." Aggie nodded and locked the door as Redd left; the house felt emptier and colder than usual tonight and she snuggled up to Cassie on the sofa, while she watched the fire crackle happily around its fresh food.

The following week saw Wolf, Aggie and Redd discussing what they might encounter once they entered the palace, when they heard a noise in one of the back rooms. They froze and Aggie felt her heart quicken. They sat in silence for several minutes, listening for any other noise and then returned to their conversation in hushed tones. Something clattered to the ground and this time Wolf got to his feet and moved quietly towards the back rooms.

Aggie made as if to stand but Redd put a hand on her arm and shook his head, while putting a finger to his lips. She stilled and they strained to hear what might be happening in the back rooms. They heard Wolf yell, there was the sound of something hard impacting with something human and then there was another, higher pitched yell.

They heard Wolf shout again but this time in surprise, "Redd! Aggie! Get in here!"

They were out of their seats before he'd finished and when they reached the kitchen area they saw Wolf standing over an unconscious Flora.

"What did you do?!" Aggie cried, crouching down to check on the unconscious officer.

"Thought she was an intruder," Wolf admitted a little sheepishly.

"She must have wanted to avoid drawing attention," Redd said as he too crouched next to the still form of Flora. Seeing that she wasn't bleeding, they lifted her by the arms and half carried, half dragged her into the main room.

Redd and Wolf sat her in one of the chairs and Redd looked at Aggie, "Forgive me," he said already looking guilty.

"For wha-" Aggie began then a look of shock crossed her face as Redd slapped Flora, "why did you-" Flora spluttered, nearly fell off the chair and opened her eyes. Aggie ran to her side and offered her some water.

"Which one of you hit me?" she asked while scowling at them; her eyes fixed on Wolf who radiated guilt.

"I'm sorry," he said while staring at the ground. "I thought you were an intruder."

"It's a good job you were only trying to incapacitate me," she muttered, then she saw Aggie's worried expression and smiled, "I'm alright."

"Are you sure?"

Flora nodded, "I can't stay long," she said taking another drink of water "I'm being watched."

"Why did you risk it?" Redd asked his voice betraying the worry he was trying to mask.

"I needed to tell you that things are looking more complicated than we'd first thought."

What do you mean?" Wolf asked, finally taking a seat.

"They've had Artists try to escape before, multiple times, they're constantly on alert."

Redd frowned, "We did think it might be a problem."

"I think it's more than a problem, we're going to have to plan everything down to the smallest detail, nothing can go wrong."

"Have you found Flicker?" Redd asked, changing the subject and suddenly hopeful.

Flora shook her head and his heart sank, "I'm sorry Redd, I've not had time, I've been shadowing the whole week. I promise as soon as I'm clear of the others I'll start looking." Redd nodded though some of his enthusiasm had diminished.

"Have you any preliminary thoughts on what we should do?" Wolf asked, taking the reins.

"I think once I've managed to get a good scope of the place, we need to plan as much as possible in here."

"Don't you think it would be better if we were all inside?" Aggie asked.

Flora shook her head and suddenly looked exhausted, "I'd like to say yes, but honestly I don't know. I'm so new that I don't know how friendly the officers are towards the Artists, I've not really seen any interaction yet. I wouldn't want to jeopardise the plan unnecessarily."

"I agree," Redd said, his face still grim. "We need to know what we're up against before we go in there. We'll probably still need to plan when we're inside but for now, let's err on the side of caution." Aggie looked unhappy but she remained silent.

"What's it like in there?" Wolf asked.

"I haven't really had chance to look around," Flora admitted. "I had a quick tour of the palace and grounds on my first day but I've mainly been shadowing other officers."

"What are they like" Aggie asked quietly and when Flora looked confused she elaborated. "The grounds."

"They're amazing," she admitted, "I've been told they have people who come in once a week and tidy them up, so they're always looking immaculate. There are some exceptional sculptures, which I've been told were made by some of the first Artist's who lived in the pala-"

"What does it matter what the grounds look like?" Redd interrupted, sounding irritated.

Aggie shrank down in her seat, "I was just curious."

"Curious about what? It doesn't matter how much they dress it up it's still a prison, and one where my brother and your mother are being held!"

Aggie's expression darkened and she sat up staring straight at Redd, "I would rather their prison were pleasant and comfortable than miserable and dank," she replied and Redd looked a little guilty.

"Aggie I-"

"You're sorry, I know," she said cutting him off. "You're always sorry." She got up from her chair and walked to one of the back rooms so the others wouldn't see the tears in her eyes.

Redd made to move but Flora shook her head, "I'll go."

"I know it's not a good place," Aggie said not looking up as Flora entered the kitchen. "I know it's a prison, but my mother sent herself there so I wouldn't miss out on my life, is it so bad that I want it to be nice?" She finally looked up and saw pity on Flora's face, the other woman smiled.

"Of course not, I would want exactly the same thing if I were in your shoes. But for Redd it's different. I think he needs to believe the palace is an awful place, and in many ways it is. He needs to believe he's rescuing his brother, freeing him from a terrible fate, to know that his surroundings are actually pleasant isn't helping his conscience."

"What do you mean?"

"Redd hasn't had any contact with Flicker since he was taken five years ago and he's been determined to free him since then. But in all honesty, how do any of us know whether Flicker is actually miserable or enjoying his new life? Redd needs to believe his brother is miserable, that he wants to be saved, so he needs to believe the conditions the Artist's are living in are equally miserable."

"But when we enter the palace ourselves he'll see for himself what it's like? So why not be prepared now?"

"I don't know," Flora said shaking her head. "Try not to take anything he says to heart, he's got a lot of demons."

Flora slipped back out into the darkness an hour later and Aggie left for home another half hour after that so as not to arouse suspicion. She declined both Redd and Wolf's offer to walk her back to her home wanting some time to think, and set off on the quick journey in blissful silence.

The spring night was cold and the sky was clear, which made her journey easier as she used the light of the moon and stars as well as the streetlights to guide her way. The streets seemed unnaturally quiet but considering the late hour she thought nothing of it. She continued walking through the quiet, empty streets and at one point drew her coat tighter around her as a chill wind began to blow.

The wind started to emit a quiet whine and Aggie felt a shiver run down her spine; she quickened her pace and rounded the next corner to see her house in sight at the far end. A soft glow emitted from the living room window, informing her that the fire was still burning, though was probably now quite low. The remaining windows were dark. She walked with purpose now towards the welcoming door and thought of Cassie and the enticing warmth just inside.

She thought she heard a noise behind her but when she glanced over her shoulder all she could see was an empty street, half covered in shadow. She quickened her pace again and heaved an internal sigh of relief as she reached her front door.

Once inside Aggie made sure the door was locked and bolted, and she crouched to give Cassie a hug. She could feel the warmth and softness of the spaniel's fur against her skin and it soothed her. It wasn't until she stood again that she noticed the slip of paper on the floor by the door.

She picked it up, assuming it was another note from Flora, maybe informing them of when she would try to meet them again but when she turned it over her heart stopped. She wasn't faced with the neat, tidy handwriting of Flora, but the hurried scribble of a stranger. There were only four words written, but they chilled her to the bone.

We're coming for you.

Chapter 21

Jackie hadn't actually said anything to him but Flicker could tell she was worried about Nilla. Neither of them had seen her since he had warned her that the Emperor's staff would be watching her. He had tried to reassure Jackie that Nilla would probably be trying to blend in and that would mean staying on the sixth floor. In reality he was quietly panicking that she might have been found out and something might have happened to her. It wasn't until a week had passed that Jackie finally revealed her real reason for being worried.

"Charlie has been asking about her." Jackie explained, sitting on a bench in the sculpture garden.

"So he's the one worrying?" Flicker asked taking a seat next to her. "I'm starting to think it wasn't a good idea letting him know she was in here."

"He had a right to know," Jackie almost scolded.

"I know," Flicker said wincing. "But we all need to keep our heads through this process, what we don't need is her husband messing things up."

"You're forgetting that he doesn't know what's going on, he doesn't know anything about what we're trying to find out. He's simply worried about his wife, he misses her, and now he knows she's here, he wants to spend time with her-"

"He wants to make up for the time they've lost,"

Flicker finished with a sigh. "I know Jack, I really do, I wish we could tell him everything, I wish we could trust him-"

"But we can't," Jackie agreed. "Not yet anyway."

They sat in silence for a few minutes then Jackie nudged Flicker and he looked in the direction she gestured; Jan was walking towards them with another officer by his side. Flicker tensed as they approached, unsure who this mystery officer was but they didn't stop to talk and Flicker realised they must be patrolling. Jan flashed a smile as they walked past and he raised a hand silently in greeting.

"Looks like a new officer has joined the ranks," Jackie muttered and Flicker gazed in the direction they had gone, trying to get a good view of the young woman at Jan's side but they had already walked out of view.

"If she's got Jan mentoring her then she might not be so bad," Flicker said nodding in the direction they had gone; Jackie agreed.

They made their way to the maze just as it approached dusk; they had promised Nilla they would remain there every day until dark had fallen and they were forced back inside. They wandered amongst the neatly trimmed shrubbery that was the maze walls, admiring the sculptures, neatly arranged flowers and topiary that littered the dead ends. The finally made it to the centre and found the group of benches deserted; they waited almost in silence for the other woman to appear, both hoping to see her stroll round the corner at any moment. As the shadows lengthened and the sun slowly vanished behind the high walls, they let out a disappointed sigh and made to move.

Flicker froze and grabbed Jackie's arm stopping her in her tracks. He cocked his head, listening intently to the silence, frowned slightly, and after listening for some time a smile broke out on his face.

"Nilla?" he almost whispered.

A shadowed figure emerged from round one of the large, foliage heavy corners and Nilla smiled at them, "I'm sorry I've not been able to meet with you until now," she said quietly, taking a seat on a wooden bench. Flicker and Jackie grinned as they joined her.

"We're just glad to see you're alright," Jackie said in her cracked voice.

"What's it like on the sixth floor?" Flicker asked with genuine curiosity.

Nilla thought back to her cosy living space, her large bedroom with its plush double bed and her new outfits and she shrugged, "It's okay," she replied. Jackie eyed her with suspicion but said nothing.

"What section are you working for?" Flicker asked eagerly.

"I'm working for Perunia," Nilla explained, trying to avoid Jackie's gaze. "I'll be spending a lot of time around the workrooms on the fifth floor, monitoring their progress and auditing them, I thought that would be the best place for me to try and find out what's really going on."

Flicker perked up instantly, "Nilla that's fantastic! If you're trusted by the others, if you get into those workrooms, we'll finally know what it is the Emperor's up to."

"If he's up to anything," Jackie interjected and Flicker shot her a look. "Scowl at me all you want Flick but the fact is we don't actually know if there's anything underhand going on."

He chose to ignore her words, "How soon do you think until you're allowed into the workrooms?"

Nilla shook her head, "I'm not sure, I've got a lot of paperwork and filing to do first and then I'll be shadowing some of the others until we all feel I'm capable of completing my work unaided."

Flicker deflated slightly but tried not to let it show, "Well we're not going anywhere," he said forcing a smile. "We've got all the time in the world."

She smiled back though it didn't feel genuine, she knew as well as Flicker that the longer everything took the more chance there was that she would be found out. "Have you seen Charlie recently?"

Jackie nodded and lost some of her hostility, "He's been asking a lot about you, he misses you."

"I miss him too," Nilla said and her voice caught. "I wish I could have seen him again today but I didn't even know if I'd be able to get down here."

"I'll tell him you're thinking of him," Jackie said softly and Nilla smiled genuinely this time.

"I'd better go," she said getting to her feet. "I'll try and get an internal message to you next time to let you know when I can meet, but I don't know when I'll be able to get away again." The other two nodded and Nilla hugged them both tightly before she slipped back into the darkness and left the others to make their way back to the palace.

Flora was enjoying shadowing Jan on his patrols, he was a lot friendlier than most of the other officers and he let her in on the secrets and jokes that had been established for months and years. The sun was beginning to set as she walked around the grounds with him and he explained some of the finer points of the job. They were approaching the sculpture garden as he talked about the various living quarters for the Artists.

"The exterior buildings are where a lot of the older, more seasoned Artists live-"

"Do you mean those who are trustworthy?" Flora asked bluntly.

Jan smiled sheepishly, "I suppose I do, yes. Those who are new or who haven't given us a reason to trust them remain in the palace. And those who really don't want us to trust them are provided with a twenty-four hour watch."

Flora stopped in her tracks, "That really happens?" she asked in surprise.

Jan nodded, "Not so much these days, but there have been one or two we've needed to monitor."

They were walking through the sculpture garden now and Flora loved looking at the complicated and intricate sculptures that adorned the grounds. They approached two Artists seated on one of the benches; one was slightly older and had grey hair tied back, the other had messy red hair and was, she guessed, around her own age.

Her attention was snapped back to Jan who was explaining what to do if she caught an Artist out of bed after hours and she noticed him grin at the Artists on the bench and wave in greeting.

"Do you know them?" she asked glancing over her shoulder after they'd passed.

Jan nodded, "Flicker there was one of the Artist's who had caused us quite a bit of trouble until recently."

Flora felt her heart skip a beat and her stomach flipped, she chanced another glance behind her but could no longer see the two Artist's on the bench. They had walked by so quickly, she wasn't even sure she'd recognise him if she saw him again.

"What kind of trouble?" she asked trying to sound normal.

"He's one of the Artist's who tried to escape," Jan said grinning and Flora cursed internally. "He didn't succeed, obviously, but he sure was inventive."

"He's not causing trouble now though?"

Jan shook his head, "He turned himself around several months ago, finally realised he's not going anywhere and might as well try to make the best of it."

He's not going anywhere yet, but I'll do what I can to change that, Flora thought grimly. *If only I could get the chance to talk to him alone.*

"And who was that he was with? Another troublemaker?"

Jan laughed loudly causing Flora to jump, "Crafts no! That was Jackie, she's one of our model residents, we all thought she'd set Flicker on the straight and narrow when she took a shine to him but it seems even she couldn't persuade him."

"He's on the straight and narrow now," Flora pointed out. "Maybe it just took a bit longer than you all thought?"

Jan laughed again and this time Flora smiled, "Maybe you're right," he agreed as they reached the gatehouse and headed inside for a hot drink.

Flora wasn't sure if she should admit it but she was enjoying her new position inside the palace grounds. The work could be seen as monotonous, especially after several years of service, but it was easy and it was safer than being on the streets of the city. She highly doubted the Artist's would be lurking with large blades down alleys or hiding with illegal firearms. She knew the goal was to help Flicker, Nilla and any other Artist's to escape the palace but if everything failed and they couldn't escape, then she didn't think she would mind continuing to work there.

Jan smiled at her over the top of his mug, "Have you any family in the city?"

Flora shook her head, "My parents died when I was young, they both caught the flu, before there was any way to treat it and didn't survive. I was an only child and went to live with my uncle, he was a retired officer and I decided to follow in his footsteps. He died a few years ago."

"I'm sorry to hear that," Jan said and he sounded genuine.

Flora smiled and took a sip of her tea, "What about you?"

Jan grinned and pulled out some pictures from his pocket, "I've a wife and two children living in the city," he explained, showing her several pictures of a pale, dark haired woman and two small boys, each with dark hair and big smiles.

"Is it difficult being away from them?" Flora asked while gazing at the pictures with a small stab of envy.

Jan nodded, "I miss them when I'm in the palace, but I get four days in a row with them and I make the most of our time together. I know I could patrol the city and see them every night, but Clarissa and I both decided it would be safer for me in here."

Flora nodded and drank her tea in silence, eventually she put her mug down and passed the pictures back to Jan, "Your family look lovely."

Jan beamed with pride, "You'll have to come over for dinner one evening when we're on our days off."

Flora thanked him and realised that she was actually looking forward to the idea of meeting Jan's family. She still didn't know where his loyalties lay, she didn't have any idea who how many of the officers in the palace were part of the underground resistance but she liked him and she thought that maybe, if she spent enough time with him that she could turn him.

Chapter 22

Aggie had found it difficult to sleep after finding the note, afraid that whoever had left it might try to break into the house. She had pushed a cabinet against the door for extra protection and it had helped a little but every small noise had her staring about in fear. Cassie could tell something was wrong and had remained awake and alert while snuggling up to Aggie, trying to comfort her.

She woke bleary eyed, cold and confused the next morning as she found herself on the sofa, then saw the scrawled writing of the note and felt a chill run through her. Cassie was curled up next to her, already alert and awake. Aggie scrunched her hands into the spaniels fur, feeling its softness and relaxed as she realised the night had passed without incident.

She showered and changed her clothes, feeling far more positive about the day and opened the front door to make her way to Redd's workshop. There was already warmth in the air that indicated spring would soon make way for summer. She froze. Someone or something had attacked the few plant pots in front of her house, spilling their contents across the pale grey pavement. Aggie felt tears prick her eyes as she stared at the chaos in front of her house and set about clearing it up.

Once clear she locked her house and thought about heading to the market where Redd would be waiting when she saw something stuffed into a crack in the wall of her house. She took a few steps towards it and pulled out a crumpled piece of paper. Her heart began to thump and her breath caught in her throat as she straightened out the paper.

The same scrawled handwriting covered the surface; the majority of the words were insults but there was one sentence that stood out from the chaos and made her blood run cold.

We're coming for you, and you won't make it out alive.

She fumbled with her keys and managed to unlock her door; she slammed it behind her and locked it again. Tears rolled freely down her cheek and Cassie emerged from the living room looking slightly bewildered but ultimately happy that her owner was back.

She collapsed to the floor and sobbed loudly while Cassie licked the salty tears from her hands and face. She whined softly and began to nuzzle Aggie in an attempt to cheer her; Aggie threw her arms round her dog and cried heavily into her fur.

She exhausted herself after an hour and forced herself to her feet. Cassie, who had been waiting patiently wagged her tail and followed Aggie into the kitchen where she drank a glass of water. Aggie looked at the spaniel and smiled, she was grateful for the company and not for the first time felt pleased that she had created her.

Aggie remained inside all day, not daring to leave for fear of who she might encounter; she had no idea who had written the notes, it could have been a neighbour, it could have been a stranger who listened to rumour, it could even be someone from the pub.

She noticed the time was approaching her shift at

The Fisherman's Fancy and she contemplated staying inside, claiming she were ill. This line of thought didn't last long, she knew if she didn't turn up that Wolf would come looking for her. They might already think something's wrong since she'd missed her shift at Redd's and could be worried about her. She actually smiled at this thought, it was nice to have people who cared for her now that her parents were gone.

Aggie took a deep breath, changed her outfit once again and got ready to walk to the pub. Her heart pounded as she unlocked the door and was about to open it when a loud knock sounded. Aggie froze and after a few seconds realised she was holding her breath. She thought about pretending she wasn't in, thought about running and hiding under her bed, then a familiar voice sounded through the wood.

"Aggie?" Redd called and there was concern in his voice, Aggie let out a loud sigh and opened the door. "Aggie," he said with a sigh of relief. "Is everything okay? When you didn't turn up this morning I was worried."

"I'm alright," she said, trying hard to sound it. "I wasn't feeling well this morning but I've been resting and now I feel a lot better."

"Are you going to see Wolf?" he asked stepping out of the way of the door, Aggie nodded as she stepped over the threshold and locked the door behind her. She could feel a small amount of panic clutching at her but she took a deep breath and walked with Redd towards the pub.

Wolf was concerned when Redd mentioned she'd not been feeling well; he had a natural paternal instinct and told her to take a break if she felt unwell again. Aggie smiled gratefully at him and worked through her shift, knowing full well she wouldn't need to take a break to rest.

She didn't stay long after the pub had closed, there wasn't a lot for the three of them to discuss; they needed to wait until Flora came to see them again.

"Why not stay in my spare room lass," Wolf said still looking at her with concern.

"I'm fine, really," she said while smiling, as if that would convince him.

"I'll walk you home," Redd offered and although she tried to protest, he wouldn't take no for an answer. "Are you sure you're okay?" he asked when they had walked in silence for a few minutes.

She nodded and when Redd looked unconvinced she elaborated, "I think I might be a bit overwhelmed with all the work, I'm feeling quite tired."

"Why not take a few days off then," Redd said smiling. "I can tell Wolf if you like?"

She suddenly felt panicked at the thought of being trapped in her house, vulnerable, "I'm sure I'll be okay tomorrow," she said while forcing a smile. "You can leave me here if you like, it's not far for me to go." Redd looked at her intensely but eventually nodded and told her to take care.

Aggie walked through an uneasy silence down the main street and started to pick up her pace. She had only been walking for a few minutes when she thought she heard voices behind her; she froze and glanced around, wondering if Redd had returned. The street was empty but she quickened her pace again. A few more anxious minutes passed as she walked and she swore she could hear people whispering in the shadows.

She glanced around again not stopping this time, hoping that her mind was playing a trick on her. She could feel her heart thumping in her ears and her breathing was short and quick. Aggie thought she could hear footsteps and suddenly felt panic bubble up inside her.

She took a deep breath and finally broke into a run; she hurtled down the street, not daring to glance around her for fear of what she might see. She threw herself into her house and locked the door behind her, sinking to the floor in a fit of shakes and sobs. Cassie emerged from the living room to nuzzle and lick her face.

She still didn't mention anything about the note to Redd or Wolf the following day and had even convinced herself that she'd been hearing things the night before. She felt calm and happy as she went about her day and insisted on walking home alone the following night, convinced that she was safe.

Nothing happened to begin with, Aggie walked through the quiet street in peace; she felt relaxed and happy strolling through the peaceful night. It wasn't until she neared the street her house was on that she thought she could hear whispered voices again. She tried to ignore them, tried to convince herself that they were just the wind but deep down, she knew they weren't.

Her breathing quickened as panic rose but she willed herself to stay calm, to not let whoever it was know she was scared. The voices seemed to get louder and Aggie tried to quicken her pace, hoping to leave them behind, but they stayed with her. She couldn't make out any specific words, though she thought she could guess what was being said.

A loud crash sounded from one of the alleys and she froze; the voices also stopped and for a moment, everything was silent. She turned her head slowly towards the noise and saw a dark figure in the alley; she couldn't see their face but she knew they were staring at her waiting.

Her breath caught in her throat and her heart pounded against her ribs; she sprinted towards her house and above the pounding in her ears, could hear the hammering footsteps of her pursuers. She felt a sense of dread course through her as she neared her house, *What if they're waiting for me?*

She reached the front door and fumbled frantically with the keys until she was able to slot one into the lock and turn it quickly. She had turned the handle and started to push the door when someone grabbed her roughly from behind and threw her onto the hard pavement. Staring down at her, ugly snarls on their faces were Jason, Stephie and several others she couldn't quite see.

For a second the world stopped as Aggie realised what was about to happen, as she came to terms with the fact she probably wouldn't live through it, and then with a loud rush of sound, the world started up again. Stephie was the first to move, she kicked Aggie in the side, grinning now; Jason joined in, stamping on her legs, calling her names. The others started jeering and spitting at her, one of them kicked her in the head.

Too scared to fight back Aggie tried to curl into a ball, pain throbbed and seared through her and all she could hear were the yells of her tormentors. Then she heard barking, *Cassie*, she thought with relief and fear; her loyal spaniel had managed to get through the door. Cassie started to attack Stephie, who screamed in terror while some of the others attempted to detach her from Stephie's leg. Jason was still beating Aggie, but with his hands now; she remained curled in a tight ball and wished it would all be over. She heard the yells of Stephie and the others as Cassie growled and continued to cause some pain. She heard Jason's harsh voice as he threw insults at her as he continued to beat her and she heard her own sobs and rough breathing as she waited in agony for the end.

She heard several shouts followed by Cassie yelping and then a loud thud. She felt her heart break as she knew her beloved spaniel had lost the battle. Tears, which had already been flowing from the pain, began to stream down her face as she thought of how she would never see her happy dog greet her, tail wagging. She would never again nuzzle into her soft fur and feel her rough tongue lick away the pain and uncertainty she frequently felt. Her heart broke again.

Something erupted around her; a deafening roar, primal and furious. Jason stopped kicking her and she heard the group fall silent. Aggie dared a glance towards the street and saw a blurred mountainous dark form lunge towards her former classmates. She watched in terror as they were thrown into the street like ragdolls, where they groaned but didn't move.

The shadowed, hulking form strode towards her and Aggie let out a small whimper. As the figure moved closer, familiar features came into view and she felt an overwhelming sense of relief wash over her as Wolf bent down to scoop her into his arms. She clung to him like a small child and sobbed uncontrollably into his shoulder. Wolf shifted Aggie in his arms, picked up the still form of Cassie and carried them both into the house.

"It's alright Aggie," he said gently, once he had settled onto the sofa; Aggie continued to cling to him and he stroked her hair comfortingly. It took her a long time to calm down enough to explain to Wolf through stray sobs and hiccups about the notes she had received and what had happened.

"C-Cassie?" she asked in a small voice and erupted into fresh sobs when his expression looked sorrowful and pained.

"I'm sorry," he said softly as her sobs settled down to a sniffling whimper. She continued to cling to Wolf, continued to cling to the only thing now that made her feel safe. She had somehow managed to stop crying though her breathing was uneven and her chest hurt with every ragged breath. Her face was still buried in Wolf's shoulder and she refused to surface, to look around the familiar surroundings, which now felt alien and hostile.

She tried to think of anything but Cassie, tried to stop the flow of silent tears as the spaniel bounded around behind her closed eyes. She felt Wolf's large, rough hand stroking her hair gently, trying to soothe her and eventually, somehow she fell asleep.

Chapter 23

Nilla woke bright and early with the warm, spring sun streaming through her curtains; she was desperately trying not to get used to her current lifestyle, but it was proving difficult. She dressed in one of her new outfits; a dark blue shirt with black, trousers and grabbed something to eat from the dining room on the same floor.

Several of her colleagues were already there, including Lucie, and they waved her over to the table they were sitting at.

Lucie smiled pleasantly as she arrived, "Looks like you'll be going into the field today," she said in her calm voice.

"The field?" Nilla asked with confusion.

"Perunia is extremely pleased with your work and she wants you to start auditing the workrooms."

Nilla thought Lucie was watching her carefully for anything that might betray her; she took an internal deep breath and smiled calmly, "It will be nice to take a break from writing reports."

"You say that now," a young man called Damien said with a grin. "But after a few weeks of it you'll be begging to write reports again." Several of the others laughed and Nilla joined in.

She was starting to worry ever so slightly, she knew nothing about this new appointment was going to happen quickly and she was having to be patient but the more time she spent around these people, the more she liked them. The sooner she got into the workrooms and started to investigate the better.

She made her way down to the fifth floor where she met Mickael, the colleague who would be walking her through the auditing process. He smiled pleasantly at her and they walked in silence to a wide corridor with a number of doors; several officers patrolled its length. They weren't detained as they approached and Mickael walked towards the first of the doors.

"This is the first of the workroom corridors," he explained and Nilla betrayed herself by showing surprise.

"I hadn't thought there would be so many," she said quickly after Mickael shot her a look.

"It often comes as a surprise," he said nodding. "You're obviously aware of the situation the city is currently in?"

Nilla nodded, "Perunia explained about the resources crisis," she didn't elaborate further, there was no need, everyone on the sixth floor knew about the supposed lack of trade and resources. What she didn't say is that her, Flicker and Jackie had been discussing the suspicious nature of such an explanation, which in turn had lead to her being on the fifth floor at that very moment.

Mickael turned the handle of the first door and entered with Nilla following close behind. She wondered if this was the same room Flicker and Jackie had broken into. It certainly looked how they'd described though now it was full of bustling, busy Artists. She wasn't sure how appropriate it was for her to stare at her surroundings so she snatched glances and used her clipboard to scribble notes when Mickael wasn't looking.

"I'll lead the audits for today," he explained as the Artists continued to busy themselves around the room. "Feel free to take notes, you'll be completing the audits in another workroom tomorrow while I supervise."

She nodded but remained quiet. She followed Mickael round the workroom as he evaluated the quality of the Artist's work and asked them questions relating to the amount of time they practiced and their personal daily quotas. It seemed like a very similar process to the audits Nilla had attended with Lucie, except for the question about daily quotas, that one was new.

As she continued to act as Mickael's shadow, she made notes about the layout of the workroom, the items the Artists were working on and the materials that were contained within the many drawers and cupboards around the perimeter. The labels and contents didn't seem to hold any new information which disappointed her.

She had started to drift off into a daydream when she heard Mickael's voice raised in anger and alarm. She swivelled quickly to where he was scolding one of the Artists, who was in turn apologising. Nilla edged closer to try and make out the words that were flowing thick and fast from Mickael's mouth.

"Didn't you think there was something odd about your surroundings?" he snapped though he had lowered his voice to try and avoid the others looking at them.

"I'm sorry," the young Artist said. "I've not been transferred long, I-"

"I don't care about your excuses," Mickael snapped under his breath again. "Clear this mess up and get yourself over to the next corridor!"

The young Artist began to deform the lump of clay he'd been working on and Nilla caught a quick glimpse of it; she frowned as she watched the familiar form be manipulated until it resembled nothing more than a grey lump. The Artist got quickly to his feet, threw the lump of clay into a large container and left the room without another word. She could see Mickael take a deep breath and he pinched the bridge of his nose with his finger and thumb.

"Is everything okay?" she asked tentatively.

Mickael looked at her and smiled, "Yes of course," he replied forcefully. "Just a slight misunderstanding."

"A misunderstanding?"

Mickael continued to smile but Nilla could see if was forced, "Nothing for you to worry about right now, let's get this audit finished so we can break for lunch."

Nilla smiled and started following him round the room again, making the odd scribbled note if he said something that seemed important but her mind couldn't be dragged away from what she had seen the Artist working on. Between his hands, quickly becoming deformed and misshapen was what looked like a human foot.

Flora had been patrolling the palace grounds with Jan for several days without seeing Flicker again and she was starting to worry that she might never manage to track him down. She only had one more day until she could go back into the city and she didn't feel like she could meet with Redd, Wolf and Aggie without good news.

"What do you say to dinner with my family in two days time?" Jan asked as they made their way past the large, swan filled lake.

"That sounds lovely," Flora said with a smile. She had enjoyed patrolling with Jan these last few days, they seemed to have a lot in common but she still couldn't tell whether he was on the side of the Emperor or not. She had started asking small questions about the Artists and their living situation but Jan only replied with vague, short answers.

"I hope you don't mind children," Jan continued as they entered the flower garden and were suddenly surrounded by a rainbow of colour. "My boys can be a little energetic."

Flora laughed, "Not at all," she replied suddenly thinking how much she missed Aggie. She stopped suddenly staring intently at a clump of tall shrubbery and Jan walked a few paces before he realised, he turned to back and looked quizzically at her.

"Is everything okay?" he asked.

Flora came back to herself quickly and started walking to catch up, "Yes of course," she said smiling.

"Did you see something troubling?" Jan asked looking around them with worry.

Flora shook her head, "No, I'm sorry, I thought I saw someone crouching in those bushes, but I think I was mistaken and I suppose it wouldn't matter even if I had."

Jan frowned and stared at the shrubs Flora pointed at, "We should probably check it out."

Flora looked confused, "But surely it doesn't matter? I thought the Artist's had free reign in the gardens?"

"There have been a few isolated incidences of clay rich soil being used in the gardens, I'm sure I don't need to tell you how dangerous that could be."

Flora looked shocked, "But how could that even happen? I thought the palace had strict criteria for that sort of thing?"

Jan nodded but his face was grim, "We do, but somehow, someone managed to switch the soil coming in, we're still not sure how it happened and we've been worried in case it happens again." They had reached the densely packed bushes but despite their rigorous searching, found them to be empty.

Flora was silently relieved, "It was probably an animal or something," she said and Jan nodded though he didn't look overly convinced. Her heart sank at this, it seemed that this small action proved he was in the Emperor's pocket.

Jan broke for lunch soon after the non-incident in the flower garden but Flora decided to keep wandering the grounds, feeling somewhat troubled. She wasn't sure how to explain it but she was sure that Jan would be on her side if she explained her situation. Everything about his actions in the flower garden screamed that he was in the Emperor's club but everything up until that point implied otherwise.

Of course it was very likely that he had always been on the side of the Emperor and had been sent to watch her and see truly where her loyalties lay. She couldn't quite explain why, but she was sure that wasn't true.

She had found herself in the topiary garden, one of the areas she hadn't really spent a lot of time exploring, and since she was finally alone, she decided to wander round and examine the topiary artwork. Flora didn't have an artistic bone in her body and so she always marvelled at the artwork she saw and the pieces she'd so far seen in the palace and grounds were exceptional.

She had stopped by a topiary dragon; it had huge outstretched wings and a long tail that curled up at the end. Somehow, despite being made of a densely packed large shrub, the body looked as if it glittered in the sunlight and she almost thought she could see glinting eyes in the depths of the sockets.

She shook her head and focussed on the other

topiary art around her when she saw a familiar face and stared hard in order to be certain. Before they could slip out of sight Flora hurried over, making sure no other officer was around. She approached the small, grey haired woman and tapped her shoulder lightly; Jackie spun round, a scowl on her face which softened the moment she saw the officer's uniform.

"Can I help you dear?" she asked in her cracked voice.

Flora paused, unsure what to say first, Jackie looked at her quizzically, "Do you know Flicker?" she finally asked.

Jackie's expression changed instantly to suspicion, "That depends," she replied.

"On what?"

"On what you want with him."

Flora fell silent again, desperately trying to read this woman, to know if she could be trusted, "How long have you known him?"

"I don't believe I said I *did* know him," Jackie replied with a frown.

Flora sighed in exasperation, "I already know you know him," she said placing her hands on her hips; Jackie looked unimpressed. "I saw the two of you together."

Knowing she'd been caught out, Jackie finally spoke slowly, still unsure what to make of this new officer, "I've known him since he arrived, I looked after him."

"So, he trusts you?" Flora pried.

Jackie looked indignant, "Of course he does," she almost snapped and Flora's mouth turned up in a half smile.

"Good," she said smiling fully now. "If Flicker trusts you, then I can too."

She opened her mouth to speak again but Jackie held

up a hand instantly silencing her, "You might be able to trust me, but who says I can trust you?" She stared accusingly at Flora who sighed heavily and looked around for a bench, she indicated one close by and the two women sat down.

"I've never met Flicker," Flora admitted and Jackie looked like she was going to get up and leave. "I know his brother, Redd."

This made Jackie pause and she stared into Flora's green eyes, "You know Flicker's brother?" she asked and Flora nodded. "I think you're going to have to explain yourself," she said, settling herself back down and folding her arms.

Flora took a deep breath and explained almost everything about her, Redd and Wolf; she didn't want to reveal too much just on the off chance that Jackie couldn't be trusted or that someone was hiding and listening nearby. She didn't say anything about Aggie, not yet anyway, there was no point risking the girl's life unless there was no other way. Jackie sat patiently through it all until the end, and Flora felt both exhausted and lighter once she had finished.

"Flicker always thought Redd must have been trying to contact him, that the officer's weren't letting mail in or out of the palace, looks like he was right."

"Do you know where he is?" Flora asked eagerly, "I need to see him, he needs to know about his brother."

"Hold on," Jackie said holding up a hand, her expression still wasn't friendly. "How do I know this isn't some sort of trap?" Flora looked confused so Jackie explained, taking her time to say the words. "How do I know that you've not been sent here to find out what the Artist's are really feeling? Tracking down families isn't hard, we all know you keep an eye on them, you might know Redd or you might simply know of him. How do I know that you're really here with the underground resistance?"

Flora sighed in exasperation and got to her feet, she started pacing, "I'm not a spy for the Emperor," she said but Jackie's expression remained neutral. "I've spent months trying to get in here, to find Flicker, to tell him his brother has been working tirelessly on a plan to help him esc-" she stopped suddenly and clamped her mouth shut, realising she may have said too much.

She shot a glance at Jackie who was smiling faintly, the other woman got to her feet and walked towards her, she took hold of Flora's hands and held them tightly, "Now I trust you."

Chapter 24

Wolf had taken Aggie to The Fisherman's Fancy the following morning after burying Cassie in the back garden of Aggie's house. She had barely stopped crying since he had started to dig the small grave for the spaniel and as they sat in the small rooms above the pub she clung to him as if she were six years old again and scared of the monsters under her bed.

Eventually he managed to coax her down with him and she was currently sat at the small table by the window nursing her injuries. He had tried to patch her up as best he could, but he wasn't a doctor and he hadn't been sure if some of her cuts needed stitches.

She seemed small and fragile as she cowered in the corner while he busied himself and for the first time, he wondered if Redd hadn't been right all those weeks ago because right now, she didn't look strong enough. At that moment a sharp knock came at the door and Wolf saw Aggie shrink back even further into the corner trying to merge with the shadows, he sent a reassuring smile her way and walked towards the door.

"What in the Emperor's name happened?" Redd asked as he burst through the door before Wolf had fully opened it. "I got your message, where is she?" Wolf pointed to where Aggie was curled up on her seat and Redd rushed towards her. "Aggie I'm so sorry," he said with sincere concern. "Are you okay?"

She nodded slowly but didn't say anything, Redd looked to Wolf and he shrugged, "She hasn't said much since last night," he explained taking a seat near the young girl. "They beat her up pretty bad."

Redd looked again at Aggie, at her numerous injuries, then back to Wolf, when he next spoke his voice was low, "She can't be a part of this now, you must see that?"

Wolf nodded, "Aye, I do, I think it would be best if she remain here."

"Please don't," came a small voice and they both turned to look at Aggie, who had finally uncurled herself and was sitting up, her eyes wide and full of fear.

"Don't what?" Redd asked. "Aggie, you're terrified! I know you've been through something awful and I'm so sorry that it happened, but you must see that you're not capable of helping us in the palace, events could easily take a turn for the worst." Tears brimmed in her eyes and Wolf felt a jolt of guilt at the thought of abandoning her; he turned to Redd who instantly looked annoyed. "No Wolf, you just agreed-"

"Aye, I did but I'm sorry Redd, I can't leave her here alone, I can't abandon her, you didn't see her last night, you didn't see what they did to her, what they did to her pup."

"What good will she be to us?" Redd asked in irritation.

"I don't know," Wolf admitted. "Maybe none at all, but at this moment I actually think she'll be safer with us in the palace that out in the city on her own."

Redd sighed heavily and Wolf could see defeat in his eyes, "Alright," he said finally and Wolf smiled in triumph while a small knot of worry twisted in his stomach.

It took several days but Aggie finally started to feel like herself again; she knew she was safe at The Fisherman's Fancy, knew that Wolf would never let anything happen to her. She had started to calm down, had stopped seeing danger at every turn and had instead started to be annoyed at herself for how she had acted. She had tried to apologise to Wolf but he wouldn't hear of it and had told her to keep resting and get herself better.

Redd was a lot harder to please, she had apologised for her behaviour and for being weak and he had simply grunted in return. Wolf had shot him a cold look but Redd had ignored it and continued to scribble on some paper.

"I really am sorry," she said again as Redd continued to ignore her. "I'll do better next time."

Redd glanced up that time, took in her bruised and battered appearance and suddenly he felt cold and cruel, his shoulders slumped and he forced a weak smile. "You have nothing to apologise for," he finally said. "I should apologise for being so hard on you all the time."

Wolf stopped dead in his tracks, "Did I just hear you correctly?" he asked in astonishment. "Did you just admit you were in the wrong?"

Redd smiled somewhat sheepishly and turned back to Aggie, "I know I've said this to you several times now, but I am sorry for how I treat you. I sometimes forget you're only sixteen and that you don't know how to defend yourself."

"I'll start learning," she said quickly. "I want to learn," she added with a glimmer of determination. "I don't want to be in that situation again, I never want to feel that helpless again."

Redd smiled kindly at her and he placed a hand on hers, "Then I'll help you, I'll teach you what I know, it's mainly the basics, but hopefully it will be enough."

"I'll help you too lass," Wolf said as he reached the table with drinks. "Anything I can do to make you feel safer, I will."

Another week passed uneventfully, Aggie's wounds had almost healed and she felt determined to gain some courage. Redd had started to worry about Flora since she still hadn't turned up and he was sure that her days off had now been and gone. He was visibly agitated and while Wolf had done his best to try and reassure him, he and Aggie had left him to brood in the corner by the window.

"Alright Aggie, I'll show you a few basic self defence moves first, are you ready?" Aggie nodded and felt fear surge inside her despite only being faced by Wolf, who she knew would never hurt her. She took a deep breath and scolded herself internally.

She was terrible; she was still in some pain and occasionally flinched when Wolf made a move towards her. Her strength was laughable. She felt miserable despite Wolf's encouraging comments; all she needed was a glance in Redd's direction to know how she was really doing.

They stopped after only an hour, Aggie feeling deflated and a failure, Wolf placed a reassuring hand on her shoulder and spoke kindly to her.

"I wouldn't worry lass, neither of us expected you to be perfect first time. These things take practice, but we'll get you there, I promise." His words had actually helped and she had felt momentarily hopeful until she caught another glimpse of Redd's expression and then her heart sank.

"It's hopeless isn't it," she said, looking at Redd rather than Wolf. "I'm terrible, we can all see it, tell me the truth, is this a waste of time?"

Redd opened his mouth, saw Wolf's expression and closed it again. He took a few minutes to choose his words carefully before he spoke. "Look, I'm not going to lie to you and tell you you're good, you've already proved you know that's not true." Aggie deflated further. "But Wolf is correct, you were never going to be an expert the first time, and considering what you've recently been through it's understandable that you would be hesitant."

Aggie stared at Redd with an odd look on her face, "Is that your way of trying to tell me I'm not a lost cause?" Redd smiled at her and Aggie grinned back. "I'll get better," she said looking between them, "I promise."

With still no sign of Flora, Wolf sent Aggie to bed while he finished cleaning the pub; Redd continued brooding in the corner.

"Chin up lad," Wolf said as he dried the last of the glasses. "She'll be okay, you know she will."

"I don't know Wolf, I'd have thought she'd manage to get word to us somehow, like last time-"

"Crafts!" Wolf said loudly and Redd turned quickly to look at him thinking he'd cut himself. "Last time she left a note it was at Aggie's."

Redd's eyes widened, "Have you got the keys?"

Wolf nodded and threw them over, "Be careful lad," Redd nodded and left the building quickly while Wolf started to upturn the chairs onto the tables.

It was dark in the streets and bitterly cold, Redd looked up at the cloud covered sky and exhaled deeply; his breath misted and swirled around in front of him. His footsteps echoed in the empty streets and he felt unusually uncomfortable. He usually relished the dark and the quiet, and enjoyed walking through the city alone, but tonight, something felt different.

He quickened his pace, suddenly feeling uneasy until he saw Aggie's dark house come into view. He relaxed momentarily then heard the clatter of something behind him; he froze for a split second then continued at a slightly quicker pace on hearing footsteps behind him. He began to hear harsh whispers and stopped a second time looking around the dark empty streets.

"Try it," he said in a deep threatening voice. "I dare you."

He heard retreating footsteps and felt his shoulders relax as silence reigned once more. It didn't take him long to reach the small house and he let himself inside; he looked around the dark hallway and fumbled for the light switch. The room was soon bathed in a soft, warming glow and Redd saw with a glimmer of hope, several folded slips of paper on the floor. He picked them up and went into the living room, which was as cold as the rest of the deserted house. He sat in the large, soft armchair and opened the first slip of paper; he shuddered at the words:

Next time you'll join your mongrel

With some reluctance, he opened the next one and found an equally threatening statement. He opened two more and scrunched them into balls almost instantly as a knot of anger formed in his stomach, *How long has she been receiving these notes?* Redd thought with a deadly expression on his face, *and why didn't she say anything to us?*

His face suddenly fell and the knot of anger was replaced with one of guilt as he realised it was probably his fault that she'd stayed quiet. He was the one who had thought she was too weak to be of any use, he was the one who had been cold and distant towards her, he was the one she was trying to prove herself to. He let out a frustrated breath and saw that there was one final slip of paper still in his hand. He opened it with apprehension and his expression softened instantly as he saw Flora's familiar handwriting:

> *Still being followed,*
> *have found someone who knows Flicker,*
> *will try to see you all soon.*

His heart lifted slightly now that he knew Flora was okay; he had known she would probably be followed to begin with until she was trusted by the other officers, but he hadn't realised it would be this rigorous. He realised with some annoyance that they probably wouldn't be able to act on their plan as quickly as he would have liked. Then he thought about Aggie, and perhaps delaying the plan would be useful, he and Wolf could spend this extra time getting her prepared for what they might face inside the palace.

Redd managed to make it back to The Fisherman's Fancy without any trouble and showed the threatening notes to Wolf when he entered.

"What in the Emperor's name? Redd, where did you get these?" Wolf asked in shock.

"They were waiting for me when I got to Aggie's, I don't know how long she's been getting them, but I think it's safe to say that beating wouldn't have been a onetime thing. You made the right decision bringing her here, and I think you're right in saying we can't leave her in the city alone."

"I had no idea things were this bad for her," Wolf

said as he almost collapsed into one of the chairs by the window. "Why didn't she tell us?"

Redd swallowed his guilt and shook his head, "I don't know."

"Should we ask her about them?"

Redd paused then shook his head, "I think right now it will only make things worse, you've seen how she is, she's still fragile, we need to focus on the positive, we need to keep *her* positive."

Wolf nodded in agreement as he continued to stare at the threatening notes, "Was there anything from Flora?" he finally asked, suddenly remembering the reason Redd had gone there in the first place.

Redd nodded and handed him the final note with Flora's neat handwriting on, "She's making progress," he said with little enthusiasm and Wolf looked up at him.

"Give her time," he said and Redd shot him a questioning look. "I know what's going on in that head of yours, you wanted us to be in and out within weeks of Flora entering the palace." Redd opened his mouth to protest but Wolf went on. "You did, you know you did, now you're realising it's not going to be as easy as you thought and you're starting to feel frustrated." Wolf got to his feet and placed a comforting hand on Redd's shoulder. "Flora's only been in there a couple of weeks and she's managed to find someone who knows Flicker, that's fantastic and you know it. The palace houses hundreds if not thousands of Artist's, did you really think she was going to find him on her first day?"

Redd sighed heavily, "No, I guess not, and you're right, I need to learn how to be patient, it's just I've been waiting for this moment for-"

"I know lad," Wolf said taking a seat again and after a moment Redd sat with him. "I've been with you since the beginning, I know what this means to you, I really do, but you've come so far, and to be impatient now would be reckless."

"You're right, I know you're right, I've waited five years to see my brother again, I can wait a little longer."

Chapter 25

Nilla met Mickael by the corridor of workrooms for another round of audits, which she was going to complete while he appraised her and decided whether she was ready to start auditing on her own.

"How are you feeling?" he asked as he made a few notes on his clipboard.

"Nervous," she admitted.

"Don't be," Mickael said with a smile, "you've picked up things up pretty fast, I've no doubt you'll do the same with this." Nilla smiled back and they both entered the workroom; it looked identical to the others she had been in though she knew she had never actually audited this class before.

She took a deep breath, smiled at the teacher and began to walk round the room, looking at the students work and asking them questions. She was fully aware now that these workrooms were set up to produce resources. Perunia had made it very clear that the city was suffering from a serious lack of certain resources that could only be retrieved from across the borders. For close to ten years now the ties between Shanora and the other cities had been strained and all trade had ceased, though no one would tell her why.

The Artists in the palace were trained up until they were deemed flawless, then they were moved to the fifth floor where they created resources to be used in and around the city. Nilla understood that it was an important task that needed to be completed, though she still didn't like the circumstances under which it was completed.

The individual resource quotas were progressing well this week for this class, which meant they would likely be on target for hitting their group quota at the end. She smiled at Mickael who watched her from the front of the room and continued talking to a young woman who was working on what would become a steel slab.

"And how are you finding the work? Are you having any anxiety issues with regards to your quota?"

"Oh no," the woman replied brightly, "this work is far easier than what I was doing before."

"You mean the work on the lower floors?" Nilla asked while making notes.

The woman shook her head, "No, I mean the other workrooms." she looked at her with a confused expression so the woman elaborated. "For the last couple of years I've been on the offence team but my standards began to slip and they transferred me to the defence team." Nilla continued to look confused but before the woman could say anything more Mickael had reached them.

"Is everything okay?" he asked with insincere concern.

Nilla smiled, "Yes of course, this young woman was just telling me how much she's enjoying the work." Nilla and Mickael moved away from the woman and Nilla completed the remainder of the audit with Mickael at her side.

"Well you passed with flying colours," he said once they were back in the corridor. Nilla let out a genuine sigh of relief and Mickael laughed. "You can't have been that worried really?"

"No matter how confident I might have felt this morning the nerves still got to me and I worried I might have made a silly mistake."

"Even the best of us make mistakes," Mickael said with a smile that didn't reach his eyes. "You'd better get that report written up for Perunia before lunch." Nilla nodded and they made their way back to the fifth floor.

The remainder of her day was taken up with writing reports and completing paperwork. She actually found she enjoyed this side of the job as much as the auditing; it was methodical and relaxing and she found she could let her mind wander. Right now it drifted back to what the young woman had said, about being transferred from the offence team to the defence team.

"The offence and defence teams," she said aloud to herself. "What in the Emperor's name are the offence and defence teams?" She continued her filing as she pondered the possibilities, it was clearly linked to what they were doing in the workrooms but she had been in them, she knew what they were doing. "Maybe there are certain resources that are created in the various workrooms?" She shook her head immediately. "That sounds ridiculous."

Her filing finished she began to pace her office in frustration, she wished she could find Flicker and Jackie and talk about this to them, but she knew she would have to wait until the evening if she didn't want anyone to see them. She wished she could just ask Perunia or Lucie about the different teams but it was likely they hadn't mentioned them to her for a reason. Maybe they still didn't trust her. "One thing's for certain, there's definitely something else going on here," she told her empty office. "And I'm going to find out what it is."

It wasn't until she was on her way to meet with Flicker and Jackie that she suddenly remembered the human foot she thought she'd seen. She wondered whether that might have been linked to the offence and defence teams and she made a mental note to mention it to the others when she saw them.

She was approaching the entrance to the maze when she was grabbed from behind and dragged to the side and into some bushes. She tried to cry out but a large, dark hand clamped around her mouth. Her eyes were wide as she was held in place for several minutes; she was sure she'd been found out.

"Don't be afraid," came the quiet, familiar voice of her husband.

She relaxed instantly and he released her from his grip, she swivelled to face him and smacked him round the head. "What in the Emperor's name are you playing at?" she hissed as his hands flew up to protect himself.

"I'm sorry, I needed to talk to you in private."

"So you crept up on me and dragged me away? You could have just asked!"

"I'm sorry, I panicked," Charlie said sheepishly.

Nilla sighed and lost her hostile exterior, "What's wrong?"

"I need you to tell me what's going on, all of it," he said and she looked both concerned and afraid.

"What do you mean?"

"You know exactly what I mean Nilla, I wasn't born yesterday, you're taking a great risk to keep meeting with those two and there's obviously a reason."

"They're my friends Char-"

Charlie snorted, "Do you really think I'm an idiot?" he said with an undertone of hostility. "What's going on?

Are you planning an escape?"

"Escape?" Nilla asked with surprise. "Of course not," Charlie's expression altered to something she couldn't quite work out. "Were you hoping we were?"

"I feel like I've been here for an eternity Nilla, I've missed you and I miss our daughter, I want to see her, I want the chance to get to know her."

She put a gentle hand on her husband's arm, "I know you do, but I'm sorry Charlie, we're not planning an escape, not anytime soon anyway."

"Then what *are* you doing? And don't give me the, 'they're my friends' rubbish." Nilla stared at him for what felt like hours and tried to decide whether she could trust him. "Nilla please, I'm still your husband, what's going on?"

She sighed heavily, "I don't know," she admitted and as he looked at her sceptically. "I really don't, we think there's something not quite right here, that there's something going on behind the scenes but we don't know what it is."

"Behind the scenes? Is that why you took the administration position?" his eyes were wide but Nilla shook her head vigorously.

"I took the administration position for the original reason I told you, I'm not an Artist and I don't think I'd have lasted long before they found out. It wasn't until I started my new position that I uncovered a few things that seemed odd-"

"Like what?" Charlie asked a little too eagerly.

Nilla looked at him intensely, "Why are you so interested?" she asked slowly and Charlie seemed to visibly reign himself in.

"I've been feeling like something isn't quite right here for some time, but it's so hard to find anything out and it's difficult you know who you can trust. We're always being watched."

She nodded slowly, trying to decide how much to tell him, "I heard from one of the Artist's on the fifth floor that there's an offence and a defence team, which I'd never heard of. I decided to see if Flicker and Jackie knew anything about it."

"Is there anything else?"

Nilla shook her head, "That's the only thing I've noticed so far."

Charlie seemed disappointed, "I'll see if there's anything I can find out," he said with a smile. "And you keep me updated on what you uncover okay?" Nilla nodded as Charlie embraced her and she felt his warmth comfort her momentarily but when he pulled away and left her to enter the maze, she felt an overwhelming sense of unease.

Flicker and Jackie were sat on one of the benches in the centre of the maze, wondering whether Nilla would be able to join them.

"It's been a while since we last saw her," Jackie pointed out.

"It's probably difficult for her to slip away, I wouldn't be surprised if they had someone checking in on her from time to time until they're satisfied that she won't betray them."

Jackie chuckled, "They're in for a treat then."

Flicker turned to face his friend, "Tell me again about this new officer-"

"Flora," Jackie interrupted.

"Fine, tell me about Flora," he repeated while sighing, "Do you think she can be trusted?"

Jackie nodded, "I know she can, she's on our side

Flick, I promise you."

"How can you be sure?"

"I don't know how to explain it, call it a gut feeling but I know she's on our side, I really think you should meet with her."

"I'm not sure Jack, what if it's a trap?"

"I can't guarantee that it isn't but it just doesn't feel like it, you didn't see her Flick, you didn't feel her sense of urgency at finding you."

Flicker remained silent for a long time before he responded, "Okay Jack, if you trust her then I trust her, do you know how to set up a meeting?"

Jackie nodded as Nilla walked round the corner into the clearing, "Nilla!"

Nilla smiled and gave Jackie a tight hug, "Hi Jack, Flick, I've really missed you two."

"We've missed you too dear," Jackie said with a grin.

"Have you found something?" Flicker said and Jackie shot him a scolding look. "What?" he said defensively.

"You've not seen her for days and that's the first thing you ask? Not, how are you? Not, how is the work? But, have you found something? You're hopeless."

Flicker felt suddenly ashamed and looked apologetically at Nilla who was stifling a laugh, "It's fine," she said with a wide grin. "As a matter of fact, I think I have found something, I'm not sure what it means yet, but it's definitely something." The other two sat up straight and looked at her expectantly, she took a deep breath. "There's two things really," she explained as her friends looked on silently. "The first is that, I think someone was sculpting a foot-"

"An animal foot?" Flicker interrupted and Nilla shook her head.

Jackie elbowed him in the ribs, "Don't interrupt."

He grimaced and Nilla continued, explaining about the auditing session where she thought she had seen a human foot being sculpted before the Artist was evicted and the one where she had heard about the offence and defence teams.

"I've never heard anything about any teams," Jackie said quietly, "I don't know what that might be about."

Flicker shook his head, "Me neither, but I wonder whether the foot might have something to do with-"

"That's what I thought," Nilla said, "I wish there was someone up there that I could trust enough to ask but I think it's just us for now."

"It's not really something you can just drop into casual conversation," Jackie agreed and Flicker let out a loud bark of laughter.

"Yes I've finished those reports and I'm all ready for tomorrow, oh by the way why was someone sculpting a human foot the other day?"

Nilla laughed, "If only it were that easy."

"How many of the workrooms have you actually seen?" Jackie asked, still straight faced.

Nilla sobered quickly, "I've mainly been dealing with the workrooms down the first corridor."

"And how many corridors are there?" Flicker asked, suddenly catching on to Jackie's train of thought.

"I'm not sure," Nilla said slowly as she counted in her head. "Maybe five or six…" she trailed off and Jackie smiled. "You want me to try and get into one of the workrooms down another corridor?" she said quietly and they nodded.

"I know it won't be easy but it will still be far easier for you than it would be for us," Jackie said and she nodded her agreement.

"Exactly, "Flicker said. "If you're found by someone you can simply tell them you're auditing th-"

"Except I only audit the first corridor," she said with an undertone of worry, the other two opened their mouths and she pressed on. "I'll still do it, just don't think it's going to be easy for me simply because I already work up there."

Jackie suddenly looked concerned, "If it's too risky-"

"Honestly Jack it's fine," she said smiling. "We all know there's something strange going on and if we don't take the risks we'll never move forward. I'll get into one of the others rooms, let's just hope I don't get caught."

Chapter 26

"It's weird Jack, I mean a human foot, why on earth would someone be sculpting that?" Flicker asked as he picked at the dry clay under his nails.

Jackie shook her head, "I don't know Flick, if we knew what the offence and defence teams were I reckon we'd have a better idea of the signifi-"

"The Artist's are meant to be creating resources, right?" Flicker interrupted.

"It seems that way."

"So why in the Emperor's name do they have the newcomers sculpting animals? What do they have to do with wood and metal and everything else?"

Jackie fell silent for several minutes before she answered, "It must be about accuracy," she finally said while Flicker stared at her sceptically. "Think about it logically," she explained. "Certain resources have incredibly fine detail that might be missed by someone who isn't already trained to think and examine that way. It actually makes sense that the Artist's would be made to sculpt animals first because they're required to make then look as lifelike as possible."

She paused while Flicker digested the information, "So they'll apply that same level of detail to the resources they're sculpting and then there won't be any problems with them."

"Exactly!" Jackie said with a smile. "Perhaps the Artists on the fifth floor are required to do the same thing but with human body parts in order to keep themselves well trained."

"I suppose that could be the case," Flicker said slowly with a hint of scepticism. "But it doesn't explain what the offense and defence teams are."

Jackie nodded slowly, "Yes, that one's a right mystery, let's just hope that Nilla manages to find out something useful that will help us solve the riddle."

Their discussion was cut short a female officer with short dark brown hair walked towards them in the flower garden, "Sorry I'm late," she said with a sigh. "It was murder trying to get out of the palace, there's some new recruits and they're causing trouble."

"Perhaps they should send them your way Flick," Jackie said with a cackle and Flicker shot her a look.

"I'm not that person anymore Jack," he said forcefully.

"I hope that's not true," Flora said and the other two turned to look at her.

Flicker folded his arms across his chest and stared at her, "Okay, let's have it."

Flora took a seat opposite them and chewed on her bottom lip as she tried to decide where to start. As if reading her mind, Jackie spoke, "Try starting from the beginning."

Flora smiled, "I've been an officer since I left school, I liked the idea of protecting people, of helping to enforce the laws that governed our city but it turned out that being an officer wasn't quite how I'd imagined it to be. Everyone and everything seemed to be corrupt. And then there were the spies, those that took pleasure in ripping Artist's from their families and sending them to spend eternity here.

"I started to think that the laws I was meant to uphold weren't as good as I had once been lead to believe. I started to think that there must be a better way for the Artist's to be controlled; locking them away and forbidding them to see their families couldn't be the answer.

"I went looking for an alternate path. At first I wanted to leave the force, I wanted to do something else but while I was walking home one evening I saw an officer on patrol and he was telling someone to run and hide. He told them they weren't to leave their home for several weeks and when they finally did, they were to leave the city as quickly as possible. After the person had left I approached the officer and asked him if he'd just let an Artist escape; he pulled his firearm on me."

Flicker and Jackie's eyebrows lifted in surprise and Flora smiled sheepishly, "I was young," she said before taking a deep breath to continue. "Clearly the officer didn't shoot me and once he trusted me he told me about the underground resistance, about officers who help Artists to escape the city rather than be sent to the palace. I joined and it wasn't long after that moment that I met your brother, Redd.

"I'd heard rumours through the underground that an artisan, whose brother had already been taken, might be in trouble so I went to check it out. He was in a pretty bad way." Flora locked eyes with Flicker and he nodded with a grimace that she should continue. "He'd clearly found some blood that he believed to be yours and he…tried to make himself an Artist-"

"He did what?" Jackie asked in astonishment, she turned to Flicker whose face was hard.

"Keep going," he said with little emotion.

Flora nodded, "He'd cut himself and it was pretty deep, he was lucky he didn't slice through an artery. He tried to mingle what he believed to be your blood with his."

Jackie's eyes were so wide the irises were now completely ringed with white, "That's madness," she whispered.

"Losing Flicker devastated him," she locked eyes with the young man. "You were his little brother and he'd been unable to protect you, at that moment he would have done anything to get into the palace and be back with you.

"I helped him get back on his feet but it wasn't easy. He didn't trust me to begin with and in all honesty I don't blame him, I'm not sure I would have trusted me either. But eventually the walls came down and we began to hatch a plan; we were inexperienced and reckless to begin with and while conspiring in one of the pubs we were overheard by the owner. Rather than turn us in he kept his mouth shut and offered to help us, turns out his wife was an Artist but she fought back when they came for her and the officers killed her."

Flora stopped to take a breath and noticed Flicker staring at her with eyes similar to his brother's; she felt a shiver run down her spine. "It's taken years of planning; the palace isn't an easy place to break out of as I'm sure you already know." Flicker half smiled and Jackie let out a quiet cackle. "When we finally decided that I should get transferred into the palace it became a waiting game and now I'm here the game has continued but we need to speed things up, we need to get you out of here."

"So that's what all of this is about? Breaking me out of the palace? But how? You know as well as I do that breaking out is near enough impossible," he said.

"True," Flora agreed. "Except this time there's someone on the inside who has access to the front gates, as long as we can overpower the other officers we'll be fine. Once we're out we'll have to lay low until the chaos has died down but once it has we can find a way to leave the city."

Jackie and Flicker looked at one another; both were frowning, "It's not the right time," Flicker finally said and Flora's mouth dropped open.

"Not the right time?" she asked in astonishment. "Not the right time?" she asked again but louder and with an underlying note or irritation. "We've been planning for almost five years, I finally manage to get into the palace and find you and you tell me it's not the right time? What in the Emperor's name am I supposed to tell Redd?!"

"Calm down," Jackie said in as gentle a tone as her cracked voice could manage. "We didn't say we didn't want to leave, we just said we might need to delay things a bit."

"Why exactly?" Flora asked through gritted teeth.

Jackie and Flicker exchanged another look and Flora inhaled loudly, "Alright," Flicker said holding up his hands in defeat. "We'll tell you." He paused and considered his words carefully. "Things don't quite add up in here," he said and when Flora looked at him with exasperation he continued quickly. "We've noticed odd things happening in the workrooms and they don't make sense, they don't seem to be in line with the creation of resources. We think there might be something more sinister going on, something to do with offence and defence teams."

"Offence and defence teams?" Flora asked, clearly puzzled.

"I take it you've not heard of them?" Flicker deflated

and Flora shook her head.

"Do you think you could listen out for anything relating to them?" Jackie asked and Flora nodded, flashing her a smile.

"Anything I can do to get you out of here quicker, I will because believe me, Redd won't wait another five years to see you."

Flora met with Jan an hour later to continue patrolling inside the palace, she was mulling over what Flicker and Jackie had said about offence and defence teams but couldn't think of anything to explain them.

"Everything okay?" Jan asked.

Flora nodded, "Sorry, I was off in my own world."

"What's bothering you?"

Flora glanced at Jan as they rounded a corner and were greeted by a large sculpted bear, and wondered how much she could tell him. After a few minutes of internal debate, she decided to be blunt. "What do you know about the offence and defence teams?"

A puzzled look crossed Jan's face and Flora's heart sank slightly, "Where did you hear about those?" he asked with little emotion.

Flora's heart rose again, "I heard something mentioned up on the administration floors," she replied trying to sound casual. "I wondered what they were."

He glanced in her direction and she noticed a concerned look on his face, "I don't know what they are," he finally said and Flora let out a disappointed sigh. "I've heard the terms used once or twice amongst the others but I learnt early on it's best not to pry into things that don't concern us."

Flora frowned, "How do you know it doesn't concern us? You don't even know what they are."

"If it concerned us then we'd have been told about it."

"Do you really believe that?" Flora had stopped now and was staring at Jan with a pleading look in her eyes, *Come on Jan, don't be like all the others.*

"Of course it is, and if you know what's good for you it's what you'll believe too." He continued walking and she followed behind feeling deflated. They walked in silence for several more minutes until she could no longer take the unfamiliar tension that was growing between them. She stopped again and Jan turned to face her when he finally noticed.

"What's wrong?" he asked with a sigh.

Flora stared at him, "I thought maybe you were different," she finally said and when he shot her a confused look she just shook her head. "Never mind," she said walking towards him. "It doesn't matter." She walked past him and continued round a corner and out of sight, Jan shook his head and followed.

When he turned the corner he found the corridor to be empty and although he called out to her, Flora didn't reappear. He shrugged his shoulders and continued his patrol without her. He still wasn't sure about this new officer and whether she could really be trusted. He knew she wasn't really interacting with any of the other officers and that in itself was suspect. But she was the only officer to really take an interest in him and his family and that made him want to trust her.

"Can I trust her?" he asked aloud as he wandered past sculptures of badgers, foxes and rabbits. "I need to find out once and for all if she supports the Emperor, only then will I know." His face was set into a slight frown as he rounded the next corner and marched out of sight, determined to find Flora and see where her loyalties lay.

As his footsteps became quieter, Flora emerged from a store room and heaved a great sigh, "Looks like I made the right decision on holding back the information I knew," she said with regret. "I'll have to be careful what I say around him from now on." She turned away from the direction Jan had gone and began trudging in the opposite direction, feeling frustrated that the only officer she had liked was on the opposing team.

Flora halted suddenly and cocked her head as if listening for something, then she gasped and turned back to look at the sculptures that lined the halls. She stared at them intensely for some time and wondered whether maybe it was possible. "Could they be here to defend the palace?" she whispered to herself as she stroked one of the badgers muzzles. "Is the Emperor having the Artist's make these animals in case of an attack?" It seemed a bit farfetched to her but why else would they bother keeping the sculptures? Why would they potentially waste tons of clay?

She continued to stare at the finely detailed animal sculptures and chewed on her bottom lip in thought, *Didn't Redd once tell me that the clay was better unfired for animals?* "So if this really was an army, why would they fire the sculptures?" She continued to stare, willing the answer to come to her and eventually shook her head in defeat. "I'd better talk about this to Flicker and Jackie, maybe they can think of something I can't." She finally turned on her heel and marched back down the hall and out of sight.

Jan peered round the corner at the now empty corridor, an unreadable expression on his face, "I'm going to need to keep an eye on her."

Chapter 27

"You're a talented artisan Aggie," Redd said as he nodded approvingly at her work. "You've picked everything up incredibly quickly, you should think about this as a career."

Aggie grinned as she continued to mould and shape the large vessel in front of her, "There's nothing I love more than working with clay," she replied as she easily manipulated the cool, soft material.

"Flicker loved making things too," Redd replied with a hint of regret in his voice. "He had talent like you and he loved this job, if only he hadn't been afflicted with that damn curse."

Aggie winced and looked up at Redd who was turned away from her, "It's not a curse," she said quietly and Redd spun round with a look of thunder. "Well it's not," she said with more force. "I can see why you'd think it was since your brother's in the palace, but his gift isn't the problem, it's the Emperor who's the problem, he's the one who's keeping them locked away. If he wasn't here then maybe Artists would be able to stay with their families."

Redd, whose mouth was open in anticipation to argue closed it and he remained quiet for some time before he finally answered her. "You might be right," he said and Aggie's look of shock made him chuckle. "I don't always take the difficult route to the truth you know," he said running a pale hand through his chestnut hair. Aggie caught sight of the large scar down his left forearm but quickly looked away so he didn't notice her staring. "You're allowed to ask about it, it's okay," he said without looking at her and Aggie blushed.

"I don't need to know," she replied and continued working on the vessel.

"I tried to make myself an Artist," Redd explained and Aggie looked up sharply, her hands frozen mid sculpt.

"You what?"

"I won't go into the details, but after Flicker was taken I tried to make myself an Artist and this was the result." He pointed at the large, ugly scar and Aggie found herself staring in disbelief as her mind raced through ideas of what he had tried to do. She eventually managed to drag her gaze back to the vessel and continued to work on it, throwing all of her energy into it, rather than the desire to pry more into Redd's past.

"Morning Redd," came a deep, gruff voice from the front room where Redd had gone.

"Good morning officer," came Redd's reply. Aggie felt her heart rate increase; she glanced nervously towards the door but continued to work on her vessel, adding fine decoration to the surface.

"I believe it's time for your six monthly check," the officer said and Aggie heard Redd sigh in exasperation.

"It's been five years, are you still unsure whether or not I'm an Artist in disguise?"

"Now Redd, you know how these things work, Artistic ability can manifest at any time and at any age. Your brother is an Artist, so there's a good chance you'll manifest the ability at some point."

"Except it's not a genetic ability," he pointed out.

"Even so," the officer replied.

Redd exhaled in exasperation and held out his hand towards the knife the officer held, "Let's get this over with then." He took the knife from the officer's grasp and pressed the tip against his index finger; a small bubble of blood rose to the surface and he smeared it onto a small mound of clay on one of the workbenches.

Something clattered in the back room and Redd cursed under his breath as the officer's hand went to his firearm, "Who've you got in there?" he asked suspiciously.

"Just my new apprentice," Redd replied as he started to mould and sculpt the clay. "Hope a mouse is okay."

The officer marched towards the door leading to the back room and Redd cursed under his breath a second time. The door was thrust open and the officer pointed his firearm at a terrified looking Aggie. "You!" he said staring at her. "Out here," she trembled as she scurried past him and ran straight to Redd who placed a protective arm round her shoulders.

"Don't worry," he said calmly. "Everything will be okay," he stroked her forearm before the officer grabbed her shoulder and dragged her away. He continued sculpting his small mouse and Aggie stared at him in confusion.

"You!" the officer said again at Aggie. "Who are you?"

"I-I'm Redd's apprentice...Aggie," she stammered and started hugging herself.

"Take the test," the officer said, holding out the knife to her.

Aggie trembled as she clasped her hand round the handle and glanced quickly at Redd who winked discretely at her. She glanced down at her hand and noticed with a flood of relief that he'd managed to put a smear of blood on her palm. She positioned herself over a small mound of clay and in a way that the officer couldn't quite see what she was doing, pretended to press the knife into hand where the smear of blood was.

The officer watched as she pushed the blade into her hand and then smeared a drop of blood onto the clay mound, he was about to step towards her when Redd sighed in exasperation. "Okay I'm ready," he said and the officer walked towards him. Aggie took the opportunity to tie a scrap of fabric round her hand to avoid suspicion.

"Do it," the officer ordered pointing his firearm at Redd's face. Redd breathed on his imperfect mouse and waited. As expected nothing happened and the officer made a note in a small pocket notebook. He turned back to Aggie as soon as he was convinced the mouse wasn't coming to life and saw she'd also quickly sculpted a small mouse. "Now you," he demanded.

Aggie took a deep breath and tried to slow her hammering heart, then she exhaled. To her relief no wisps of coloured smoke left her mouth and the small, sculpted creature failed to come to life. Several seconds later the officer seemed satisfied and made another note in his pocket book before turning back to Redd.

"Next time there's a change at your place of business we expect to be informed immediately." Redd opened his mouth to reply but the officer swept out before he had chance.

Aggie let out a sigh of relief and collapsed to the ground, "Thank you," she said looking up at him.

"Don't mention it," he replied letting out his own relived breath.

"Sounds like a close call," Wolf called from one of the back rooms as Aggie continued to set up the tables and chairs in the pub.

"I thought we'd been found out," she admitted as she began giving the tables a quick wipe, then she corrected herself. "Well actually I thought *I'd* been found out."

"That was quick thinking on Redd's part," Wolf said, entering the main room while wiping his hands on his apron.

She nodded in agreement, "It it hadn't been for him I'd probably be in the palace right now. I know that's ultimately what we want but-"

"But not quite yet," Wolf finished as he unbolted the front door and opened it to let the cool spring air circulate. Aggie started to light the fire while Wolf busied himself behind the counter.

"I wonder when we'll next hear from Flora," She said as the fire crackled and began to lick greedily at the paper and sticks. Wolf started a reply but never finished as several officers walked into the building and began to look around.

"Evening officers, what can I get you?" Wolf asked in a slightly strained voice.

One of the officers eyed him suspiciously before walking towards the counter, "Do you own this establishment?" he asked in a nasal voice as he wiped his greasy black hair from his sallow face.

"Aye, that I do," Wolf said calmly. Aggie noticed the same officer she'd met earlier and began to move slowly towards the back rooms.

The sudden movement caught the sallow faced officers attention and he turned his hawk eyes on her; she froze, "Who are you?"

Aggie opened her mouth to reply but no sound came out; Wolf came to her rescue, "She's my niece," he said quickly and Aggie clamped her mouth shut in order to hide her surprise. Her heart began to pound and she hoped that the officer she'd met earlier didn't recognise her.

"I know you," he said suddenly and her heart sank, she noticed Wolf stiffen but he didn't move or speak.

The sallow faced officer turned to his comrade, "How do you know her? Who is she?"

The officer pulled out his pocket notebook and flipped to the right page, "Her name is Aggie, she's an artisan's apprentice, she tested clean."

The sallow faced man stared at her again with violent intensity, then finally turned back to Wolf, "I've been hearing rumours about this place," he said and began to walk round the large front room. "Some patrons of yours think there's something underhand going on." Wolf stiffened again but didn't say anything so the sallow faced officer continued. "They think you're selling on the black market, but we think that maybe your hiding some Artists."

Aggie stifled a gasp but Wolf remained neutral, his posture now relaxed, he folded his arms and eyed the officers with dislike, "This is because of my background isn't it?"

The sallow faced officer grinned, which only made his features become more distasteful. "There have been reports of secret meetings, and some of your patrons claim to have seen people slip in and out of your establishment after hours."

Aggie felt her heart race, her mouth was dry and her palms suddenly felt clammy; Wolf remained impassive. "I've a friend who often stays past closing, that's no secret, and once we're done talking he slips out the back to avoid causing a disturbance. I hardly see that as breaking the law."

"I think we might need to search the premises, just to be sure, and unless you want a repeat of what happened to your wife, I suggest you both stay out of our way."

Wolf clenched his fists but didn't move from his position behind the bar as the officers began unnecessarily overturning tables and chairs in the main room. Aggie, suddenly caught off guard by the commotion cowered next to the fireplace until they had passed her, then she scurried over to Wolf who put a protective arm round her.

"Don't worry, we'll be okay."

"But Wolf they're destroying the place."

"I know Aggie, I know."

"Why are they doing this? You've not done anything wrong!"

Wolf smiled down at her as several of the officers stomped up the stairs, "Haven't I? Technically I am hiding an Artist," he whispered.

"Yes but they don't know that," she whispered back.

"No lass, but this is a warning, and unless we're more careful with our meetings, things might get a lot worse." Redd entered at that moment and on seeing the destruction looked around for some sort of weapon. "It's okay Redd, we're fine."

He looked towards the ceiling where loud crashing noises were emanating, "What's going on?" he asked as he made his way across the debris strewn floor.

"We've had a visit from some officers," Wolf explained and Redd's eyes widened as he stared at them. "It's okay, they don't actually know anything, but some of my apparently disloyal patrons have been spreading rumours."

"What are they doing up there?" Redd asked, setting a chair back into its rightful position so he could sit down.

"Throwing furniture around by the sounds of it," Wolf sighed. "We better hope we can move forward with our plans soon, or things could get very tricky round here."

Redd nodded, "I wish we could get word to Flora, it might be better to try and meet at the workshop from now on, this place clearly isn't safe anymore."

"I'm not sure anywhere is going to be safe for us soon," Wolf sighed.

"Couldn't we leave a note at her house?" Aggie asked tentatively. "Like she did with me?"

Wolf and Redd fell silent for a few minutes and all that could be heard was the crashing and clattering upstairs. "We could try it," Redd replied with a nod. "I'll go tonight, they'll probably keep some officers lurking around to keep an eye on you two."

Wolf nodded, "You'd best leave now before they come back down, it's best if they don't know we're associated with one another. One of them already recognised Aggie, we don't want them recognising you too."

Redd nodded and got to his feet, "I'll see you both tomorrow," he swept out of the pub quickly and seconds after he'd left, one of the officers re-entered the main room, followed quickly by the others.

"Looks clean," the sallow faced man said as he walked past Wolf towards the open door. He stopped suddenly and stared at the chair Redd had been sitting on. "Who's been here?" he asked sharply.

"No one," Aggie replied in a clearly wavering voice and Wolf got ready to come to her rescue. "I was unsettled by your arrival and I needed to sit down but when I heard you coming down the stairs I ran back to my uncle."

The sallow faced man stared at her with such piercing eyes that she was sure his gaze would leave marks on her flesh and Wolf hugged her a little tighter. After what felt like an eternity the officer turned away from them and marched out of the door with his colleagues following quickly behind.

"Quick thinking lass," Wolf said with a sigh and then surveyed the carnage that surrounded them. "I suppose we'd better get this place cleaned up."

Chapter 28

Nilla made her way somewhat nervously down to the fifth floor to begin her weekly audits. It was amazing how much more strict they were with these Artists compared to the ones lower down. But then, considering the work these Artists were doing, she could understand their need for perfection.

She made her way along to the first of the workshop corridors, took a deep breath and walked straight past the opening and along to the fifth corridor. The officers on guard didn't even give her a second look as she walked past them and knocked on the first workroom door.

The room was much like the others she had audited on the first corridor and contained approximately fifteen Artists busily moulding and sculpting various lumps of clay or applying fine detail to their sculptures. Nilla smiled and nodded towards the female teacher at the front of the class and began to scribble notes on her clipboard in order to make her visit look like an official audit.

The teacher walked over to her and Nilla felt her heart pound in her chest, "Good morning," the teacher said in a cool, light voice. "I didn't think we were due to be audited until tomorrow."

"Change of plans," Nilla said in her most authoritative voice. "Several teams require a more watchful eye."

The teacher looked concerned but returned to her desk at the front of the class and Nilla continued making notes. She began walking round, asking the Artists about their workload and examining the items they were currently sculpting. It took all of her effort not to gasp when she saw several human looking limbs strewn across the benches. Instead she took an internal deep breath and smiled at the creators before moving on to the next row of Artists.

The first Artist she came to appeared to be working on a horse's head and Nilla frowned as she made a note on her clipboard. The Artist noticed her expression and looked nervous, "Is there something wrong?" he asked.

Nilla forced a smile, "No, of course not," she replied as calmly as she could. "I'm sure you'll be adding finer detail to your specimen won't you?"

The look on the Artist's face sent a shot of guilt through her, but he nodded slowly, hung his head and carried on with his work. Nilla walked away, hating herself ever so slightly for hurting the feelings of the young Artist but it had been the only way to cover herself.

"Everything looks satisfactory," she said to the teacher, who tried to hide a look of shock.

"Sa-satisfactory?"

"There seems to be a lack of fine detail on several objects," she answered and tried to sound authoritative. Then she had a risky idea. "If this laziness continues the Artists, and yourself will be removed from the offence team."

As she had hoped a look of fear crossed the teacher's face, "Please accept my sincerest apology," she said quickly and got to her feet. "I'll personally check everyone's work and I'll make sure the standards are met."

"See that you do," Nilla replied and left the room. She walked confidently past the officers on guard and back towards the first corridor where she should have been auditing. She headed for one of the central workrooms, took a deep breath to calm the adrenaline currently surging through her veins and knocked loudly.

She entered the now familiar workroom and smiled at Oscar, an elderly man who was almost bald and should really be wearing glasses. He was currently walking round and examining the Artist's work.

"Good morning Nilla," he said pleasantly and his eyes crinkled as he smiled.

"Good morning Oscar, sorry I'm late, I was held up."

"I was beginning to worry," Oscar said, "you're usually so punctual."

"How have the Artist's been this past week? Is everyone performing as expected?"

Oscar nodded then gestured she follow him to the front of the room, "We've had a slight problem with one of the transfers," he explained quietly and Nilla cocked her head in interest. "Harney recently came up from the ground troops and he's finding it difficult to adjust to this area of the work."

"You'd like to transfer him?" Nilla asked, following his train of thought.

Oscar nodded, "I wondered whether he might be better suited to the offence team since he's so used to that line of work and it seems to be his area of interest."

Nilla nodded and made a note on a fresh sheet on her clipboard, *Crafts! This is getting ridiculous, even the teachers know what the teams are. I'm going to have to talk to Perunia. How in the Emperor's name can I do my job properly when I don't even know the whole story!*

"I think I'll start with Harney and see whether he'd be a good fit for the offence team." Oscar nodded and took a seat at his desk as Nilla moved off around the room.

She was back in her office mid-afternoon completing paperwork when a short, sharp knock came at the door and Perunia walked in.

"Good afternoon Perunia," Nilla said with a smile when she looked up from her reports.

"Good afternoon Nilla, you wished to see me?"

Nilla nodded as the plump woman, her hair neatly in a bun, took a seat opposite her, "I have some questions I need answering," she explained and Perunia gave her a look that suggested she should elaborate. "I keep hearing about the offence and defence teams," she paused to see Perunia's reaction but none was given so she continued. "But I've no idea what they are. Today one of the teachers in a workroom I was auditing suggested transferring one of the Artist's to an offence team since he'd be better suited and I had no idea what he was talking about."

"How did you handle the situation?" Perunia asked, touching her immaculately styled blonde hair as if it could possibly have escaped its prison. She failed to display any emotion towards Nilla as she spoke.

"I acted as though I knew what was going on of course," Nilla stated.

Perunia finally smiled, "Good, that's what I'd expect of my team."

When she failed to say more Nilla pressed on, "Perunia please, what are the offence and defence teams?"

"They're nothing for you to concern yourself with at this moment in time," Perunia replied and Nilla sighed in exasperation.

"Then what am I supposed to do about the transfer request?"

"Fill out the application and send it to Mickael, he deals with all transfer requests and will determine whether the Artist is truly better suited to alternative work." Nilla opened her mouth to protest but Perunia rose from her seat and walked towards the door. "Be careful Nilla," Perunia said softly, still facing the door. "The Emperor doesn't care for inquisitive minds." With that she left and Nilla felt a cold chill run down her spine.

Flora was patrolling the grounds in the hopes that she'd run into Flicker or Jackie, she desperately needed to talk to them about her new theory. The more she thought about it and turned over the idea in her mind the more ridiculous it seemed, why on earth would the Emperor use animals to defend the palace? But there was definitely something else going on, she could feel it and she was sure they were close, they would have to be careful.

"Hi Flora," came Jan's familiar deep voice and Flora flinched slightly before turning round with a smile on her face.

"Jan, it's good to see you," she said with only a hint of insincerity. Despite now firmly believing Jan wasn't to be trusted, she still liked him. "Is everything okay?" she asked when Jan began looking at her with a curious expression.

Jan smiled, "I was going to ask you the same thing, you've been patrolling these grounds like you're on some sort of mission. Are you looking for someone?"

Flora smiled back but it was partly forced, "I've got a

few things on my mind," she admitted.

"Anything I can help you with?"

She shook her head, "It's kind of you to ask but I'm okay, I just need to work through a few things."

Jan nodded and they began to patrol together, Flora wished he would leave her alone so she could try and find Flicker and Jackie but he seemed determined to stay by her side. *I wonder if he suspects something.*

"Are you happy here?" Jan asked suddenly and Flora looked visually surprised by the question.

"Of course," she replied trying to regain her composure, "why do you ask?"

"No reason," Jan replied and fell silent for several minutes before speaking again. "We've had problems in the past," he finally said.

"What kind of problems?" she asked a little nervously.

"A few years back we had a new batch of officer transfers, everything seemed fine to begin with but on one of the Emperor's rare visits to survey the Artist's he was attacked by two of the newer officers-"

"What exactly are you implying?" Flora asked coldly as she stopped dead in her tracks and stared at Jan.

"I'm not implying anything," he said coolly. "But I can't deny there are similarities between those conditions and yours."

"Like what?"

"You distance yourself from the other officers, you spend most of your time patrolling alone or talking with the Artists, it's not exactly normal behaviour for an officer."

"You're not exactly best friends with the other officers either," she countered and Jan smiled.

"True," he replied with a sly smile. "Now doesn't

that tell you something?"

Flora stared at him with a mixture of anger and confusion, "I honestly don't know what you're implying Jan but if you've something more to say then I suggest you say it."

Jan's smile fell away and he sighed, "You really need to learn to trust me Flora, only then will you get the answers you're looking for."

He started to walk away from her and she stared after him in confusion, *He does know something,* she thought with slight horror but then her features showed confusion again, *but why didn't he just come right out and say it?* With very little thought to whether she was making the right decision or not, Flora ran to catch up with Jan and grabbed his shoulder.

He turned to stare at her with an unreadable expression on his face, "What?"

"Tell me what you know," she said, her hand still clamped on his shoulder.

He shook his head, "That's not how this works, you need to give me something first, you need to trust me."

She stared into his eyes, trying to read them, trying to see what lay behind them; she took a deep breath, *I really hope I'm making the right decision.* "I'm part of the underground resistance," she almost whispered and her heart raced as she put Redd's plan in jeopardy.

Jan nodded and his faced remained impassive and unreadable, "Why are you here?" he asked. "What can you hope to achieve in here?"

Flora shook her head, "I've already told you more than I should, especially since I still don't know if I can trust you."

He finally smiled, "You can trust me."

"Are you part of the res-"

He shook his head and Flora felt her heart skip a beat, "But I'm not fully in favour of the Emperor either."

She let out a sigh, "So what are you? How do I know I can I trust you?"

"I'm just an officer trying to provide a living for my family, but Flora you're my friend, you're the only officer who's taken an interest in me and my life, and because of that, you can trust me and I promise I'll keep your secret. I still don't know what it is you hope to achieve in here but I promise I won't stop you."

"Will you help?" Flora asked, half hopeful.

Jan paused for some time before replying, "I don't think that's something I can answer while I'm still in the dark, so you'd better think long and hard about how much you're willing to tell me and then I'll give you my answer. But no matter what it is, I still promise I won't interfere with your plans."

She smiled and finally relaxed her grip on Jan's shoulder though her stomach churned with worry about how much he now knew, how much more she should tell him and what it would mean if he betrayed her. She desperately needed to find Jackie and Flicker; this wasn't a decision she could make alone.

Chapter 29

There were raised voices as Nilla made her way closer to the centre of the maze and she wondered whether Jackie and Flicker had been found and were being questioned by the officers. She began to tread carefully, trying to make as little noise as possible when she suddenly realised that she knew another of the voices. Her pace quickened and she no longer worried whether she was audible or not to others.

"What's going on!?" She demanded as she rounded the corner; four sets of eyes fell on her along with four frowns. She panicked immediately when she saw a female officer with cropped, dark brown hair and pale skin standing amongst the others.

"Why in the Emperor's name is he here?" Flicker demanded pointing at a bristling Charlie.

"I'm her husband, I've more right to see her than you!"

"The Crafts you do!" Flicker shot back and drew himself up to his full height.

Nilla positioned herself between them, "For the love of the Emperor will you two be quiet!" she hissed. "What's going on? Is there some sort of problem?" she asked looking at the officer.

"Don't mind her," Jackie replied calmly. "We'd like to know why your husband's here." Nilla remained silent, not willing to reveal anything in front of the unknown officer. Jackie sighed. "It's okay Nilla. Flora knows Flickers brother, now please explain how your husband knows we've been snooping around the palace."

"Because I told him we thought there was something off."

"Crafts! Nilla, how could you be so stupid?!" Flicker yelled as he threw up his arms and stormed away from her.

"Stupid?" Nilla asked folding her arms, "how exactly am I stupid?"

Flicker scoffed loudly and stormed back towards her and Charlie, "How do you know he can be trusted?"

"He's my husband Flicker he-"

"He's been in here for fifteen years Nilla," Jackie said calmly. "And in those fifteen years he's not been your husband, he's been an Artist, and he's been working for the Emperor."

"You've been here far longer," Nilla pointed out. "And you're not fawning over the Emperor. Charlie's my husband and I trust him, he's not told anyone about me has he?" An uncomfortable silence fell and Nilla took that to mean she'd won. "Let's just get this over with shall we."

"I'm not happy talking about this in front of *him*," Flicker spat and Charlie bristled.

"Him?" Nilla's eyes flashed angrily. "What about her?" she jabbed a finger in Flora's direction. "She might claim to know your brother but she's an officer. How can she be trusted?"

"She's proved herself," Flicker said hotly. "She's here to help-"

"Wait!" Flora's sudden outburst silenced them and they turned to stare at her unkindly. "You're Nilla?" Nilla nodded her head and Flora gasped. "I know your daughter, I know Aggie."

Time felt as though it had stopped, she stood frozen, mouth open in shock, staring at Flora as she explained how Aggie had started working by chance in the same pub that her and Redd met in.

"So she's okay?" Nilla whispered.

Flora nodded, "she's being looked after by good friends, they're taking care of her, I promise. She's part of our team now, I'm here to help you as well as Flicker-"

"Help them what?" Charlie interrupted. "Escape?"

Something in his tone of voice made Flora hesitate, "No," she said finally and Charlie deflated. "We're all trying to help figure out what's really going on in here-"

"How can they help from outside?" Charlie asked. "What good can they do?"

"There's more going on outside these walls than you think Charlie," Flora said carefully. "There's probably more that they can do out there than we can do in here." Charlie looked unconvinced but he remained quiet and Flicker turned to Nilla, the hostility finally absent from his hard features.

"Have you uncovered anything new? Anything about the offence and defence teams?"

Nilla shook her head, then nodded it, "I don't know," she finally admitted.

"Tell us what you've found," Jackie said gently.

"I've not been able to find out anything else about the offence and defence teams, no one will tell me anything," she said.

"I tried to do some digging around them too," Flora admitted, then shook her head. "None of the officers seem to have heard anything about them."

Nilla nodded, "The Artist's in the workrooms I audit

know what they are, and they seem to think that I do too but I've asked my superior and she's told me I don't need to worry about them right now." She shrugged and finally took a seat. "I'm not sure what more I can do with regards to them, I don't want to keep asking, I've already been warned once."

"What do you mean?" Flicker asked worriedly.

"Perunia, my superior, she told me the Emperor doesn't like it when people pry."

"That in itself seems suspicious to me," Flicker said. "Why would the Emperor be bothered about someone asking questions unless he's got something to hide?"

"My thoughts exactly," Nilla agreed and silence fell once more.

"Is there anything else?" Flicker asked and Nilla cocked her head to one side in thought.

"No," she said finally. "That's everything."

"I suppose we'd better get ourselves inside then before someone comes looking," Jackie said and she got to her feet, Charlie was already walking towards the gap in the hedge.

"Just a minute," Nilla said and they all stopped, Nilla turned to her husband. "It's okay Charlie, you don't need to stay, I just want to catch up with Jackie and Flicker, it's been a while since we've had chance to gossip." He nodded, then looked to Flora, who smiled at the others and followed him out of the maze.

"What's going on?" Jackie asked.

"I know I said I trusted him but-"

"Your husband was awfully quiet throughout that whole conversation," Flicker said.

"And he seemed a little too eager when he thought we might be trying to escape," Jackie added. Nilla nodded.

"So there's more?" Flicker asked.

"Yes," Nilla admitted. "Though I'd hoped Flora would have been here too."

"Not to worry," came Flora's quiet voice. "Charlie knew the shortcuts out and when I was sure he was out of sight I ran back in."

"So what else have you found?" Flicker asked eagerly.

Nilla shot them a wide grin, "I managed to get into one of the other workrooms and I think you'll like what I found." They waited with baited breath for her to continue, she glanced quickly round and lowered her voice. "Body parts," she finally said.

"What?" they asked in unison.

"They were sculpting body parts, plus a few horse heads."

Her response was met with more puzzled and confused expressions, "Human body parts?" Flora asked.

"Yes," Nilla replied. "The only items the Artist's were working on in that workroom were human body parts and horse's heads."

"What in the Emperor's name are they creating up there?" Flicker asked, turning his eyes to the palace.

"Perhaps I could try to get assigned guard duty down those corridors?" Flora suggested. "I don't know whether I'll learn anything but it's worth a shot."

Jackie nodded, "I think at this point we need to try everything and anything we can," she turned to Nilla. "Is there anything else? Anything at all?"

Nilla shook her head, "I'm sorry, that's all I've been able to find. I know it's not much but without asking someone direct-" she stopped suddenly and the others turned to look at her.

"What is it?" Flora asked, suddenly feeling nervous.

"One of the workrooms I audited today had a young Artist, newly transferred to us but Oscar, the teacher, thought he would be better suited to the offence team."

"Does that mean you're auditing the defence team?" Flora asked.

Nilla nodded, "But that's not what I'm thinking about, I'm thinking about Harney, the Artist," she clarified. "Maybe if I get him on his own after he's been transferred, maybe he'll tell me about the offence team?"

"It could be risky," Flicker said.

"Me simply being here is risky," she pointed out. "I might as well try, I mean, what have I got to lose?"

"Plenty," Jackie said with a sad smile. "But I agree that it's worth a shot."

They were about to leave when Flora stopped them, "I need to run a theory past you," she explained and they all took their seats again. "It might be crazy and if it is then tell me and I'll think no more about it."

"What is it?" Jackie asked.

"I was patrolling the interior corridors the other day when I started thinking about the sculptures."

"What about them?" Flicker asked.

"Well," Flora began and she realised suddenly how nervous she was. "What if they were real?"

The other three stared at her sceptically, "What do you mean real?" Nilla asked.

"I mean, what if they could be made real? What if the Emperor had them created so they could defend the palace in a crisis?"

They sat in thought for some time pondering the idea until Jackie swept it aside without a moment's hesitation, "It's a nice theory," she said with a smile. "But I don't think it's feasible"

"But surely it's possible?" she pressed on.

"I don't think so," Flicker said and Flora looked a little disheartened. "There's no control over where the Artists go, there's nothing to stop them breathing life into them. In fact I would guess at least one Artist would have attempted it over the years."

Flora's shoulders slumped, "You're right, I hadn't even thought about that."

"It was a good theory," he said with a smile.

"It's better than anything we've come up with so far," Jackie agreed.

"I guess it's back to the drawing board then," Flora said with a grim smile.

They dispersed soon after with Flicker, Jackie and Nilla heading back to the palace, while Flora made her way to the gatehouse. It was almost completely dark now and dim lights twinkled around the grounds, illuminating her way. She was walking past the sculpture garden when she heard hushed voices and froze; she was sure she recognised one of them.

Flora began to creep towards the voices and managed to hide herself amongst some shrubbery as she drew nearer. She peered out through a small gap in the leafy bush and stifled a gasp. Charlie was talking to one of the officers. She strained to hear what they were saying but could barely make the words out.

"...trust me they're up to something..." she managed to hear Charlie say.

"...fifth floor?" The officer asked and Flora saw Charlie nod. *Thank the Emperor Nilla sent him away when she did,* Flora thought but then her blood ran ice cold as she managed to grasp a few more muffled words.

"...an officer helping them..."

"Crafts!" Flora cursed under her breath.

"I think she's new," she heard Charlie finally say and the officer facing him smiled.

"I know just the one," Flora heard, clear as day, then the officer left the area and Charlie scurried off in the opposite direction. She remained where she was for several minutes, cursing internally and wondering whether she'd be transferred back into the city. *If they transfer me, Flicker and the others will know there's a leak, they'll have to know it's Charlie and the officers' won't get any more information.*

"What should I do?" she whispered to herself. "Should I confront Charlie? Or pretend I know nothing?" She sighed under her breath and glanced around at her surroundings which were now well and truly deserted. She clambered to her feet, backtracked until she was out of the sculpture garden and decided to patrol the grounds in the opposite direction to the gatehouse.

She was desperate to talk to Flicker and Jackie but she knew they wouldn't be meeting again for another few days since tomorrow she would be back in the city.

"It'll be at least another four days until I'll see them again and can tell them what I saw," she muttered to herself as she walked in the cool night air. "For the love of the Emperor, don't let that weasel gain the upper hand."

Chapter 30

The key turned and clicked in the lock of Flora's home and she sighed internally as she entered the quiet, small building on the outskirts of the city. It seemed unnaturally quiet inside and for the first time she felt uneasy in her own home. She stepped carefully inside, turned on the lights and noticed several letters on the floor by the door; she collected them and took them into the small living room.

Once the fire was blazing happily, Flora took a seat in a very battered, pale green armchair and opened the first letter who's handwriting she didn't recognise. She glanced quickly at the signature and saw it was from Jan:

> *Flora,*
>
> *You need to be careful, some of the officers are suspicious. I don't know how important your task is, but if you can lay low for a few weeks then I would. I know whatever you're doing includes Flicker and Jackie, if I were you, I'd stay away from them for a while until the heat cools. They're going to be keeping a close eye on you from now on and there's only so much I can do to help.*
>
> *Jan*

Flora sighed loudly, "I suppose I should have expected something like this to happen," she said to no one in particular before opening the second letter. She skimmed the contents but it was simply her new rota for the next few weeks; there were a few odd changes to her patrol partners and she guessed this was linked to the other officers suspicion towards her.

The third letter was from Redd, she could tell that handwriting anywhere:

Flora,

There's been some trouble at The Fisherman's Fancy. Everyone's okay but Wolf is under suspicion of sympathising with the Artists. The officers have had reports of people coming and going in the middle of the night and they think he's helping Artists hide and escape. They ransacked the pub and I think they'll probably watch it from now on. It's not safe to meet there anymore. If you can, come along to my workshop on the second night of your leave, we'll be waiting.

Redd

"It looks like events are beginning to escalate," she said quietly while continuing to look at the familiar scrawl of Redd's handwriting. She was about to make herself something warm to drink when a quick tap at the door made her freeze. She remained immobile for several long seconds until she became frustrated with herself. "This is ridiculous, I'm in my own home and I'm alone, it doesn't matter who's at the door, I'm the one with the authority not them." Despite this confident sounding outburst, she threw the two letters on the fire before walking to the front door.

Jan looked worried as she opened the door and he pushed his way inside quickly before she could protest. "They've taken us off patrol together."

"I know," she replied. "I've just seen the new rota, and your letter."

247

"I would have told you in person, but honestly I don't know if they're following me too and I've got to think of my family."

"I know," she suddenly looked concerned. "Should you be here now? Is it safe?"

Jan shrugged, "I don't think I was followed but Flora, they're really not happy with you, what on earth are you planning?"

"We're not really planning anything," Flora admitted. "Not at the moment anyway."

"Flora, you're going to have to tell me everything, I need to know what I've inadvertently gotten myself into."

"I don't know Jan," she replied, biting her lip. "Surely the less you know the better? What if they try to get information from you?"

"Flora please," Jan had a pleading look in his eyes. "I need to know what I'm dealing with here."

She sighed, slumped back into the faded armchair and gestured for Jan to do the same in its twin opposite. "Originally I came into the palace to try and break Flicker out."

"Flora are you mad? No one can escape the palace, you should know that."

"No one can escape because they only way out is guarded, but if one of the guards holds a key to the front door…"

Jan shook his head, "You're playing with fire you know."

"I know."

"Wait," Jan suddenly looked puzzled. "If you're goal is to break Flicker out, then why haven't you done it already? I'm no expert but surely acting fast would have been to your advantage? What's changed?"

"Do you remember when I asked you about offence

and defence teams?" Jan nodded but remained silent. "Well we think there's something more going on and they're part of it."

"What are they?"

She shook her head, "That's just it, we don't know."

"Then how do you know there's something strange going on?"

"Because one of the administration staff has seen the Artists on the fifth floor sculpting body parts."

For several minutes the gentle crackle of the fire was the only sound until Jan finally found his voice, "Body parts? As in human?"

Flora nodded.

"Why on earth are the Artists sculpting human body parts?"

"That's exactly the question we're asking."

Silence fell again until the lengthening of the shadows snapped Jan out of his thoughts, he got quickly to his feet. "I should be going, Laenaia will wonder where I am."

"Jan you can't tell anyone any of this, not even your wife, you know that don't you?"

He nodded, "I told you before you can trust me and I meant it, whatever happens, I'll keep your secret." They walked to the door and Jan hesitated before giving Flora a one armed hug. "Look after yourself Flora, and watch your back, I'll see you in a few days." Flora nodded and in one swift movement, he had been swallowed by the night.

Flora hoped she had made it to Redd's workshop unseen and that they too hadn't been followed. She was relieved to see her three friends unharmed and sitting huddled in the back room sipping warm tea.

"I hope you've saved some for me," she said quietly.

Aggie snapped her head up and a wide grin spread across her face, "Flora!" she said in as loud a voice as she dared. "You made it!" The young girl ran over and hugged Flora tightly and the older woman smiled fondly at her.

"We were worried you might not make it," Redd said with a grimace.

"So was I," she admitted taking a seat and sipping the warm, soothing drink that was placed in front of her. "Events aren't panning out quite as we'd hoped in the palace," she admitted.

"What's happened?" Wolf asked.

"It seems that Flicker and Nilla aren't quite ready to leave yet."

Redd's mouth hung open in astonishment, "They're what?"

Flora suddenly turned to Aggie who had a hurt look on her face, "Your mother misses you very much Aggie, she wanted me to tell you that she's thinking about you every day."

"Then why doesn't she want to come home?" Aggie asked with a tremble in her voice.

"What's going on Flora?" Redd asked firmly.

She explained, once again the events that had taken place in the palace, that they thought there might be something more sinister going on, that there were offence and defence teams and that Nilla had discovered the Artist's were sculpting body parts.

"Body parts?" Redd asked incredulously.

"As in human?" Aggie asked.

Flora nodded, "They want to stay and find out what's happening, they're worried something terrible is going to happen and I'm inclined to agree." She glanced briefly at Aggie, then took a deep breath. "There's something else."

"What is it?" Wolf asked.

"You're probably not going to like it," she said looking at Aggie.

"I can handle it," Aggie replied, trying to sound confident.

"I'm not so sure," Flora admitted but one look from Redd made her continue. "I've met your father-"

"What?!" Aggie said excitedly. "What's he like? Has my mother seen him? Has he asked about me?"

Flora held up a hand and Aggie managed to silence herself, "Aggie…I don't know how to tell you this but…"

"What?" Aggie asked with a sudden sense of dread. "Is he dead?"

Flora shook her head, "No, nothing like that, but…I-I don't think we can trust him."

"What do you mean?" Aggie asked.

"I think he's working for the officers, I saw him talking to one of them, I think he was telling them about the conversation we'd just had with your mother and-"

"You think?" Aggie frowned. "You've got no proof then?"

"Well no but-"

"If you've got no proof then you could have misunderstood, you could have misheard."

"Aggie I don't think I-"

"You have no proof," Aggie reiterated.

She closed her mouth and looked to Redd and Wolf for support, she was grateful when Wolf changed the subject.

"From what you're saying, it seems like perhaps we should fast forward our plans."

"Are you saying we should get into the palace sooner?" Redd asked.

Wolf nodded, "If we're there, maybe we can help unravel this mystery faster, then we can all get the Crafts out of the city once and for all!"

"I agree, we need you in there and at this moment in time I think we'd all be safer."

"For the love of the Emperor!" Redd said loudly and the others looked at him with puzzled expressions but he was grinning. "Couldn't you have come up with this revelation several days ago?"

"What's wrong?" Flora asked.

"Redd was tested the other day," Aggie explained a little coldly. "They won't test him again until next month."

"Don't you worry about that," Flora said with a smile, "I'll handle everything and maybe this will help to get the other officers off my back. Just make sure you've got both Aggie's blood and Aggie close to you over the next few days."

"In there, I saw him!" Redd heard Flora's voice, unusually hard and cold as he put the finishing touches to a clients order two days later. He froze and glanced at Aggie who had just emerged from the back room.

"I think I'm about to get taken," he said and Aggie nodded staying close to him. They'd have to be careful, if they didn't get it right the officers would see it was Aggie who was the Artist instead of Redd.

"That's him!" Redd turned to look at Flora and an unknown male officer standing in the large, open doorway of his workshop.

"Can I help you?"

"You need to be tested," the unknown officer said curtly and pulled out a thin dagger.

Redd shot them a smile and tried to remain steady, "I

think if you check your records you'll see that I was tested several days ago and I was found to be clean."

"We know," Flora said in her coldest voice. "Sarl and I were tipped off earlier that you've found a way to cheat."

Redd tried his best to look shocked and surprised, then opened his mouth to speak but before he got the chance Sarl spoke. "You girl, you'll be tested again too." Aggie nodded, trembling a little with fear; they had to get this right.

Sarl held out the thin knife to Redd who took it and sliced into his finger, handed the knife back to the officer and turned to smear blood onto a small pile of clay.

"Wait!" Sarl said; Flora and Aggie held their breath as Redd turned slowly to face him.

"What?" he asked as a small drop of blood slid off his finger and fell to the ground.

"I want to check it's your blood going into that clay."

Redd cursed under his breath but did as Sarl demanded before kneading the clay to allow the blood to mingle. Seemingly satisfied the officer leant back against one of the benches and in that moment, while still kneading, Redd slipped the vial of Aggie's blood from his pocket and allowed several drops to fall onto the surface of the clay.

It didn't take him long to sculpt a small rabbit from the clay in front of him and as the others watched and Aggie carefully positioned herself to the side of Redd. They both took a deep breath and exhaled. Because Aggie had managed to obscure herself from Sarl's view, it looked as though Redd had given the breath of life.

For a long few seconds nothing happened, then the clay began to change from a slate grey to a pale brown flecked with white. The ears and nose began to twitch as the rest of the body solidified and stiffened. The once smooth surface of the clay began to puff out as clumps of fur formed and softened. The rabbit was far from perfect having been made quickly but it was good enough. Sarl killed it swiftly before taking out a pair of cuffs, he edged towards Redd while Flora trained her weapon on him.

"Crafts!" Redd said with a grin, "I guess you finally caught me."

Sarl slapped the cuffs on Redd's wrists and shoved him towards the front door, "Check the girl while I sort this one," he snapped at Flora who nodded immediately and headed towards Aggie.

"It worked?" Aggie asked excitedly and Flora nodded.

"Redd will be taken straight to the palace for an induction. They'll come for you and Wolf later tonight, stay safe and I'll see you soon." She gave Aggie a quick squeeze and left to accompany Sarl back to the main headquarters. Hopefully word would spread that she'd been involved and the officers in the palace would back off.

Aggie remained where she was for at least half an hour, then she locked up the workshop and headed quickly to The Fisherman's Fancy to warn Wolf. She had barely explained to him what had happened when the officers burst in and Aggie noticed with slight horror that it was the sallow faced man.

"Well, well, well," he said as he walked slowly towards a scowling Wolf. "Seems as though I was right about you all along, you *are* harbouring Artist's." Wolf continued to scowl but remained silent. "Get them both tested," he said to a couple of officers behind him.

Wolf, after secretly adding a few drops of Aggie's blood to the ink, began to sketch an incredibly awkward sparrow. It was one of the easier animals that Aggie had taught him to create and the only one he felt even remotely confident trying.

Aggie had managed to place herself close to Wolf without the officers looking too concerned. She watched as he clumsily sketched the sparrow, then opened his mouth to exhale. Aggie's lips barely moved as she took a breath and exhaled at the same time. Pale yellow mist tumbled from her mouth but looked to have come from him.

The parchment began to quiver and slowly, as if unaware of the several pairs of eyes that watched it, hawk like. A small, feathery body began to rise up out of the parchment. It took a few minutes for the sparrow to have completely extracted itself from the sheaf of paper and once it had, it stood, ruffling its feathers on a now aged piece of parchment.

The sallow faced man clamped a pair of cuffs round Wolf's wrists immediately and grinned devilishly at him. "You've no idea how happy this makes me." He turned quickly to Aggie. "Now you."

She was pushed towards another bottle of ink and a knife was thrust into her hands. She took a deep breath, feeling unnecessarily worried; the hard part was over, she was the only Artist, she wouldn't have a problem getting herself caught. It didn't take her long to sketch a small hedgehog and it had been so long since she'd drawn anything that she almost forgot about the officers surrounding her. She became lost in adding detail; she could have spent hours working on the drawing but eventually a hand grabbed her roughly and dragged her away from her illustration.

"You're done," he said with a growl.

Aggie nodded, took a deep breath and exhaled,

allowing the pale yellow wisps of mist to twirl around the parchment. The paper began to quiver, just like before and a small, spiked body crawled out of the paper and started to twitch its nose. It looked quickly around, then curled up into a small spiked ball.

Neither animal was allowed to survive for long.

Aggie had a pair of cuffs placed round her wrists and the sallow faced man's grin was even larger, "Such a good haul today," he said gleefully to himself. "I'll be well rewarded for this."

He marched out of The Fisherman's Fancy, upending one of the tables as he went, while Wolf and Aggie were roughly manhandled towards a waiting transport vehicle, which would take them directly to the palace. Unknown to the officers surrounding them, they were smiling.

Chapter 31

"I think we need to get into those rooms," Flicker said as he threw a small pebble into the lake; several swans and a lone duck eyed him.

"It didn't exactly go according to plan the first time we did it," Jackie pointed out and Flicker grinned.

"I think it's safe to say we've got a bit more of an idea what we're looking for now, we'll be more efficient."

"We need to keep Nilla out if it," Jackie said pointedly. "If we fail or get caught then I want to know that someone else can keep looking."

Flicker nodded in agreement, "Can you get some more kindling?" he asked with a mischievous grin.

"What do you think?" she replied with an equally playful smile on her face.

Flicker waited on the 5th floor in the shadows that night and almost held his breath until he heard the yells of several officers' two floors below. He took a deep breath, took out a small bottle of oil and coated a pair of red curtains, then he grabbed a match and set them alight. The oil caught fiercely and it wasn't long until the curtains were fully ablaze and it was trying to spread to the paintings that adorned the walls. He felt a small pang of guilt as the flames finally made the leap onto a wooden frame, then turned and fled down the corridor.

He scrambled behind another set of curtains as he

heard more shouts and yells and several pairs of feet thundered past him towards the corridor he'd just come from. *How in the Emperor's name have they reached here so quickly?* He thought as he sprinted from his cover towards the corridors filled with workshops.

Jackie was waiting for him.

"You took your time," she mused as he drew up beside her breathing heavily.

"Let's just get this over with before the guards get back," Flicker said and they made their way to the sixth corridor. Flicker picked the lock of the first room and they slipped inside; Jackie flicked on the lights and the room was suddenly bathed in a warm, soothing glow.

"It doesn't look promising at first glance," Jackie noted and Flicker's face showed he agreed.

"Let's just have a good look round, you never know what we might find."

They began to search through cupboards and drawers for anything that might provide a clue as to what was being produced there but all they found were sculpting supplies and large quantities of clay. After a thorough search of the workroom they had turned up empty handed.

Flicker exhaled loudly in frustration as he leant against the wall behind the desk, he banged his head backwards and froze. Jackie stared at him, then looked past him to the wall he was leaning against. Flicker tapped his head against the wall again and they both heard the same hollow sound.

"This wall should be solid," Flicker said quietly.

Jackie nodded and walked towards him, "Start looking, there's got to be something here."

It was Jackie who found the concealed handle that proved there was a door; miraculously it was unlocked.

Jackie turned the handle and tentatively pushed the door away from her; it swung open effortlessly and they held their breath as they entered a small, dark box of a room.

"I'm not sure what I was expecting," Flicker said as he felt his heart sank. "But it definitely wasn't this."

Jackie had found a light switch and now they were looking upon several more boxes of supplies and a handful of animal statues that had yet to be fired.

"I really thought this was it Flick," Jackie said with a sigh as they left the box room and made their way to the workroom door. Flicker put his ear to the door and listened intently but heard nothing on the other side. They slipped back out of the workroom and the door clicked behind them, locking itself.

"We'd better get out of here before we get caught," Flicker said as they emerged from the corridor to find the area still empty. "We'll talk about this tomorrow and hopefully we'll be able to talk to Nilla."

The pair waited for Nilla just before dusk in the sculpture garden, it was far more risky that she'd be seen but they'd started to wonder how safe and secure the maze was. Neither Flicker or Jackie trusted Charlie and it almost seemed as though being out in the open was more private than hiding in the maze.

"Sorry I'm late," she said as she took a seat on the bench next to Jackie.

The pair looked at her quizzically; she was wearing what looked like a long robe and had a thin scarf wrapped round her head. "What exactly are you wearing?" Flicker asked.

"I'm trying not to get noticed," Nilla said, glancing around.

"So you chose to wear an outfit that will make you

stand out?" Jackie asked slowly, Nilla scowled, grabbed the scarf and pulled the robe up over her head. She wore plain clothes underneath.

"That's far less conspicuous," Flicker said with a nod.

Nilla scowled again, "I've not been able to find out anything else I'm afraid," she admitted with a disheartened tone.

"Neither have-" Flicker began but Jackie interrupted.

"We broke into one of the workrooms," she said.

Nilla looked shocked, "You what?"

"We wanted to have a good look around," Jackie said.

"We wanted to see for ourselves the human body parts," Flicker clarified.

"Don't you trust me?" Nilla asked, suddenly feeling hurt.

"Of course we do," Jackie said giving Flicker a nudge in the ribs. "We thought that if we had a rummage and saw them with our own eyes that we might be able to come up with a theory."

"And did you?" Nilla asked hopefully.

Flicker shook his head, "There wasn't anything there."

"What do you mean?"

"He means what he says," Jackie said. "We couldn't find anything. Whatever they're making during the day, it's not there at night."

"That's not possible," Nilla said in disbelief. "I saw them, they were there!"

"We don't doubt you," Jackie said, patting her arm reassuringly. "But maybe they're storing them somewhere else overnight, maybe there's another store room further along or at the end of the corridor."

"We didn't have that long to look," Flicker admitted. "We could easily have missed something."

Nilla shook her head, "No, I'm sure you were as thorough as you could be, Jackie's probably right, they must store everything somewhere else, probably to keep it cool so-"

"Of course!" Jackie said. "The basement!"

"The what?" Nilla asked.

"The basement, it's where sculptures are stored before they're fired, I'd almost forgotten it existed."

"So what you're saying is we need to check the basement?" Flicker asked.

"It's worth a shot," Jackie said with a grin. "We've not got much else to go on now have we?"

"Why on earth are we breaking into the classrooms when we want to be in the basement?" Flicker asked as he picked the lock to Jackie's classroom.

"We might need a distraction," she replied as Flicker finally heard a, 'click' and the door opened. Jackie strode past him and into her classroom towards the large sink and placed the plug in the hole.

"You're going to flood your own classroom?" Nilla asked.

Jackie nodded, "I doubt they'll suspect me, I've played by the rules for far too long."

"What about me?" Flicker said nervously. "There are still those who don't believe I've really changed."

"To be fair to them, you haven't," Jackie said with a chuckle. "But they also know I'm one of the few friends you've got, what would you gain from flooding my classroom?"

"She's got a point," Nilla said as Jackie turned on the taps and allowed the sink to begin filling with water.

"We'd better get down to the basement," Jackie said as she strode past Flicker once again and out of the door.

Flicker sighed, "I'm really not sure any of this was needed Jack," he said as he glanced over his shoulder at the rapidly filling sink.

"Quite possibly not," Jackie replied.

"Then why bother?" Nilla asked with confusion.

"Because I've played by the rules for far too long."

Flicker and Nilla raced after her, not bothering to close the classroom door behind them. They made their way silently down three flights of stairs until they reached the basement; they'd been lucky that they hadn't yet met any of the officers. Nilla felt incredibly nervous and fidgeted continuously with her hands.

The basement was simplistic; stone corridors with plain wooden doors and large padlocks keeping them secure.

"Any idea which one to choose?" Flicker asked with a grimace.

"I suggest we start with the closest and work our way along," Nilla said with a shrug.

"You do know picking locks isn't easy right?" Flicker said with underlying annoyance as he approached the first door.

"Oh hush Flick, just get on with it," Jackie said as she glanced back up the stone steps towards the ground floor.

Flicker worked as quickly as the locks and his limited skills would allow. He could feel the others' eyes on him and he slipped up several times as a result. He cursed softly under his breath, trying to get the pins to line up when footsteps above them made him freeze. Jackie peered round the corner and up the stairs but it was empty. The footsteps died away and Nilla heaved a sigh of relief.

"Must have been an officer on patrol," Jackie said quietly, her cracked voice sounding even more so.

"How are you doing over there?" Nilla asked, trying not to sound too anxious.

"Almost got it," Flicker mumbled as the last pin finally clicked into place and the lock sprang open.

They hurried into the first storage room and Nilla fumbled for the light switch. Bright light illuminated a large quantity of clay animals, clearly in the process of drying. Their hearts sank collectively but Jackie put on a determined expression.

"Might as well give this place a good searching," she said as she started to weave between the animals. "Took long enough to get in."

"You two stay in here, I might as well get started on the next room," Flicker said with a sigh.

"Try several doors down," Nilla suggested. "I've a feeling the next few will mimic this one."

Flicker nodded and left the two women to search of the storage room. There seemed to be a theme running through the room, with the majority of the animals consisting of predatory birds. There were a few other wild mammals thrown in for good measure but Nilla felt as though it must mean something.

"Jackie," she whispered and the other woman looked over to her. "Just suppose the clay that was used for these animals already had Artist blood in it," Jackie opened her mouth to speak but Nilla pressed on. "Just suppose," she said again with more emphasis and Jackie closed her mouth. "What would happen if an Artist, any Artist gave the breath of life?"

Jackie was silent for some time before she answered, "They would come to life," she said slowly. "But Nilla-"

"Do it," Nilla interrupted.

Jackie stared at her with wide eyes, "You want me to what?"

"Give the breath of life." Jackie shook her head. "Why not?" Nilla asked, folding her arms in annoyance.

"Let's say you're right," Jackie said as she weaved between the animals to get closer to Nilla. "And just for the record I don't think that you are, but for arguments sake let's say you are, what do you think would happen if I gave the breath of life right now?"

"The animals in this room would come to life."

"And what about all of the other rooms down here?" Jackie asked pointedly and Nilla frowned. "You see in all my time here I've never known the Emperor to experiment with an Artist's range. I could breathe and all of these animals could come to life, and whatever is in the next room could come to life and-"

"But surely if Artist's had a greater range than initially thought any Artist who breathed would bring everything to life in ever part of the palace? It's not as if the officers can stop you."

"Which is why I don't think anything in the palace contains Artist blood, except for during some of the audits, and the items being created on the 5th floor."

Nilla shook her head, "But then where are they being stored?"

"Hopefully down here-"

"But that doesn't make sense," Nilla protested.

"I know," Jackie said with a small smile.

Flicker appeared at that moment in the doorway, "I've made it into another of the rooms and I think you'll want to come and see this one."

"Body parts?" they asked in unison.

Flicker shook his head, "Afraid not, but it's worth a

look anyway.

They left the first room, making sure to place the padlock back in position before moving three rooms down. The next room they entered was nothing like the first, it was far larger for one thing and it housed some very different items.

"Are those what I think they are?" Nilla asked as she manoeuvred her way around a horse.

Flicker nodded, "The same firearms used by the officers, plus a few larger looking specimens."

"What are they doing down here?" Nilla asked in awe.

"More importantly," Jackie said as she looked around the room. "What are they doing in a room full of horses and wolves?"

Nilla shook her head, "This doesn't make any sense."

They suddenly heard several yells on the floor above and Jackie shot the other two a grin, "I guess that means they've found the leak."

"I'm not sure we should risk spending any more time down here," Nilla said nervously.

Flicker had a look of concentration on his face, then suddenly looked up towards the others, "I don't think this is it."

"You don't think this is what?" Nilla asked.

"I don't think this is the real basement, I think it's a decoy."

"A what?" Jackie asked, baffled.

"I think there's a sub-basement and I think there are things being stored here with Artist blood in them, but I don't think they're here, I think they're further underground where out power can't reach."

Jackie shook her head, "Flicker do you know how you sound right now?"

"Jackie look at this animal," he said while pointing to one of the wolves. "Tell me what you see."

Jackie walked over to where he stood and began to examine the wolf; Nilla joined them and also began looking at it.

"There's no fine detail," Nilla said with shock in her voice before Jackie had finished looking. "If this animal were to become real it wouldn't act the right way, yes it would be close but it wouldn't be perfect."

Flicker nodded, "It's the same with the horses."

"What about the weapons?" Jackie asked.

"I couldn't say, I don't know enough about them."

"A sub-basement you say," Jackie said with a grin. "The plot thickens."

Chapter 32

The workshops would be in full swing when Nilla arrived but she'd wanted it that way so no one would notice what she was doing. Harney's transfer had been granted and Nilla had volunteered to escort him from his old workshop to his new one. Perunia, clearly not sensing any foul play welcomed the gesture and provided Nilla with the details of the new workshop.

She had meant to arrive first thing, when the Artist's were starting the day's work so Harney could become accustomed to how his new workshop was run, but that would leave very little time for talking. She had allowed herself to get distracted that morning, which meant the Artist's would now be completely focused on their work and the guarding officers would have relaxed.

She knocked loudly on the workshop door and walked in, smiling at Oscar as she made her way to Harney. The young man looked up and she could tell he was nervous.

"Don't worry," she said in as soothing a voice as possible. "You're just being transferred."

"To the offence team?" Harney asked, suddenly perking up.

Nilla nodded, "If you want to follow me, I'll take you to your new workshop."

Harney stood quickly, brushed himself down and

smoothed his short blonde hair; Nilla walked to Oscar and explained what was happening.

"You'll have another Artist brought to you in the next few days to help even out the work."

"Thank the Emperor," Oscar said in relief. "You've no idea how hard it's getting to fill our quotas."

Nilla looked confused, "Everything seemed fine in the last few audits."

Oscar grimaced, "I may have bent the truth a little."

"What?!"

Oscar frowned, "The quotas have been increased recently, the Emperor demands more from us but doesn't increase our numbers. We can only achieve so much and sometimes standards start to slip. Anything that doesn't pass the control checks won't be used and then we're under even more pressure-"

"And so the cycle continues," Nilla finished with concern, Oscar nodded. "Let me have a talk with Perunia, there might be something we can do, perhaps we can increase the class numbers."

"Thank you Nilla," Oscar said as Harney joined them.

"Okay," she said, turning from Oscar. "Let's go."

They left the workshop but instead of turning right and heading to the main corridor, where the entrances to the others were, she turned left and Harney could do nothing else but follow.

"I thought you were taking me to my new workshop," Harney said nervously.

"I will," she said as they reached the end of the corridor and turned left towards a stairwell, there she paused and turned to the young man who looked nervous and fidgeted constantly.

"Have I don't something wrong?" Harney asked.

Nilla shook her head, "Harney I need your help with something." He looked at her expectantly and she took a deep breath, "I need you to tell me about the offence and defence teams."

Harney looked at her in confusion and then with fear, "Is this some kind of test?" he asked while glancing round.

"No Harney, this isn't any sort of test, I just need you to answer me truthfully."

"I don't understand, shouldn't you know?"

Nilla sighed in exasperation, "You would think so wouldn't you but apparently I'm one of the few that hasn't been privy to that information yet."

Harney shifted uncomfortably, "I'm sorry Nilla but I don't think I feel comfortable telling y-"

"Let me put it this way," Nilla interrupted and she took a step towards the fidgeting man. "I still have a lot of influence and if I decide the offence team, whatever that may be, isn't the right fit for you, then you'll go back to making wooden planks, do you understand?"

Harney stared at her with a mixture of disbelief and fear. It wasn't strictly true, she didn't think she had any pull over who went where, but Harney didn't know that, she just had to make him believe she was telling the truth.

Finally he nodded and cleared his throat nervously, "The defence team create resources for the city."

Nilla nodded, "I suspected as much."

"The offence team," Harney began and then he paused and seemed reluctant to continue, Nilla shot him a look and he cleared his throat again. "The offence team are creating an army."

"They're what?" she asked, unable to keep her composure.

"They're…creating an army," Harney repeated.

"Ready for when the other cities invade."

Nilla shook her head in disbelief, *An invasion? Can that really be the case? I know it's been rumoured but could it really happen?*

"When were you told this?"

"Just before I was moved up to these floors, I and a few others were briefed by one of the administration team, they wanted us to know we were providing valuable assistance."

Nilla nodded and gestured for Harney to follow her as she walked back towards the corridor they'd left. She dropped him off at his new workshop and threatened him into keeping silent. She didn't like pretending to be cruel, but she knew it was the only way to stop him talking and to keep herself from getting into trouble.

When the lunch hour arrived, Nilla weaved her way round the dining room until she found Oscar. The older man was sitting by himself and seemed to be enjoying a plate piled high with the dish of the day.

"Do you mind if I join you?" she asked and Oscar shook his head. "I just wanted to let you know that Harney seemed very happy in his new workshop, I think he'll make a good job of contributing to the Emperor's army."

Nilla watched the man for any sign of a reaction but none came, he simply continued shovelling food into his mouth. She sat there for several more minutes until he finally looked up and acknowledged her.

"Oh Nilla I'm sorry, I didn't realise you were still here," he said, setting his knife and fork down. "Is there something else I can help you with."

She sat quietly, trying to decide how best to phrase the question, "Aren't you ever worried Oscar?" she finally asked.

"Worried about what?" he asked looking slightly confused.

"That the other Artist's will find out about the sub-basement and bring the army to life?"

Oscar cocked his head as if considering her for the first time, then he shook his head, "It will never happen, the Emperor wouldn't allow it."

Nilla smiled inwardly, *So there is a sub-basement,* she thought. "The Emperor can't know everything. I've heard about rogue Artist's, what's to stop one of them bringing the whole army to life?"

Oscar shook his head again, "You're worrying for nothing Nilla, you're forgetting about our range, even at the top of the stairs to the sub-basement our range is too short."

Nilla smiled and let out a little laugh, "Of course," she said. "I was getting so worried and worked up it completely slipped my mind," she laughed again and Oscar smiled.

"It happens to all of us at some point," he said. "You're still fairly new, it's only natural that you'd worry for the Emperor's safety."

She smiled again and got up to leave, "I'm sorry to have taken up so much of your time, I hope I've not ruined your lunch?"

"Not at all," Oscar said and grinned. "It's always a pleasure to talk to you." She started to walk away and Oscar's smile dropped to a frown.

Nilla spent the afternoon in her office catching up on paperwork and reports. It wasn't the part of the job she liked, which was why she saved up all her paperwork to do in one afternoon. Perunia had tried to get her to space it out, but she had so far resisted.

A polite knock came at the door and Perunia entered, her stylish outfit looking as though it had just been pressed. *I hope she's not going to lecture me on paperwork again*, she thought with an internal sigh. She smiled pleasantly for her superior.

"Good afternoon Perunia, what a pleasant surprise."

Perunia's face remained troubled and a frown decorated her expression, "I wish I could say the same," she replied.

"Is there something wrong?" Nilla asked and her hands suddenly felt clammy; she tried her best not to fidget.

Perunia took a seat opposite her and still her professional exterior didn't break, *This isn't going to be good*, she thought trying to swallow the lump that had formed in her throat.

"Perunia, what's wrong?" she finally asked.

"Why don't you tell me?" the other woman asked.

A look of confusion crossed Nilla's face, "I wasn't aware anything was wrong," she said slowly. Perunia folded her arms and looked hard at Nilla who felt herself flush. "Have I done something wrong?" she asked nervously.

Perunia's icy exterior finally broke but there was little warmth behind her words, "Why don't we start with how you audited the wrong workshop, and end with how you've been snooping for information that doesn't concern you."

Nilla sat in stunned silence, her face felt hot and her insides squirmed while Perunia's gaze pierced her like a knife, "Perunia I-"

"What in the Emperor's name were you thinking Nilla? Do you even know how serious this is?"

She snapped back to herself as if she'd been slapped, she sat up straight and levelled her gaze at her superior. "What exactly was I supposed to do Perunia? Even the Crafting Artist's know more than me around here! I had to know what was going on, I had to know what I was dealing with! How the Emperor expects me to competently do my job without knowing what the offence and defence teams are I'll never know!"

"I had already told you it was none of your concern," Perunia said firmly.

"You did," Nilla confirmed. "But when Artist's are coming to me and requesting a transfer to something I know nothing about it makes me and this department look like idiots!"

Perunia got to her feet, "You will remember your place Nilla! I could easily have you sent back down to the classrooms!"

"Do what you must!" Nilla said, her voice getting louder as the weeks of frustration finally tumbled out. "But don't think sending me back down there will solve anything, people other than me are asking questions Perunia!"

"Who? What questions?" Perunia asked and Nilla saw a hint of worry.

Realising she'd said too much, her brain raced as she thought of a way to cover herself, "Whether the Emperor even exists," she finally said and a cold smile crept across Perunia's face.

"Well that will be easy to answer," she replied turning to leave. "Because the Emperor wants to see you."

Nilla's skin went cold.

Chapter 33

It had been a gruelling week for Redd, Wolf and Aggie; they'd had to endure countless questions about who they were, what they did, who their families were and so many others that Redd's brain had started to ache. Following that, they'd been forced to sit through endless presentations regarding the Emperor. It was clearly a tactic to try and brainwash the Artist's into believing what the Emperor was doing was for the good of the city and that they in turn were helping by being there.

Redd didn't doubt that Shanora was in crisis, he was almost certain that there was a severe lack of resources. However he didn't understand why the Emperor wasn't trying to negotiate with the other cities, and he didn't think imprisoning the Artist's and forcing them to work was the way forward.

Once the presentations, most of which Redd had slept through, were over they were stripped of their clothes and any possessions, and provided with a simplistic uniform, which consisted of brown trousers and a white shirt. As he pulled the shirt over his head, he wondered how many of the uniforms were actually created by the Artists.

He entered another of the classroom's where a small number of new Artist's were already sat, including Wolf and Aggie and took a seat of his own. He looked down at the desk and saw a detailed map of the palace and its grounds.

"You are permitted to use these maps to find your way until you become familiar with your surroundings," a stern looking female officer said at the front of the room. "They will be removed from your possession in one week so I suggest you study them carefully. Wait here while I summon my colleagues who will show you to your new rooms and classrooms."

She left the room momentarily and Redd took the opportunity to get Wolf and Aggie's attention.

"Are you two okay?" he asked as he looked between them.

The other Artists in the room kept their heads down and pretended not to notice. "I'm okay," Aggie said with a shaky smile, Wolf just nodded, which was enough confirmation for him.

The female officer re-entered the room with a handful of her colleagues who were each assigned to escort the new Artist's to their permanent rooms and classrooms. He was separated from Wolf and Aggie almost instantly as a tall, burly officer with neat, blonde hair ordered him and another male Artist to their feet.

They left the small building and were greeted with light drizzle as they crossed what Redd had to admit were pretty amazing grounds. They walked through a colourful flower garden before entering into what appeared to be an area of lawn games. *I wonder how much free time the Artist's actually get,* he thought while staring at the games. *They probably don't even get a chance to enjoy something like that.*

He scowled at the palace as they continued to walk towards it, hoping that maybe the Emperor was watching them from one of his many windows. They passed through another garden full of elaborate topiary pieces and Redd actually found himself marvelling at the detail and intricate designs. Then he scowled again and cursed himself internally, *Crafts! Redd, pull yourself together! This artwork shouldn't be confined and these Artists shouldn't be confined! The Crafting Emperor has them all in the palm of his hand!*

"I need to fix this," Redd muttered so quietly that his two companions couldn't hear him.

They finally reached the palace and entered through the large wooden doors flanked by officers. They eyed the newcomers suspiciously and Redd found himself scowling at them. They made their way to the third floor and along several corridors until the officer finally stopped at a door with no number.

"This will be your room," he said to the other Artist accompanying them.

The young man looked terrified and stared at the unmarked room, "How...how will I be able to find it again if it's unmarked?" he asked in a trembling voice.

The officer with them smirked, "Do you mean to tell me that you haven't been paying attention? You were given a map, what exactly do you think it was for?" He turned on his heel and beckoned for Redd to follow him then called over his shoulder to the other Artist. "You will meet me downstairs by the main enterance in fifteen minutes where I will then show you to your new classroom."

Redd glanced over his shoulder at the young Artist who simply stared at them in terror as they abandoned him. He took a deep breath and faced forwards, following the officer who still had a smirk on his face. Redd's face darkened and he had to make a conscious effort to stop himself from attacking the man.

They made their way back along several corridors,

which Redd didn't bother to memorise until the officer turned a corner and made his way halfway along before he stopped in front of another unmarked door.

"This will be your room," he said gesturing, he waited for a response but none came, so he went on. "I will expect you downstairs in ten minutes so I can show you to your classroom." Redd nodded and as the officer turned away from him he made to follow. "If you follow me," the officer said without turning round, "I'll shoot you and claim you attacked me."

Redd froze and anger surged through him as the officer sauntered away down the corridor and out of sight. He went into his new living space and found it highly undesirable; a small, single bed with thin sheets, an old, battered desk with what looked like an incredibly rickety chair and a small, grimy window. He sighed loudly, left the room and looked at the doors either side to see whether they had any distinguishing features.

They didn't.

Redd went back into his room and looked around for anything he could use but there were no hidden corners and the only items residing inside were the ones he'd already seen. Instead he went to the sheets on his bed and ripped a thin strip from the edge, then he left the room and tied the piece of fabric round the handle of his door.

He nodded in satisfaction and made his way down the corridor, exactly the same way that the officer had gone, and counted the doors to the end.

"Eleven from the end," he muttered as he turned the corner to the right and continued down another corridor. He made a mental note of the direction.

Somehow, and he suspected luck was on his side, he managed to find a staircase and eventually made it to the ground floor where he noticed the officer was waiting for him and the other Artist. The officer looked at his watch as Redd arrived, "You're cutting it a bit close," he said with a smug smile. "Only a minute left."

Redd looked anxiously round for the other Artist and hoped he would make it in time. The final minute felt like agony to Redd as he willed the young man to come racing down the stairs, but no one came and the stairs remained empty.

"Times up," the officer said gleefully. "Looks like it's just you and me."

Redd spun round and glared at him, "You can't seriously leave him wandering, how will he know where to go!?"

The officer unholstered his firearm and casually aimed it at Redd who stiffened, "Let me make one thing clear," he said almost lazily. "What I say goes and you don't question me, if you do, you might just get a bullet between the eyes."

Redd seethed and clenched his fists but kept his mouth shut. Eventually the officer holstered his weapon and gestured Redd to follow. They made their way to the second floor and walked for several minutes until the officer stopped by one of the doors and walked inside.

An older woman, who was small in stature and had grey hair tied back in a bun looked up towards them and scowled.

"What do you want Kento?" she asked in a cracked voice.

"Careful Jackie," he said as he walked towards her.

She scoffed, "Threaten me all you want Kento," she said as she got to her feet. "I'm not afraid of death."

Redd raised an eyebrow as Kento seemed to back down, "I've brought you a new Artist," he said eventually.

"I was informed I would be receiving two," she said with a frown.

"The other one couldn't keep up," Kento replied with a smirk.

"For the love of the Emperor Kento!" Jackie said coming to stand inches from him. She looked tiny in comparison to his large frame but this didn't seem to bother her. "Get him down here immediately!"

Kento's hand slid to his firearm and Redd could tell he was seriously considering shooting her. Jackie however seemed unconcerned by this movement and continued to stare him down.

Finally Kento's hand moved from his firearm and he ran a hand through his neat hair laughing loudly. "You need to lighten up Jackie," he said with a grin that had an underlying tone of anger. He turned on his heel and left the room, slamming the door behind him.

Jackie's face suddenly softened and she turned to smile at Redd, "Sorry about that," she said as she took a seat behind the desk. "Some of those officers are pure brutes."

Redd suddenly noticed how quiet the classroom was and he chanced a quickly glance at the Artists. They were all working calmly and silently as if the incident moments ago had never happened. Redd turned back to Jackie who was still smiling at him.

"Welcome to my classroom," she said in her cracked voice. "What's your name?"

"Redd," he replied.

Jackie gasped.

Jackie dismissed the other students early as lunch approached but asked Redd to stay behind so she could get him accustomed to the classroom. The other Artist still hadn't turned up and when Redd had queried it, Jackie had informed him that Kento wouldn't bother trying to find him for at least another few hours.

"What's wrong with the officers in here?" he asked in a disgusted tone.

"They aren't all as bad as him," Jackie explained. "He's just a particularly nasty one.

"So what more do I need to know?" he asked looking round the classroom.

Jackie grinned sheepishly, "I must confess I've kept you here under false pretences."

"You're not going to talk to me about the classroom?" She shook her head and Redd folded his arms across his chest which revealed the ugly scar on his left forearm; she eyed it. "What's going on?" he asked firmly.

"I needed to talk to you in private and this is about as private as it gets."

"About what?"

"About your brother."

Redd froze, "What do you know about him?" his tone was threatening.

Jackie raised an eyebrow, "I'd advise you not to take that tone with me," she replied. "I'm not easily intimidated."

He forced himself to relax and placed his hands by his sides, "Sorry. Do you know my brother?"

Jackie smiled, "Oh I know him alright, for a long time Flicker was my only source of entertainment in this place!"

"You know him well then?"

She nodded, "I'm helping him try and uncover whatever's going on in here, I'm assuming Flora told you everything?"

"You know Flora too?"

"There aren't many people in here that I don't know," she replied with a grin.

"Where's Flicker?" he asked, suddenly eager. "When can I see him?"

"I know you won't like this but I think you need to wait until tonight," Redd opened his mouth to speak so Jackie pressed on. "We've potentially got eyes on us, eyes we don't want and I'd rather they didn't see us fraternising with the newcomers so openly, they might get suspicious."

Redd nodded then sighed, "Why is it that no matter how close I get to actually seeing him again, he always seems just out of reach."

"I promise you won't have to wait much longer," Jackie said placing a comforting hand on his arm. "He's been waiting for this moment just as long as you have and I guarantee he's just as anxious to see you again too."

"I hope you're right Jackie," Redd said as a slight frown settled on his face.

Chapter 34

It was late but the spring weather meant the sky was still light as Jackie and Redd made their way to the centre of the maze; she'd sent a cryptic message to Flicker, which had explained when and where to meet and she prayed he'd received it.

Redd was nervous and apprehensive, not the emotions he expected to feel about finally seeing his brother after five and a half years. *What if too much time has passed?* He thought to himself. *We're probably very different people now.* He frowned to himself and Jackie glanced back at him.

"Cheer up," she said with a grin. "Anyone would think I was leading you to your death."

Redd forced a smile, "I'm worried Jackie," he admitted.

She halted, "Worried about what?" Redd gave her a slightly ashamed look and she sighed heavily, folding her arms. "You've spent over five years trying to get back to your brother, I'm not about to let you chicken out now that you're feeling insecure."

"What if we're not the same people we-"

Jackie snorted loudly, cutting him off, "Of course you're not going to be the same people as before! But that doesn't mean you're not still brothers! Now come on, before I have to drag you by the ear."

She started moving and he made sure he kept pace with her; he grinned to himself. *She sure is something,* he mused as Jackie walked purposefully in front of him. *I wish I'd had someone like her on the outside.*

They rounded the final corner and Redd came face to face with his brother; he ground abruptly to a halt. Flicker looked momentarily disbelieving, then shot him a wide grin and Redd launched himself at his brother. They hugged fiercely and Redd had to force himself to laugh to stop himself from crying.

"You've no idea how good it is to see you little brother," Redd said as he pulled away and looked Flicker over.

"What took you so long," Flicker said, still grinning, Redd thumped him on the shoulder before turning to Jackie.

"Thank you," he said to the older woman, who smiled at them, but said nothing. "I wish I knew how to find Wolf and Aggie," Redd said as a familiar voice floated towards them.

"Don't worry, we're fine," Wolf said as he and Aggie turned the corner and walked towards them.

Redd grinned, "Glad to see you've both survived your first day."

"We've been skulking around the grounds looking everywhere for you," Aggie said with a grin. "We finally saw you as you were walking in here and decided to follow." Introductions were made between the small group and Jackie walked up to Aggie, smiling kindly, "So you're Aggie." The young girl nodded, smiling. "I thought you must be when you walked round the corner, you look so much like your mother."

"Have you seen her lately?" Aggie asked eagerly.

Jackie cocked her head, then looked at Flicker, "Is

she meant to be coming tonight?"

Flicker nodded, "I think so, but it'll depend on how easy it is for her to get away. I saw Flora earlier too, she's on patrol this evening so she might try to stop-"

Aggie squealed as both Flora and Nilla walked into the clearing and she threw her arms around her mother, squeezing her tightly. Both mother and daughter cried as they embraced one another and Aggie desperately tried not to let go as her mother started to pull away.

"It's okay Aggie," she said as she finally extracted herself from her daughter. I'm not going anywhere." Aggie reluctantly let go of her mother, then threw her arms round Flora.

"I honestly didn't think we'd ever see each other again," Redd finally admitted and the others fell silent.

Nilla nodded, "I know what you mean," she said as she smiled lovingly at her daughter, then she looked at Wolf and Redd. "I take it you're the ones who've been looking out for my daughter?"

"It was no trouble," Wolf said, smiling fondly at Aggie.

Another round of introductions were made between those who hadn't yet met and there was a brief period of calm. Suddenly, Nilla's face grew serious, and she turned to Jackie and Flicker, "I've got some news."

"I hope it's good," Flicker said with a grin. "You wouldn't want to ruin the party now would you?" Nilla sighed and Flicker's face fell, "It's bad then?"

"I don't know for sure, but I'd take a guess that it's bad."

"Has someone found us out?" Jackie asked with concern.

Nilla shook her head, "I honestly don't know."

"What is it?" Flicker asked frowning.

"The Emperor wants to meet me."

The group were stunned into silence; Jackie finally choked out some words.

"The…Emperor?"

Nilla nodded.

"What does he want?" Aggie asked, suddenly clinging to her mother as if her life depended on it.

"Perunia found out I'd been looking into the offence and defence teams, I think she told the Emperor what I'd been doing and-"

"Wait!" Flicker said, suddenly excited. "Does that mean you found out what they are?"

She nodded and Flicker grinned, he opened his mouth but Jackie shot him a look and he closed it again.

"What did Perunia say?" Jackie asked, knowing they could discuss the positive news later.

"She wasn't happy," Nilla said, taking a seat. "Actually that's an understatement, she was furious."

"What do you think will happen?" Jackie asked.

Nilla shook her head, "I honestly don't know, I doubt they'll send me back down to the regular classrooms, I know too much, but I doubt Perunia is going to be happy with me working for her from now on. Maybe I'll be taken off active duty and will end up confined to my office," she shrugged. "I really don't know."

"We'll figure something out Nilla," Flora said gently. "If necessary we'll speed up our plan, we're not going to let anything happen to you."

Nilla smiled, "I suppose I should tell you what I found out before Flicker explodes." They looked at the young man, who seemed to be trying to disintegrate Jackie with a glare, she clapped him round the head.

Nilla took a deep breath, "I found out exactly what

the offence and defence teams are."

"Really?" Flicker asked almost unable to contain his excitement.

She nodded, "The defence team relates to the lack of resources, the Artists are creating them and the officers are pretending to bring them into the city from the outside. The offence team," she took a deep breath. "They're creating an army."

"They're what?!" Flicker asked with a mixture of disbelief and excitement.

"Why would the Emperor need an army?" Aggie asked.

"I can answer that," Flora said and the others looked at her. "Endore and Flintai have allied themselves against Shanora, it's no secret that friendships have become strained. But I've heard they've ceased all trade with us. I've heard that our spies believe they're going to attack us, and rather than put people's lives at risk the Emperor has been making the Artists create an army to protect the city."

Nilla nodded, "Those body parts I saw are part of the army, they make limbs separately and attach them together, then they store them in the sub-basement. It's far enough underground that an Artist can't bring them to life."

"Even if they did I'd wager wherever they're being stored is locked," Flora added.

"We really need to find that sub-basement," Flicker said and the others nodded.

Aggie would never admit it to the others but she was actually enjoying her time in the palace. She felt guilty for admitting it to herself. She knew the Emperor was evil and she knew, overall, that the palace was a terrible place to live out the rest of their lives. But she knew she wouldn't be there for the rest of her life. Her and the others would break out soon, so why shouldn't she pick up some tips for her artwork?

Her teacher, Lieam, had been instantly impressed with her work and the first time she'd experienced a class audit, the administration staff had seemed impressed too. Despite her natural talent there were intricate skills she hadn't yet mastered, and she was enjoying taking the time to learn them. They were in this place to create art, she might as well learn something about it.

"I bet in a few months you'll be sent upstairs," a male Artist in his mid thirties said as he admired her squirrel sculpture. "Bet they'll have you on the offence team," he shook his head. "Lucky," he muttered under his breath.

Aggie frowned, "Lucky? Why am I lucky?"

The other Artist looked at her incredulously, "Didn't you listen at your induction? The whole point is to get upstairs and help with the offence and defence teams."

"Yes of course," she said forcing a smile. "But, wouldn't you rather be living out there?" she gestured with her arm, indicating the city beyond.

"How could I help the people of Shanora if I was out there?" he replied, then frowned. "Don't you want to help the city?"

"Of course," she said quickly. "I suppose it just feels a bit like we're prisoners."

"Prisoners? We're taken care of in here and we're protected by the officers."

"I suppose I just think we'd all work better if we were with our families, or at least able to see them once in a while."

The Artist's frown deepened, "Don't you want to be

here?"

Aggie forced a smile while her heart began to pound, "Yes of course. I'm pretty new and this is all strange to me. I just miss my family."

The Artist nodded in understanding but continued to frown, "You'll settle in soon enough. Just remember that by being here you're helping to protect them."

She nodded and continued with her work while the other Artist turned away to work on his fox sculpture. *This isn't right*, Aggie thought as she continued to frown. *These Artists' deserve to be free.*

She managed to find Wolf at midday and practically collapsed next to him, sighing heavily as she did so. He smiled at her in a fatherly manner.

"What's up lass?" he asked as he shovelled warm stew into his mouth.

"I don't think it's going to be enough Wolf," she replied distractedly.

He glanced at her questioningly, "What isn't?"

"The plan," she replied vaguely and when he shot her a look she took a deep breath, then lowered her voice. "I don't think it's going to be enough just getting our group out of the palace. The other Artists, don't they also deserve to be free? To be reunited with their loved ones?"

Wolf studied her carefully before exhaling loudly, "Aye, you're right, but I'm not sure what we can do. I've noticed some of the Artists are beaten down, unhappy, but many of them seem to like it here and I'm not sure there's any fight in those that don't."

"Maybe we need to light a fire under them," Aggie said with a mischievous grin.

Wolf laughed loudly and several Artists stared at them, including Charlie who looked at them suspiciously. "I like you're enthusiasm lass," Wolf said putting an arm round her and giving her a squeeze. "Perhaps we'll run it past the others."

"Run what past the others?" A cracked voice asked and Jackie smiled down at them.

"Nothing Jackie," Wolf said. "At least nothing to worry about right now."

"Is everything okay?" Aggie asked.

Jackie nodded, "Just thought I'd check up on you both, I don't think we'll manage to all get together again for a few days, it's harder to avoid the officers now there's more of us."

"What'll happen if they catch us?"

Jackie shrugged, "Isolation, questioning, twenty-four hour guard, torture," Aggie looked shocked at the last comment and Jackie tried to smile reassuringly. "I'm sure it wouldn't be anything that drastic, but it's better to err on the side of caution."

Wolf nodded in agreement and Jackie shuffled away. "Don't worry lass, if we keep a low profile we'll be fine."

"We're planning on exposing the Emperor and breaking out of the palace," Aggie pointed out. "Just exactly how are we supposed to keep a low profile?"

"Jackie!" Charlie's voice called out to her as she left the dining room. She froze, frowned, then turned to face the bustling room. Charlie jogged towards her with a less than genuine smile on his face.

"Charlie, how can I help you?" she asked in as polite a tone as she could muster. She still didn't trust this man and the less time she had to spend in his presence the better.

"Who were those Artist's you were just talking to."

Jackie's heart skipped a beat, should she be the one to tell him? "Newcomers," she replied carefully.

"Newcomers?" Charlie repeated with a frown. "You seemed awfully friendly with them."

Jackie snorted, "I'm friendly towards everyone Charlie, you know that. It's hard enough adjusting to life in the palace, seeing a friendly face can make all the difference."

Charlie nodded slowly but didn't seem convinced, "Have they been here long? The girl looked familiar."

She should, Jackie thought as she stood looking at the man she was sure would betray her in a heartbeat but finally she sighed and stared him straight in the eyes. "She's your daughter."

"M-my what?" Charlie stammered.

"She's your daughter, she's Aggie," Jackie repeated.

Charlie narrowed his eyes, "How do you know that? How do you know she's mine?"

Jackie rolled her eyes, "I've talked to your wife enough to know what she looks like and how many people are there going to be in the city that are called Aggie who fit the description?"

"My daughter," Charlie whispered turning back towards the dining room to get another look at her. "My beautiful Aggie."

Chapter 35

Nilla shifted in her seat and glanced at Perunia, who sat next to her, alert but stony faced. Perunia had been silent as soon as they'd reached the seventh floor and at that moment Nilla's nerves had gotten the better of her and she'd had to put all her energy into not vomiting. She played nervously with her hands and glanced at Perunia again who simply ignored her and stared straight ahead at the wall.

After they had waited for what felt like days, a thin, balding man emerged from a dark, wooden door with a clipboard. He looked down the page, levelled his pen halfway down and looked at Perunia over narrow glasses.

"Ah Perunia," he said as she gave him a tight smile and nodded stiffly, then he looked at Nilla and the urge to vomit resurfaced. "Nilla?" she nodded slowly and tried to calm her nerves. "The Emperor is ready for you."

He walked back towards the dark wooden door; Perunia got to her feet stiffly and began to follow, while Nilla lurched to her feet and felt incredibly unsteady as she trailed behind.

The seventh floor, like the others, was a labyrinth of corridors and rooms and it wasn't long before Nilla felt well and truly lost. She was grateful to the man acting as their guide, there was no chance she would have been able to find her way otherwise. The man finally stopped outside another dark wooden door, that could easily have been the first, and considering the amount of twists and turns they'd taken, she wouldn't have been surprised if they'd ended up back at the beginning.

Their guide knocked three times on the door and opened it without entering, he then gestured for the two of them to go in and closed the door silently behind them. Perunia and Nilla waited by the door and Nilla took the opportunity to look round the large room.

As far as she could tell there was no one in it except for the two of them, though it was so huge that someone could easily have been hiding and they'd never see them. The carpet was a deep crimson and many of the elaborately decorative items, including candelabras, clocks and small trinket boxes appeared to be gilded and painted. There were a number of plush chairs in the room, all covered in a midnight blue fabric, that looked as though they'd never been sat in. There were a number of shelves adorning the walls, which she could see contained a variety of books and manuscripts and there seemed to be a large, elaborate wooden writing desk at the far end.

Nilla suddenly realised that there wasn't any art in the room, it didn't contain any sculptures, tapestries or paintings. She frowned.

A door opened in the wall to their right and a tall, well built man with thick dark hair that mimicked a lions mane strode through. She saw Perunia stiffen even further while she found herself trembling. The man, whom she assumed was the Emperor took a seat in one of the plush chairs and stared at them.

She felt her breathing quicken and her stomach churned as his eyes pierced her; she was sure he'd be able to see through her lies. He stared for what seemed like an age before he finally spoke.

"Everett!" he yelled, looking past the two women.

The door behind them opened and the tall man entered, "Yes Emperor?"

"I wish you to witness this conversation," the Emperor's voice was deep, clear and commanding.

Everett bowed deeply, "Of course Emperor, it would be an honour." He scurried out of the room and returned seconds later with a writing pad and a pen.

The Emperor then turned his attention back to the two women, "You are Perunia?" he asked, looking to the older woman.

She bowed low, "Yes Emperor," she replied.

"You will sit," he commanded and Perunia walked stiffly towards a wooden chair that the Emperor was pointing to. He then turned his gaze on Nilla. "You are the one who has been prying into my affairs."

It wasn't really a question but she felt she should answer him anyway. She mimicked Perunia's bow and tried to sound calm as she spoke, her voice wobbled against her better judgement, "Yes Emperor."

"You admit your actions then?" he almost sounded surprised.

She glanced to Perunia, who gave nothing away, then bowed again before she answered. "Forgive me Emperor," she said as she stared at the floor, unable to hold his gaze. "I know it was wrong, but I didn't feel I was able to do my job properly when I hadn't been furnished with all of the information." She finally looked up and saw a hard, impassable expression on the Emperor's face, then she noticed he was looking at Perunia and not her.

"You didn't explain to her?" he asked in a calm voice that was clearly menacing.

Perunia somehow remained motionless, "She's new,"

Perunia explained calmly. "I wanted to be sure we could trust her before she was supplied with all of the information."

The Emperor narrowed his eyes at Perunia, then turned back to Nilla, "What caused you to pry into my affairs?"

Nilla bowed again, though she wasn't sure she actually needed to, "The offence and defence teams had been mentioned to me on several occasions, including a transfer request. I was almost unable to handle the situation professionally-"

"Almost?" came the deep, smooth voice.

"I-I lied Emperor." She saw the ghost of a smile on the Emperor's lips. "You lied in order to protect yourself."

"Not myself," she said finally holding his gaze and feeling suddenly brave. "You."

The Emperor raised an eyebrow at her and she thought she heard the faintest of gasps emit from Perunia, "Explain," he said.

She took a deep breath, "I know there have been problems in the past with some of the Artist's, and I also know that it's not just the officers who keep the peace, it's us, the administration team. We're authority figures, but we're also Artist's, we have something in common with the other residents."

She took another breath and found herself calming, "If the other Artist's found out that a member of the administration team hadn't been trusted with information provided by the Emperor, if they thought that they weren't trusted by the Emperor, then why should any of the Artist's trust them? And why should they trust you?"

"You think they would rebel?" the Emperor asked, almost amused.

"I think it's better not to give them that chance," Nilla replied.

The Emperor studied her for several minutes, "Very well," he said looking to Everett. "I believe her reasoning is satisfactory and I do not feel it necessary to punish her."

"Very good Emperor," Everett said scribbling in his notebook.

"Perunia," the woman stiffened again. "See that she is furnished with the necessary information to competently do her job." Perunia nodded and the Emperor rose from his seat and walked towards the door to their right. "You are dismissed."

"I thought you said there were plans of the palace stored in here?" Flora said with slight annoyance as she and Jan continued to rummage through several drawers.

"They should be," Jan replied in a worried tone. "Everything of use to us is meant to be in here."

They stopped searching and took stock of their situation. They were in a small storeroom with no windows and a fading central light. It was located to the left of the gatehouse. Flora and Jan were the only ones inside, which allowed them to talk freely.

"I assumed you'd already know where to look," Flora said folding her arms.

Jan looked a little sheepish, "I've never actually seen the plans myself," he admitted and Flora looked suddenly annoyed. "But they should be in here, how else would we get copies?"

"I wish we could use the one I was given when I started here," Flora sighed. "They must really want to keep the sub-basement a secret."

Jan sighed and ran a hand through his hair as he sat,

"You know even if we find the plans there's no guarantee they'll include the sub-basement."

She nodded, "I know. I'm starting to think we should just start snooping around the basement instead."

"Isn't that a bit risky? The other officers have only just started to trust you."

Flora shrugged, "I'm concerned we might be running out of time, the sooner we can find out what's going on, the sooner we can get out of here."

They slipped into the basement easily; being officers, and with Flora no longer under suspicion, the others didn't question their motives.

"There has to be a door around here somewhere," Jan said as they walked further into the gloom.

Flora grinned, "There are doors everywhere Jan."

He scowled at her as they walked down a corridor with doors lining either side, "You know what I mean."

They wandered around in the gloom for a couple of hours before Jan finally called them to a halt; they'd had no luck uncovering a secret door and they'd made sure to check the walls and even the floor.

"We've been searching for too long, someone's going to notice our absence."

"You go back," Flora said as she moved off again down the corridor. "I'm going to keep looking."

He sighed and followed, "Exactly how long are you planning on wandering down here?"

"Until I find the sub-basement," Flora said with a grin that Jan probably couldn't see."

"Honestly anyone would think you've got some sort of-"

Jan yelped and was suddenly lost from view as the wall he'd been running his left hand along vanished and he toppled down a short flight of stairs.

"Jan!" Flora yelled and rushed to help him to his feet.

"Looks like I might have found something," he said with a groan.

"Are you hurt?" she asked, trying to check him over in the half-light.

He shook his head, "Nothing serious," he assured her and turned to examine the thick, heavy set, wooden door at the bottom of the small flight of stairs. "Do you think this is the sub-basement?"

"It's possible," Flora said with excitement in her voice. "Is it locked?"

Jan nodded, "Got any experience with lock picking?"

Flora shook her head and frowned, "Do you?"

"Afraid not."

They stared at the locked door for some time as if willing it to spring open. Flora examined the thick, steel padlock and wondered how easy it would be to unlock without a key. She felt in her pockets for anything remotely useful, but came up empty; Jan followed suit with the same result.

"Doesn't look like we're getting in here today," Jan said.

Flora looked deflated, "We've come so far."

"Unless you've got magic lock picking fingers I think you'll have to admit defeat, at least for now."

She nodded reluctantly and they began to make their way back to the main staircase.

"If anyone asks, we'll say we thought we saw an Artist come down here and were trying to find them."

Flora nodded. It took them half the time to get back to the ground floor than it had to find the door, since they were no longer searching for the entrance to the sub-basement. They passed several officers who barely paid them any notice and walked out into the failing daylight.

"How are we going to get it?" Jan asked quietly as they made their way back to the gatehouse.

"I've no idea," Flora replied. "There's obviously a key somewhere…but I'm not sure that's going to be a viable option."

"There's no way for us to get the key without looking suspicious," he said.

"Exactly. I think the only way we're going to get in is if we try and pick the lock ourselves."

"Except neither of us know the first thing about lock picking," Jan pointed out.

"Perhaps I should ask the others," she half muttered. "They might be able to help."

"do you want me to come along?" Jan asked.

Flora looked at him with an odd expression on her face, "I'm not sure that's wise."

"I've known Jackie and Flicker a lot longer than you, I don't think they'd-"

Flora shook her head, "It's not about that Jan, you've got a family, a wonderful family and you shouldn't do anything to risk yourself or them. You're probably already doing too much and I don't think any of us would forgive ourselves if something happened to you, or to them."

Jan nodded though Flora could tell he wasn't happy with the situation. *I'm sorry Jan,* she thought as they entered the gatehouse, *but this is the only way to keep you safe.*

Chapter 36

Redd and Flicker roared with laughter while several Artist's nearby shot them odd looks and the officers watched them suspiciously.

"I can't believe I let you go through with that!" Redd laughed, wiping a tear from his eye. "You looked so ridiculous!"

"I'm pretty sure you still owe me money from that," Flicker pointed out.

"You didn't get anywhere, I saw that woman hit you."

"She only hit me after," Flicker said mischievously.

"You don't expect me to believe that do you?"

Flicker grinned, "I could take the same challenge in here, I'll bet I'd still get a girl to kiss me."

"No way am I taking that bet! You'd just get Jackie to do it!"

"Jackie? She'd wallop me one, no way I'd ask her!"

They burst into laughter again and this time a burly officer with neat blonde hair strolled over to them; they tried to compose themselves.

"What's going on here?" the officer said; Redd looked up and realised it was Kento, the same officer who'd left an Artist to wander the corridors alone.

"Nothing officer," Redd said as he tried to remain straight faced.

"Not going to let me in on the joke then?" Kento asked and there was something Redd didn't like in his voice.

This could get dangerous, he realised.

"There's no joke," Flicker said with a grin. "Not one you'd understand anyway."

Kento smacked Flicker round the head with the butt of his firearm. "Saying I'm stupid are you?" he growled.

Redd jumped to his feet and stepped between Kento and his brother, "No one's saying you're stupid," he said in as calm a voice as possible. "He's my brother, we were talking about our childhood."

Kento looked between them for several minutes as if trying to decide whether they were telling him the truth. He growled and punched Redd in the face, dropping him to the floor, then he smacked Flicker with his firearm and marched away.

Redd shook his head and instantly regretted it as his vision swam; he glanced over at his brother who was clutching his face on the ground next to him. The other Artist's around them were pretend not to notice what had just happened. Redd got to his feet and pulled his brother's hand away, seeing a small oozing cut near his eye.

"Are you okay?" he asked.

Flicker nodded, "Yeah, I'm fine. Nothing I can't handle," a spot of blood trickled down his face and he wiped it away quickly.

"You're not fine, you're injured," Redd pointed out as he tried to look at the wound.

Flicker pushed him away, "I'm fine Redd, I promise. That was nothing I haven't dealt with before."

Redd's expression was unreadable, then it darkened, "The officers do this to you often?"

Flicker shook his head, "Not anymore, it only happened when I was being disagreeable."

"You mean when you were trying to escape?"

Flicker nodded, "I promise you I'm okay," he said reassuringly but he had lost his playfulness. "Why are you doing this Redd?"

"Why am I doing what?"

"Why are you here? Why have you risked your life to be here? You were free, you could have just carried on, you *should* have carried on."

Redd's expression was stern, "Could you have carried on if it had been me who'd been taken?"

Flicker didn't reply but his expression answered Redd's question.

"You're my little brother and I'm supposed to look after you. I couldn't have moved on with my life knowing you were in here, knowing you were going to be imprisoned for the rest of your life. We've spent our whole lives looking out for each other Flick, when you'd gone, when you were taken from me, I was lost. You're the only family I've got, I wasn't about to let the Emperor keep you from me."

His brother was silent for several minutes, "You know there's no guarantee we'll get out of here."

Redd smiled and shrugged, "It doesn't really matter now does it? We're back together, that's what's important."

Flicker frowned, "And what about the others? Redd I'm pretty sure they didn't sign up to stay here for the rest of their lives, they came here knowing they'd get out again."

"Everyone knew the risk," he replied flatly. "We'll do what we can to get out, but we all came in here knowing there was a slim chance we'd die in here, naturally or unnaturally."

Flicker cocked his head, "What aren't you telling me Redd?"

"Nothing."

"I can tell when you're lying, what are you planning that they don't know about?"

Redd's expression softened slightly and he forced a smile, "I promise I'm not planning anything little brother, I only came in here to help you get out, that's all I've ever wanted."

Flicker stared at his brother and frowned; there was something he wasn't saying.

It was getting harder for the group to meet in the evenings without the officers noticing so they had decided they might as well simply have their meetings during the day. It wasn't unusual for groups of Artist's to spend time with one another, they just needed to make sure they kept a low profile while they talked.

Aggie and Wolf were two of the last to arrive in the sculpture garden; the location for today's meeting. Aggie looked round and frowned at the absence of her mother.

Flora spoke before Aggie could ask, "There's been no news about your mother amongst the officers."

"Is that a good thing or a bad thing?" Wolf asked.

Flora paused, then spoke carefully, "It means that no one has been asked to dispose of a body."

Redd looked at Aggie, expecting to see worry and panic in her eyes and was surprised to see they were hard and firm. She looked to him and gave a slight smile as if to prove she could handle the situation calmly and rationally, then she glanced at Flicker and her expression turned to a frown.

"What happened to you?" she asked, voice full of

concern.

Flicker shrugged and smiled, "One of the officers had a disagreement with us, it's no big deal though, nothing I can't handle." The others looked unconvinced and Flicker forced his smile to be larger, showing teeth. "Seriously, I used to deal with far worse, Jack can testify to that." He looked over at the older woman who stared back with a frown. "Not you too Jack, I'm fine."

"Fine doesn't normally look like that," Jackie replied curtly. "But that's not the point, what were you doing to attract attention? We're supposed to be keeping a low profile."

Redd looked sheepish, "I'm sorry Jackie, that might have been my fault. We were reminiscing about old times, we got a bit carried away." Jackie shook her head and Redd felt a wave of shame wash over him. *How can a look from one woman make me feel so guilty?* he wondered as he studied her.

"I think we need to focus," Flora said, snapping the others back to reality. "I think I've found the entrance to the sub-basement." There were murmurs of excitement from the others and Flicker shifted excitedly.

"What did you find?" Jackie asked eagerly.

Flora suddenly looked deflated, "Well technically nothing." The others shot her puzzled and disappointed looks. "I couldn't actually get in, the door is padlocked. I'll keep working on it but I've not really got any lock picking experience so it might take some time."

Jackie let out a bark of laughter and nudged Flicker, "Looks like she's in need of your particular skill set Flick!"

"What skill set?" Flora asked.

Flicker grinned mischievously, "Let's just say I've become rather familiar with the padlocks in the palace."

"Of course!" Flora said slapping a hand to her forehead. "How could I forget that!"

"When should we go?" Wolf asked.

Flicker frowned, "I'm not sure it's wise for us all to go, it's hard enough getting together at the moment in the open, trying to sneak all of us down to the basement, it seems far too risky."

"Surely there's safety in numbers?" Wolf said.

Jackie shook her head, "I think it would be easier if only a few people went along, in fact the less the better. It makes sense for only Flicker and Flora go, after all they're the only ones who actually need to be there."

"Why not have one more person," Redd suggested. "I don't think it's wise to risk yourself unnecessarily without some sort of guard."

"What do you think I am?" Flora asked in irritation. "I'm an officer Redd, if there's anyone who can get us out of trouble if we get caught it's going to be me."

Redd frowned but said no more.

"That's settled then," Jackie said as silence fell. "Flora and Flick will enter the basement two nights from now. If anything looks or feels off, then don't bother risking yourselves, we've got plenty of time to get this right, it's not like we're going anywhere anytime soon," she laughed but Redd cut her off.

"Aren't we?" he asked getting to his feet, a hint of anger in his voice. "I was under the impression we put ourselves in her, put our lives on the line, so we could get you out."

"Easy Redd," Flicker said putting a hand on his brothers shoulder to pull him back down to the bench. "Of course we're going to get out of here, but Jackie's right, there's no rush and if there *is* an army in the sub-basement then we might be able to use it to our

304

advantage."

Redd folded his arms and stared with a stony expression at Jackie who seemed unfazed by the experience. Aggie's voice eventually broke the silence, "I've been thinking," she said as all heads turned to look at her. "Maybe we shouldn't just be focusing on getting us out of the palace."

"What do you mean?" Jackie asked.

"I don't think all of the Artist's are happy in here, in fact I'm sure most of them would rather be out there," she gestured towards the large, imposing walls and the city beyond. "With their families."

"What's your point?" Redd asked.

"I think we should try and get them to help us."

The others looked at her sceptically, except for Wolf who was looking at her with a kindly expression, "I'm not sure that would work," Flicker eventually said. "A lot of these Artist's have started to think like the Emperor, they really believe they're doing something good, they believe *he's* doing something good."

Aggie shook her head, "I'm not so sure they do, I think that might be a cover, I think they-"

"I'm sorry Aggie," Jackie said shaking her head. "I just don't see us managing to get a large enough group on our side."

"Don't they deserve the chance to be free too?" Aggie asked stubbornly.

"Of course they do," Redd replied gently. "But I think right now we need to focus on us. If other Artist's see what we're doing and want to join us then great, but we've got to make sure we're the ones who get out. After all that's the reason we came here, we can't lose sight of that."

Aggie nodded miserably, and hung her head as the

group dispersed.

Chapter 37

Charlie watched his daughter from a distance as she talked and laughed with a tall, broad man. He frowned as the man smiled at her in a fatherly way, then put an arm round her and squeezed tightly.

Who does he think he is? He thought bitterly as his hands balled into fists. *Thinking he can take my daughter from me, well there are ways to stop that!* Charlie glanced around and saw one of the more, 'influential' officers on patrol, he smirked to himself and walked towards them.

"Good afternoon Kento," he said.

"What do you want Charlie?" Kento asked with hostility.

Charlie's smile fell from his lips, "I want a favour."

Kento scoffed, "A favour? Why in the Emperor's name should I do you a favour?"

Charlie drew himself up to his full height, "I've been your informant for years Kento," he pointed out, "I've put my life on the line just so your lot could look good for the Emperor and find traitors."

Kento shrugged, "I still don't see why I should do you a favour."

He grunted in annoyance, "My daughter is in here Kento," he said gesturing to where Aggie sat with Wolf, and the officer raised an eyebrow. "She arrived last week but she's being influenced by the wrong people."

"And I should care why exactly?" Kento asked with little interest.

"Because they might be planning to break out of here."

Kento snapped his head back to stare at Aggie and Wolf, then stared intensely at Charlie, "Do you have proof?" Charlie shook his head. "Then don't bother me with your petty problems until you do."

Kento turned to leave and Charlie grabbed his arm; the officer spun and struck him in the face causing him to fall to his knees. "Don't you dare touch me again!" he spat then kicked Charlie in the stomach and marched away.

A large hand appeared in front of him, offering help, "Are you alright lad?"

Charlie glanced up and saw the same man who had been with his daughter with a worried look on his face. He looked around quickly and saw that she was still sitting on the bench; she looked shocked. Charlie reluctantly took the hand that was offered and was helped to his feet.

"Thanks."

Wolf looked at him with concern, "Are you sure you're okay?"

Charlie nodded, "I'm fine."

"Are they all like that?" Wolf asked.

"Like what?" Charlie replied.

"Do they all attack the Artists without cause?"

Charlie stared at him in confusion, then slowly it dawned on him, "Some of them do," he said slowly as he rubbed his chin. "They're not all like that though, he's just a particularly bad one."

"I'm Wolf," Wolf said holding out a hand. "I'm pretty new here, any advice you can give I'm always willing to listen," he grinned and Charlie found himself disliking the man even more.

"My name's Charlie," he replied shaking the man's large hand. "And I'll give you a piece of advice right now. Watch your back."

Wolf looked taken aback, "Excuse me?"

Charlie forced a smile, "The officers, they like to, 'play' with the new ones."

Wolf's expression softened and he nodded, "Thanks for the tip," he said before walking back towards Aggie.

"And keep away from my daughter," he growled under his breath.

Charlie found Jackie in the dining room eating alone, he slid into the seat opposite her and she looked up in surprise.

"Hello Charlie," she said slowly while putting her fork down.

"I want to see my daughter," he said.

"You've already seen her," Jackie pointed out. "It's not like she's going anywhere, you can see her whenever you want."

Charlie scowled, "I want to talk to her."

"So talk," Jackie said; Charlie's expression darkened. "What exactly do you want from me Charlie?"

Jackie's face was firm and he knew he wouldn't be able to intimidate her, he didn't actually know of anyone who could. He sighed and tried to relax, "I want you to introduce me to her."

Jackie smiled, "Was that so hard?"

"Will you do it?" he asked.

Jackie nodded, "Of course, she has the right to meet you." *Despite the fact I think you're working for the Emperor.*

"Thank you Jackie," he said with a smile. "You have

no idea what this means to me, I'm worried about her."

"Worried? What makes you worried?"

Charlie shrugged, "I don't like the people she's been hanging around with, I don't trust them."

"I was under the impression she was being looked after by my lot," she said coolly.

Charlie remained impassive, "Well there's at least one person staying close to her that I don't trust."

You're one to talk, Jackie thought. "I'm sure she's fine Charlie, I've been keeping an eye on her so stop worrying."

"You're a good friend Jackie," Charlie said as he got to his feet, then he left the dining room leaving her alone once more. She picked up her fork but suddenly didn't feel hungry anymore.

"Should I warn Aggie?" she muttered to herself as she pushed her food around her plate. "Or should I try to get word to Nilla?" she sighed. "I miss the days when all I had to worry about was Flicker getting himself killed.

Charlie waited nervously in the flower garden for his daughter to arrive. He glanced around at the brightly coloured plants and smiled, *She'll like this,* he thought.

"That newbie still causing you trouble?" A familiar voice sounded from behind.

Charlie turned to see Kento, "That depends," Charlie replied.

"On what?" Kento asked.

"On what it's going to cost me."

Kento smirked, "Oh I'll think of something, just know that you'll be in my debt."

"Aren't I always," Charlie said with a grin.

Kento smiled but it wasn't friendly, "I believe it was you who first came to me all those years ago wasn't it?

And haven't I helped give you a better life in here?" Charlie nodded. "Exactly, so keep an eye on the people your daughter is spending time with, get me proof of their escape plans and I'll make sure they disappear." Kento grinned and sauntered away towards a small group of officers.

"Should I have done that?" Charlie said almost with a feeling of guilt. "Perhaps I'm overreacting, perhaps..." he trailed off as he noticed Jackie and Aggie walking towards him and his mood lifted. Instantly it soured as he saw Wolf was with them and the feelings of guilt vanished. *Who in the Emperor's name does he think he is?*

"Aggie," Jackie said in her cracked voice as they reached Charlie. "This is your father."

Aggie had a wide grin on her face and she looked as though she was struggling to keep still. *Should I hug her?* Charlie wondered to himself, but before he had chance to react Aggie threw her arms round him. He felt momentarily stunned, then tentatively wrapped his arms round his daughter, thinking back to the last time he'd done so.

Aggie had only been a baby really, not even a year old, but she'd smiled up at him and his heart had melted. It had always melted when he had looked at her. He felt it now, holding her again, his heart melted and he didn't remember why he'd been so angry a moment earlier.

She pulled away and looked up at him still smiling, "Sorry," she said taking a step back.

"What for?" he asked.

She looked embarrassed, "It's been a long time since we saw each other, I just presumed it would be okay to-"

Charlie smiled, "Of course it is, I'm your father."

Aggie smiled again and gave him another hug, "I've dreamt about this day so many times," she said in a muffled voice.

"So have I," he said quietly, then he held her at arm's length. "Now let me take a look at you." Aggie gave him a twirl and he smiled; she had his dark hair and green eyes but she was lighter than he was and looked so much like her mother. He gestured for Aggie to sit on one of the benches with him and she obeyed. He glanced quickly towards Jackie and Wolf who appeared deep in conversation.

"Aggie what happened?" he asked and his daughter looked confused. "I've seen your mother, I've spoken to her, she told me she took your place, she told me you were safe."

Aggie swallowed hard, "I got caught," she said slowly. "I've never been good at ignoring my gift, I tried to only use it in the house, but someone saw and they reported me."

Charlie nodded and placed a comforting arm round her shoulders, "And who's that man who seems to be acting as your bodyguard?"

Aggie looked over at Wolf and smiled, "That's just Wolf, we were brought into the palace at the same time, he's just looking out for me. We've seen what some of the officers do round here and I think he wants to make sure I'm okay."

It was a lie of course but she had promised Jackie she wouldn't reveal everything about their plans, and that included how she knew Wolf from the outside. She hadn't thought it was necessary, he was her father after all, if she couldn't trust him then who could she trust? But Jackie had made her promise, and she wouldn't break that promise.

"I think you can probably tell him I'll look after you from now on," Charlie said tightening his grip on Aggie's shoulders.

Aggie looked up at him frowning, "But he's my friend."

Charlie forced a smile, "I'm sure he is, but I've been here a long time, if anyone can protect you in here it's me."

Aggie shifted uncomfortably and Charlie dropped his arm from around her shoulders, *She doesn't trust me*, he thought with a flash of anger. *She would rather have him take care of her than her own father!* He tried to push down the feelings of anger and hatred towards the broad man but they bubbled to the surface. *He'll get what's coming to him.*

Charlie cleared his throat, "What do you think of the palace? He asked, trying to change the subject.

Aggie perked up, "I love it," she admitted. "I'm learning so many new skills and I love being able to work with my hands."

"You're happy to be serving the Emperor?"

Aggie frowned internally but tried to maintain her exterior smile, "Of course," she said and her father smiled. *Did he say that to keep up appearances?* she wondered. *Or was Flora right, is he on the Emperor's side?*

"Why don't you tell me everything I've missed," Charlie said with a smile.

Wolf and Jackie watched as Aggie chattered away at her father; Jackie looked concerned and Wolf had a frown on his face. "I don't know Jack, I'm not convinced she should be meeting with him."

"It doesn't matter whether we think she should meet him or not, she has a right to. Think how mad she'd be with us if she knew we'd prevented this from happening."

"I don't like him Jack, he's got a shifty look about him."

"I don't like him either," Jackie admitted. "But that still doesn't give us the right to keep Aggie from him."

"She won't tell him anything will she?" Wolf asked with sudden concern.

Jackie shook her head, "I made her promise not to."

Wolf nodded, "How's all the planning going?"

Jackie shrugged, "Flora and Flick have been organising their little journey to the sub-basement but other than that there isn't much to do."

"Any word from Nilla?"

Jackie suddenly looked worried, "No, nothing. I don't know what to make of it Wolf, I've tried everything I can to get information but no one's talking."

"We've got to hope that no news is good news, maybe it's too hard for her to get away?"

Jackie nodded stiffly, "I hope you're right, because if you're not, if something really has happened, then that girl is going to cling to the only family she's got and I doubt that'll be a good thing."

Wolf folded his arms and opened his mouth to speak, someone barrelled into him.

He yelled in surprise as an officer thumped him in the face while a second jumped onto his back as he got to his feet. He spun quickly and threw the second officer to the ground, where he knocked into Jackie causing her to collapse. Wolf saw Aggie scream and try to run towards him but her father grabbed hold of her.

That's probably for the best, he thought as he smacked the first officer in face and felt their nose crunch beneath his fist. The officer yelled and threw his hands to his bleeding face; Wolf kicked the front of his knee hard and the officer dropped. The third officer had been keeping his distance, clearly wanting to see how the situation played out. He was larger than the other two and clearly kept himself in good shape.

The second officer launched himself at Wolf again and managed to get a few good blows in before Wolf managed to head butt him and he fell backwards in a daze. Wolf squared up to the third officer as if daring him to make a move.

"Kento!" Jackie yelled, getting unsteadily to her feet. "What in the Emperor's name are you doing?"

"Stay out of this Jackie," Kento said balling his hands into fists. "This doesn't concern you."

"The Crafts it does!" Jackie yelled taking another step towards Kento. The officer turned and hit her, knocking her quickly to the floor. Aggie screamed and broke free from her father's grasp, Charlie stood stupefied and Wolf roared, launching himself at Kento.

They fell to the floor grappling with one another; Wolf bit, kicked and punched the other man all the while roaring like a wild animal. Kento somehow managed to scrabble away and got to his feet; he stood several steps away from Wolf, who suddenly looked twice as big as he had done a minute ago. Wolf stood rigid, breathing heavily, growling quietly.

Kento pulled out his firearm.

Aggie screamed again and threw herself between Wolf and Kento, "Please," she begged, tears running down her face.

Kento stared at her, then at Wolf, whose fists had unclenched and who now stood silently. He lowered his weapon, then walked towards Wolf who braced himself. The officer spat in his face and smacked Wolf across his head with the butt of his firearm before helping his comrades to their feet and marching away. Wolf dropped to the ground and Aggie collapsed at his side crying.

Charlie finally ran over to them and helped Jackie to

315

her feet, "Are you okay?" he asked while checking her over; she would have a black eye in a day or so but otherwise she looked unharmed.

Jackie nodded, "I'm fine," she said coldly making her way to where Wolf lay with Aggie sobbing beside him. "He'll be okay Aggie," she said soothingly.

Aggie looked up, "Why would they do this to him?" she asked.

Jackie shook her head, "Kento is known for his rough treatment of new Artists," she said touching her left eye gingerly.

Wolf groaned and stirred, then he opened his eyes and cracked an uneven smile at Aggie. He sat up and put a hand to his head as he felt a wave of dizziness wash over him; he looked at Jackie, "Are you okay?"

Jackie nodded, "I'll live, I'm more worried about you."

Wolf grunted as he got to his feet, "I'll be fine," he replied as Aggie threw her arms round him; he winced.

"Sorry," she said, quickly pulling away.

Wolf smiled, "Don't you worry lass, I've been in worse pain."

Jackie frowned, "Wolf you need to watch yourself, Kento isn't happy you showed him up, he's going to try and get revenge."

"Good," Wolf growled. "I wouldn't mind a rematch."

Jackie slapped him and he cried out, his already burning face flaring with pain, "Stop being foolish! The officers have firearms, and they aren't punished for, 'accidentally' killing Artists. You're lucky they didn't use the-."

At that moment a shot rang out and an Artist some distance away dropped to the ground like a stone. Silence fell heavy as lead around the grounds and several Artists started to scurry indoors.

"Crafts," Wolf whispered, "I didn't think they'd actually use them."

Jackie nodded sombrely, "You'd be surprised how often Artists bear the brunt of the officers' bad moods."

Wolf looked to Charlie, "I guess you were right after all."

Charlie started, "What?"

"You warned me about the officers, I guess I should have paid more attention."

Charlie shrugged, "I've been here a long time, I know how things work."

Jackie narrowed her eyes at the man but said nothing.

"Aggie why don't I take you back to your room," her father said holding out his hand to her.

She looked at him, then back at Wolf, "I think I'd like to stay with Wolf," she replied not looking at her father.

Charlie stiffened, "Aggie it's not safe for you, it would be better if you stayed in your room."

Aggie drew herself up to her full height and stared her father in the eyes, "You don't have any right to tell me what to do, I'm staying with Wolf."

A stunned silence fell, then Charlie forced a smile, "That's fine, perhaps we can catch up again another time." He turned to Wolf and Jackie. "I hope you both feel better soon," then he walked towards the palace with a face like thunder.

It had taken a couple of hours but Wolf had managed to convince Aggie to get an early night with the promise that he would do the same. Once he'd left her room, he and Jackie had gone to the empty dining room, where they both sat with troubled and bruised expressions.

"I'm not saying he hasn't wanted to," Jackie explained, an bag of ice over her left eye. "I can see in his eyes he's wanted to hit me for years, but I honestly didn't think he ever would."

"How often does that sort of thing happen?" Wolf asked.

Jackie frowned, then winced from the pain, "It used to happen more often, but….it's been a long time since someone was killed."

"Suppose it was due then," Wolf said shrugging.

Jackie shook her head, "Something isn't right, there's something we're not seeing."

"Like what?" Wolf asked, removing his own bag of ice to look at her.

"I don't know, I just feel like there's something we've overlooked. It's as if Kento has more information than he should."

Wolf shrugged, "I'm just glad Aggie was talking to her father, I'd hate to think what might have happened if she'd been with us."

"He seemed agitated."

"Who did?" Wolf asked.

"Charlie, when it was all over, he was too quiet and he kept fidgeting."

"Probably just shocked."

"You heard him, he's been here for years, he's seen worse than that."

"Then he was worried for Aggie," Wolf said with a shrug.

Jackie was silent, then she looked up at him, "Don't you think it was odd he picked you?"

Wolf shrugged, "I'm new."

"You were stood with me, I'm respected enough by

most that it just doesn't happen."

"What about Flicker?"

"They never attacked Flick when he was with me."

"What are you saying Jackie?"

"I think it was planned."

Wolf cocked his head, "What do you mean planned?"

"I think Charlie asked Kento to attack you."

Wolf looked taken aback, "But why? What have I ever done to him? I don't even know him!"

Jackie shook her head, "I've seen some of the looks he gives you when he thinks no one's looking. I don't think he likes that Aggie's so close to you-"

"You mean he's jealous?" Jackie nodded and Wolf snorted. "Well I'm not sure beating me up got him the result he wanted."

"You need to be careful Wolf," Jackie said putting her hand on his arm. "You're going to have to watch out for Kento *and* Charlie now."

Wolf scowled and put the bag of ice back on his face, "I think they're the ones who are going to have to watch out for me."

Chapter 38

Nilla paced her room for what must have been the hundredth time; she was starting to get restless and angry. She walked to the door of her lavish rooms and opened it revealing two officers standing guard.

"You're still here then," she said with irritation.

The officer on her left, who was a tall man with short dark hair turned to look at her, "Until you've been cleared we're instructed to-"

"Keep an eye on me. Yes, yes I know all that but really, do you think the Emperor himself would have instructed Perunia to let me into her secret little club if he didn't think I could be trusted?"

The guard shifted uncomfortably, opened his mouth, closed it again, then turned to face forwards. Nilla huffed loudly and slammed the door. Instantly there was a light knock and the door opened to reveal the second officer; a short woman with long dark blonde hair tied back in a knot.

"What?" Nilla asked coldly.

"Forgive me ma'am, but you're not confined to your quarters, you're allowed to leave just as everyone else."

Nilla folded her arms, "Yes and I'll have a wonderful officer escort while I do so."

The officer frowned, "I'm not sure I understand why you're reacting this way ma'am, we're all on the same side."

"Seems to me that I'm on the side of the Emperor and you're on the side of Perunia," Nilla replied.

The officer stiffened and she frowned, "I serve the Emperor and only the Emperor."

"Then why are you bending to Perunia's will?"

"The Emperor told her-" the officer began.

"The Emperor told her to provide me with the information to do my job properly and instead she's given me an *escort* and is preventing me from doing my job at all."

The officer looked as if she was going to speak but Nilla's expression made her falter, she glanced at her comrade, then back at Nilla. "Perhaps you'd like to spend some time in the gardens? If we happen to lose sight of you well…" the officer trailed off and a slight smile rose to Nilla's lips.

"I suppose it might be good to allow myself some fresh air," she stepped from her room and into the corridor with the two officers falling into step behind her. She felt a flutter of excitement at the thought she might be able to see her daughter. It had been days since they'd last spoken and she worried for her; she knew Wolf, Redd and the others would be looking after her but they'd already spent so long apart, she didn't want to do it again.

How in the Emperor's name did Redd and Flicker manage for so long?

They reached the main set of stairs and were about to descend when a familiar female voice spoke from behind.

"Nilla," Perunia said in her high pitched harsh tone.

She spun on her heels and faced the older woman, arms folded, "Yes Perunia?"

Perunia looked angry, no she looked far worse than

angry but there was also something else in her expression, something she couldn't quite figure out.

"The Emperor has asked to see you."

Nilla's eyes widened, "Again?" she asked trembling slightly. Perunia simply nodded and walked away; she followed and after a brief pause the officers turned and also followed.

Crafts! Has he found me out? Has he changed his mind? Maybe Perunia found me out, maybe she told him I can't be trusted. Crafts! What does he want with me?

She opened her mouth to ask if Perunia knew but thought better of it. They climbed the elaborate staircase until they reached the seventh floor and headed for the same small room where they'd waited the first time. Everett was waiting for them.

"Ah Perunia, thank you for bringing Nilla back to us, the Emperor was most insistent about talking with her again."

"Of course Everett, whatever the Emperor needs."

Everett nodded, "Right this way," all three moved forwards while the two officers waited, Everett paused by the door and looked surprised to see Perunia with them. "My apologies Perunia," he said with a slight bow. "The Emperor asked to speak to Nilla alone."

Perunia looked as though she'd been slapped and Nilla winced at her thunderous expression. She composed herself a moment later however and produced a perfect bow in return.

"Of course Everett, please let me know if there's anything further I can do to assist the Emperor."

Everett smiled and Perunia reluctantly withdrew, though she made sure the two officers remained inside the room to wait for Nilla.

"Shall we?" Everett said as he reached for the handle.

Nilla put a hand on his shoulder and he paused, "Everett," her voice was unsteady. "Am I in some sort of trouble?"

Everett looked at her and smiled, then he turned the handle and they began the same twisting journey as before. It wasn't long until she felt completely lost once again, that is until they stopped before the dark, wooden door, the one she knew the Emperor was behind. Everett knocked three times as he had the first time and entered the same large, beautifully decorated room.

The Emperor was already inside.

He was seated in one of the large, plush, midnight blue chairs reading a small, battered looking book. He looked up as she entered and smiled; he gestured for her to take a seat in the chair opposite and she obeyed, not wanting to make him angry. Everett took a seat at the writing desk, a pen in his hand and looked ready to record their conversation.

The Emperor studied her for several minutes before he finally spoke, "You are curious."

Nilla remained silent, unsure what, if anything, she should say.

"I've been informed that Perunia has all but confined you to your living quarters and prevented you from completing your work."

"Yes Emperor," Nilla said feeling her palms become hot and clammy.

"And during that time you've challenged the guards multiple times and claimed they aren't on my side?"

She felt her cheeks go hot, *How does he know all of this?* "That is correct Emperor."

"What made you say these things? What made you think Perunia wasn't working under my command?"

She opened her mouth to speak then closed it,

Doesn't he remember what he said when I was last here? Or is this some kind of test? "The last time I saw you Emperor you informed Perunia that I was to be provided with the information necessary to do my job competently. It seemed to me that she was going against your wishes."

The Emperor stared at her for several minutes before finally nodding his head, "You are correct. Why do you think Perunia is acting the way she is? Is she not loyal to me?"

"She's incredibly loyal Emperor," Nilla said quickly, "she loves her job and she loves being a part of your administration team."

"Then what is the reason for her actions?"

She shifted in the large chair and looked uncomfortable.

"Speak," the Emperor commanded.

"I believe she might be jealous Emperor," she had no trouble speaking the lie.

"Jealous?"

She nodded, "I think she may believe I'm getting special treatment…from you Emperor."

He let out a loud, deep laugh which put her on edge rather than making her relax. "Everett," he turned to the small man. "You will ensure Perunia feels appreciated." Everett nodded and turned back to his notebook which was full of scribbled handwriting. The Emperor turned back to Nilla. "I appreciate all of those who help to maintain the peace in the Palace," he said, as if making something clear to her. "However I am also aware that different people have different talents."

Nilla nodded but remained quiet, she sensed that now wasn't the time for her to speak.

"Nilla, I appreciated your honesty the last time you were here, it is not something I experience often. The others, they do not treat me like a man but like a God and although I am blessed with exceptionally long life and good health, a man is what I am."

She nodded again.

"When people start to see you as a God, they fear you, they are afraid to tell you the truth and so they lie. Nilla, when my people lie, even if it is done with the best intentions it is an attack on me. They are implying I can't handle knowing what is really going on in my palace, but how can I improve the situation if I don't know what my people are actually thinking?"

She nodded for a third time but still didn't dare speak. *What's he getting at?* She thought as she studied his unreadable expression. *Does he know the Artist's are unhappy? Does he want to change things?*

"I have a proposition for you," he finally said after being silent for several minutes. "I would like you to work with Everett and try to find out what is really going on in the palace. I want you to work together and find out if there is any unrest, any plots against me. I want you to find me the Artists and officers who aren't loyal."

Nilla felt a cold dread wash over her but she nodded her head and smiled at the Emperor, "It would be an honour," she said.

It was after midnight when Flicker finally heard footsteps on the stairs; he slunk back into the shadows growing tense. The footsteps grew louder until they eventually reached the bottom of the staircase, there was a long silence, then he heard Flora's whispered voice.

"Flicker?"

He emerged from the shadows and Flora instantly relaxed, "I was worried you wouldn't be able to get away, the officers seem rather alert."

Flicker shrugged, "I'm used to sneaking around this place late at night. Did you have any trouble?"

Flora shook her head, "Jan's covering for me."

He nodded, "Remind me to thank him for everything he's done for us when this is all over."

They moved further into the basement, Flora leading the way. The duo walked in silence for several minutes until they were sure they'd be out of earshot.

"Do you think you'll be able to get the lock open?"

Flicker shrugged in the gloom, "I won't know really until I see the lock, but I'm hoping so."

They passed the rows of thick, wooden doors that held the clay decoys and Flicker wondered, not for the first time why they were being stored there and what they would be used for. It seemed like a waste of good clay to him, especially since they seemed to genuinely be in a resource crisis.

"What do you think the Emperor plans to do with everything in there?" he asked, gesturing to the rows of doors.

Flora shook her head, "I've no idea, I'm convinced they're still active, otherwise it seems like a waste."

Flicker cocked his head and considered her words, "I'm not so sure, I mean anyone could give the breath of life to them if they tried, I could do it right now."

"But it doesn't make sense otherwise, there would be no logical reason to keep them," Flora argued.

Flicker sighed, "I don't know what to say. I can see where you're coming from and a large part of me agrees, but it just doesn't make sense to have them so close to the Artists when someone could easily trigger them."

They continued on in silence, twisting and turning down the various dim, stone corridors until Flora finally stopped before a dark opening.

"The door is at the bottom of these stairs," she said.

Flicker nodded and made his way to the bottom where he examined the lock, he drew in a sharp breath, "It's not going to be easy," he called to Flora.

"Can you do it?" she asked.

Flicker nodded, then realised she couldn't see him, "I can do it, but it might take a while."

"There shouldn't be any patrols down here, so as long as we're quiet, we should be okay."

Flicker set to work while Flora remained at the top of the small flight of stairs to keep watch in case any stray officers found their way to them. Flicker studied the lock for several minutes before he set to work with his handmade picks and tools. It wasn't all that different from the locks he'd picked before; it looked just like the ones on the workshop doors in fact, but he was fairly certain that this lock had actually been made by an Artist and anything made by an Artist could be subtly altered from the original.

He worked slowly and carefully, making sure to be precise in his movements; he could tell Flora was growing impatient. He could hear that she'd started pacing, but she'd just have to wait, you couldn't rush these things, especially if an Artist had been involved in the construction.

Another few minutes later and Flora peered down at him, "How's it coming?" she asked with a slight edge to her voice.

"Another few minutes and I'll be done," he said, not looking at her. Flora bit her lip, then went back to pacing.

Flicker heard an almost inaudible, 'click' and the padlock finally sprung open; he heaved a sigh of relief and called to Flora.

"We're in."

Flora practically scrambled down the steps and held her breath as he pushed the door open; it creaked quietly as if it hadn't been opened in years. Blackness lay before them.

"Do we have some sort of light?" Flicker asked.

Flora took a step into the blackness, "In theory there should be a switch here somewhere." She started fumbling along the walls just inside the door and eventually the room was illuminated with a pale glow.

They both gasped.

The room was in fact more like a cavern. Large stone pillars stood at regular intervals, clearly providing structural support. The remainder of the room was filled with statues and sculptures similar to those in the rooms above, only these were far more realistic. If Flicker hadn't known any better he'd have thought they were already alive.

He walked up to the first member of the Emperor's, 'army' ensuring his mouth remained closed and he breathed through his mouth. He started to examine the first statue closely; it was a tall female, who looked to be well built. She wore what he assumed was going to be the army's uniform and there were two pistols holstered at her hips. He glanced at the figures either side of her and although their gender was different they looked almost exactly the same.

After walking amongst the statues for several minutes he'd finally concluded that they were all the same, or at least they'd been based on the same model; tall, broad, muscular. Clearly what the Emperor hoped would be the perfect army.

Flora joined him a moment later, "Is it just me or is this all just a little creepy?"

Flicker nodded, "It's creepy alright. Have you found

anything other than people?"

Flora pointed further along the cavernous room, "I think I could make out a mass of horses over in that far corner."

They walked towards where Flora had pointed and it took them far longer to reach the horse statues that Flicker would have thought it should. After walking for well over half an hour the first horse came into view. He studied it carefully, paying attention to the amount of detail that had been used in the creation of the beast.

It was almost perfect.

He had noticed some slight imperfections but nothing that would deter from the horse from believing it were real. "This is incredible," he said as he stared at row upon row of sturdy, well-built horses. "With animals like this to ride or pull supplies the army could ride for days without needing to rest."

"That's the point isn't it? The reason the Emperor is creating this army? They're his perfect soldiers; they won't need food or sleep and if they've been created properly they'll be so lifelike they'll already know how to fight."

Flicker nodded looking suddenly distracted, "I wonder what would happen right now if I-"

Flora grabbed his arm, "Don't you dare!"

He looked at her and grinned, "Aren't you even a little curious?"

"Not so curious that I'm willing to risk both our lives!"

Flicker shrugged and she let go, "So what do we do now?"

Flora looked around them and bit her lip in thought, "I guess all we *can* do is report back to the others and tell them what we've found."

"I think we need to keep this in mind for a potential

distraction," he said indicating the large motionless army around them."

"As a last resort perhaps," she said looking less than convinced. "But I don't want to put anyone, including the officers, in any unnecessary danger." They began walking back towards the open door.

"Seriously Flora? The others up there, they're not your friends, they're not on our side, if they're killed because they serve the Emperor then I'm not going to lose sleep at night."

"And what about Jan? Or the other Artists?" Flora asked.

Flicker paused, "Alright, we'll use it as a last resort only," he said, though he could tell she wasn't convinced by his words. *I'm sorry Flora,* he thought as they reached the main door, *but if it's a case of us or them, then I choose us and I'll do whatever it takes to get us out of here.*

It took them twice as long to find the main staircase once they'd left the sub-basement as they'd taken several wrong turns. By the time they'd finally arrived Flicker felt exhausted and couldn't wait to curl up in bed. They were about to climb the stairs when Flora placed an arm across his chest to stop him; she cocked her head.

"Damn," she said under her breath, then she turned to him and whispered. "I think there's some officers up there."

"What should we do?" he asked.

"I'll go up first, I'll tell them I thought I heard someone down here and came to look, when I've got them distracted you'll have to sneak past."

Flicker nodded and Flora started up the stairs, he heard the officers at the top call out as they heard her footsteps and she called back to them. He made his way after her carefully and quietly, ensuring he made as little noise as possible.

When he poked his head round the corner he saw all three officers with their backs to him and he edged his way across the floor behind them until he reached the large staircase. He took them two at a time, hoping that the heavy carpet would muffle his footsteps and once out of sight raced down the corridors until he reached his room.

He breathed heavily as he leant against the inside of the closed door and sank slowly to the floor in a heap of exhaustion.

Chapter 39

"Please Aggie, let me explain," Charlie said as his daughter turned and stomped away from him.

"I don't want to talk to you," she replied, making her way to where Wolf sat, still bruised and battered.

"You don't need to talk, you just need to listen," he said as he caught up to her.

She stopped abruptly and spun, staring at him with anger and betrayal, "Is it really true?" she asked and the question seemed to catch Charlie off guard.

"Is what really true?" he asked.

"You know perfectly well what!" she replied gesturing towards Wolf who was now watching them with caution. "I take it that's why you want to talk to me? You want to explain why you goaded the officers into doing such a thing?"

Charlie paused, opened his mouth and closed it again, Aggie's expression turned to shock and anger.

"You can't can you!? You can't even come up with a good enough reason for what you did!"

Charlie's expression darkened slightly, "Why do you even care Aggie? You barely know that man and you're acting like...like he's-"

"My father?" she finished folding her arms. Charlie looked at her with an expression she couldn't quite place and she turned away from him. "He's more of a father to me than you," she said quietly, "I don't think I want to see you for awhile," she walked away quickly.

Charlie clenched his fists as he watched his daughter sit next to the man he hated. *You'll pay for this,* he thought as he felt his anger rising, *if it's the last thing I do, you'll pay for this.* He watched them for several minutes as Aggie laughed at something Wolf had said when a shadow fell across him; he glanced to his right and saw Kento.

"You don't look too happy," the officer said lazily.

Charlie tried to make himself relax, "I'm fine Kento."

The officer scoffed, "Is that why you're stalking your daughter and that Artist?"

"I'm not stalking them," he replied through clenched teeth. "She's my daughter, I'm allowed to keep an eye on her."

"Right," Kento said, leaning against a nearby tree. "You know you've given us some relatively helpful information recently, in return we could do something more permanent to deal with him."

Charlie shot Kento a look, "What do you mean?"

"I think you know exactly what I mean. The boys and I, we're not too happy with what he did to us, we'd like to get our revenge."

Charlie smiled wickedly, then his expression faltered, "She'll know," he said bitterly and when Kento looked questioningly he elaborated. "Aggie, she'll know it was me who made you do it, she'll hate me."

"I'm sure we can find a way to work around that little fact. If we attacked her-"

"Don't you lay a hand on her!" he growled.

Kento held his hands up in mock surprise, "Hey, calm down, we won't *actually* hurt her, because you'll save her. The other guy, he can simply be caught in the crossfire."

"You promise Aggie won't get hurt?"

Kento placed a hand on his shoulder, "Charlie, we're on the same side aren't we? You have my word she won't be harmed."

Charlie nodded but said nothing and Kento walked away with a wicked grin on his face. He took a deep breath; *I guess I should make an effort.* He walked towards his daughter and Wolf and the other man looked up as he approached.

"Hello Charlie," Wolf said in his gruff voice.

Aggie scowled, "What do you want father?"

Charlie forced an apologetic smile, "I wanted to apologise to your friend here," he turned to Wolf. "Look, I'm sorry, I really am, I was a jealous fool and I acted poorly. Really I should have been thanking you for taking care of my daughter. Please forgive my selfish actions" He held out his hand and after a few minutes Wolf shook it.

"Don't mention it," Wolf half grunted.

Charlie turned to Aggie who looked unconvinced, "I hope you'll be able to forgive me too?"

Aggie stared at him for several minutes before she slowly nodded her head; he moved closer to her and opened his arms to hug her but she drew back and he faltered. "I forgive you," she said, folding her arms. "But that doesn't mean I'm going to forget what you did. I can't act like this didn't happen; I'm going to need some time."

He nodded but his heart sank and his anger rose, *What will it take to get her on my side?* "I'm sorry you feel that way Aggie, but I'll do my best to make you trust me again." He smiled as warmly as he could at them and walked away, feeling his hands ball into fists once again.

"You didn't need to do that, lass," Wolf said once Charlie had left them.

"I know," Aggie shrugged, "don't take this the wrong way Wolf, but I didn't do it for you, I did it for me." She smiled at the older man. "I know he's my father but I don't know him, and that's been made very clear these last few days. I was naive to think he'd be how I imagined him, how my mother described him. It's been fifteen years and he's been stuck in here, doing what he can to survive. I need to find out who he is before I can let him into my life."

"That's a very wise thing to do," Wolf said giving her shoulder a squeeze. He looked up as Jackie and Redd came quickly towards them. "Is everything okay?" he asked as they arrived.

Redd nodded, "I've just seen my brother, they want us to get together this evening by the lake."

"The Emperor only knows why he chose the lake," Jackie said as she shook her head. "Those Crafting swans hate him."

"Do you think my mother will be there?" Aggie asked hopefully.

"I've tried to get a message to her," Jackie said. "I hope she's able to get away and let us know what's been happening up there," she gestured to the upper floors of the Palace.

"As long as the Emperor doesn't know about us then I don't really care what's been going on," Redd said as he sat down on the warm grass.

"I do," Aggie said getting to her feet. "My mother's never been worried about risking her safety before to come and meet us, which means something must have happened up there to make meeting us even more dangerous."

Jackie nodded, "Nilla will be keeping her distance not only to protect herself but also to protect us."

"I suppose you're right," Redd said. "I guess we should be grateful to her."

Aggie nodded in satisfaction.

They were silent for a few minutes, then Redd looked towards Wolf and Jackie, "How are you two holding up?"

Jackie grinned, "It'll take more than a black eye to keep me down," she said though she winced as smiling clearly caused her some discomfort.

"I've been through worse," Wolf agreed.

Nilla slipped out of her room towards dusk, *This is ridiculous,* she thought as she crept down the empty corridor towards the stairs. *I shouldn't feel like I'm doing something wrong.* She peered round the corner to make sure the coast was clear and quickly made her way down the large staircase. *I'm technically working for the Emperor now to find traitors; I can go where I please, when I please, so why do I feel so guilty?*

She continued down the elaborate staircase, with wooden carved flora and fauna running along the length of the banister and nodded to Artists and officers who passed her. *Perhaps it's because I'm technically a traitor, really I should just hand myself in and be done with it.* She smiled a little at that.

She relaxed as she arrived on the ground floor and walked with more confidence towards the palace gardens. The air was cool and the sky was clear as she walked down towards the gardens; she had no idea where Aggie and the others would be this evening, so she'd just have to walk round and hope that she found them.

It would be good for her to have some fresh air, and if any of the officers whom she assumed would have been asked to keep an eye on her were around, it would look like she was doing as the Emperor asked. She needed to get close enough to groups of Artist's that it would look like she was eavesdropping, without actually being noticed.

Of course she had no actual intention of revealing any, 'traitors' even if she found them. She wasn't really sure why she'd accepted the position the Emperor had offered; perhaps it was because she hadn't felt as if she could actually say no.

"Good evening," came an unfamiliar male voice.

Nilla glanced to the side and saw a tall, broad, blonde officer walking towards her; she smiled, "Good evening officer."

"Are you one of the administration team?" he asked eyeing her non-standard outfit.

She nodded, "Yes, I'm just out for some fresh air.

"I didn't think the administration team came out to fraternise with the other Artists," he said sliding a hand to where his firearm sat at his hip.

She took an internal deep breath and leant closer to him, "I'm under special orders from the Emperor," she said in a low voice and the officer raised an eyebrow.

"What special orders?"

"He suspects there are those who aren't loyal, he's tasked me with finding them."

"Proof?" the officer asked.

Nilla had thought this might happen and had thankfully had the good sense to mention it to Everett, he'd written her a note, which she now handed to the officer.

The officer read the note then scoffed, "You want to

know who's not loyal? I can tell you that right now!" She looked taken aback and the officer started to laugh. "You think it's some big secret that Artist's aren't loyal?"

She shook her head, "I didn't realise it was so openly talked about."

"It is between the officers," he replied fingering the butt of his firearm. "We target the ones who aren't loyal."

She nodded slowly, trying not to look horrified.

The officer grinned, "Look for the ones with bruises, they're the ones you want and when you take them to the Emperor, don't forget to mention my name," he began to walk away.

"What is your name?" she called.

"Kento," he said over his shoulder.

She stood frozen for several minutes as she watched the brash officer walk away, then she shook her head and scanned about for Aggie or her friends. She couldn't see them in the immediate vicinity so she continued on, making sure she headed in the opposite direction to Kento.

Eventually as she neared the lake, she noticed a small group, trying to remain inconspicuous by the water's edge. She smiled at their obvious failure to be hidden and made her way towards them.

Aggie was the first one to notice her and she squealed before jumping to her feet and throwing herself at her mother who hugged her tightly. After several minutes of struggling to breathe she managed to extract herself from her daughter and joined the others.

"It's been a while," Flicker said, nodding in her direction.

"We've been worried," Jackie added with a concerned smile.

"I'm sorry," she said, taking a seat, "things upstairs

got a little...complicated."

"Complicated how?" Jackie asked in a worried tone.

"No one knows anything," she assured them. "At least I don't think they do. I-" she paused as she took in Jackie and Wolf's appearances. "Wolf! Jackie! What happened?"

They smiled as if it was nothing and Wolf tried to brush her away as she attempted to examine him, "We're fine lass," he said in a jovial tone. "Just a little run in with the officers."

She paused, suddenly looking terrified.

"What is it?" Redd asked.

She turned to them, "I've just had a run in with one of the officers myself," she said quietly. "He told me they target those they believe are traitors," she turned back to Wolf.

He smiled and shook his head in return, "I don't think you need to worry, I'm pretty sure this had nothing to do with that."

She opened her mouth to protest when Aggie interrupted, "It was my father," she said quietly.

Nilla turned in towards her, "What?" she asked almost in a whisper.

Aggie looked ashamed and it was Jackie who eventually explained, "It seems that Charlie didn't like Aggie being around Wolf, he asked Kento and his friends to teach him a lesson."

Nilla's mouth hung open and her eyes were wide.

"I know he looks bad," Jackie said. "But you should have seen the state of the officers when he'd finished with them," she chuckled trying and failing to lighten the atmosphere.

Nilla shook her head, "I can't believe it," she looked at her daughter. "If anyone but you had told me, I wouldn't have thought it possible. Your father was such a kind, gentle man when I knew him."

"This place can change a person," Flicker said solemnly.

She nodded in reply feeling her heart break, then forced a smile, "I suppose I should tell you everything that's been happening upstairs over the past few weeks."

They leant towards her and she started to explain.

The group were stunned into silence once Nilla had finished recounting her tale; it was Flicker who finally spoke up.

"You're working directly for the Emperor?"

Nilla nodded and they continued to stare at her in disbelief.

"So who's this Everett person? Jackie finally asked, "I've never heard of him."

"As far as I can guess he's the Emperor's personal assistant. He seems to do everything for him, and I'm pretty sure he's the one the administration team managers actually talk to. When Perunia and I met with the Emperor the first time, she acted as if it was the highest honour."

"I'm not sure I like this," Flicker said, "you're putting yourself in even more danger."

Nilla smiled, "The way I see it I'm in no more danger than when I first arrived. I'm not an Artist and I'm still planning to help other Artist's escape."

"But you're in direct contact with the Emperor," Flicker protested.

"Not really, I'll mainly be reporting to Everett and he's hardly as threatening as the Emperor."

Flicker frowned but said no more.

"Does this mean you'll have more freedom?" Aggie

asked hopefully.

Nilla nodded, "I'm required to observe the Artist's when they're at their most vulnerable, which means I'm required to be out here when they are." She smiled as her daughter beamed, then looked round the ever growing group of potential escapees. "I think we need to start being smart about meeting. You're too conspicuous and I can't keep being seen with you in case the Emperor becomes suspicious of *my* loyalty."

"You don't have any loyalty to him," Redd pointed out.

"Well yes, but he doesn't know that does he, and I'd rather he didn't find out. I'm in a fortunate position right now, I might be able to uncover some useful information."

"Speaking of useful information," Flicker interrupted brightly. "Flora and I entered the sub-basement." The waited expectantly for him to continue and as he revelled in their suspense; Jackie punched him on the arm. "Alright," he said rubbing the area she'd just hit. "It's just as we suspected."

"The army?" Wolf asked.

Flicker nodded, "There's a huge cavern beneath the palace and basement, and it's filled with clay men, women and horses. The Emperor has an army ready to do his bidding, and as soon as an Artist gives the breath of life they'll be awaiting his orders."

"Do you think you could get in again?" Redd asked.

"I should think so, with Flora's help," Flicker replied. "What are you thinking?"

Redd smiled, "I'm thinking that we could use the Emperor's army as a nice distraction when we escape."

Chapter 40

Nilla sat with Everett in silence pouring over the books he had given her. She wasn't quite sure why it was important to read them, but he had been quite insistent. She sighed heavily and he looked up at her across the table.

"Is something wrong?" he asked in his calm, polite tone.

She glanced up quickly, clearly unaware she had sighed audibly; her cheeks turned pink, "I'm sorry, I'm doing my best with these," she indicated the pile of books next to her on the table. "I just don't see how it will help me with the Emperor's task."

Everett leant back in his chair and eyed her over his glasses, "How easy do you think it is to keep the palace running smoothly?" he asked.

Nilla shrugged, "I've no idea."

"It's not easy at all," he replied leaning towards her. "The administration team feel they're superior to everyone else and therefore believe they should be entitled to certain privileges, half of the Artist's are unhappy and try to break out several times a year and the officers act so superior to everyone, it can be difficult to keep some of them under control."

"I hadn't realised it was so complicated," she replied.

"No one ever does. And because the Emperor is far

too busy and important to deal with what's going on out there," he gestured wildly with his arms. "They all come to me."

"I'm still not sure how this will help with my-" she began.

"I'd like you to help me with the enquiries," Everett said interrupting her, she opened her mouth but he rushed on. "I need help and the Emperor trusts you, which means I trust you. He has also tasked you with finding traitors and what easier way than to get them to come to you."

She cocked her head, "I don't understand."

Everett leaned back again and placed his fingertips together, "I've long since suspected that half of the people who make their way to me are actually disloyal to the Emperor but I've no proof. But you have the ability to meet them, talk to them and then follow them into the gardens to see what they do."

Nilla felt her insides squirm. She had liked Everett as soon as she'd met him, he was calm and polite and had seemed completely harmless, but right now, seeing the look on his face she felt uneasy and wished to be anywhere but there.

She smiled, "Of course, I understand the importance now." Everett smiled back at her and she buried herself in the next book, trying desperately to forget the expression on his face.

She must have read the introductory paragraph regarding the palace officers five times before she realised it wasn't going to sink in. Her mind kept flitting back to her daughter and the fact she hadn't seen her in what felt like weeks. Since their last meeting, when she had been sure she'd be able to get into the gardens and see her more often, Everett had decided that she needed background training before she continued the Emperor's work. Then when she'd managed to get out into the gardens it had either been too late or too early for the others to be around.

Of course it wasn't really Everett's idea and she knew that; Everett spent half of his morning's meeting with the Emperor to discuss the agenda for the day and it was in those same meetings that she was certain they discussed her as she sat mere feet from them. It always made her uncomfortable to think they were talking about her and she wondered what they might be saying. Did they really believe she was loyal? Or was this all an elaborate hoax to try and catch her, Aggie and their friends?

She would never know what went on in those meetings, Everett refused to tell her, he claimed what was spoken between him and the Emperor was confidential unless specifically stated. Nilla herself had seen the Emperor only a handful more times since she'd first been offered her new position. She didn't feel any more comfortable meeting with him. In fact she was certain the more times she met him, the more convinced she was that he must have found out her secret.

Her mind drifted back to Aggie and she hoped her daughter was okay. She knew Wolf and the others would be looking after her, but she was becoming increasingly worried about Charlie. There had been a hint of something when they'd been together, flickering and fleeting, lurking beneath the surface, but it had never risen.

The closest he had come to snapping had been not long after they had become an item. They had gone for a drink at one of the local pubs and she had made her way to the bar to get their second round of drinks. She had known the barman since childhood and they began chatting as he poured their drinks. She had been laughing at something he had said when Charlie had appeared at her side and placed his arm possessively round her shoulders. He'd spoken to the barman in a stern tone, his expression had been firm, he'd clutched her a little too tightly.

She hadn't really thought anything of it at the time, after all what was wrong with a little jealousy? But after hearing what he'd had done to Wolf…she felt uneasy and restless, she needed to get back into the gardens to find her friends, she needed to know that they were all okay.

She put a hand to her head and squinted a little at the pages in front of her; Everett glanced up, noticed her expression and spoke.

"Are you okay?" there was softness and concern in his voice, all traces of his momentary hostility were gone.

"Just a headache," Nilla said with a pained smile. "I'm sure it will pass."

Everett frowned, "Perhaps you should stop for the evening," he said glancing at the clock. "It should still be light outside, why not get some fresh air to clear your head."

Nilla smiled gratefully, placed a marker in the book she had failed to read and rose from her seat, "Thank you, I'm sure the fresh air will clear my mind."

Everett nodded and she left the room, making her way down the now familiar maze of corridors until she reached the main set of stairs. She smiled and nodded to the guards on duty and they nodded curtly in return. She continued to smile as she made her way towards the ground floor and palace gardens.

Oh Everett, she thought with a grin, *you're so predictable*. It wasn't the first time she'd feigned a headache or illness to get out of reading those mind numbing books and he'd

345

always responded with one of two options. 'Go and lie down' or 'take a walk in the gardens'. He'd answered her in exactly the way she had wanted, now she just had to hope that this time Aggie was outside.

Aggie was making sure she spent all of her time with Wolf when she wasn't in class. He'd told her she was being silly and there was no need, but she was certain the officers were just waiting for a time when he was alone. They seemed to be following him, stalking his every move. She didn't care how many times he told her he could handle himself, she wasn't about to let him out of her sight.

They were taking a walk around the sculpture garden, passing the time before their next meeting with Flicker. He would be talking to Redd and Jackie at the moment and then he'd update them on their progress. It wasn't easy and she was sure he was beginning to feel like a messenger but her mother had been right, they'd started to become too noticeable and if they wanted to continue with their plan, they needed to be smart.

She smiled as Wolf inspected an elaborate statue of a peacock; he loved walking round the sculpture garden, she knew it was his favourite place. He'd explained that he admired all forms of artwork, especially because of his own lack of talent, but he was fascinated by the sculptures. He felt it required a more practiced eye in order to make them appear realistic.

"What I wouldn't give to have talent like this," Wolf said as he stared with his nose an inch away from the peacock's beak.

Aggie giggled, "It's all about practice, I've seen your work, it's not that bad, if you practiced you could be as good as this."

He shook his head, "You need careful hands for this type of work and that's something I simply don't have. I'm a fighter not an artisan."

"Wolf," she hugged him tightly. "You're one of the kindest, most gentle people I know."

"Quiet lass," he said with a chuckle, "we don't want to break my cover." She pulled back from him still with a grin on her face but it quickly turned to a frown as she glanced to his side. "What's wrong Aggie?" He followed the direction of her gaze and saw five officers walking towards them. Kento was at their head. Wolf sighed and set his jaw. "Keep behind me Aggie, I don't want you getting hurt."

Aggie remained where she was, "It's not me I'm worried about Wolf, I think they're still angry about what you did to them."

He smiled down at her, "Don't worry about me lass, I can take them."

She shook her head, "Unless you've got a firearm hidden away then I'm not sure you can."

Wolf looked again at the oncoming group and saw with shock that the officers' firearms were already in their hands and pointed at him. Aggie stood in front of him, her heart pounding as they drew closer.

"Aggie what are you doing? They'll shoot you," he started to move in front of her but she slipped beneath his arm and faced the officers as they stopped several feet from them.

"They might leave me alone," Aggie whispered, her voice trembling audibly. "They're friends with my father remember."

Wolf grabbed her by the shoulders and dragged her so she was behind him again, "Don't be a fool Aggie, this isn't worth us both getting hurt."

Kento grinned at them, "Listen to him girl, we're not interested in you."

Aggie struggled against Wolf's grip but he held firm and she could only partially see the group of officers, "Please!" she shouted desperately. "Please don't hurt him."

Kento grinned again but it was twisted and full of malice, "Sorry girl, I don't think that's going to be possible."

He raised his firearm and aimed at Wolf's chest.

"Stop!"

The officer's wavered and glanced around to see Charlie running towards them, Kento scowled, "What do you want Charlie?"

"Don't hurt them," Charlie said with a pleading expression. "I don't want this to happen, I don't want to lose my daughter over this."

"Too late Charlie a deal's a deal."

"Father what have you done?!" Aggie asked, eyes wide.

Charlie placed himself between Wolf and the officers, his arms outstretched towards them, he peered over his shoulder and looked at his daughter as she stared back at him with his eyes. "I'm so sorry Aggie, I wanted revenge, I wanted to have you all to myself, but I realise now that this isn't the way to make that happen." He turned back to Kento and the officers. "Walk away Kento, before you do something you'll regret."

Kento barked a laugh, "Regret? Charlie I could kill all three of you right now and I wouldn't regret a thing. In fact I'd probably be doing the world a favour."

"Do you really think the Emperor would congratulate you for killing three of his Artists?" Nilla said as she strolled towards them, arms folded, expression stern. "I'd have thought you'd know better than that."

Kento swivelled and levelled his firearm at her and Aggie yelped in fear. Nilla looked unfazed at the weapon pointed directly at her chest. "I wouldn't do that either," she said calmly.

"Why not?" Kento spat. "Four dead Artists sounds even better than three! I could tell the Emperor you were all traitors and I know he'd congratulate me for that!"

"That could work on those three," she waved her hand at the others. "But you know it wouldn't work for me. I know the Emperor personally remember and I've been tasked with finding traitors as well you know, I sincerely doubt he'd believe I was one myself."

Kento's expression faltered and he whirled back round to point his firearm at Charlie, "Deal's off Charlie, no more letting you look like a hero in front of your girl, we're through, which means now you're just one of them and you're fair game."

His finger gently squeezed the trigger but his shot was thrown wide as something large barrelled into him and sent him sprawling to the ground. The other officers stumbled back in surprise and in that moment Wolf hurled himself at them. Nilla grabbed Aggie and tried to drag her away from the chaos.

"Please mother stop! We've got to help them!"

Nilla looked over at Wolf who was throwing the officers around like they were ragdolls and beating them with their own weapons and then at Flicker, who was the one who had rammed into Kento but was now struggling against him. "Alright."

She grabbed for Kento's firearm but his grip remained strong so she kicked him twice in the head to make him let go. She swung the weapon towards him, smacking him in the face with it, then levelled it at his head. He froze instantly.

"I think that's enough," she said calmly though her heart was thumping in her chest. "Let's call this one a tie and all walk away unharmed."

"It's a little late for that," Kento snarled, struggling to his feet, blood dripping from his nose. "You think you're saving these Artist scum?" he spat and blood spattered across her clothes. "You haven't saved them, you've simply signed their death warrants, along with your own!" He snatched the firearm from her hands, shoved her roughly to the ground and pointed his weapon at her, his finger resting on the trigger. Nilla held her breath, hoped Wolf was shielding Aggie and prayed it would end quickly.

"What in the Emperor's name is going on here!?" Everett's normally calm voice rang through the sculpture park clearly and the officers froze. They looked towards him and saluted, holstering their weapons immediately.

"Sir," Kento said, standing to attention. "I apologise for what you've seen, we were just dealing with some troublemakers."

"Troublemakers?!" Everett asked as he helped Nilla to her feet. "The Emperor forgive you Kento, this is Nilla, she's one of the Emperor's most loyal subjects!"

Kento's expression darkened for a split second before turning neutral again, "My apologies Sir, but she intervened with a punishment."

"What punishment?"

"I have become suspicious that *these* Artist's could be traitors."

Everett's eyes narrowed and he turned to Nilla; he spoke in a low voice, "What do you have to say about all of this?" he asked and there was a hint of malice beneath the calm.

Nilla took a deep breath and kept her voice as low as his, "Everett, I must apologise, I should have told you this sooner but I feared for their safety." He shot her a look and she took another breath before continuing. "These Artist's are my family."

Everett inhaled sharply then narrowed his eyes as he leant in closer and practically hissed at her, "Explain yourself."

Nilla pointed to where Wolf and Aggie were standing, the latter clinging to the former in terror, "That's my daughter and with her is my brother." *Hopefully he won't comment on the lack of family resemblance.* She then pointed to where Charlie and Flicker were stood. "That's my husband and with him is an old family friend of ours. I know I should have informed you of this as soon as I began to work closely with you but I was terrified that someone else might find out and would try to use them against me," she shook her head. "And it looks like that has already happened."

Everett stared at her silently for what felt like an age and Nilla had to throw all of her effort into looking ashamed and guilty.

Eventually Everett sighed and nodded once, "I understand," he said quietly before turning back to Kento. "Leave these Artist's alone, they are no longer your concern."

"But Sir-"

Everett drew himself up to his full, unimpressive height, "Are you questioning me?!"

Kento shook his head quickly, saluted and turned to leave with the other officers.

"And Kento," the officer turned back to him and visibly shuddered at the hostile expression on Everett's face. "If I hear that one of them has suffered an 'accident', you might just find yourself on the Emperor's bad side."

Kento nodded once, then ran to catch up with his comrades.

"Everett I'm so-" Nilla began but Everett held up a hand to silence her.

"Nilla I think we should return to the office and discuss what must be done with your family, they cannot possibly remain in the open."

"But, where could they go?"

"Perhaps we should consider placing them under guard, until Kento has calmed down."

"You don't think the threat of the Emperor will stop him then?"

"Unfortunately, no. I've known Kento a long time and he's not one to let a grudge fall easily. Having your family remain indoors under guard will be the only way to ensure their safety. Come, let us move them upstairs."

Everett began walking towards the Palace and Nilla looked to the others, a look of apology on her face, "If you'll all follow Everett, we're going to move you upstairs for a few days."

"Nilla what in the Emperor's name did you tell him?" Flicker hissed.

"I told him you were all part of my family and now he wants to keep you under guard for your protection."

"Are you kidding me?! Nilla I came to say we're ready to implement the plan."

Nilla looked startled, "So soon?" she asked.

"Redd didn't see any reason to wait but now you're going to have to find him and tell him to hold off, either that or you need to convince Everett that we don't need to be guarded."

"I'll talk to Redd, I promise."

"You better," Flicker almost growled. "Or none of us will leave this place alive."

Chapter 41

"Are you sure it's really necessary?" Nilla asked as she stood,
arms folded opposite Everett.

"Nilla we've been over this," Everett replied in an exasperated tone. "They won't be safe in the open with Kento around."

"So they're being locked up? Everett they haven't done anything wrong, if anything Kento-"

"Kento is only doing what he's been told," he interrupted sternly. "He's one of our best and I won't have him locked up like a common criminal."

"But you'll happily lock up my family instead?"

Everett looked up at her and saw the thunder in her expression, he sighed, put his pen down and placed his fingertips together. "Nilla that's not what I meant."

"Then what did you mean?" her voice was getting dangerously loud and Everett raised a grey eyebrow at her.

"Believe it or not I'm thinking of their safety, as well as yours. It doesn't matter how high up you are, if Kento wants to see you suffer, he'll make sure it happens and unfortunately your family seem to have got on the wrong side of him."

"I still don't see why he's getting away-"

"He is loyal," Everett said sternly. "You of all people

should know the importance of that."

Nilla sighed and her shoulders sagged as she slumped into the chair opposite, "How long do you expect them to remain in custody?"

"They have not been arrested," Everett started to explain.

"But the guards-"

"The guards are there for their protection, your family are not restricted in their movements, but they will have guards accompany them and I do not think it wise for them to leave the palace at the moment."

She remained silent for some time, wondering whether they could still make their plan work but eventually she had to admit defeat; they would have to wait a little while longer.

"Everett I'm sorry," she said sighing heavily.

"For what my dear?"

"For getting angry at you, for snapping, I know you're only doing what's best."

"That's quite alright, I understand that your family are very important to you."

"They are, they're the most important thing to me," she admitted, almost forgetting who she was talking to. "And they've been helping me with my task for the Emperor," she added bringing the conversation back to something more relevant.

"Have they?" Everett asked with intrigue.

"I know you wanted me to keep it to myself, but they're as loyal to the Emperor as I am," she smiled inwardly at this, knowing she wasn't technically lying. "It's no wonder Kento was suspicious of them, they probably *were* acting odd as they were being my eyes and ears around the palace and grounds when I couldn't be there myself."

Everett nodded thoughtfully, "You're lucky to have them with you."

Nilla nodded and smiled but remained silent and eventually Everett went back to writing his reports.

"I'm so sorry," Nilla said as she took a seat next to her daughter, "I didn't mean for this to happen, I've been trying to get Everett to remove the guards but he's adamant it's for your own safety."

"It's okay," Wolf said with a half smile. "If you hadn't stepped in Kento would have probably killed us, I'd rather be alive and in here than dead out there."

Nilla smiled at him then noticed Flicker's glowering expression, "Flicker I'm sorry, I really am, this wasn't what I intended, I-"

"Have you spoken to my brother yet?" she shook her head and Flicker scoffed in annoyance. "How do you know they've not started the plan?"

"They can't, not without you," she pointed out and Flicker scoffed again. "If anything's happening right now it'll be that they're trying to find you, I don't think we need to worry just yet."

"You'd better hope not, if anything happens to my brother because of this I-"

"Stop it!" Aggie rose noisily from her chair. She scowled at Flicker who looked surprised at her outburst. "She said she's sorry, why can't you just accept that?! Wolf's right, if my mother hadn't stepped in to help we'd all probably be dead right now!"

She fell silent and Flicker suddenly looked ashamed; he stared at the floor and when he spoke there was no hostility in his voice. "Nilla I'm sorry, I know this isn't your fault," he looked up and met her eyes. "I thought this was it, I thought we were going to get out…"

"I know," she said softly. "Sometimes I forget how long you've been in here, I understand, I really do and I'll do whatever it takes to get Everett to drop your guard as soon as possible, I promise."

She reached out and squeezed Flicker's hand and he smiled at her, "I know you will."

"Do you think he's really doing all of this out of concern?" Wolf asked. "Everett I mean."

"Why wouldn't he?" Nilla asked almost in surprise.

"Well in his mind we're only Artist's, surely we're expendable?"

Nilla shook her head, "I don't think that's the case, if Shanora really is in as much trouble as we're being lead to believe then the Emperor needs all the Artist's he can get and Everett knows that, it's why you're still to go about your normal day."

"And you're sure he believes you?" Aggie asked quietly.

"Believes me about what?"

"About us, that we've been secretly helping you?"

Nilla smiled reassuringly, "He's no reason not to. Trust me, you're safe, at least for now."

"I hope you're right," Flicker said. "And I hope our guards aren't close friends with Kento."

Nilla looked suddenly startled, "I-I hadn't thought of that," she stammered and glanced towards the closed door where the officers stood on the other side.

Wolf chuckled, "If that Everett is as smart as you say he is he'll have thought about which officers to place with us."

Nilla nodded absentmindedly but made a mental note to check out those guarding them.

"So what are we going to do about Kento?" Flicker said and the others looked at him quizzically. "Well we're in here because of him, because he needs to calm down, which I highly doubt is going to happen anytime soon, I get the impression he likes to hold a grudge."

Nilla nodded in agreement, "What we need is to get you all out of the palace and out of the city."

"But that's not going to happen with Kento prowling around," Wolf pointed out.

"So we need to find a way to get him occupied with something else," Aggie suggested. "Or get rid of him," she added to the shocked expressions of the others.

"Aggie!" her mother exclaimed.

Her daughter shrugged, "It's true mother, Kento is the problem and the best way to be able to do what we need to would be to get rid of him."

Nilla looked at Wolf, "What exactly have you been teaching my daughter while I've been in here?"

Wolf tried to stifle his laughter and Flicker spoke up, "She's got a point, try talking to my brother, if anyone can think of a way to get Kento out of the picture it'll be him."

Nilla's expression turned to shock, "We're not killing him," she said forcefully.

Wolf's laughter stopped and he looked suddenly serious, "Why shouldn't we? He'd have killed us without a second's hesitation."

"That doesn't mean he should die!"

"It doesn't necessarily mean he should be allowed to live either," Aggie muttered and when her mother looked slightly horrified she continued. "He's an evil person mother, he's beaten Wolf, he's threatened me, he hit Jackie! Tell me he doesn't deserve-"

"He does not deserve to die! And you certainly do not have the right or the authority to decide his fate. I'll talk to the others about a non lethal way in which we can incapacitate him."

She stood before the others could protest and left the room with an uneasy feeling in her stomach that they were right.

She thought about heading down to find Redd but found herself standing outside Charlie's room instead. The two guards nodded to her as she knocked and pushed open the door; Charlie was staring out of the window and he didn't turn to look at her.

"Hello Charlie," she said as she took a seat on the edge of his bed, he still didn't look at her. They sat in silence for several minutes before she spoke again. "What happened Charlie? What happened to make you…like this?"

He finally tore his gaze away from the window and looked at her; his eyes seemed hollow and there was no expression on his face, "I don't know what you mean," he replied without tone.

"You're not the man I married, what happened to him?"

At that he snapped and his face twisted, "I've had to survive Nilla!" he spat and she drew back from him. "I've spent fifteen years in here alone! Without you, without Aggie! I did what I had to in order to survive and if that means I've changed a little then so be it!"

"A little?" she asked getting to her feet. "The man I married would have *never* put his daughter in danger!"

He winced at that but his expression remained dark, "I wouldn't have had to do that if that *man* hadn't tried to take her away from me!"

"No one was trying to take Aggie away from you Charlie," she said, her voice calming. "Wolf is a good man and he's looked after our daughter, he's kept her safe, you should be grateful of that."

"Is there something between the two of you?"

Nilla was taken aback, "Of course not! How could you even ask that!?"

"You seem awfully close to him and those others."

"They're my friends Charlie and I'm thankful to Wolf for taking care of our daughter when I couldn't."

"He's no right; she should have come to me!"

"She doesn't know y-"

"She doesn't know him either! But for some reason she's attached herself to him! And he's let her! He should have brought her to me, should have let me take care of her!"

"She was scared and alone Charlie, Wolf was with her when she got here, it's only natural for her to form a bond with him and it was only natural for him to be suspicious of you, after all, he didn't know who you were and neither did she."

Charlie snorted, "I can't believe you're defending him over me! I'm her father Nilla!"

"Then start acting like it, instead of a jealous child!"

He got to his feet and took a step towards her, "There's something not right about that man, I've been here long enough to smell a traitor when I see one and that Wolf is a traitor and if you're with him then you're one too."

She slapped him and he took a step back, "If anyone's a traitor in here it's you! You betrayed our daughter by harming someone who's been looking out for her, and I doubt that's something either of us will forgive you for."

Charlie clenched his fist and took a step forwards but Nilla had already turned and stormed out before he had a chance to respond.

She leant against the closed door and breathed heavily, forcing herself not to cry. The man she had married wasn't in that room, he'd gone and been replaced with someone else, someone she knew she could never love. Her heart broke. The guards either side of her stared at her awkwardly until one of them finally asked if she was okay. She forced a smile, told them she was fine and made her way to the main stairs; she would need to find Redd and Jackie as soon as possible despite her desire to lock herself in her room and cry until there were no tears left.

She took a deep breath and made her way to the dining room, hoping her friends would be there and she wasn't disappointed, though she was surprised to see Flora with them.

"I didn't think this was part of the patrol route," she smiled as she approached them.

"That's the good thing about being an officer, I can convince just about anyone that what I say is true."

"Is everything okay?" Redd asked, seeing the slight redness around her eyes.

Nilla took a seat and thought about what she needed to say, "There's been a bit of a problem."

"What's happened?" Redd asked suddenly tense.

"Everyone's fine," she reassured them. "But we can't proceed with the plan, not yet anyway."

"What do you mean?" Jackie asked.

She took a deep breath and explained the events that had led to Flicker and the others being put under guard, while those with her looked on in shock and in Redd's case anger. He remained silent until she had finished but cursed loudly as soon as she had done so.

"How are we supposed to get out of this place

now?" he hissed.

"We'll think of something," Nilla said with an exhausted sigh. "I promise."

"What about Everett? Can't you get him to send the guards away?"

"I've tried, but it was his idea to have them guarded in the first place, they're not confined to their rooms, so there's a possibility we could get them away."

Flora shook her head, "It won't work, the moment the officers lost track of them they'd sound the alarm and every officer in the palace would be looking for them."

Redd cursed again.

"I'm sorry," Nilla said with another exhausted sigh.

"It's not your fault," Jackie said kindly and patted her hand. "You were only trying to help."

Redd took a deep breath, "I'm sorry Nilla, I know I'm taking this out on you and Jackie's right it isn't your fault, you were stopping them from getting hurt, or worse."

Nilla smiled and Redd looked quizzically at her, "You and your brother are so alike."

Redd smiled too at that, "What about the Emperor? Is there anything he could do to help?"

"The Emperor?" Nilla asked in surprise. "I-I'm not sure, I've only seen him a few times and most of those have been with Everett, I don't usually talk to him, I'm not sure I could ask him for such a large favour."

Redd looked suddenly thoughtful, "How easy is it to get into his rooms?"

"Whose rooms?" Nilla asked in confusion.

"The Emperor's."

The three women stared at him with puzzled expressions, "Why on earth do you want to know that?" Jackie asked with a suspicious glint in her eye.

Redd shrugged and leant back in his chair, "No reason, I just thought it might be useful in case we want to hold him hostage or something."

"Why would we hold him hostage?" Nilla asked.

"In case we need leverage to have our friends released."

"Redd think about what you're saying," Flora said. "If you took the Emperor hostage there's no way the others would be released, you'd be proving yourself to be a traitor."

Redd shrugged again, "It was just a thought."

"Don't worry, we'll think of something," Nilla assured him.

"Perhaps I could get myself on the guard rotation for them?" Flora suggested. "At least if I'm there we've a better chance of having the other guards distracted."

Nilla nodded, "Give it a try." She yawned suddenly feeling a wave of exhaustion wash over her.

"Get yourself some rest," Jackie said gently. "We'll keep thinking of ideas and we'll meet again tomorrow."

She nodded and made her way to the door but before she could leave Redd placed a hand on her shoulder.

"What is it Redd? Do you have a message for your brother?"

Redd shook his head, "I need you to tell me how easy it is to get to the Emperor."

"Redd we just talked about this, taking him hostage won't work."

"You don't know that, we have to think of every option."

"We could get ourselves killed."

"Please Nilla, it could be important."

She sighed, "The floor is always guarded, there are

officers at the base of the stairs and the top, and there are officers that patrol periodically. They don't bother me because I'm there all the time, but I wouldn't be able to bring anyone else onto the floor without written permission from Everett or the Emperor himself."

"What about if you-"

"I have no idea what the layout is like. I've only ever been in the offices and the main living room area where the Emperor entertains Artists," she said pre-empting his next question. "I've no idea what his other rooms look like or even how many there are. I have no idea where he spends most of his time and I'm often working with Everett so I've never had the opportunity to explore."

Redd looked irritated and Nilla softened her expression, "I promise you we'll find another way to get the guards away from your brother and the others."

Redd forced a smile as Nilla left the room, then clenched his fists.

Chapter 42

Late spring moved into early summer mostly uneventfully with Flicker and the others seemingly no closer to losing their personal guards and all of them no closer to escape. Aggie was handling it the best, and being around her meant Wolf remained calm and collected. But Flicker, who was actually more used to this type of treatment than the others, was not coping well.

The other two didn't know much about his time in the palace before they'd arrived and he'd tried to keep it that way but when the twenty-four hour watch had started up again he'd become increasingly irritable and each day was a slow descent into anger and frustration. This type of guard was actually worse than before since they were being followed around the building. Before, he'd been guarded at night but he'd been allowed to roam free during the day since the palace and grounds were crawling with officers. With Kento on the loose and out for blood however, it was deemed too risky to let them walk around unescorted.

He'd tried to remain calm, he'd even tried to ignore them, but it was no use, he could feel their presence, even if they were stood outside the door to his classroom. He knew they were there and a dark cloud was growing around him.

The only benefit was that he was able to see his

brother and Jackie, though they weren't able to talk about anything important for fear of the guards overhearing, which meant they were unable to come up with a plan to get rid of those same guards that shadowed their every move, or Kento.

It all came to a head one afternoon when Flicker was trying to give Jackie a message for Redd. He'd scribbled it down on a piece of scrap paper earlier in the day and was trying to find a way to pass it to her without his personal guard seeing. They'd become a little paranoid on his behalf lately and didn't seem to trust anyone or anything.

"Keep your distance," a dark skinned officer with a bald head and a stocky build said to Jackie as she tried to lean in close and grab the slip of paper.

Flicker rolled his eyes, "Calm down Trip, it's just Jackie, I see her all the time."

Trip frowned and took a step towards them, "I think I'd prefer it if you both kept your distance."

"For the love of the Emperor Trip! What's she going to do? What do you think she's got hidden beneath her uniform?"

"You can take a look if you want?" Jackie chuckled, lifting the hem of her shirt.

Trip blushed but his expression remained firm, "Everett has instructed us to keep alert and check out anything that seems suspicious and-"

"And this is suspicious to you?" Flicker asked, his voice louder than it should have been. "I'm chatting with the person I've seen practically every day since I entered this place?"

Trip shuffled uncomfortably and his companion, a petite female officer with hardened features joined the conversation; her voice was as stern as her expression. "We do not need to explain ourselves to you," she told him sternly. "We do the work of the Emperor, now keep your distance."

Flicker's hands clenched into fists, "Do you have any idea how ridiculous you sound Rosa?"

She took a step towards him, "I don't really care how ridiculous I sound, I'm doing my job and I'm not going to take orders from the likes of you."

She spat at his feet and something inside Flicker that had been building for weeks finally snapped. He threw himself at her, knocking her to the ground where he began throwing his entire weight into his attack. He only managed to get a couple of good hits in before the surprise of his attack passed and she was able to throw her arm up to deflect his blows.

She managed to throw him off and got to her feet just as he lunged for her again but this time she was ready for him and a swift kick brought him down. He moved as if to attack her again and she brought her firearm out. He paused, then sank to his knees. Unseen by either Rosa or Trip, Jackie grabbed a slip of paper from the ground and slid it into her pocket.

"I think you had better leave," Rosa said to Jackie without looking at her.

"I'll see you soon Flick," Jackie said as she turned to leave.

"I doubt that," Rosa said with a rare smirk on her face. "Attacking an officer, that'll leave you in solitary confinement for at least a week."

Flicker clenched his fists again and growled quietly under his breath but he made no further move until Trip grabbed him by the shoulder and hauled him to his feet.

Nilla had been slowly trying to chip away at Everett's armour in order to have her daughter and her friends released from their personal guards with little result. They were sat in their large office examining the productivity reports for the last quarter. Everett was once again going over the quotas and explaining why they were increasing.

"The Emperor is concerned that the other cities are ready to make their move on us, his spies have brought back disturbing information."

"Surely if we just explained to the Artist's what was going on they'd be more than happy to increase their productivity, after all we're talking about keeping their homes, their families and their city safe?"

Everett shook his head, "It's too risky, they may see it as a way out."

"A way out of what?"

Everett carefully put his pen down and looked at her over his glasses, "Nilla it's no secret to you that not everyone here is happy."

She nodded, "That's why I'm doing what I am, trying to find the traitors for the Emperor." She smiled inwardly at how easy it had become to lie to Everett.

"Indeed, but what do you think those traitors would do if they learnt there might be an invasion? They could start decrease their productivity, find a way to sell our secrets to our enemies; they could cause the downfall of Shanora and our Emperor."

She thought carefully about how to respond. What she wanted to say was that the Artist's would be more productive if they were allowed to see their friends and families, but she knew that wouldn't go down well with Everett. She'd tried that line before, besides she needed him to keep thinking she was on his side, that she believed the best place for the Artists was in the palace.

"Yes, of course you're right Everett, as always," she finally said with some reluctance.

Everett nodded, "Exactly, and we can't let that happen, we cannot allow our city to fall into enemy hands."

She nodded and Everett went back to his work but her stomach churned and she felt uneasy; she needed to get Aggie and her friends out of there. "Everett," he looked up at her again. "There's been no sign of Kento trying to find my family, surely now we could relax the guard on them?"

Everett tilted his head as if considering the request and Nilla's heart sank, she'd seen this move too many times and she knew what it meant. In truth she was starting to worry he'd never relax the grip on the others

"I think for now it's safer to keep them watched, you wouldn't want anything to happen to them now would you?"

She sighed in exasperation, "I don't understand why you don't just remove Kento from service, he's clearly the problem here."

Everett slammed a fist onto the table, which made her jump and his face had once again become twisted, "He is not the problem Nilla! Kento is doing the Emperor's work, he's following orders, it's the Artist's who are always causing trouble, they're the problem!"

"But they weren't causing trouble! They hadn't done anything!"

"Nilla," he said her name with such venom that she flinched. "If you would like to keep your job and if you would like your family to remain safe then I suggest you drop the matter."

She fell silent and began to look over the books in front of her; Everett had also gone quiet and a glance up at him showed his features to be calm and unthreatening.

"Now I'd like to continue going through last

quarter's reports to see who might be best suited for a promotion," he smiled at her warmly and Nilla smiled back more uncomfortably.

"Of course Everett, why don't we-"

A knock came at the door and an officer walked in looking a little battered and bruised.

"Is everything okay Rosa?" Everett asked.

"Everything's fine Sir, but I wanted to inform you that the Artist Flicker who we have been guarding is now in solitary confinement."

"What!" Nilla shouted rising from her seat, "why?!"

Rosa looked to Everett who nodded for her to continue, she made sure she avoided Nilla's gaze. "He attacked me Sir, it was unprovoked."

"That is ridiculous!" Nilla said making her way to Rosa. "You're lying, Flicker wouldn't-"

"Nilla," Everett's voice was calm but she heard the underlying venom and she fell quiet. "I'm not surprised this has happened, it is not the first time he has been in trouble for scuffling with the officers. One week should suffice, he'll soon remember what it's like in there and I'm sure he'll do what he can to avoid a repeat visit."

Rosa nodded and left the room silently, a grin on her face. Everett turned back to Nilla, "Now where were we, ah yes, the reports," he smiled and she sat back down, seeing and feeling his hostility. She pointed at the section they had been looking at previously but said nothing.

They worked for several gruelling hours before Nilla took a break. She closed the door to the office behind her and let out a long breath that she felt she'd been holding in since the incident with Rosa. She didn't believe for a second that Flicker had acted rashly; she'd heard stories from Jackie about what he'd been like for most of his time in the palace but he'd changed over the past year. There was a chance at freedom and she knew he wouldn't have done anything to jeopardise that without good reason.

Unfortunately when she tried to go and see him she was refused, apparently even her high status in the palace couldn't get her past the officers. She sighed and went back up to the seventh floor where she suddenly thought about what Redd had said to her weeks earlier.

Heart racing, she made her way to the Emperor's living area and knocked; there was no answer so she pushed open the door and peered inside. The room looked the same as it always did though it was unlit and she noticed with relief it was empty. She looked in several of the drawers and cupboards in the room but on finding them empty of anything potentially useful turned to go until she saw the door at the far end; the one the Emperor always came through.

Slowly, heart still pounding, Nilla made her way across the room towards the door, checking behind her in case Everett suddenly appeared. She pressed her ear against the door and on hearing nothing from the other side, gently turned the handle and pulled it open.

The room was dark and she fumbled for a light switch; a familiar click sounded and a single bulb in the centre of the room struggled to life leaving the room only slightly brighter than before. She frowned and began to look around, though seeing now that the small corridor of a room she had entered contained only a long, plain cabinet and a simple rug it didn't take long. She walked towards the cabinet and found the doors to be locked, she frowned again.

"Something doesn't feel right," she whispered to herself as she stared at the bland, empty room that was completely the opposite of the one she had come from. She turned around, taking in the sparse furnishings and noticed another door opposite the one she had entered through. She walked towards it and once again placed her ear against the wood of the door, then quickly pulled back as she heard a voice on the other side.

She made her way quickly and quietly out of the bare room and across the living area, closing the door as quietly as possible when she had made it back out into the corridor. The door clicked quietly and she heaved a sigh of relief.

"Nilla?" her heart froze and she spun round in shock to see Everett looking at her. "What are you doing?"

"Everett," she tried to sound relieved, "I've been looking everywhere for you."

Everett cocked his head and frowned, "I was in my office, as usual, why were you looking for me in the Emperor's chambers?"

Nilla's heart raced and she tried to scramble her thoughts into something that would make sense. "I thought you had a meeting with him," she glanced at the clock on the wall and feigned stupidity. "Oh that's not for another hour, Everett I'm sorry I'm all turned around today."

He inspected her closely, his face still set in a frown, Nilla held her breath, hoping he would believe the lie. Everett straightened and smiled, "I couldn't tell you the number of times that's happened to me, once I almost missed a meeting with the Emperor," he shook his head as if reprimanding himself internally. "What was it you wanted to see me about my dear?"

Nilla's face, which had started into a smile as relief flooded her froze momentarily before she forced it, "I've had some ideas regarding promotion and increasing productivity," she replied quickly.

"Ah, excellent, then let us head to the office and discuss them."

Her heart continued to pound as she followed Everett into the large room that was practically her second home and prayed that he wouldn't ever see through her deception.

"I'm telling you Jackie it was practically empty, nothing like his main living area,"

Jackie looked at the young woman and smiled reassuringly, "Don't let him get in your head."

"Who?" she asked.

"Redd of course, he's got you thinking about the Emperor and now you're making a mountain out of a molehill."

"So you don't think it's odd?"

"He might very well be a humble man," Jackie suggested. "Perhaps he's trying to put on a show by making that one room lavish, while keeping everything behind the scenes simple."

Nilla frowned, "I don't know Jack, it seemed odd to me, I mean the cabinet was locked, it was locked! Why?"

Jackie shrugged as Redd approached, "It probably wasn't even a real cabinet, just something that was made, it's not unusual."

"What's not unusual?" Redd asked as he took a seat next to Jackie.

Nilla explained what she'd seen in the Emperor's living quarters again and Redd leant forwards with interest.

"I think you might have found something," he said while Jackie sighed in exasperation.

"Really Redd, he's probably just-"

"Sorry Jackie but I think you're wrong, I think there's more going on here than meets the eye." He leant in close to Nilla. "I think you need to try and go further, keep looking."

She shook her head, "I'm sorry Redd but it's too risky, Everett caught me leaving the living area last time, I can't do anything to risk my position, I need him to keep trusting me."

Redd exhaled in frustration, "If we're going to make our move then we need to figure out a way of going forward, this could be it!"

Jackie shook her head, "Nilla's right, she needs to proceed carefully, and we should focus on trying to get the others away from their guards."

Redd leant back in defeat and annoyance, "And how do we do that? Flora's been unable to get on the rota so we can't get eyes and ears on them at all times."

Nilla sighed, "There's something else," they both looked at her. "The fight Flicker got himself into, it's landed him in solitary confinement for a week." She braced herself expecting Redd to explode but he remained quiet, she looked to Jackie. "You knew?"

Jackie raised an eyebrow, "I've seen Flicker get into enough scuffles with the officers to know the consequences."

"It puts everything on hold again," Nilla said and Jackie nodded though Redd looked thoughtful.

"Not necessarily."

"He's in solitary Redd, even I couldn't persuade the officers to let me see him."

"All we need to do is overpower the officers, then we tie them up and in the ensuing chaos we can escape."

The two women considered this option until eventually Jackie shook her head, "I think we need Flicker to unleash the army at the same time we overpower the guards and that won't happen while he's in solitary."

"What we need is to get Kento out of the picture, incapacitate him somehow so he's no longer a threat," Nilla mused.

"Have you any thoughts on how we do that? I've been watching him, he's almost always surrounded by those thugs of his."

"I'm not sure it's just Kento we need to worry about anymore, his companions probably want revenge just as much as he does," Jackie added.

Nilla sighed in exasperation, "I'm telling you Kento is the key, if we get him out, his companions won't make trouble."

"Then what do you suggest?" Redd asked.

"We need a power shift."

"A power shift?" Jackie laughed but not unkindly. "I'm sorry Nilla but I've been here many years and no one's even come close to knocking him off his pedestal."

"It's the only way I can think to get him off our trail for a while."

"And how do you propose we convince someone to challenge him?"

"We don't."

They looked at her with confusion, "I think you're going to have to elaborate," Jackie said and Nilla smiled somewhat mischievously.

Redd waited nervously by the basement stairs for Kento to walk by on his rounds. He could see Jackie talking to Flora and Jan some way off; they were slowly making their way towards him and Jan seemed oblivious to what was happening around him.

Redd stiffened in his hiding place at the top of the

basement stairs as he heard Kento's harsh laugh and realised the man wasn't alone; he swore under his breath, there was no way they could pull this off if he wasn't alone. His mind raced as he thought of a way to separate Kento from his companion and just as he was about to emerge from where he hid, he heard Nilla's voice ring clearly down the corridor.

"Morn, could I trouble you for some help?"

Redd peered round the corner and saw Nilla struggling with a large object, he smiled, *She's a crafty one.*

Morn smiled at her and made his way over, while Kento scowled and waited for his friend by the top of the basement stairs. He began picking at his nails while glancing with disgust at Flora and Jan who had almost reached him with Jackie. He turned away from them and spat into the darkness of the basement as they walked past. At the same moment Redd dashed from his hiding place, barged into Jan who in turn spun around from the force and stumbled towards Kento. Redd concealed himself round a corner, held his breath as his heart pounded and peered towards the basement stairs just in time to see Jan push Kento.

Kento cried out in surprise before tumbling down the stone steps to the basement, landing with a sickening thud at the bottom. Jan looked in horror at what he'd done and turned pale as he faced Flora and Jackie. Morn and Nilla both dropped the sculpture they were carrying, which crashed to the floor and shattered. They raced towards the stairs, Nilla feigning worry. Morn raced down the steps while Nilla looked genuinely shocked at the crumpled mess that was Kento.

Jan made as if to hurry down the stairs to help but Flora put a hand on his arm to stop him and he looked at her questioningly. A number of other officers arrived in time to help Morn bring Kento up the stairs where they laid him down and checked him over. He groaned quietly.

"How did this happen?" Morn asked as he looked over at Flora and Jan.

Jan shook his head, "Morn, I'm so sorry I-"

Flora took a step forward, "Looks like Kento had a nasty accident."

Morn looked at her with some confusion before his expression darkened, "You did this!"

Flora smiled sweetly, "Me? Why on earth would I push Kento down some stairs?"

Morn took a step towards her, "You've allied yourself with the wrong people," he growled.

"I told you," she replied still smiling sweetly, "I didn't do anything."

Morn took another step towards her but Jan stepped between them, "It was me."

Shock spread across Morn's face, "You?!"

"Yes, I-"

"You did this?!" Morn's hands clenched into fists. "Mark my words you'll pay for this."

Jan opened his mouth to protest but Flora stepped from behind him, "Are you sure about that? Are you sure you want to threaten us? After all you've seen what happens to those who do."

Morn growled again and looked like he might lunge for them but became distracted when Kento moaned as he came to, "This isn't over!" he spat and turned to his friend.

Jan whirled to look at Flora in shock, "What in the Emperor's name was that about? It was an accident, you know that."

Flora shrugged, "I'm tired of Kento and his thugs thinking they own the place, so I used what happened to our advantage."

"Our advantage? Flora they could kill us! I've got a family remember!"

"Jan calm down, Kento's in no shape to do anything to anyone and I doubt his friends are going to do anything without him by their side. They wouldn't get away with half of what he does."

Jan shook his head in disbelief and started to back away from her, "You're crazy, I can't believe what you've done."

"Jan wait!" she called as he turned on his heel and walked quickly down the corridor. She sighed. "Did we do the right thing Jack? What is Jan's right, what if Morn and the others want revenge?"

Jackie put a hand on her arm, "I wouldn't worry about that lot, I've watched them a lot over the years and without Kento in the lead they're all talk. Jan will come around and at least now we've got Kento out of the way and a chance at getting out of here."

Chapter 43

"You did what?!" Wolf asked as they all stared at Nilla in disbelief.

She sighed, "It was the only way to get Kento out of the picture."

"I know we suggested it but I didn't actually think you'd go through with it," Flicker, who was grateful to be out of solitary, shook his head.

"For the record all I did was distract Morn, Redd was the one who organised everything."

Flicker chuckled, "Yeah that sounds like my brother," he glanced at Nilla and on seeing her troubled expression placed a hand on her shoulder. "You know it had to be done."

She nodded, "I know and I agreed to it but it doesn't mean I feel good about it."

Aggie squeezed her tightly, "Just remember it's our only chance to get out of here," she nodded and squeezed her daughter back.

Wolf sat up, "So with Kento out of the picture, does that mean Everett will drop the guards?"

"I don't know," Nilla admitted. "I haven't had a chance to discuss it with him yet."

"Surely he can't object to letting us go now, there's no one to threaten us," Aggie pointed out.

"That's what I'm hoping, but Everett has been a bit

unpredictable lately, I'm starting to wonder whether there's something he's not telling me."

"I'm sure there's plenty he's not telling you," Flicker pointed out."

"Let's just hope he sees sense and removes those officers, I'm finding it harder to keep my cool," Wolf growled softly.

"Trust me Wolf you'll keep calm, you don't want to end up in solitary."

"And you don't want to jeopardise the plan," Aggie pointed out. "We've got Flicker back and Kento out of the way, now's the time to act."

Wolf nodded, "I know lass."

"Let me talk to Everett about the guards this evening, once we've got rid of them we can organi-"

The door opened and Everett strode in with a serious expression, "Nilla, come with me please."

Her heart started to pound and she gave her daughter one last hug before following Everett from the room. The door shut quickly behind them and a heavy silence filled the air.

"You don't think he knows do you?" Aggie asked in a worried tone.

"I'm sure everything's fine," Wolf said reassuringly but with a concerned expression on his face as he continued to stare at the door.

"Let's get out of here," Flicker suggested. "Maybe we can find Redd and Jackie."

Nilla followed Everett in silence as they made their way to the top floor. Her heart hadn't slowed and her mind was racing, he'd never sought her out personally before, he'd always sent messengers. Did it mean he knew something about her? Or about what they'd done to

Kento? She tried to breathe steadily and calm her nerves but it was no use, she was about ready to confess everything as they entered the familiar office but managed to restrain herself as she took a seat opposite Everett. He looked at her quietly for several minutes before finally speaking.

"Nilla I'm worried about you."

She was unable to hide her shock, "Worried? Why are you worried?"

Everett cocked his head as if he were contemplating his words, "I've heard that you've been spending a lot of time with your family recently."

She let out a breath in relief, then looked confused, "Is there something wrong with that?"

"Everyone in the palace knows your position, they know you're working closely with me, how do you think it looks to others when they see you with common Artists?"

"But they're my family," she pointed out.

"And only you and I know that," he retaliated. "So why would someone of your stature be spending time with common Artists? It looks suspicious."

She bristled, "Are you telling me I can't see my family? My daughter?!"

"I'm simply explaining that if you'd like to stay up here in the Emperor's *personal* service, then you might want to think about reducing your visits to your family."

"Why not remove their guards? It's not as if Kento is a threat anymore after his accident."

"I thought I told you not to speak about that!" he snapped and she got to her feet.

"Perhaps you should tell me *why* you're so insistent on keeping my family under guard, what's really going on Everett?!"

He looked at her with a thunderous expression but for once she didn't back down, she was tired of pretending, and she was tired of the lies, she wanted answers. Finally, after several minutes of lethal silence, Everett finally spoke and gestured that she take a seat.

"It's no secret that I'm an old man and that I'm past my prime." Nilla opened her mouth but Everett held up a hand and she closed it. "The Emperor himself has voiced his concerns that my mind is no longer what it was, he wants me to choose a replacement."

She nodded, seeing the sense it made but not seeing the relevance.

"I want you to be my replacement Nilla."

Her mouth dropped open in shock and she sat in stunned silence for several minutes while Everett looked at her carefully.

"Do you think you'd be willing to take on the challenge? It's why I chose you to help me, it's why I've been training you all these months. I knew there was something different about you when I first met you, I knew you were the one to replace me. It's also why I've been keeping your family safe for you, I didn't want anything to happen to them that might, cloud your judgement."

She continued to stare in silence at him, taking in what he said but barely believing what she had heard. Maybe she could do it, and maybe if she did then they didn't have to escape, with her in charge she could change the rules. She could allow visitors, she could let the Artist's return to their families and live with them, she could get rid of Kento and his thugs. She could change things for the better…Only, she couldn't, because Everett wasn't the one in charge, the Emperor was, and he was the one who made the rules and he'd never allow what she wanted to happen.

She forced a smile, "Everett I'd be honoured."

He beamed and clapped his hands in celebration. She continued to smile though internally she was grimacing because she knew they needed to get out of here as soon as possible, they needed to start the plan.

Flora had finally found Jan amongst the lawn games but he didn't look happy to see her.

"I really don't want to listen to what you have to say Flora," he got to his feet and made to walk away but she sprinted towards him and blocked his path.

"Please Jan, I owe you an explanation and more than that I need you to know what's going on, especially since I've put you in the middle without your consent."

He sighed and sat back down, "Fine, talk."

"Do you remember when I wanted to get down into the basement?" Jan nodded. "Well I found something down there, something that's been troubling me for a while."

"What was it?" Jan asked with a hint of curiosity.

"It was an army Jan, the Emperor has an army hidden in the basement."

"An army?" he asked and she nodded. "Sorry you're going to have to elaborate, are they locked up? Or simply hiding down there? And why keep them in the basement? Wouldn't they be better out on the streets?"

"Sorry Jan I should have explained better, it's a clay army."

"A what?"

"An army, made entirely of clay, we think the Emperor's going to use it to march on the other cities."

"Well I suppose that would explain all the body parts you found but what does it have to do with your friend pushing Kento down the stairs and blaming me?"

Flora looked shocked, "How did you know?"

"He rammed into me Flora! What I can't figure out is why you wanted Kento out of the way and why you implied I'd pushed him."

Flora put her head in her hands, "I'm so sorry Jan, none of it was supposed to happen like this but we've had to improvise."

Jan sighed loudly, "Flora, either you tell me exactly what you and your friends are doing or you leave here right now and never say another word to me."

Flora chewed her bottom lip then took a deep breath, "You know I initially came here to get Flicker out," Jan nodded. "But then we thought there was something else going on, something we weren't being told."

"The army?"

Flora nodded, "The Emperor has two, 'teams' for lack of a better word, those dedicated to creating resources and those dedicated to creating an army. This army that wouldn't need food or sleep, it would keep going until they're cut down. It's an army that could raze the other cities to the ground or surround them and wait for the other cities to run out of food. Once he's conquered the other cities, who knows what he'll do."

"But you don't know this for certain," Jan pointed out.

"I'll admit it's more of an assumption but Jan why else would he have spent years, maybe even decades building an army? Has there ever been any real threat from the other cities?"

"I don't know," he said truthfully. "Now you've found the army, what will you do?"

Flora hesitated for a long time before answering,

"We're going to bring it to life and escape."

Jan inhaled sharply and stared at her in disbelief, "You're serious aren't you?" she nodded and Jan got to his feet; he started pacing. "Are you crazy? You have no idea what's really going on! What if there really is a threat? What if this army is our only defence? Have you seriously thought this whole thing through?"

"Honestly Jan it no longer matters, I need to help the others get out of here, it's no longer safe and the longer they're here the more dangerous it'll become."

"Why?" A heavy silence settled over them. "Why Flora?" Jan pressed.

"Because they're not all Artist's Jan!" she threw her hands to her mouth and he stared at her eyes wide.

"Say that again."

Flora lowered her hands, "Redd, Wolf and Nilla, they're not Artist's. I need to help get them out, I need them to be safe."

"If they're not Artist's then how in the Emperor's name did they get in here?"

"Nilla took her daughters' place so she wouldn't have to spend her life in here, the others tricked the officers, they used Aggie's blood and Aggie's gift to create."

Jan shook his head again, "I can't believe what you're telling me!"

"There's more," she said and Jan put his head in her hands. "Kento became suspicious and he threatened them, so Everett placed them under guard to keep them safe and-"

"You couldn't get out if they were under constant guard," Jan finished. "You had Kento injured to get rid of him in the hopes Everett would remove the guard."

Flora nodded, "We need to move, we need to get out, it was the only way."

He started pacing, not looking at Flora as he digested what she'd told him. It was a good ten minutes before he finally stopped and turned to her. "I told you months ago I couldn't be involved in this, I told you I needed to protect my family and you've gone and endangered them anyway."

"Jan they're not in any danger I promise!"

"Can you really promise that? Do you think Kento only has allies in here?"

"Jan I'm sorry I-"

"You didn't think did you?! Not about anyone other than yourselves!" He shook his head again and his face showed disgust, "I am not a part of this Flora and I won't help you."

"Jan please don't-"

"I'll keep your secret, but I need to protect my family and I need to make peace with Kento."

Flora's eyes widened, "Jan you can't!"

He turned on her, "How dare you tell me what I can and can't do! You've put my family in danger without a second thought! I won't tell anyone what you're planning, I promise you that, but I will not pretend I pushed Kento down those stairs."

Flora wilted and dropped her head, "I'm so sorry, I didn't mean for it to turn out this way."

Jan's shoulders slumped and his face lost all hostility, "I understand why you did it, but you need to see it from my point of view."

She lifted her head and there was pain in her eyes, "I do and I'm sorry, I really am. Tell Kento it was me, tell him I pushed him, keep your family safe."

Jan nodded and walked away.

"We need to move, we need to get out of here," Nilla said

as she paced around by the lake.

"What's happened?" Jackie asked.

"Everett's asked me to take over for him."

There was a brief stunned silence then Redd grinned, "Nilla that's great, think about what you could do!"

"I've already thought about it Redd, Everett's not going anywhere yet, and you seem to be forgetting that the Emperor is ultimately in control. I can't keep pretending anymore, we have to go."

Jackie nodded, "I think you're right, we've put this off for far too long."

"But what about the guards? Has Everett agreed to remove them?"

"Not yet," Nilla replied. "But I've got a plan," Redd looked at her questioningly. "Just trust me, what we need to do is figure out when we're going to do this."

"I'd suggest soon," they jumped as Flora's voice joined the conversation; she looked worried.

"What's happened?" Jackie asked.

"Kento will soon know it was you Redd."

"How?" Nilla asked in alarm.

Flora shook her head, "It's a long story, but he'll soon know and once he does he'll be out for blood."

Redd shrugged, "We knew it was a possibility, don't worry."

"Don't worry? We were trying to get Kento out of the way and now it looks like we've made things worse!"

"Not quite, he's broken his arm so he's on light duties for the next few months *and* he's not allowed a firearm right now."

"*He's* not but I bet his thugs are." Nilla said worriedly.

"If I've learnt anything about Kento during my brief stay here it's that he likes to get his revenge himself, he won't let anyone else pull the trigger." Redd replied.

"I hope you're right," Nilla said quietly.

Nilla made her way back to the top floor where she had a meeting with Everett, she gathered a small pile of documents she'd drafted earlier and wandered along to their shared workroom.

"Good afternoon Nilla," Everett smiled as she entered.

"Hello Everett."

"I thought we might go through a few of my duties you won't be aware of."

"Of course Everett, I wonder if you might be able to sign the promotion and productivity documents before we commence?"

"Ah yes of course," he replied with a smile. She handed him the documents nervously. Everett scrawled his signature across the bottom of each document without glancing at the contents before handing them back to her. She smiled pleasantly and tucked them into a folder.

"I'll make sure I distribute them to the appropriate departments."

"Thank you Nilla, I can't tell you how pleased I am to have someone like you on my side."

She smiled again and they began discussing Everett's non-essential roles. The meeting felt as if it dragged on for days and she found it difficult to keep still; she was itching to leave and sort the documents.

Everett continued to drone on while she took insufficient notes until the sun had dipped beneath the horizon. "Oh my, Nilla I am sorry it looks as though I've chattered on."

She smiled, "No need to apologise Everett, I hadn't

even noticed how late it had become."

"We had best stop for the evening and you had better get some rest, we've a busy day ahead of us tomorrow." She smiled again and left the room, clutching the folder to her chest.

She placed the majority of the documents by their relevant administration representative's name, then made her way to where Aggie, Wolf and Flicker were being held. She handed over the final document from the folder and one of the officers on watch scanned it quickly then nodded to her.

"We've been dismissed," he said to the others and waved them all away.

She breathed a sigh of relief and went into the room currently doubling as a communal area, Wolf and Aggie were inside but Flicker was absent.

"Where's Flick?" she asked nervously.

"In his room I think," Wolf replied. "What's going on?" he asked as he noticed there were no officers by the open door.

"The guards have been dismissed, we need to move quickly."

"You got Everett to agree with you?" Aggie asked.

"Not quite," she replied ushering them out of the room. They reached Flicker's room and knocked.

"Come on guys just leave me be for five minutes!" came a muffled voice.

"Flicker? It's Nilla," she pushed open the door and Flicker sat up from his position lying on the bed."

"Is everything okay?" he asked getting to his feet, then noticed the lack of officers, "where are the-?"

"There's no time, we've got to move, I tricked Everett into signing a document dismissing your guards."

Flicker grinned, "Why Nilla, I didn't think you had it

389

in you."

She cuffed him round the ear, "Redd could be in trouble, we've got to move."

Flicker turned serious, "What's happened?"

She explained briefly and they hurried through the palace towards the dining room where they hoped both Jackie and Redd would be.

It took far longer to find them than Nilla would have liked but eventually they tracked down Jackie and the others in the centre of the maze. Redd grinned as he saw them approach and gave his brother a tight hug.

"You've finally made it out without your entourage."

"Redd you're okay," Nilla said with a sigh.

"Of course I'm okay, why wouldn't I be?"

"Because of what's happened with Kento," Flicker said suddenly showing concern.

Redd shrugged, "Oh that, I wouldn't worry about that, I doubt there's much he can do."

"He could kill you Redd," Nilla pointed out, and being that he's an officer and you're an Artist, everyone would believe his side."

Redd shrugged again, "I really don't think there's anything to worry about."

"We need to get out of here soon," Nilla urged; Jackie, Redd and Flora looked confused. "I forged a document releasing this lot of their guard, Everett signed it but if he finds out what I've done he'll be furious."

"That was risky," Jackie pointed out.

"I know, but with Kento out for Redd's blood I figured the risk was worth it."

"So we need to make a move," Wolf said and Nilla nodded forcefully. "How about tonight then?"

"Tonight? so soon?" Flora asked.

"No time like the present," Wolf said. "There's a

chance Nilla's already created confusion with that forged document, why not create a bit more."

Chapter 44

They waited until it was fully dark; Flicker, Jackie and Flora made their way to the sub-basement where they would unleash the clay army on the unsuspecting palace. They reached the top of the stairs and Flora paused,

"How long do you think you'll need?"

Flicker shook his head, "I honestly have no idea."

Flora frowned, "I think it would be best if I tried to get a key for the main gate, none of this will mean anything if that door remains locked."

"We have no idea how long this will take," Flicker pointed out. "You could be waiting hours, you could get caught."

She nodded, "I know but it's also possible I won't."

He looked at Jackie for backup but she shook her head, "I actually agree with Flora, I think she needs to get that key if we're to have the slightest chance of getting out of here."

"I think we need to stick together," Flicker persisted. "We could also go once the army is out, there's more of a chance we'll be able to overpower whoever is on guard."

"There's also more of a chance of one or more of you getting shot."

"We have that chance anyway," he pointed out.

"Then we shouldn't do anything to increase it."

"Flicker," Jackie said softly. "I think you need to

accept you're not going to win this one."

He stared intensely at Flora for several minutes before his shoulders sagged, "Fine, *we'll* unleash the army, you get the key, but Flora," she looked at him. "Please be careful."

She smiled, "Same to you." She raced off towards the main palace door and Flicker sighed in exasperation.

"You could have at least tried to be on my side Jack."

"I could have," she admitted. "But I happen to agree with Flora on this occasion, now come on, we'd best get this over with."

Flora strolled out into the warm summer night, trying to act as if she were on regular patrol around the gardens when she heard a rustling behind her. She swirled round and came face to face with Charlie.

"What are you doing out here? It's past nightfall, you should be inside the palace."

"I was wondering what *you* were doing," he said in a dark voice.

Flora folded her arms, "It's none of your business what I'm doing Charlie."

Charlie smiled, "Why exactly were you letting those two traitors go into the basement?"

Flora stiffened, "I don' know what you mean."

Charlie laughed, it wasn't a kind sound, "Oh Flora, there's no use lying to me, I saw you just now talking to them. So what is it they're doing? And what's your part in all this?"

"I told you it's none of your business, now get back inside and I'll say no more about it."

"What's down in the basement anyway? Supplies? Weapons? A secret passage out of this place? Come on

Flora let me in on the secret."

"There's no secret Charlie, now get inside before I make you."

He laughed again and it cut through the night like a serrated blade; he grabbed her wrist as she reached for her firearm and drew close to her. "You're part of it," he hissed and she flinched as saliva speckled her face. "You're another reason my daughter and my wife hate me, you've helped turn them against me. Well not for much longer!"

She kicked out and Charlie let go of her wrist as he thudded to the ground. He scrambled to his feet and snarled at her but she had her firearm out and aimed in his direction. "Go back inside Charlie," she said sternly. For a split second he looked as though he might charge her but he finally turned away and walked towards the soft glow of the palace.

"Watch your back Flora," he said as he blended with the night.

It had taken longer than Flicker wanted to find the door to the army large cavern it had been so long since he'd last been there he'd taken a few wrong turns.

"I hope we've not worried them," he said to Jackie as he began to pick the lock.

"I wouldn't worry about it Flick, they'll just carry on as normal until they hear the signal."

"I wish Nilla hadn't had to go back to meet with Everett, what if he found out what she did?"

"Everyone needed to act as normal as possible," Jackie pointed out. "For Nilla that's attending her nightly meeting with Everett. Try not to worry too much Flick, she's a smart one, and good at thinking on her feet."

"I know," he replied, sliding the second wire into the

lock. "I just don't want anything to happen to her, or any of them."

"Neither do I Flick, and with any luck we'll all get out unscathed."

The lock finally clicked open and Flicker pushed the door gently; they watched as it swung slowly inwards.

"Breath through your nose Jack," he said as they walked into the dark. He flicked a switch and several dusty bulbs sprang to life, glowing faintly around the cavernous room.

Jackie went to gasp and threw a hand over her mouth as she stared wide eyed around the room, "I had no idea there would be so many," she whispered.

"I know Jack, the Emperor's been building this army for years at least."

"Longer than that," Jackie said taking a few steps towards the nearest row of soldiers. "This room goes further back than you think, but it looks like the bulbs have long since blown."

Flicker squinted into the distance, "Crafts! Jackie you're right, we're going to have to somehow find the centre of this place, there's no point giving the breath of life if it won't reach those at the back."

He made to move but Jackie placed a hand on his shoulder, "Are we doing the right thing Flick?"

He shook his head, "Honestly I have no idea, if the threats against the city are real then we're putting everyone in danger, but this is our only way out and the others are counting on us, so we can't turn back now."

She nodded and they made their way slowly to what they thought was the centre of the room, weaving amongst the clay soldiers, horses and hounds.

"Do you think we'll be able to control them?" Flicker whispered, suddenly feeling as though the clay soldiers might hear them."

"I don't know Flick," Jackie whispered back. "I haven't heard of anything like this ever being done before, I don't even know if there's a rule for this sort of thing." She was still in awe of the sheer number of beings in the cavernous room, the amount of work that had gone into sculpting and crafting them was immense.

Flicker finally stopped some way ahead of her and began to scan the room, "I think this could be it," he said as she caught up to him. "Would you like to do the honours?"

Jackie shook her head and pressed her lips together; Flicker grinned, took a deep, long breath. He exhaled slowly, sending swirls of pale yellow mist from his mouth. It began to expand and split into multiple tendrils, swirling through the cavern, glowing faintly and began to twirl around the clay creations.

Once every being had been engulfed by the mist they began to change. Skin paled and darkened around them, showing a range of colours from the palest pink to the deepest brown, while hair lifted away from the scalp starting from the forehead and cascading like a waterfall to the back of neck. Flicker found it fascinating; there had been nothing on the clay statues to distinguish between red or blonde hair, grey or brown, yet here was an army that had previously been the exact same shade of grey and was now a range of colours and shades. Clothing began to loosen, lift away from the skin, then settle against it, armour became tough and impenetrable, clinking softly as it settled into place.

The animals started to paw the ground and snort in frustration which jolted Flicker out of his hypnotised state.

"That took a lot longer than I thought it would," he

whispered to Jackie as the soldiers stood still and silent, facing forwards, barely blinking.

"Well there's significantly more here than we're used to," Jackie whispered back, a slight quiver in her voice as she eyed the army surrounding them. "What now?"

"Now I guess we see if they'll listen to us."

They stood in silence for some time staring at the large army that remained, apart from the animals, as stationary as when they'd been clay. Finally Jackie nudged Flicker and he glanced down at her. She gestured around them.

He cleared his throat but none of the army looked at him and he began to feel nervous that their plan wouldn't work. "Army!" he shouted, not knowing what else to call them. "The Artists in the palace are in danger." No one moved. "We are being held prisoner in this place by armed officers, they carry firearms much like your own but they do not have the gift. They are holding the Artists against their will and must be stopped! Anyone outside of this room with a firearm is an enemy!"

Instantly the army began to move around them as if they were one mind. Flicker choked in surprise, he hadn't quite finished his speech, suddenly worrying for Flora and Jan who he knew would both be carrying weapons. He grabbed Jackie by the arm and started to drag her towards the door.

"We've got to get out of here before them Jack! We need to warn Flora and Jan."

"Crafts! Couldn't you have been more specific Flick?" she half joked.

He grimaced as they tried to push their way through the marching army.

Aggie and Wolf were sat in the dining room when they

heard a faint rumbling beneath them.

"Do you think that's the sign?" Aggie asked quietly, her voice trembling.

"It's either the sign or an earth tremor," Wolf replied getting to his feet. "Come on lass, we best find your mother, there's no way she'll have heard that."

"What about Redd?" she asked looking around them. "Where did he go?"

Wolf shrugged, "Said he had some business to sort before we got out of here, don't worry, I'm sure he'll turn up." He grabbed Aggie's hand and they raced to the stairs.

Officers and Artists were looking around them in confusion as the rumbling beneath their feet got steadily louder. Wolf and Aggie raced past them and made their way up the numerous flights of stairs to the top floor.

They were both exhausted by the time they reached the seventh floor and panting heavily. The officers at the top eyed them suspiciously

"What are you doing up here? And how did you get past the lower officers?" The second question was answered first as the officers from the base of the stairs came hurtling to the top to help bar the way.

"They slipped past us!" one of the officers said angrily.

"What are you doing up here?" the first officer asked again.

"We need to speak to Nilla," Aggie gasped, her hands on her knees as she tried to catch her breath.

"If you'd like to speak to her you'll have to ask for an appointment."

"She's my mother," Aggie said straightening up. "Please it's important."

"No unauthorised personnel are allowed on this

floor."

"Please," Aggie begged. "I really need to see her, it's urgent." She made to move forwards and one of the officers grabbed her shoulder to detain her.

"No one gets past us without authorisation," he spat.

Aggie looked into his cold eyes and started to yell, "Mother! Please help u-" a hand clamped over her mouth and an arm pressed against her neck forcing the breath from her.

Wolf stared with fury at the man holding Aggie and growled, "Let her go."

The officers smirked, "Or what?" one of them asked.

Wolf half smiled and launched himself at two of the officers, knocking them to the ground. He began throwing punches at the two of them as they struggled to manoeuvre themselves away from him and grab for their firearms. The other officers lunged forwards, grabbed Wolf and pulled him off their now bloodies comrades.

They tied Wolf's hands behind his back and threw him roughly to the ground; he was about to clamber to his feet when a firearm was held in front of his face, "Don't even try it," the officer hissed. Wolf glanced at Aggie who was also being tied up and slumped back to the ground.

Several more officers came panting up the stairs, "something's happening down there," a young female officer said, a worried look in her eye.

"What is it?"

"I-I think it's an army."

"Crafts! Leave these two here, we must defend the palace and the Emperor!"

The officers rushed back down the stairs leaving Aggie and Wolf alone, "Don't worry lass, we'll get to your ma'."

She nodded and they both started to struggle against their bonds with little effect. Aggie gave up quickly, realising there was little she could do but Wolf continued to struggle and curse loudly, his wrists becoming red raw. Suddenly he fell silent and still; Aggie was about to ask what was wrong when she heard it; two shots rang out followed by heavy footsteps on the stairs. Wolf frantically tried to loosen his bonds and Aggie braced herself.

Chapter 45

Flora had just reached the gatehouse when she heard a low rumble beneath her feet, *Is that the army?* She thought as she slipped inside and smiled at the guard on duty.

"Evening Phinn,"

Phinn smiled, nodded, then went back to the book he was reading.

"Sorry about this," she said, and as Phinn looked up at her she hit him over the head with her firearm and knocked him out cold. She fumbled around trying to get the keys from his belt that would unlock the drawer where the main keys were located. She glanced around but no one had heard anything and she was still alone as she grabbed the keys to the main gate and rushed to unlock it.

"What are you doing?" came a soft, male voice from behind as she turned the key in the lock. She swivelled round and visibly relaxed as Jan stood before her.

"I think you already know the answer to that," she replied steadily.

"So, you're really going through with it?"

Flora nodded, "Look Jan, if I were you I'd leave here now, go and find your family, stay indoors and wait for everything to calm down."

"What do you-" there was a loud commotion emanating from the palace and it looked as though a number of fires had broken out. Jan gasped and sprinted towards the chaos.

"Jan! Jan stop!" Flora's voice was lost amongst the noise from the palace; she cursed and began to run after him, hoping she could reach him in time before he got hurt.

Something barged into her and she was thrown to the ground; the air was knocked from her and she struggled to see what had hit her in the darkening grounds.

"Who's there?" she called as she reached for her firearm and with a pang of horror, realised it was missing. *Did I leave it in the gatehouse?* She wondered as she tried to search the immediate area around her.

"Looking for something?" came a cool, sinister voice.

"Charlie?" she asked peering through the gloom to make out a tall figure in front of her.

"What's going on in there Flora? What have you and those traitors done?"

"Give me my firearm Charlie and walk away from here."

"You're a traitor Flora, you need to be punished

She threw herself to the side as he fired, then scrambled towards him as he turned and tried to take aim at her again. She reached him before he had a chance to shoot and tackled him to the ground. They wrestled on the ground for several minutes, Charlie biting and kicking like a feral animal while Flora attempted to grab her firearm from him.

"You'll never win," Charlie growled; his breath hot and rancid.

They continued to struggle for the weapon, Charlie's finger was still on the trigger but it was pointed towards the sky. Flora tried to manoeuvre herself so she was on top of the Artist, using her strength to ensure a more strategic position. She had almost managed to overpower him, when he shifted his weight and she toppled from him. She still had his arms in a tight grip and he rolled towards her as she fell; the firearm lowered towards her and Charlie's finger started to squeeze the trigger.

The shot that rang out was deafening and both parties froze momentarily, then Charlie's grip on the weapon slackened and Flora was able to take it from him. She scrambled away and stared in a mixture of shock and horror as a bright red stain spread across the front of Charlie's shirt.

Flora dropped her firearm and scrambled back to Charlie, who was staring at her with a look of surprise on his face.

"I'm so sorry," she whispered as blood trickled from his mouth.

"Aggie," he rasped with one final breath before he coughed, convulsed and eventually fell still. Flora cursed loudly, stumbled to her feet and turned back to the palace, which was now a blazing inferno on several floors.

Wolf heaved a sigh of relief as Redd reached the top of the stairs, a wide grin on his face.

"Where have you been?" Wolf asked as Redd began to untie them.

"It's not important," he replied. "I'm glad I found you, it's getting crazy down there. Where's Nilla?" Aggie pointed towards the main door that would take them into the labyrinth of the seventh floor and the Emperor's personal rooms.

"I guess we'd better start looking, someone's started some fires and it won't take long until the entire building is ablaze."

Aggie and Wolf got to their feet and the three of them made their way into the maze of corridors. Aggie began calling for her mother while they checked the various rooms with little success and it wasn't long until they were well and truly lost. They had been searching for several minutes when they eventually found themselves in familiar surroundings.

"Crafts!" Redd cursed as they all recognised the main door they'd entered through. "This could take all night!"

"We don't have all night," Wolf pointed out.

"Well we'll just have to keep looking; we can't leave Nilla here to burn."

They set off again through the labyrinth, checking any new rooms they came upon and eventually managed to stumble across Nilla as she was leaving one of the many rooms they had thought they'd already searched.

"Mother!" Aggie cried and Nilla swivelled to stare at them, eyes wide. Aggie threw her arms round her mother and Nilla remained frozen for several seconds as she processed the three people in front of her. Aggie opened her mouth again but her mother placed a finger over her mouth and ushered them away from the room she'd recently exited.

Once they had reached a safe distance, she spoke to them in a whisper, "What are you doing up here? How did you even manage to get up here? You have to go now before Everett sees you."

"It's time Nilla," Wolf said calmly. "The army has been unleashed and it sounds like the Artist's are rioting, we've got to get out of here now while we can."

She nodded curtly and started to lead them back to the main staircase, they had almost reached the main door when Wolf realised Redd was no longer with them. He searched frantically back the way they'd come and eventually they found him staring down one of the corridors, eyes unfocused.

"Redd!" Wolf shook him roughly by the shoulders and the other man snapped back to reality.

"What?"

"What are you doing? We've got to get out of here!"

Redd shook his head, "There's something I need to do."

"What do you mean? We're already in the middle of something, we're trying to get everyone out!"

"There's something else I need to do," Redd replied clenching his fists.

Wolf grabbed him arm as he turned to leave, "It's not worth it Redd."

"Isn't it?" The Emperor has been terrorising us all for far too long, he needs to be stopped!"

"Think about what you're saying lad, think about what you're doing. This isn't the way to do things, we came here to free Flicker, that's our priority, now let's get back downstairs and find him before we leave this place for good!"

Redd stared at Wolf, almost as if her were considering his words and he made a small movement as if to follow. Wolf smiled and turned back to Nilla and Aggie who both had looks of horror on their faces. Wolf fell to the floor as the butt of a firearm smacked him in the side of the head. Nilla took a step forward but Redd shook his head.

"Leave it Nilla, it's not worth it. Please tell Wolf I'm sorry, and tell my brother I love him."

"You don't have to do this Redd, we could find another way."

"Where are the Emperor's rooms?"

She shook her head, "I won't let you do this."

Redd yelled in frustration, "I'm going after the Emperor whether you help me or not!"

She stared defiantly but as he turned away her shoulders slumped and she spoke, "Down that corridor, first left, then the second right, the door is highly decorative."

He turned back briefly to nod his thanks and looked at Aggie who was now crouched by Redd, "Take care of yourself Aggie, and take care of Wolf for me." Then he sprinted down the corridor and out of sight.

Flicker and Jackie had only just made it out of the basement before the large army, and had headed straight for the gardens to find Flora and hopefully Jan before they were attacked. They had rushed out into the palace grounds but it was already dark and they weren't able to see whether Flora was still by the gate. They turned back to the palace in time to see the first few soldiers emerge from the basement steps, their expressionless faces snapping towards anyone with a firearm.

Shots rang round the ground floor as officers were shot dead without a moment's hesitation. Flicker flinched, wondering whether he'd done the right thing, after all they had no way of knowing how many of the officers were actually loyal to the Emperor.

"Jackie what do we do? Should we wait by the gate or start searching for them?"

The older woman shook her head, "I don't know Flick," several more shots rang out and the Artists began to scream and run in terror. "I don't think we should stay here though and wait to be caught in the crossfire."

"Let's make for the gatehouse, it's where everyone should try and meet."

Jackie nodded and they made their way outside into the cool air. Flicker tripped and stumbled down the concrete steps as a shot rang out loud and clear in the dark.

"Crafts! I think I missed," came a cold, cruel voice.

Flicker struggled to his feet and was instantly grabbed by several large officers; Kento swaggered towards him.

"I guess we might not have such a quick getaway as we thought Jack," he said light-heartedly and was met with silence. A cold dread spread through him. "Jackie?" he almost whispered. A quiet groaning sounded from his left and he tried to turn and peer through the gloom but the officers either side of him held firm.

"Jackie!" he yelled, panic rising. "Jackie!"

Kento scoffed, "I don't think she'll be able to help you this time. Now, where's that traitor brother of yours?"

Flicker growled under his breath and stared pure hatred towards Kento, "Even if I knew I wouldn't tell you," he spat.

Kento roared with laughter and aimed his firearm against Flicker's head, "Are you sure about that?"

Flicker started to struggle against his captors though he knew it was useless, "I don't know where he is, I swear to you I don't know! Please let me see Jackie, she needs help!"

Kento smiled coldly, "She got exactly what she deserved, no one can help her now." He glanced briefly at the dark mass on the ground, then back to Flicker. "One last time or you'll join your friend here, where's Redd?"

"I don't know!" Flicker screamed and Kento shook his head in disappointment as his finger squeezed the trigger, Flicker hung his head in despair, waiting for the end.

The shot never came and as he glanced up he saw Flora holding her weapon against Kento's temple; the officer looked scared.

"You're going to do exactly as I say," she said calmly staring at the officers who held Flicker and they nodded. "Let him go." They did as she ordered and Flicker scrambled towards Jackie's still form. "Now get out of here." The two officers ran quickly in the direction of the gatehouse but Kento turned to look her in the eye; the firearm was still placed against his head.

He grinned and spat in her face, she stumbled back and in that moment he pulled his firearm up and aimed it at her. He fired but she had already moved out of the way; her shot however found its mark and he crumpled to the ground, still grinning.

Flora turned to see Flicker crouched over Jackie and she rushed over, a feeling of dread in the pit of her stomach.

"I'm sorry Jack," Flicker whispered as he cradled the older woman in his arms.

"I think we both knew I wouldn't get out of this place alive," she rasped and Flicker felt tears rolling down his cheeks. "It's okay Flick," she gasped for breath and Flicker held her tighter; she leant painfully towards his ear. "Thank you for being a good friend, and for making the last few years of my life more entertaining that I thought possible."

"I love you Jackie," he said through the tears. "I'll never know anyone like you again, you're the best friend I could ever have asked for."

She smiled sadly, then closed her eyes.

Flicker rocked slowly with Jackie's lifeless form still in his arms. Flora placed a gentle hand on his shoulder and crouched beside him, "We have to go Flicker, we need to find the others and get out of here." Flicker shook his head and clutched Jackie tighter. "Flicker please, we won't have another chance, it's now or never."

Reluctantly, he laid Jackie down in the grass, got to his feet and followed Flora into the chaos of the palace.

Chapter 46

Nilla and Aggie hadn't managed to drag Wolf very far when he eventually came round; he lay on the floor for several minutes until his head cleared and his vision settled and then, very slowly, he sat up and looked at them.

"Where is he?"

"He went to find the Emperor," Nilla said quietly.

Wolf cursed and god to his feet, "Get yourselves to safety, I'll find Redd and we'll meet you by the gate." He turned and raced down the corridor, surprisingly quickly, Aggie made to follow him but her mother stopped her.

"We have to get out of here and find the others Aggie, we have to make sure they're safe."

"But what about Wolf and Redd?"

"I'm sure they can take care of themselves, now we need to take care of ourselves."

Reluctantly Aggie followed her mother to the main stairs and they started to make their way down to the ground floor. Around them chaos reigned. Artists were fleeing their rooms in panic; they shoved one another out of the way as they clambered to get down the stairs and out of the palace. Nilla and Aggie made their way carefully down the stairs, trying their best not to get separated. Every now and then shots would ring out as the stern faced army roamed the corridors and shot all officers in sight, without hesitation.

Among the shouts and screams of the Artists and officers was the crackling of fires as several floors blazed happily; ceilings and floors creaked as the raging flames licked greedily at them and the terrified citizens of Shanora raced around, weakening the structure.

Mother and daughter raced down the main stairs and had almost reached the third floor when several of the soldiers grabbed them and began to search them thoroughly.

Nilla tried to push them away and screamed in fear, "We're not officers! We're Artists! We're unarmed, please let us go!" The soldiers ignored her and finished their search before moved on wordlessly. She grabbed Aggie close to her and they continued down the stairs until they almost collided with Flicker and Flora.

They fell into one another in relief and exhaustion and then both parties looked worried.

"Where's Redd and Wolf?" Flicker asked.

"Where's Jackie," Aggie asked at the same time.

Silence followed, then Flicker shook his head, "Sh-she didn't make it," he said sadly. The others looked stunned and Aggie felt tears prick her eyes.

"Redd and Wolf are on the seventh floor," Nilla said carefully, sensing how fragile Flicker was at that moment.

"What? Why? What's happened?" he asked frantically, searching around as if he'd find them.

"Redd's gone after the Emperor."

"What?! What didn't you stop him?" Flicker almost erupted.

"Because I need to get my daughter to safety, I won't have her in danger any longer!"

Flicker shot her a look of hatred, "You do what you want, but I'm not leaving without my brother."

411

Nilla looked helplessly at Flora, who looked away, unable to hold either her or Aggie's gaze.

"We need to go back," Aggie said urgently as Flicker began to make his way up the stairs.

"No Aggie, we need to get you out of here."

Aggie shook her head, "No, we have to help them. Redd and Wolf looked out for me when no one else would, I can't just leave them here."

Nilla's shoulders slumped and she nodded reluctantly; they turned to make their way up the stairs when Flora placed a hand on Aggie's shoulder.

"There's something I need to tell you," she said with a look of guilt and pain on her face.

"Can't it wait?" Nilla asked, feeling uneasy, Flora looked at them both for several seconds and eventually nodded but felt the knot of guilt in her stomach tighten.

Redd cursed as he took another wrong turn, he couldn't understand how he'd managed to get so lost when Nilla's directions had been so simple.

"Crafts! She lied to me!" He yelled and kicked a small statue by one of the doors, it smashed against the wall and he stared at the area it had impacted. There was an elaborately decorated door next to it; Redd grinned, clutched his firearm and headed for the door.

The lavish living room was dark when he entered and he flicked on the lights, raising his firearm in case someone occupied the room, but it was empty. Seeing the highly decorative furniture made him even angrier and he toppled a number of elaborate items before making his way to the only other door in the room. He entered the dull, bare corridor room and looked interestingly at the few items within but he didn't linger long, his eye was drawn to the door opposite, the one Nilla hadn't managed to get through. He made his way slowly towards it; firearm held out in front of him in case someone came through unexpectedly and held out a hand towards the handle.

The door opened slowly away from him and the room on the other side was dimly lit. Redd made his way carefully forward and swept the room with the firearm in case someone was inside, but once again, it was empty. There were a few more items in this room, though it was still dull and bare compared to the main living area. He edged forwards, checking frequently behind in case someone had followed him but he was alone; he made his way to another door along the opposite wall and held his breath as he turned the handle and pushed the door open.

It was as sparsely furnished as the other rooms he'd been in; there was a small dresser against the wall to the left and a rickety looking desk and chair next to it. A small grimy window was located directly opposite with tattered, filthy curtains barely covering it and finally a small, single bed on which a tall, broad man sat hunched over, his thick, dark hair obscuring his face.

Redd stepped loudly into the room and pointed the firearm at the man who looked up in surprise. On seeing Redd he got to his feet, set his face into a frown and tried to look imposing.

"Are you the Emperor?" Redd asked, unfazed by the man's actions. He nodded but said nothing. "Good! Do you have any last words before I shoot you? Do you want to apologise to all of the families you've ripped apart? To all the Artists whose lives you've ruined?"

The Emperor's face fell and he sat back on his bed heavily, his shoulders sagging as if they were carrying a great weight. "I'm sorry," he said in a small voice. "None of this was my idea."

Redd scoffed, "What do you mean it wasn't your idea? You're the Emperor! This was all your idea!"

The Emperor shook his head, "No, it's not what you think, I'm a prisoner too, just like you, just like all of the Artists."

Redd scoffed again but slightly lowered his firearm, "Explain," he commanded.

The Emperor sighed, "Hundreds of years ago, a young Artist called Jeremy was travelling the land, trying to escape something terrible. He was lonely and so he created me to be his companion. He treated me like a friend and we had many adventures together; I hadn't wanted those times to end. Eventually we came upon a small settlement; it was Shanora, this city. Jeremy met other Artists like himself, only they didn't know the extent of their power, they didn't know all the wonderful things they could do. Jeremy promised to train them, to show them the upper limits of their gift if they'd help him in return and they agreed. They helped to build him a house, while he taught and trained them to use their power in more and more elaborate ways.

"But then they were done. They had finished his house and Jeremy had no more to teach them. That should have been the end of it, we should have been able to live happily there but Jeremy had changed, he'd become twisted with power, he wanted the other Artists to admire him; he regretted teaching them.

"He paid some of the local officers to help him kidnap the Artists and imprison them in his house and once they were there he forced them to create for him. He had them create the very bricks that would eventually become the great wall that imprisoned them. He made them create gold so he could afford to pay building merchants a handsome sum to build him a larger house; a palace.

"I tried my best to stop him, I tried to persuade him to let the Artists go but he threatened to destroy me and I feared death, I had started to enjoy the world and I wasn't ready to leave it. I know now that was a mistake."

He looked up with sorrowful eyes and Redd felt a stab of pity towards the man; he had completely lowered the firearm now and it hung loosely at his side. He gestured for the Emperor to continue.

"As time passed Jeremy tried to convince the Artists that they were contained within the palace for their own safety, that there had been mutterings among the regular citizens, that they no longer trusted the Artists. After years of spreading the lies, they started to become truth.

"Years passed with Jeremy ruling like a God, except that he started to age and I remained the same. He hated me for staying young and he envied me. What started out as verbal hatred turned into physical violence and torture; being what I am, I had a higher tolerance of pain, but it still hurt and the beatings still haunt me.

"Jeremy died suddenly when he was seventy and I wasn't sure what to do. I'd never been allowed out of my room, I'd never even seen the inside of the palace. I remembered one Artist that Jeremy seemed to have been quite friendly with, so I asked one of the officers to bring her to me. I explained what had happened and she comforted me, she acted so kind and concerned, it's no surprise that I listened to her every suggestion."

"She took over," Redd said in an expressionless voice.

The Emperor nodded, "She told me the Artists had become settled and it wouldn't be wise to throw them out and fend for themselves, after all, the normal citizens were wary of them now. She told me she would be my advisor and that I should call myself the Emperor so they had someone to look up to. I listened to her; I was naïve.

"It was longer than I care to admit before I realised what Sela was doing but when I tried to stop her she beat me and when she couldn't physically beat me anymore she created beasts to attack me. Eventually I gave in and I let her rule, using me as a pawn in her game. This system continued for hundreds of years and as the rulers became more paranoid, relations with the other cities became strained until eventually we closed ourselves off altogether.

"It's no longer a secret to the other cities what's going on in here, their spies have uncovered the truth and our spies uncovered their plans to invade, to try and free the Artists."

"That's why you created the army in the basement," Redd said, edging closer to the Emperor.

He nodded, "We would have been ready for them."

"The army you had created will no longer serve your purpose, they're killing the officers as we speak."

The Emperor nodded, "That's probably for the best."

"Aren't you angry?"

The Emperor smiled, "Haven't you been listening? I am not, nor have I ever been the one pulling the strings in this city, I am the puppet not the puppeteer."

"Then who is?"

A shot rang out and Redd slumped to the ground suddenly struggling to breathe while the Emperor looked on in horror.

"What have I told you about talking to people without my supervision," Everett said in a disappointed tone as he crouched next to Redd.

"Why?" Redd gasped, turning to look Everett in the

eyes.

Everett smiled but there was no warmth behind it, "Because I like ruling this city, and I can't have you ruining that for me, despite how hard you're trying." He straightened as Redd began gasping painfully for breath; his body jerked slightly.

"Make sure you dispose of the body," Everett said as he grabbed Redd's firearm and left.

The Emperor crouched by Redd and took one of his hands, "I'm sorry," he said as Redd struggled to focus. "I wish it didn't have to end this way for you." Redd opened his mouth as if to speak but the light in his eyes dimmed and his grip on the Emperor's hand slackened.

Chapter 47

It took far longer than they would have liked to reach the seventh floor; Artists, officers and soldiers crowded the corridors and stairs, clamouring to escape the burning building and each other. They made it through the first door and several officers waited on the other side; they looked up in surprise and before they could draw their firearm's Flicker and Flora hurled themselves at them.

"Find Redd and Wolf!" Flicker yelled as he tried to grab the officer's firearm from his holster. Nilla grabbed Aggie and they raced down the corridor and out of sight. They ran for several minutes, Nilla practically dragging her daughter as she twisted through the maze of corridors, heading for the Emperor's room. The hurled themselves round a corner, ran into something solid and fell back; Nilla pulled Aggie towards her in fear and then relaxed as Wolf helped them to their feet.

"What are you doing here?"

"Looking for you and Redd," Nilla replied, "I thought you'd have found him by now."

Wolf shook his head, "I got all turned around in here, can't find my way in or out of this place."

"Follow me," she said and led the way until they reached an elaborately decorated door. "This is the Emperor's living room," she said as she opened the door carefully. Wolf barged past her and strode into the room to make sure it was safe. Nilla pointed towards the far door and they made their way carefully towards it. Once through Nilla started slowly towards the next door but Wolf strode past and kicked it open, she held her breath for a few seconds until she realised there was a similarly empty room beyond.

They continued to make their way, Nilla and Aggie carefully, Wolf recklessly until they finally reached a door that was partly ajar; a voice could be heard talking gently. Wolf slammed the door open and froze at the sight of Redd's still form and the tall man crouched next to him.

He roared and threw himself at the Emperor who did very little to defend himself. Nilla and Aggie tried to pull him off but he was like a wild animal; he battered the Emperor mercilessly and still the Emperor did nothing to prevent it. Nilla and Aggie tried again to pry Wolf away; they grabbed his arms and did everything they could to pull him back, eventually the Emperor threw a firm kick at Wolf's stomach and he fell back.

Wolf growled and looked ready to pounce again but Nilla placed herself between the two men. "What happened here?" she demanded and the Emperor looked sorrowful.

"He was killed by Everett," the Emperor replied in a small voice that took Nilla by surprise.

"What? How? Why? What's going on?"

The Emperor sighed and tried to recount as little of his tale as was necessary as he knew they were running out of time. "Everett wanted to you to take over for him, he thought you were just like him."

Wolf laughed coldly, "He got that part wrong, she's not even an Artist."

The Emperor smiled and nodded, "I know."

They looked shocked, "How?" Nilla asked almost in

a whisper.

"I was created by an Artist and as such I'm able to sense them."

"Why didn't you tell Everett the truth?"

"Because I had hoped you would put an end to all this," he gestured at the surroundings. "I'm tired of being a prisoner, of being a puppet for someone's cruel game. I want to be free."

Nilla took a step towards the Emperor, her hand outstretched but at that moment Wolf, who had been standing near the door stepped to the side of the room.

"We've got company," he said gruffly.

Wolf threw himself at Everett as soon as he walked through the door, knocking the firearm instantly from his hands. Aggie lunged forwards and scooped up the weapon before either of them could try to grab it. The two men struggled frantically on the ground and although Everett was older he was still able deal Wolf some nasty blows. Wolf however had revenge in his eyes and he managed to block most of Everett's attacks before landing his own well timed punches to Everett's face creating a bloody mess.

Eventually Nilla screamed at him to stop and Wolf sat back from the bleeding, groaning man.

"He deserves this," Wolf growled.

"He needs to pay for what he's done the right way," Nilla replied.

Wolf started to rise and Everett began a gargled laugh, "I'll never pay fo-" Wolf crouched and snapped his neck before he could utter another word.

"I'm sorry Nilla," Wolf said stepping away from the bloodied corpse.

Nilla shook her head, "It-it's okay Wolf...I understand."

"We need to get out of here," Aggie said quietly, still holding the firearm she'd grabbed from the brawling pair. Wolf gently removed the weapon from her grasp and threw it across the room, then he bent to pick up Redd but the Emperor stopped him.

"Let me carry him," he said in a gentle voice. "It's the least I can do to try and make up for the crimes that have been committed in my name."

"What is your name?" Aggie asked in a small voice as the Emperor stooped to collect Redd's body.

"I don't remember," he admitted with a hint of sadness, "Jeremy named me long ago but I no longer remember what it is."

"Would you like a new name?" she asked and the Emperor nodded.

Aggie looked at him for several seconds, "Tobias."

The Emperor looked thoughtful then nodded, "I like that name."

They raced back along the corridors, the Emperor – Tobias – carrying Redd's body with ease and almost crashed into Flicker and Flora who were desperately trying to find their way. Flicker froze as he saw the limp form of his brother, fell to his knees in despair and let out a primal scream.

"What happened?" he asked hoarsely.

Wolf crouched in front of him, "Everett."

Flicker locked eyes with him, "Did he pay?"

Wolf nodded and Flicker hung his head just as a loud rumble sounded and the building around them shook violently.

"The palace is becoming unstable," Tobias said and made to move towards the main staircase.

Flicker jumped to his feet and barred his way, "Who

is this? And why is he carrying my brother?" his voice was low and menacing.

Nilla stepped forwards and placed a hand on his arm, "Not now Flick, he's helping, let's just leave it at that."

The building shook again and Aggie was thrown to the ground; they started to stumble their way to the main staircase where they saw a number of gaping holes in the ground and ceiling around them; the palace was collapsing.

The bodies of Artists, officers and soldiers littered the corridors and staircase as they made their way quickly and unsteadily to the ground floor just as one of the upper levels of the palace collapsed, creating a billowing cloud of smoke and debris.

They dashed out into the gardens as another thunderous crash sounded behind them and saw the main gates had been flung wide open. Artists were hurrying towards them, making a wild dash for freedom, while the officers continued to try and stop them and the soldiers in turn prevented an Artist massacre.

Another crash sounded as a large portion of the once dazzling and perfect palace shattered and crumbled to the ground throwing flaming debris towards the small group fleeing for their lives. Aggie was hit in the back by something large and heavy, and tumbled to the ground. Wolf was at her side in an instant, helping her to her feet and made to move on; she froze, then screamed. The others turned to look at her and Nilla let out a loud cry; Charlie's body lay inches from them.

"What happened? What happened?" Aggie sobbed as she tried to reach out to her father.

"In the Emperor's name," Nilla said in a hoarse voice, then glanced at Tobias before looking back at her husband's body.

Flora stepped forward, "Aggie, Nilla, I…I need to tell you something."

They looked at her expectantly, "What is it? Did you see who did this?" Nilla asked taking a step towards the officer.

Flora swallowed, "I-"

Several shouts sounded close by and the group swivelled to see Kento's comrades stumbling towards them, firearms raised, wavering unsteadily. They each pulled the trigger and two shots rang out loud and clear in the night.

Aggie cried out as she was thrown to the ground by Flora and Flicker yelled in surprise as Tobias shoved him roughly sideways. Two soldiers emerged from the shadows and instantly despatched the two officers with little trouble, eyed the group, then moved on.

Nilla hurled herself towards Aggie and saw with relief that she was unharmed. She turned to Flora and went to thank the woman through grateful tears when she saw the dark stain spreading rapidly.

"Flora! Flora!" she yelled as the young woman began breathing erratically.

"Flora!" Aggie cried, hugging the woman tightly, tears flowing.

Flora, opened her eyes and focused on Aggie, she leant close to her and whispered with slow, ragged gasps, "I'm…sorry Aggie…it was…an…acc…accident."

Aggie sobbed into Flora's shoulder, "It's okay, it doesn't matter, please don't leave me."

Flora smiled crookedly, "You…you have…to take…care…of them."

Aggie looked into the young woman's eyes, then sobbed louder as Flora's eyelids closed and she released her final breath. Wolf stepped forwards, gently pried Aggie away and lifted Flora into his arms.

"We'll take her with us lass, we'll give her and Redd a decent burial."

Aggie nodded and Nilla helped her to her feet, "Is everyone else okay?" she asked shakily.

"I believe I have been shot," Tobias said from where he stood, still carrying Redd's body.

Flicker, who was back on his feet, eyed him, "Where? I can't see any blood."

"I believe it is in my shoulder but I'm in very little pain, we should leave quickly."

They began to make their way to the large, open gates, avoiding trouble where possible and Flicker looked sideways at Tobias.

"The bullet would have hit me wouldn't it?" it wasn't really a question.

Tobias didn't glance at him, "Yes. I nudged you so they would hit me instead."

"Why?"

"Because your life is more important than mine, after all, I'm not real."

"What do you mean you're not real?" Flicker asked slowing slightly in confusion.

"This is not the time," Tobias replied, picking up the pace in the hopes Flicker would follow. The other man grabbed his arm and forced him to stop.

"Who are you?" He demanded as the others, realising they had lost two of their party, stopped and retraced their steps.

"Flicker can't this wait?"

He shook his head, "I'd like to know who I owe my life to."

Tobias sighed, "I was once known as the Emperor,"

he said as Flicker's eyes widened and his hands balled into fists.

Nilla immediately placed herself between them, "It's not what you think Flicker, he's a creation, he was being held prisoner. Everett was the real Emperor, Tobias was simply a puppet, a pawn."

Flicker took a deep breath and his hands relaxed, "Were you there when my..." he trailed off unable to finish.

Tobias nodded, "I'm sorry about your brother, I'm sorry I couldn't save him, but I was with him at the end and I hope he found peace."

Flicker nodded stiffly, "Let's get out of this place."

They finally made it through the gates and into the city beyond, which mirrored the chaos of the palace; fires raged, people screamed and ran in terror, bodies littered the streets as the army hunted for the officers.

"We need to get out of the city!" Nilla yelled above the deafening noise.

They rounded a corner and skidded to a stop as a dark figure emerged from the shadows. Wolf made to move in front of them, when Flicker took several steps forwards staring intently at the stranger.

"Jan?"

The figure moved into the light and smiled briefly before his face fell at the site of the two bodies being carried.

"What happened?" he asked taking another few steps forward.

"Long story," Flicker replied shaking his head. "We're getting out of the city Jan and if you've any sense you'll get your family out too."

Jan nodded, "That's where I'm heading now.

Perhaps we'll meet again someday."

Flicker smiled, "I hope that we do."

They shook hands, embraced one another and Jan moved off towards the centre of the city while Flicker and his friends began to run for the city gates.

They stopped just short of the large, imposing wooden gates, seeing a couple of armed officers still on guard.

Wolf gently laid Flora's body on the ground and grabbed Flicker, "Come on Flick, we can handle those two." Flicker nodded and they moved slowly towards the officers, keeping to the shadows as much as possible.

They approached from behind taking the officers by surprise; they had no chance to grab their firearms and appeared inexperienced with hand to hand combat. Wolf managed a couple of good blows to the head and the officer went down while Flicker kicked the second officer in the back and sent him sprawling. Each grabbed for the officer's firearm and used it to knock them unconscious; Flicker continued to hold the firearm to cover Wolf as he ran back to the others to retrieved them and Flora's body.

Flicker had the gates open as they arrived and the small group exited Shanora for the first time in their lives; they didn't bother to close the gates. It was unnervingly quite outside the city; they had quickly become used to the shouts, screams and sounds of destruction in Shanora and now they were walking towards the coast it seemed almost too peaceful.

They walked along the coast for several hours in the dark with only the stars and moonlight to guide them. Once Wolf felt confident that they hadn't been followed he set Flora carefully on the ground and looked at his friends.

"We need to decide where to go."

Nilla nodded, "I think if we keep following the coast we should reach Endore but I don't know how far it is and we haven't any food. She shook her head. "We really should have planned better."

Aggie smiled, "I think Flicker and I can handle the food mother."

Nilla looked surprised, "You can't be serious?"

Flicker smiled too, "I'll admit it isn't going to taste very nice and it won't be as nutritious as the real thing but if we fail to catch anything then we can certainly make something."

Nilla shook her head, then looked at their two fallen friends, "When should we...I mean where should..." she trailed off.

"Why not here," Flicker said, looking at their surroundings, "Redd always loved the sea, I think he'd enjoy spending eternity by it."

They took their time, and once finished they stood for several minutes staring at the sea, listening to the waves crash gently on the shore. The air was cool and the smell of salt filled their lungs.

Tobias looked around the small group, "Thank you," he said quietly.

"What for?" Wolf asked.

"For setting me free."

"We're all free now," Flicker said with a smile. "Let's hope it stays that way."

Wolf clapped him on the shoulder and they began to walk once more along the coast. Flicker gave one final look at the graves and smiled sadly, hoping his brother had finally found peace before following the others as they made their way towards Endore and the hope of refuge.

ABOUT THE AUTHOR

Vicky was born in North Yorkshire, which will always be her one true home. She studied English Language at Lancaster but ended up completing a masters degree in Object Conservation at Durham University.

An objects conservator by trade, she enjoys everything history related and loves the fact that she has been able to help restore some of the most amazing objects in Britain. She has dabbled in sword fighting and knife throwing and is a keen baker. A complete lover of books, especially fantasy, she's also a self-proclaimed geek and has always wanted a pet dragon, unfortunately she'll have to settle for a temperamental cat.

Keep up to date with everything Vicky gets up to on her website www.vickygarlick.com including her (mostly) weekly blog, updates on her current writings and occasional short stories.

70768096R00241

Made in the USA
Columbia, SC
13 May 2017